I0681210

SiXPointz
HiTopOLis

SiXPointz HiTopOLis

By the author of

Five Points Akropolis

The God's Cycle
†

And

Fantastic Travelogue:
Mark Twain and CS Lewis
Talk Things over in The Hereafter

SiXPointZ
HiTopOLis

s. dormAn

SiXPointz HiTopOLis

s. dormAn

In Loving Memory of

The Elder Dormans

SiXPointz HiTopOLis

Baby

Where did you come from, baby dear?
Out of the everywhere into here.

Where did you get those eyes so blue?
Out of the sky as I came through.

What makes the light in them sparkle and spin?
Some of the starry twinkles left in.

Where did you get that little tear?
I found it waiting when I got here.

—

Where did you get this pearly ear?
God spoke, and it came out to hear.

Where did you get those arms and hands?
Love made itself into bonds and bands.

Feet, whence did you come, you darling things?
From the same box as the cherubs' wings.

How did they all just come to be you?
God thought about me, and so I grew.

—

George MacDonald
1824-1905

SiXPointz HiTopOLis

s. dormAn

events

SiXPointz HiTopOLis

s. dormAn

ANNO DOMINE 1900

Meantime by the Stone Wall of the
Akropolis Rural Cemetery

It was 1900 A.D.

They were gathered round the z-pod in Tu's hand. Huddling
with the FivePoints 2017 CE gang, by a stone wall of the dark
Akropolis Cemetery, HBBBAH rubbed the sweat out of his dark
broom'do. He looked about him with that special CossycSystems eye
of his. He said with disgust, "A line of 0's and 1's."

Pomala, the albino girl with blue tattooed face, smiled off into
the pod-lit dark, saying, "Or, x's and o's!"

Eyes zoned in concentration, fringe of black hair hanging
over his symmetrical Osiian features, Tu had again worked the
Hadesthon calculations. He worked them just as the battery gave
out. The game display was suddenly dark. Disconcertingly so to the
other five gang members. The battery was dead. And the cemetery
around them, which they had not been attending to while gathered
round the z-pod, was dark like a pit surrounded by hidden fire.
Gaslight and some thin old-fashioned household electric glowed
down from beyond the walls. On the west side, great monoliths of
high school and church hunkered as black shadows.

Outside the Cemetery stood the venerable neighborhood of
Five Points Akropolis 1900 A.D., rhythmic that evening, with
nightlife of horse-and-carriages, pool halls, bars, and neighborhood
sociability ebbing and flowing—including a game of kick-the-can.
Certain areas of the city had been in tumult but it seemed quieter
now, the riots perhaps abating. Remote fiddling and the tinkling of
an upright piano drifted to them. The gang from FivePoints 2017 CE
were wearing their jackets again, full of hope. Ready for November,
2017 CE—the fresh twinkle in time, courtesy (they were hoping) of
the *Hadesthon*. Longing for streaming, games, apps and naChooos.

As the pod flicked off, Tu felt a great elation and would have jumped in the air and floated, hovering and gently crowing the fact. But he was Tu, so instead he said only, "Got it. And just in time."

He explained. "Nothing to do with the calculations, but this one glitch kept happening. Shooting Baltoid on Persesus29 fails the first five times, every time, then launches the P29 module gimmex.lld, causing bribell27.xee to gobble mega percentages of its CUP sickles—well, not mega, but you know what I mean."

"Sure we do" said HB.

The six members of FivePoints 2017, including Fabian, Quadri and Jayrai, scrambled for the wall to sit in line, await the recall in Time. Shyly, feeling just a bit weird and surprised by the suggestion, they held hands. Then maneuvered for position. Conversation happened.

The massive church-tower clock began tolling toward 11. Fabian and Quadri were covertly praying. And Pomala. HBBBAH was thinking about the Grandmaster. *Who was that big dude?* Jayrai was thoughtful about holding hands, her biomechanical fingers clasping small Quadri's hand.

Pomala stopped praying. "Look," she said, considering.

Holding the right hand of the little girl, Parry strolled toward them from the oldtime intersection of Five Points. Boy and girl. It was the little girl who never spoke. Pomala had been saying to the gang before that this little girl needed help of a kind they didn't have in 1900 CE. "We could help her," Pome explained now.

Holding her hand, and with the great clock beginning to strike the eleventh hour, Parry came past the cemetery where his brother worked grounds-keeping and digging graves. It was late. Willie had gone to put the rake or the mower, or something, back in the tool crypt. He should have been home. Parry saw the others on the stone wall ahead. The strange kids from the Grandmaster's minstrel show (as his own gang thought them). It was past bedtime.

s. dormAn

HISTORY IN THE ALTERNATE UNIVERSE

Lost Nation

Meantime, somewhere among the folds of the Grandmaster's garments, 'twas *Anna Damini* 1521, the past of a parallel universe. Someday (in this land of the alternate universe) would be condominiums, malls, an Olympic Village with industrial works underground. In a suburb just west of the great city of HiTopOLis, but a scant league past the neighborhood of SiXPointz, in A.D. 1521, 'twas a camp of the *Ehio*—the *Eihoerrian*, or Caht People.

In a cave in the rock half-a-league from the encampment lived a friar. Here great ice had disappeared leaving massive rocks abut, stones older than what underlay as bedrock. In a cave, not damp, nor full of badgers and worms, was the friar's stone cell with books and manuscripts in wooden racks. Though small, made of twigs and slender, these racks were tied together with deerskin thongs, sturdily. Other furnishings he had: deer-tallow candles alight on the rock floor by his knees, a small stone hearth with embers glowing, surmounted with rough-split oak mantelpiece. On this mantle two small earthen bowls held fragrant herbs and conifer smoldering, mingling with the friar's upsending prayers.

Father Domino knelt in ragged homespun on a mat of cornstalks woven by his own hands during winter, sometimes in the cell, but often sitting with believing native brothers and sisters outside in the bright *Elios-light* when weather proved mild. He had lived with the Caht People (as some knew them) long enough to convert but a score to the faith, and these had all become neighbors and friends by virtue of his mild manners and quiet smile; and because he taught them strange but believable things.

His chanting was quiet, almost a whisper, sometimes a humming, or wistful thrumming in his chest; almost never heard outside the cave. "*Raison d'être, Raison d'être.*" His friends rarely heard but knew he was in here—behind thickets, in summer hiding

13

an entrance which, in winter, was hung in deer hide to shield from cold. Father Domino had decided soon to take down these skins draping antlers wedged in the rocks. He would need to make a skin garment now his robe was rags, and the bugs of spring to be biting.

He paused, and stood to take out a precious hand-copied codex, opening to a particular spot. All in this, the Next World, was hand-made. The revolution in machine-making, of which some of his books ere made, was not yet among these A'ndyans, natives of the Next World. Letters here in this book were lit, some, as with gilt fire. While he scanned them, candlelight leapt over the glistening mica-stone walls, reflecting on the page. It glittered also across his now upraised and dreaming eyes. No one was there to see it, no one to hear him murmur, no one to feel the salt water trickle down his tallow brown cheek and caress it—as did the spirit accompanying him.

"...A vesture dipped in blood...."

The words, of course, were spoken in Latinum, a translation of Grake made by himself before he came to the Ehio to witness these very truths to Caht People. The Caht People, whose cloaks were fringed with cat-tails, named themselves Ehioerrian, or *People of the Lake and Other Waters.*

He put back the book and gazed down at the embers, heedless of faint scents—conifer gently wafting a bit of smoke through the small cell. Up and out the smoke hole among rocks above the hearth, up and out went the smoke and too his breath, and the last of his prayer.

It must mean his own blood. Must it not? Must it not mean the blood of Raison d'être?

Thoughtful, he pushed back the curtain of gray deerskin and peered through the thicket beneath. Steep and high, the ledge above, and crowned in conifer, with others hardwood stems soon to unfurl. Tall trunks of oaks, walnuts, and maples stood against the rock, dark and wet, but as yet without leaves. These would come, in due course with spring showers, but latterly would follow summer thunderstorms, always short-lived and not unwelcome. For the Ehioerrian loved wild nature.

No one was without. Slowly he stepped through swollen red stems, droplets soaking his ragged shoulders, deerskin-and-thonged feet dampened in leaf mold of uncounted years. A little later he saw the family of Geagosasa moving down through morning mist beyond the thicket stems, down toward springs easing into the Little Ehio River, tributary to the Bigger—some miles below the land they all inhabited *at present.*

This present was a time of hiding. For all waited hidden, hoping for news of the truce. A truce was what they wanted with the

Bird-Crested People, as they were known to the Ehio A'ndyans. These enemies knew them as Caht People for the many panther tails fringing their cloaks of deer or panther skin—taken from creatures in the hunt.

But this was the trouble, these cat skins and tails of the Caht People (or *Nation du Chat* in the tongue of Father Domino). The Bird-Crested People wanted the vain cat-killing stopped. But that was before-this-time, when the Caht People refused, saying all here belong to them for their use. The others, known to themselves as *Haudenosuni*, were a Confederate peoples and too many (in coalition) for *Nation du Chat* in battle. Now the Ehioerrian were to be destroyed, as promised, by the Bird-Crested People. Many battles had been fought with the Bird-Crested People, who lived eastward in mountains. They came and fought in these lands south of the Great Lake bearing Caht People's name. The Ehio had defeated that nation each time, but now more were coming, many more. Too many to kill in battle. But more, these enemies have thunder arms from strangers. The *Haudenosuni* vowed utterly to destroy them, take them in slavery, empty these lands of Ehio until the great cats should return.

"Geagosasa, *ma dame*," said the friar. Though chilled, he approached with such quiet almost to startle—had not this princess been used to such silent approach. As leader of the clan, this is what she was, to Father Domino—the princess. For the He-suit, being Frankish and Usi'opan, thought always of royalty and authority and how best to practice courtesy as a matter of course.

"Much Birdsong and sweet fern and goodness to you, and may Our Lady Mother and the Holy Father of Us All bless you, *ma dame*," said he.

Geagosasa had bent to pluck the pale green curled heads of bird-fern, sprouting from earth. Her rush pouch was rapidly filling. Down toward the tributary, her daughter Leaping Fawn also bent to damp earth for the spring harvest. Antipatihee, big brother, was with her, tall and lithely muscled. He was maybe eight-and-ten summers, and she but fourteen. Her black braid hung down to the ground as she stooped, and it trailed among spring spears of green, and the wet brown leaves plastered to earth by winter snows.

Geagosasa stood. Her black braid but threaded with silver-gray trailed down her bosom vested in doeskin. Soft 'twould be to the touch, but Father Domino had schooled himself not to notice these things. Geagosasa, as with all girls and women, were not made for the elements of his manhood, but for *dieu*. And for themselves and their husbands. Father Domino would not be ashamed on the last day.

First, she answered his blessing with one of her own. Then she said to the slender shivering friar, "You want to know of the treaty, *jeune père*. The friar looked younger than but was several summers the elder of Antipatihee.

"We have no word... as yet," she said. "The envoy is missing these several days since you went to study your signals."

She knew what he did in the cell behind thickets hid in the rock. She knew he had what he called holy letters, codes; like the signals etched in trees, sent up in smoke, or whistled forth — as if from one of the creatures (in warning or reply to other signals).

...But his skin signals were different....

She had seen the books and parchments from overseas, and how beautiful of pattern, and of elemental seriousness of purpose. The marks of his own making from his own dyes were not so beautiful, but she knew about their hidden message (hidden from her if not from Leaping Fawn). And that his marks were as important, almost, as those made so pleasantly shining and colorful by far older hands. Hands that, he had said, were now dust but leaving these wonderful signals behind. Others might now see the visions they conjured. Indeed, Geagosasa had seen these visions by words he spoke from them.

Everything here was dim with mist. They four—three natives and the friar—seemed alone in this land of making and breathing and slow-springings to life from the Maker Father Domino told of. She had no check to her learning of this, as had some of the Caht People. As soon as he told them, by the fire in the evening many moons ago—after he came in summer before—she knew on the instant 'twas true. There was a Greatest One. One to start everything. What she understood not was why *all* had not the impress to tell them 'twere so. The friar said it was so meant, but that neither she nor he might say why.

"Old Father," said Leaping Fawn, joining them, her girl's face with high cheekbones and black eyes animated. Her rush pouch was slung full on her arm. "Blackberry has had her babies. Five in all. You must come see them."

Geagosasa put her arm around her daughter's slender shoulders as they stood together.

"Blackberry, Blackberry... now let me see," said tall Antipatihee coming behind her. "It's bound to be either skunk or rat. Which is it, sister? Skunk or rat?"

"She happens to be raccoon, terrible brother. But if she were skunk or rat. What? They each are fine, too." She showed him smug eyes.

Together they went down, treading through tips of skunk cabbage, and twigs of sweet fern emerging with tiny leafbuds... down toward the Little Ehio River, its mumbling waters there in soft morning mist.

"Horn-in-Morning will return soon, will he not?" said Father Domino. He wanted peace seated within their spirits again.

Then Geagosasa frowned slightly. Gazing at her children, who watched her intently, she wondered what would happen to them in this land if the goodwill effort failed. "I will pray to the Father and Mother you speak of. Will you not?"

"*Je l'ai fait,*" said he. "*Toujours.*"

The one thing Father Domino sometimes misses here among the Nation is the scholarly community of his brothers northeast of the great lake. North of the Great Lake Ehio was a Brothery where *missions* met at whiles to share knowledge and books. Father Domino was always learning and desiring to share knowledge with others. However, some learning *experiences* were not congenial to him. Such as this now with young Leaping Fawn at the raccoon's den where, in this moment, the mother of kits slept as they suckled. Raccoons be nocturnal. The smell of the den into which the two peered was of musk, musty and full of crushed fir needles, rank beasts' smells. Here the two crouched together whispering nigh the rock crevice not far from his own, more comfortable, cave. In the same steep ledge of dark but, here and there, glimmering rock.

"See how her hands are almost like our hands, Old Father?" Leaping Fawn asked this without turning or raising her eyes to him. Delicately she lifted one of Blackberry's small paws.

He stooped a little behind her, for in truth he was afraid. It was a massive bitch coon. The raccoon, he doubted not, would not like him. She would not want him near nor even looking upon her and the kits. Leaping Fawn however was a friend (so to speak) of the family. She knew all the elder kits (*femelles et les mâles*) from the year before and all knew and accepted her.

Now the great furred beast breathed contentedly in her sleep—a mythical creature with its black-and-white mask, its pointed bewhiskered face and pert dark ears. Leaping Fawn was near, and no matter that other strange mannish scent.... All would be well. Some of the kits squirmed, and some lay sluggish, supine or prone beneath her. All masked eyes were closed. The musk smell was very strong. Later the friar would fill his cell with the odor of smoldering balsam. Then he would sit down and write all things learned of the girl and his own observations. That was what he liked most of all in this time and place—to be somewhat *out* of this present time, present place; and among the signs of the books and careful placement of knowledge.

On leaving these thickets beneath the steep-sided ledge—to

17

walk more and talk more of what they had seen—and as they walked over deadfall and leaf mold and emerging white star and mayflowers, the friar said, "Leaping Fawn."

"Yes, Old Father."

"Leaping Fawn, I observed you swiftly climbing the eastern hillside the other night, away from the tributaries and up into heights beyond the rock ledge in which I dwell. There was, again, I saw, the quick ardor you showed once before when I looked. Forgive me...." And he thought, *But having restrained my curiosity ere now, I wonder if you may sometime consider sharing your secret with me. For I doubt not you have some wonderful mystery to share.*

"Old Father, I would say nothing now." Leaping Fawn evinced no sign of discomfort, as might one so young in another place and time.

"It may be, someday?"

"*Mais oui.* It may be."

Straight way he took up *raccoons* again. "Now you have, no doubt, a story for me concerning the good mother — or another of her kind?"

"Old Father, she is a wise woman because devoted to her kits. She shows them to wash their food, and where to den, feed, and how to be safe from enemies. She is a trickster because they learn tricks of her to survive. Upon one time she took off her mask and turned red like a fox to lead hunters astray. Man would be lead to her den but comes instead to the foxhole. He does not like to eat foxes."

"But how is he tricked? He is following what he thinks is a fox? Not liking fox flesh, why would he do this?"

"Aha. Because he thinks this fox is but trying to outwit him and so will lead him to the coon's den instead." Leaping Fawn smiled with relish and glee.

With a respectful nod, Father Domino smiled.

"You have given me much to think about today. And," with a gesture, "see how the land has lightened."

They had been looking in earnest on all roundabout them, for the leaving mist had shed shining droplets everywhere, on all twigs and buds — red and gold and green — clothing all with delicate enchantment. They walked on, speaking little but looking and smiling. And indeed they, both, were enchanted.

"What will you do with your bird-fern heads, you and your mother Geagosasa?"

"You, Old Father, must come and see. You must be very hungry after all that studying many signs."

The friar smiled, turning to her sweet exotic face with darkling eyes and fullness where her cheekbones just showed but

18

would one day be prominent. "Ah, you know me well now, Mother Raccoon," said he.

She laughed like the murmuring of a swiftling brook, leaping and fleeting.

He pulled back the deerskin over the rock entrance and went once more into the cave. Now it was dark, candle- and ember-light gone. Then he took down the hide. Light filtered in and he gathered his inks, feather quills, and parchment. He had to write while Elios shone through budding thickets on his stone table, not far outside the cell. There was much to think of. Those hands, for instance. Yes, they were much like little hands, those raccoon paws.

He was inclined to agree with Brother Augusto in the manner of the Maker's revolving creation and recreation. The similarities, hand to paw, were by no means mere coincidence. All this was planned and set in motion to begin with. Indeed, sometimes he wondered (but to himself only and to the Great One who knew all his thoughts)—sometimes he wondered if there were no beginning and no ending. If all things revolved (as do planets around Elios), if all lost parts, and gained parts, and changed parts over time. *Would this not fit with His Being in the midst, and with being both First and Last?*

Then, as he set out his inks and lay open the paper-skin. He thought now instead about the great plague as had happened in Usia two hundred years ago. And how all that death had happened in the darkness of Usia, possibly because mice with disease-bearing lice had gone there from Usi'opa. So that Usia had but few folk.

Father Domino sometimes wondered what the world had been like if events great and small had not happened as they did.

He placed the cornstalk mat on the small square rock, and seated himself before the greater sandstone rock used for the table. He placed inks and quill-pen and parchment there. He shook down his ragged sleeves to begin writing.... But he paused his quill, gazing on sprouting life as it lined all twigs with delicate coloring, some reddish of various shades, some greenish. ...And here and there golden, like those beechen candle flames about to unfurl in the thickets. He put down his quill-pen and began then to worship with fervor.

No one watching might tell it except for, sometimes, the thrumming soft, deep inside. But no one watched. The encampment at half a league's distance would be busy now. True, the hunters would be about in parties after older bucks. Precautionary for the future needs of *Nation du Chat*, no yearlings would be sought. Only the great cats (for the Ehio's vanity) were not spared. Again, on finishing worship, he thought of the words.

"...Wearing a vesture dipped in blood." And again he thought, *Il doit signifier son propre sang* (It must mean his own blood).

Now again he shook down his sleeves and began to write of the morning's findings. After, with ink and quill on a different parchment, he pursued his ongoing thought about plague aversion in Usi'opa, and how this may have changed the course of history over the face of the whole heavenly wanderer. If, for instance, the plague had not been averted by prayer a great loss of populace would certainly have delayed Madame Columba's discovery of the Next World — nearly 124 years ago in *Anna Damini* 1396. But then why, anyway, did it take so long as it did? Why did we not know about the Next World till lately? Ah yes. The Doctrine of Dryland had negated the theory of Other Worlds, that is, other *lands* in Eartha. All believed there was solely one land in a desert of ocean. There had been but the one continent in geological ages past; however the belief of but the one kept explorers from discovering the Next World far longer than need be. ...And, had it not been for lack of plague, certainly the "thunder arms," as *Nation du Chat* called them would not have so soon been invented; nor lens-glass, nor steam engines conceived (as he had heard of Brother Pinochio); nor clock works, etc. until long after these happened in fact. The slant-eyed orange people of Usia, he knew, were still very backward and sparse, and now a source of slave labor (till, as he hoped, the machines should free them). Surely 'twould not have been so had the lice and mice of Usi'opa not plagued, keeping Usia from being great. Now, also, it should not have been known among civilized peoples how the lice and the mice and the microbes made ill ... had Usi'opan medicine not so far advanced ... for that no plague. This, he thought, scratching the side of his nose with his quill (it needed a new dipping) — this would explain the robust colonization and the fabrication of things wonderful for the use of humankind.

Now. About the other.... Surely the Holy Mother in the Vanticantle of Roma would someday — may it be sooner than later — allow that making and remaking has filled the Cogmos.... Possibly there would be no brutal inquiries into these things — but only such as sane women and men might allow, meaning *la curiosité intellectuelle* — and all would certainly be well for learning, and for scholarship.

A swift fleeting rustling flicker among leaves at his feet made the friar leap onto the table, knocking askew and scattering his writing materials.

Il était là!! The Haudenosuni Moccasin! O deadly deadly! Deadly! And he had escaped *just in time!*

Oh, oh, oh. The Holy Father! Holy Mother! Oh holy ones thank you. Oh thank you, my holy friends.

But he knew not he had spoken aloud.

"Ma dame?"
"Oui, mon petit père?"
Among members of the clan, Geagosasa sat crosslegged on her mat eating coal-roasted bird-fern coils before a wide bed of ashes. All sat thus eating, happily so. Here were many families gathered to the feast of fern-heads, the children romping and feeding from mothers' and fathers' hands, or those of sisters and aunts. Elios struck down through budding mighty limbs with yellow light. Some folk sat on moldering deadfall, sometimes stirring ashes to seek out roasted fernheads.

The friar said, "We (in Franke) have a musical instrument part of which shape is like to this." Gingerly he picked out a coiled fern head and held it up for the others to see. "One plays on this instrument with a bow." He put the succulent coiled fern in his mouth, chewing and speaking around it. "Not the bow with arrows, but like this." The friar then pantomimed the play one does on the great upright fiddle.

"How sounds this music?" Geagosasa asked, head of the clan. She would they learned of the friar's strange place. "It is not like our jon-jon." She mimed beating the skin drumhead. "Is it like the bird-pipe?" She pretended the slender A'ndyan pipe.

Another nearby at the edge of the circle—a young man— picked such a pipe from his belt thong. He began vigorously to play.

All were happy, now at peace. The many men and women, the children playing, all were merry and forgetful of trouble. Horn-in-Morning and the envoy had returned with news of truce. No formal treaty had been crafted, but the promise was theirs that attack would not be imminent.

Only Leaping Fawn, the friar noticed, looked distant, withdrawn. And this was not usual for her. She was the first to make merry when it were decorous. Antipatihee, the friar saw, also noticed and fell silent. Geagosasa gave her daughter a coaxing look and spoke a few words to her.

Leaping Fawn took her gaze off the embers and pulled close her doeskin cloak with a shiver. She but glanced at her mother then back toward the embers. Sounding under the camp's merriment, tree frogs trilled in deep woodland. The stream below, murmuring, fell rippling out of sight under a leaf strewn bank.

Tumbling Beaver knocked into Leaping Fawn as he ran from his tormentor, little Broad-stroke. The girl grabbed Tumbling Beaver, fiercely, before he could glance away. Leaping Fawn hugged him and spoke softly into his ear. But he squirmed mightily. She let him go. Then he clung to her, giggling.

21

Afterward, as he went upstream toward his cell, Father Domino saw her fleeting through thickets, noiseless. In fact, he but saw with the corner of his eye. He turned. Yes, it was Leaping Fawn. The friar saw her start up the wooded hillside where below the streambed bent around and out of sight. She was fierce. Climbing with great ferocity and verve. He could not see her face, but judged it, too, was fierce... and perhaps unseeing. He thought she must be enthralled. But it was not her way, he knew. So then all he might do was wonder.

And, too, he now considered the awful request made of him back at the encampment.

She had come to him next day to explain.... Perhaps?

Watching him she said the two words with subtle emphasis. "You see Old Father, it's THE DEER." She said nothing more, and he waited. He did not rush her but looked up at the sky through gently leafing limbs and twigs. Soon woodland and encampment light would be dappled dusky green but now earth and trees and sky are open—all gently almost imperceptibly breathing.

She too waited, watching him look with his strange blue eyes at blue sky and twining deeps of tall trees above. She saw the fringe of his lashes and how beautiful he looked, Old Father.

To her mother Geagosasa he was *jeune père, mon petit père,* but to her Old Father. In ways he seemed old and she felt the oldness in him as from some old culture deeper than her own. To Leaping Fawn the Ehio were ever young. *We have old stories but no one knows how old and, received, the stories also are ever young.* 'Twas the depth of his knowledge, its variety and presentation making her feel him—very old. All ancient—old like the hidden roots of trees that showed only when one of these giants fell over with thundering and upheaval. Her own people might be displaced with little effort, small power, and they *would* be so displaced (she knew). But his people could but be *thrown* down—like the tree, with great power and calamity.

Tumbling Beaver came through the buds, swiping with his small self-made tomhawk, a stick and broken flint-head (discarded by his big brother) and tied with gut.

Voice strong and piping, he said, "I know about the deer! The deer is her friend!" He came up to them and continued apace. "He's like in stories. You can't see him with your eyes. Only in your story eye is he visible." Tumbling Beaver was not as slim as some of the children, but hefty and stolid; black of hair and eye as were the Ehio.

"And have you seen him there, Tumbling Beaver?" asked the friar.

"Only when Leaping Fawn tells me of him." He looked up at her, arms akimbo, the tomhawk in his fist pointed behind him. "Only if she tells me."

"I don't tell him," she said, looking at Father Domino.

"Once she did. When we lay in the stream."

"Yes, once. But if you don't go away I can't tell Father Domino."

"Why?"

"Because too many looking at The Deer when I speak might keep him away."

Tumbling Beaver looked down at his tomhawk. "Then, I will go away... and let Old Father see him."

"Come." She opened her arms but he turned away, swiping. Walking through twigs. Then he turned back, as she knew he would, and hugged her as she bent to him. Now he looked solemnly up at both and walked off, much cheered.

"See," said the Father. "He repents and is better."

"Yes. That is a good of life. It comes from The Deer."

Gently he would correct, but thought better of it. He had her now. The deer. Kindly he said, "Tell me of your deer."

"He is not my deer. I am one of his People." She smiled softly, a challenge.

"I see." He brushed back his brown hair a moment with his fingertips.

"You should put that in a thong. Let me tie it back for you."

But he was embarrassed. She saw his face color. For a moment it grew almost as dark as Antipatihee's. She looked down at her clasped hands, sorry she had troubled him.

"You chase the deer? Is that it?"

"Not so much chasing as following after. But yesterday I chased him. He would not stay. I was troubled. Old Father?" She looked up at him.

"Please. More about the deer first?"

"Do you want him for your signals?"

"Signals? Oh, yes, signals. Yes for the words I am putting into parchments. There will be books of you all one day. And this is how we will have your stories to read in a faraway land. Not just my own land but others as well."

"Where the Franke live in great stone buildings, stone shaped as when we shape our awls, arrows and axes?"

"And others, many other, nations, lands. In many tongues the stories will be told."

"I must consider now," she said.

He bowed his head in acquiescence. The smell of simmon was deep here. He loved the sharp scent. He loved it.

23

"Old Father, will you tell me — though I have not told *you* yet what you want?"

"What is that, my child?" He took some care to use the formal more paternal term.

"Will you get the thunder arms—as they have asked you? As Horn-in-Morning asks?" Firm, she gazed at him.

"The Ehio will use them to kill their brother A'ndyans."

"That is no reason to them. They will ask you if the Franke use them on their brother enemies."

How shrewd is Leaping Fawn! He turned his face aside. Then up.

Again she saw his fringed blue eyes wide.

"I will have to tell them no," he said. He looked back at her. "Somehow."

He could not tell from her gaze, her solemn expression, what she thought of this.

"He said, "They don't need them, surely? Horn-in-Morning has a good report. Why does he ask me, I wonder."

She looked at him. "But you know, Old Father."

He nodded. "I know, young Leaping Fawn."

Came the summer with cultivation, and then harvest with the hunting, afterward the snow and winter. Father Domino had made him a garment of the deerskin and now had another, a gift of the clan, which he used for the doorway of his cell in the rock. The first of the hunt were always given to the poor — those who could not do for themselves by reason of injury, illness, or age. The friar was given the skin still slick with fat and innards, red with blood; and he prepared it himself. Now he sat quiet, meditative within, the soft sound of falling embers and scent of smoldering balsam for the comfort of his senses. He held to the deepening meditation and longing of his heart toward the Center of All Things. Outside fell the snow.

Slowly, but very slowly it grew on him that something great befell … but distantly. In the distance far, far from his inner quiet man. Far from his ears, far from the skin-covered door, from the rock in which he dwelt; far from near surrounding tall woodland, thickets and streams.

…It moved without and wakened him to its presence. With curiosity, but also with reluctance, Father Domino stood and went to the doorway. He did not pull back the skin. He had no need, for it was now in his mind: This was the attack of fierce Confederates allied against *Nation du Chat*: the Haudenosuni who dwelt in the long house, and had their nations arrayed across the mountains eastward as though a multitude of long houses built across the

24

mountains. And they were now come to destroy Ehioerrian here in woodland encampments south of the Great Lake bearing their name.

He stood quiet, without moving. Still he did not pull back the flap. He stared at the embers, sickening. It was dark in here but for that bit of glowing beneath its darkened crust, those flames roundabout guttering on candles in their pools of hardening tallow. His breath had come quickly on realization. But now—

Shoulders slumping, his neck bent, head drooping—Father Domino was cowardly, ashamed. He could not do what even now went through his mind, a headlong rush toward the camp of the nearest clan, where were believers, his converts. This was the clan headed by the wise Geagosasa, and guided in international dealings by Horn-in-Morning, who lived north of here toward the Lake. Father Domino dropped to his knees. The fall jarred him—sent sharp welcome thrusts of pain through his bones and joints. He fell on his side, moaning.

The rush of gibberish poured forth in a torrent and he but scarcely realized after some moments that he was praying in the First Tongue, the tongue of the Vanticantle's great Church by which he'd come to the Ehio.

And his mind was taken elsewhere.

And he stood on the edge of tall naked woodland where the marsh, iced and snowy, opened and prevailed: Watching the war and slaughter, men, women, children moving swiftly in the sounding chaos—screech, roar of battle. He thought not of himself or if he came in the body, soul, or spirit, but of what he saw round about him—and—he did not think—but merely witnessed.

The snow was sparse, the merest skim of pure crystal laid over everything, misting upward, clouding; and falling downward onto sheets of marsh ice clumped with sticks of cattail, leafless shrubs of laurel and other marsh plants. The shout, the *whoop*, and thundering, the screaming tumult of battle! Caht People (with long hair tied back) and some of the Haudenosuni (with bird crests), and others he might not recognize—fought hand-to-hand or with bows, arrows, spears. But many had also weaponry of cold, forged iron and steel, sending balls with explosion and smoke into human beings. Some of these targets were old men, women and children. The friar saw and recognized many of them. Little Tumbling Beaver fell beside his cousin, Broad-stroke. A great shadow passed over through mist and smoke, smelling of what he had not smelt in this world—sulfur, and he saw hands dropping cylinders from above as they moved away like dark shades, disappearing into thick dimness, dimness smelling corrosive and pale. In their wake were explosions on impact, and the gas he knew from Usi'opan warfare. It smelled— such as had been rumored there—of horseradish, making him gag, making his eyes burn. He looked down at his hands, as a cloud of it drifted past, expecting pustules and burning. But immediately his attention gave onto Antipatihee—fighting nearby with his tomhawk and coughing, screaming, hefting hand-to-hand, slashing with fleet muscular force into his bird-crested enemy (who fought so as well). Instantly Father Domino's friend the young brave was knocked to the ground; invisibly thrown, for the friar could not see whence the ball came from. Or if indeed that, though likely, was cause. Slipping and sliding on ice red-tinted with the blood of slaughter, the braves and squa (as these were known) of the Ehio hustled into, or away from, the battle. The field was overlain and dimmed with this moving miasma sent forth of these alien mechanisms of war.

How, wondered the father in detached awe, — how had these deadly and horrible munitions come to this marsh, these once peaceful woodlands? *From the Frankes!* — On the margins here in these woods, in summer, vernal pools filled with tadpoles, larva of various bugs, caddis flies, beetles, spotted salamander jelly-like eggs, and many more things found in wet lands of beauty. And he had denied such weapons to help his friends!

His gaze flew swiftly like the bird toward Leaping Fawn. It was she! Falling on the red-wet ice, clambering up again, slipping, running swiftly; in moccasins, and buckskin cloak, fringed with cat's tails, hurrying to her mother's side. But Geagosasa fell into the cattail thicket and Leaping Fawn crouched beside her. He could not see the Princess now as her young daughter covered the woman— with her own body, her cloaked form. Suddenly the girl was standing, looking about as though listening, ardently seeking. And Father Domino, who had not moved, heard it as well. The cry, great cry.

"Leaping Fawn!! Come up here!!"

The friar's gaze glanced off her and up into the treetops on the marges. He saw the antlered deer on the slope of a nearby rocky hillside.

The hillside was like a luscious tall cake, such as he knew in the great house of his childhood, white-frosted and striated with dim brown rock, and girdling tree limbs. The deer was in there! Among the thickets, iced and pure—his great rack intact though it was winter and the rut long past.

"Leaping Fawn," he bellowed in the tongue of the Caht. "Come up here!!"

The girl dashed away toward the hillside. The friar saw she was now without her cloak, perhaps left to cover her mother—he scarcely thought of it—but saw blood flying as from a fount in her side. And she was naked. She ran up the hillside and climbed through the trees where these grew in ranks ever higher.

But he could not longer watch.

For he was gone from there. And he waked on the cold floor of the cell by the hidden door, groaning.

The warfare and slaughter had taken his thought, playing again and again through his mind. He saw her naked climbing through trees, a gout of blood, her left hand to her side. Grasping the branches with her right.... Leaping Fawn.... Now she's going to Heaven. She is right—He is the Lord. The friar recognized in The Deer a creaturely form of the *Grand Créateur, Créateur* worshiped by the priest's religion and superiors. They were not alike but *the same.* —This truth sensed in the spirit of Father Domino.

He sat up. The sounds of the battle were finished—gone. How can it be? His head was in his hands, his thin frame shivering. Oh the battle! The slaughter. *The Ehioerrian.* Pray *dieu* they survive. *Prier le Grand Créateur.*

Again, he was gibbering.

A last ember died. The rock cell was silent. He was silent. He looked about his dim cave. Snowlight fell in from cracks in the rock, was bending along the margins of the skin-cloaked door. Something was moving.

"Young Father," her voice said.

It was she.

He stared in darkness... and her form was there, backlit by the doorway. Softly she pulled the skin aside. The snowlight fell on him, soft, yet pale-bright with shame. He bowed his head.

"Is... is it you, Geagosasa?"

"No, I, Leaping Fawn."

"And Geagosasa? Is she dead as well?"

"You see me alive."

"I... I saw you go to the deer."

"Yes. And I have died. And I live. I will live evermore if he's willing."

"But your mother? The Ehio?"

"All the people — my people — all gone from the land. They are gone. All but a few who go into the Haudenosuni, to serve them as they will. Even now my mother lives among them to serve them. She will be a great wise woman, sought for her wisdom. But the Ehio have become the Lost Nation. You will put it in the signals, the parchments, books you send. And they are *no more* here, the Ehioerrian. All lost.

The light, soft as it was, made him turn from her. "I am shamed," he said simply.

She came to him, kneeling, wearing her customary doeskin dress, and slung with her herb pouches made of rush.

He looked and saw the glimmering of her dark eyes, catching

the soft light from slim rock cracks behind him. He wanted to stroke her hair, her face, but refrained. He said, "Did he not take you to Heaven?"

"He took me to The Land of the Deer."

They were silent, gazing at one another. Then her look took him, lifted him up.

"It is much like this land but taller, lower. Dimmer, brighter. Fuller. Vast. —Unending as far as I might tell." She took him to the door and showed him the falling snow. "Hold." And softly she stepped into it. He could not see her for its thick falling, the endless soft falling, and falling. The snowfall. He thought of stepping in after her, tentative, fearful.

But she came back.

"Is it the snow you went into? The Ehioerrian's snow—in this land?... Or is it the snowfall of the Deer's Land? You disappeared so soon, in but a moment you were gone. I saw not the deer but that once when he called you. I saw him never when you went after him before."

"You may come with me to see many things—such as I have already seen."

"But how could you? When was the battle? I don't understand. The fire inside just went out. And why do you say Geagosasa is already great in Haudenosuni?"

"You have many questions, as always, *jeune père.*" Yes, again, she called him *young father* as Geagosasa had. She smiled a mischievous smile such as she gave to Antipatihee but a few days ago. Her smile never belittled, but included one.

"And, if I go with you—how will I write what happened to this people?" Yes, he was a little afraid. He was not ready to die and did not know if but he were already lying shivering on the cold ice marsh, on the frozen bloody battlefield among the ravened bodies of his friends. And there was no one to administer to him the last rites of mankind.

She took up his hand. Life, full of verve, went from her hand into his. Truly, he had not known the *alive* feeling until now. Now. Not ever in his whole life before.

He looked in great love and wonder on her. He felt himself tremendously braced, vivid; and yet melting, like snow falling on warm rock. Melting with love of her, and of The Deer and all things.

Gently she put back his hand by his side. "Jeune père, you will write of the Lost Nation. And of things I will show you hereafter."

He wanted to ask more about that—now that he felt himself again less alive. The thought made him desire her hand, but he dare not reach for it. The memory of life made him too humble for that.

"Then I will," he said. "I will go into the fall with you, trusting." He could not help but glance back into his cell with its loved things. He glimpsed his inks in vials on the floor by the rush mat; the melted candles, the dim racks by the far wall where snowlight fell against them. Then he snatched close his quill pen as though it were an icon or talisman.

She held out her hand. He looked, and grasped it, the life came into him. He felt his eyes shine. She smiled her solemn smile. Together they stepped into it. The snowfall. Vast fall of crystals in minute symmetries, infinite patterning. The blizzard, of purity that created all things. Just so, was Father Domino to put it on returning to his parchments: The snowfall out of which all things were formed.

For, but shortly, yet seeming many ages to him as he journeyed, he was again seated in this same cave, in his cell. It may be, he would be found here, still writing of all these things, by his C'stian brother Pinocchio, or by others, in the spring of that year in which the Lost Nation was made into history. And the good brother, or whomever, might find him living, if even thinner. For the friar had learned much of the Ehio, the *Nation du Chat*. He knew how to survive now in the wild. But the bodies of his friends were devoured by the marsh and turned into other things, like cattails and laurel and blackberries, blueberries—thence into birds-on-wing, and coyotes and other creatures such as this friar. The marsh, the friar had discovered on his travels, is a good re-maker — just as his own Maker had commanded it *be*.

HITOPOLIS 1900 EE

WIMPs

Meantime, nearly 400 years later and several kilometers east of the Lost Nation marsh, some particle physicists and technicians, head-to-toe in shiny white lab garments, sheer masks across their faces, are kneeling round the CDMS detector in the SiXPointz deep underground laboratory. The laboratory in which they work is cavernous, and gleaming with slim screen-monitors, cables and heavy equipment.

Having sprung from those who sprang from the Ultimate Imagination, these physicists and technicians were now overseeing the detection of cryogenic dark matter. They wore pale thin polypropylene gloves. One leaned over a super-cooling shaft in the floor below, intently reaching for a reddish metallic stack of six-sided objects.

Nearby, of a universe alternate to their own, six kids hovered dimly above the scientists, having slipped as if by accident into the neighborhood of SiXPointz with the particle detection. At the moment, HBBBAH, Pomala, Tu and the others weren't thinking about this strange transition as a different universe, or whether they were here by accident or design. They knew they were still together. If they were still holding hands ... this did not, at the moment, register. In fact they were holding hands—as well as dim clouds could hold hands, for these 2017 CE gang members (here called WIMPs) had been pulled across the dark gap between multiversal memBranes into a brane where they did not exactly belong. Where was here? What were WIMPs?

These WIMP onlookers, who had slipped through an interstice in spaze-time, were shadowy-dark, invisible to the eyes of these working scientists. But they were there—FivePoints gang members from an alternate universe. In the detection process they might be distinguished as WIMPs—that is, *Weakly-Interacting*

Massive Particles, a slow-moving massively spreading cloud of invisible but dark subatomic particles. One of dark matter's subatomic manifestations. As part of invisible materiality making up material existence, the gang members should be detectable in these experiments with liquid-helium-cooled crystal germanium and silicon. The most that can be said for the "look" of these basic, indivisible particles is that they are dark. Dim as ghosts, almost absent, and loosely-spreading. In essence, shadows of another, possibly similar, world.

Dimly spreading, invisibly surrounding the scientific operation, the WIMPs look on. The lab-beings, of whatever gender (it's hard at first for WIMPs to tell), kneel around a sunken coppery-bright shaft. To the WIMPs these scientists look sort of ... like deeply dimensional moving pixel shapes. Granular. Everything looks so. WIMPS do not know quite what to call the look of things they are part of.

One specialist is helping another torque a rod—clamped to a stack of these coppery-looking objects—from its berth among other such six-sided stacks in the super-cooling chamber. To the WIMPs these objects are just about the size of Nanga throwing stars, shining reddish and stacked together in their nests of six.

—You see....

Slowly, that part of the dim cloud called *His Big Black Brother Arcturus Hipster*, or HBBBAH (for short), spoke to the others: —You see.... That's how we got here.... Wherever *here* is...you hear what I be sayin'.

Past the white-garbed scientists was some coated wiring; dangling, coiled, and suspended above the workers from what look like a movable I-beam.

Tu, 1/6 part of the WIMPs, felt astonishment rise within him. He said nothing at first but, if he might be said to contain a "look" (on ghostly and lugubrious features), it would be one of astonishment. For HB had ascertained (as Tu might put it) what Tu himself had been trying to grasp with his own usually far more acute analytic intelligence. Tu's intelligence was positivist, conceptualizing of quantum theory and other physics. HB, on the other hand, was never one to go in for that—had, in fact, rather shuddered at the thought of *what* everything might be made of.

—OK, do you think they know we're here, (said Jayrai, who, in the other world, was a sleek-looking girl with wide brown eyes and biomechanical hand strong enough to crush the bones in any guy's fingers trying to put inappropriate moves on her.)   —They look ... different. Almost like pixilated...but—not. Maybe they're granules?

No one responded, either in thought or verbally. It was hard to say if they'd been directing thought—but that was how it seemed.

31

Communication, neither aural nor verbal. That part of the cloud called Pomala—the albino of the FivePoints 2017 kids—felt what she took for pressure on her own hand. It could only be from Quadri, the youngest of the WIMPs, and the most frequently in need of reassurance in these untoward adventures they had lately been having.

After a bit, Tu said, —Not as people. If it's what I think it is—and if HB is right—they'll have some evidence we are here—just not as people.

—Well, so, said Fabian. What do you think we are in that case. A gas? Some pile of ghosts. What?

He was not feeling too happy. In fact, he was still sore at Pomala for causing it all—as he sometimes thought. (He could not be sure.)

—Besides that," said the supposed offender (Pomala), and hoping to ease Quadri a little, Where *is* here? Why can't we understand what they're saying? And they look—it's almost like we can see what they're made of...at some level. Can that be Anglish they're speaking? Sounds almost.... Maybe if we listen hard.... Is this FivePoints Akropolis, or what?

—Can't be, said Tu. "This is experimentation.... I think ... they're looking for subatomic particles.... We don't have these labs in Akropolis. There is a lab underground in Minnehaha.... I *think* it's dark matter they're looking for. (For the WIMPs it now seemed that *thinking* and *saying* were the same.)

—Oh no, said HB. Here we go again. Why couldn't it be some sort of good old-fashioned séance? That's what I think. Like in the *Silents*. He referred to early 20th-century films featuring artists like Houdundy, Thebea Reab, and relying on writers like Lockshy Moles, whose stories and escapades were filmed with shockingly exaggerated facial features and heartrendingly sentimental body movements. —Can't you leave that Stephan Hiking stuff alone and get you back down to earth? Get *us* back down to earth! If these 21st-century guys called us here with this stuff let's just get on with making strange noises—maybe pull some of these wires, flick the lights, spoil us some milk.

—How do we do that? asked Jayrai. I don't even seem to have my arm. If I did I could show that off, royally. You know, make it float up there by the ceiling. Something. —How you holding up, Quad? Jayrai was not known for any overt display on the little boy's behalf, but she at least wanted to touch base, in case he was still here. She sensed a tiny edge of fear. Nobody had actually "seen" or "heard" anybody 2017 CE yet but they all seemed somehow in touch, if mysteriously, loosely. And with some sort of unknown definition.... Or was it *even* knowable?

32

Tu said, —Get used to it, HB. I've been considering it. We must be constituents of dark matter. Maybe WIMPs, MACHOS, or axions. Not neutrinos, though. We're too dark and slow for that. —Gravity. We slopped over from our universe into some other universe almost like our own. One thing is definite because we're so ignorant: *We aren't HiggsBosson. That* would be scary. And not just for us. He didn't bother to explain.

—You know.... (This from HB) I got no idea *what* you be talkin' bout. Say something I can understand. Gravity? What's that got to do with it? These guys here have gravity. What have we got? Yo, we're floating here, man. They can't see us! Then he started remembering something that had happened in the other universe—if that's what it was. When he had started that fight in Paddy's pool hall before they ran back to the cemetery, 1900 CE.

—Gravity is the force moving us from one universe to the next.

—Na-uh, said Pomala. Why are we ghosts, gas? Whatever. Why can't we be as real as they are? We were at least real in FivePoints 1900 CE when we were there and found the little girl. And I don't think you need to be sore, Fabian. I was just trying to help.

—Maybe we *are* real," said Fabian softly, now getting that she knew his thought. But just a different kind of real?

—Yes, said Tu. And this is a great opportunity for us. What we need to do is watch and see what they find. Then, because we are in this state, we will learn more about the multiverse and how it works. Can't you just be patient, HB?

—But. I. Don't. Want....

—He just wants to go back, Tu, said Jayrai. I think we're pretty much agreed. We had fun in 1900 A.D. But this here ...vagueness...is too weird. Admit it. This is so unhealthy. We can't phone, study the *Hadesthon* to figure it out. Scope the pods, apps, send vids to let'em know how we are. Nothing. All we got's.... And now she was thinking of her mother—who was uneasy, even, about being in Americle.

For the first time since they'd left 2017 CE the spookiness was getting to them: their spirits were fallen. Flat and depressive. No real bodies to speak of—they weren't, in fact, speaking, but simply virtually understanding one another.

Unconvinced, Pomala said, —What's a MACHO? It sounds better than being a WIMP, doesn't it? ...What are they doing...?

The white-garbed scientists were lifting more stacks. The technicians had climbed down from the platform, positioning robotic arms for complete removal. Some scientists crossed the spotless floors to peruse graphs on big monitors. Tu murmured, as if to

himself, *That must be for comparison.* Directing his thought he said,
—I think they're getting ready to do the math on their findings.
Then they'll know we're here. That is, what kind of dark matter, etc.
Other parameters.

He could feel the collective eye-roll.

HB grinned. Tu felt that grin.

—I'm still saying it's scientifically unrelated spiritualism.
What they be doing just *happened* to bring us in along with the
WIMPs or macros or oxymorons or whatever. Forget that shit, Tu!
We're not getting the alternate universe thing. Bogus. BoogieWoogie
man, bo-*GUS.*

But, vaporous, together they moved along after the white-clad
workers in the echoing cavernous lab: As if seeking something in
the great machinery, hardware and instrumentation. In the
monitors, materials and movements. This cloud spread and
lengthened, thinner than a vision, a questing invisible mist. As if the
mystery of their existence in this strange place of masked humans
might be understood by seeing what they did. Tu thought he knew
better. It was going to need calculus. And lots of data.

WIMPs did not, however, notice two people on the periphery
(behind every being, a part of the walls); staring at them in wonder.
Two strangers, far stranger than what the WIMPs might expect to
see in a sterile lab with such stringent codes and implementation of
design. These two strange people were clothed, not in white lab
clothes with masks, hoods, and gloves, but in buckskin—the soft
hides of animals, chewed to a delectable feel and patina, softened by
human saliva.

One of these strangers was a youthful long-haired priest,
from the neighborhood in a different age. A well traveled friar. He
had first crossed over the sea, and then the darkly wooded
mountainous continent; and come through many Next World
adventures to live among Caht People, south of the Great Lake
bearing their name. Except by this priest, Caht People had neither
seen nor been seen by Usi'opans. Nor had they heard before of the
Usi'opan Last World civilization with its fast developing steam-age.
Then the battle came with strange weaponry and materials, at the
extreme end of their national existence. Caht People had become the
lost Native Next World nation.

The other person, with a feather in her dark hair and slung
about with rush pouches, was a member of that Lost Nation, *Nation
du Chat* it was named. She was a girl, a young woman as she was
deemed though she had but fourteen summers. She had been called
from her death throes to be with THE DEER in his country, thence to
guide the good friar in his pursuit of the cataclysmic vision.

Father Domino and Leaping Fawn were come, among the

34

histories of their world, to this future time, and to this underground
lab, with its arcane experiments; in order to witness the passing of
cryogenic dark matter from one universe to another. In place, this
intersection of SiXPointz in HiTopOLis was not far from the marsh of
Lost Nation's slaughter. One or two of these academics and
scientists were local history buffs who knew of that battle and its
location, passed down from tradition and old documents,
commemorated with bronze plaque.

Here's what the priest and A'ndyan maiden saw as they gazed
silently together on the lab, on its scientists, and its guests from an
alternate existence: They saw shadowy lab people doing shadowy
experiments. ...And glowing human beings, holding hands—solid
and bright as crystals, looking on with love, and great questions
shining from their crystalline colorful eyes. These were the WIMPs,
the FivePoints 2017 gang members. As invited guests from a
different universe, they looked on. A universe slightly different,
where their own city of Akropolis, slightly changed, was here called
HiTopOLis. (Which name later they'd learn.)

The lab-dressed shadows of the friar's own world—nearly 400
years future and working on their exciting discoveries—were talking
among themselves of their work. Laughing as workers will laugh at
some joke involving their jobs. But the giant, crystalline people—
those so-called WIMPs who stood heavy, massive, tall, and glowing
roundabout them—were suddenly exclaiming. One was speaking in
consternation, even as she clung, her arm protective and encircling,
to the smallest of the colorful shimmering Giants. The historical
watchers in the walls did not yet understand her speech for these
spoke great, deep and slow. Resonant, more like to feeling (in the
chest) than to speech. The friar and A'ndyan maiden, however,
understood an expression of consternation, fear.

—1900 EE? *Oh how will we get back??!!*

—1900 CE!! The others echoed in terror. That can't be
right!

And one of them, he who was called HB, was saying —How
can this be 1900 CE!? We ain't gettin' this, girls.

—Not *CE*! They say it's 1900 EE!! *EE! EE! EE!*

—But how'd Pomala know what they're saying?

The last to speak was Tu. Even Tu, the young believer in
science. —Perhaps we'll never understand their language? How
can they be researching *dark matter* in 1900 CE??

"We've got funding!"

They had done these tests, and done them some more. And
were not yet done. But now, as Berle had proclaimed with
jubilation, and turned from the monitor to face his fellow

investigators: they were going to do *so much more.*

Someone else said, "SiXPointz is going to draw them from everywhere!"

"SiXPointz betting- bar- and brothel-land is the next center of the Darkmatter universe!" cried Berle. The turn-of-the-century, my esteemed cohorts — 1900 EE is the new beginning of the world. sHoDDylAndZ has got to go!"

And they spoke together at once, chatting, joking, hilarious in their relief and intensity of purpose. It *had* to be like this! Nothing could stop it. They were going to do all they had dreamed of doing. And more, so much more. But shieL keeL, the reverberator for *HiTop InFo* and other reverb outlets, was sitting nearby, wondering if his mockery had anything to do with his intriguingly missing wife. The molecular biologist. *Mary Bala Jones.* But maybe not. Not many people know about Mary Bala Jones. ShieL keeL had sat on it—for many months—waiting further developments without looking into it herself. Silently she negated the thought. She could not think evil of the woman.

And there were other secrets shieL keeL sat on ... for which HiTopOLis was not ready. Dangerous secrets. And made much more dangerous on revelation ... should that happen.

Tu, the WIMP from a next-door universe, thought he understood at least something and said to his subatomic friends, — That curving dotted red line is the experiment from um 1897. The blue one from uh 1898, and the dark green from 1899. The next to be superimposed will be us. The vertical scale—see the numbers, top-to-bottom, on the left? That's particle scatter—WIMPs—*weakly interacting massive particles*—indicating nuclei scattering; and the horizontal scale is for the mass of the particles."

—Plain as the nose on your face, murmured HB, watching, trying to concentrate. —But....

—But so what? said Jayrai.

—She's right, said Fabian. How's all this going to help us?

—Help, said Pomala in reflection of Quadri's pressure on what may or may not be her hand. —Said it before—so glad we're all together in this.

—Amen, as great grandma used to say. (This from Fabian.)

— I know, said HB to Fabian. When she was channeling her North Regina ancestors.

—So, Fabe answered, Think how hard it was for them to come to Akropolis from the hollers in the mountains. Maybe it was like this for them. Weirder than any words for it.

— Yo, Man. You're crazy. And talk about how hard ancestors had it—don't get me going, K? But at least she had her chewing tobacco—and teeth to chew it with! This is nothing like that. Get a grip. —So, Tu!?

—Tu, are we like channeling here, you mean? (Jayrai was asking.) Can we get somewhere, where we'll be real? Preferably back to FivePoints and the library, the pods, phones, my job.

—Job? asked Pomala.

—OK, my wanna-be. My baristaHood. I had an appointment, yo. Think I was talking about it when you grabbed the little girl's hand.

Oh no, thought Pome. —Tu??

Tu a big zero, almost felt almost a collective gaze on him.

Slowly he said, —I think we are in FivePoints but a different universal FivePoints. That may or may not mean we'd be anywhere around here—but it's to be hoped.... In the multiverse....

He felt empty, hopeless.

—What? asked Fabian, the long-hair with buzz-cut on top, the blond boy, slim jim, the (nominal) leader (all formerly).

Tu said, —Maybe—? Maybe our parallel ancestors? No. Can't be. Mine would be in Osia and Jay's in.... Oh no, we've got to forget being anything but particles, ghosts, vapor, clouds....

—Feathers and dust, finished Jayrai. House dust.

The lab, with its joking specialists, giant plastic display screens, and heavy industrial hardware seemed to grow colder, more distant. Quadri, especially, seemed to shiver and then whimper, though he made no sound. The dark cloud (as the WIMPs seemed to themselves) expanded, its nether particles escaping throughout the cavernous laboratory, darkening and filling its florescent limned upper edges with palpable gloom. But the scientists and technicians did not seem to notice. The joy of their success kept them buoyant, hopeful, alive.

—They don't even know we're here, whispered Pomala, despairing.

—They think we are nothing, an escaped nothing.... It was Jayrai. Her impression on the others now was distant, very distant. So very unlike the bold Jayrai they'd known.

Tu, by the blank disposal of his thin expressiveness seemed both analytical and bemused. —They don't know there is an *us* here in their subatomic particles ... in their triumphant quest....

—I think we should get out of here, suggested HB. His tonal quality was the most downright. And yet... to the others it seemed kind of... light. Almost feathery, as Jay had suggested, but as though a *bright* feathery-ness. As if he were saying, —C'mon, let's us be light.

It pulled them together a bit, still with that big coldness, but now they had something to try, at least *try*.

37

—How do we do that? asked Fabian. —Sneeze? Blow our noses? Hope we'll spray ourselves out through the cracks?

—I'm opting for a big fart, myself, said HBBBAH. He was grinning, they could tell.

—So, we must be underground.... (Said by Tu.) I didn't know Akropolis had iron or mafic bedding deep enough for these experiments. But—

HB said, —If we can get through the walls of the universe, how's a little iron ore, concrete and I-beams gonna stop us, chirren?

—He's right, said Pomala. —If this is FivePoints in the universe opposite to ours I want to see it.

—Not opposite—. Tu was objecting, HB saying, —Yo, think how fun *hauntin'* it's gone be. What if there's a slightly 'nother soup kitchen and we be all like scarin' the homeless?

—Can we bend spoons, think? (said Pomala)

—Just by thinking, suggested Jay.

Meanwhile they'd been lifting upward (as it would seem to one watching this dim cloud disappearing out of the company of men and women, slipping through astronomical interstices in bedrock as through the seeming vacuum of outer spaze, nothing hindering).

—But let's hold together, said the virtually disembodied Pomala. —We need each other, huh, Quad! She could suppress neither excitement nor trepidation, but he was still with her, she could tell.

—Look-at-it. We be better'n' gas! (said HBBBAH)

—We're Spidey in particles. Nothing but nothing can move like this! said Fabian.

And up they went, through concrete and forged steel, porous as the multiverse, made, as were they, out of "nothing'n'spit," said HB.

But the rocks and concrete walls, the girders and beams that were in fact as nothing, watched them, dressed in buckskin and feathers, on the periphery—amazed. For, as Father Domino and Leaping Fawn watched, like the very material of Next World's existence, these child giants (of their alongside universe) climbed with massive jewel-like hands and feet; and as though with great bones of ebony, of ivory, and skins of abalone; up through the clouds of Next's substrata. Out past great works beneath the city and its outskirts with people working in protective uniforms. Out into the open of SiXPointz HiTopOLis, with its unexpected intersections and solarized traffic, controlled by grids under the city whose ponderous labyrinth they had just escaped. To the two watching heavenly gatherers (and disseminators of visions) WIMPs were glowing crystalline giants handling the earth and its processed constituents—as though it belonged to them.

But to the WIMPs themselves—the WIMPs seemed barely existing. A veritable *nothing*. Just the barest material of questionable mass. Thought up by some unknown and unknowable, some outrageous unspeakable, Mind.

The two witnesses of their departure felt the great hands, knees and feet of the jeweled Giants stomping, pulling, kicking and punching them in a scramble to ascend and be venturing in the city on top of the earth. But Father Domino and Leaping Fawn stayed behind, corporal materials through which the WIMPs had floated away. Then Father Domino and Leaping Fawn were once again, and without harm, free to observe the white-garbed investigators of cryogenic dark matter. The workers had removed their masks and hoods and stood in contemplation of their findings as configured above them (some), though here and there stations were taken by others seated before smaller screens, making notes on small deVices with styluses.

One of these was the contractual reverberator with *Virtual Futures*, *HiTop InFo* and other outlets; and she was loading the experiment, while simultaneously recording audiovisuals.

"Better leave out the bar-and-brothel comment, shieL," said Berle over his shoulder at her. The others chuckled and another, Puce, said, "Leave in the part about the funding and draw!" More chuckles. Then silence settled in the cavernous laboratory for a time, shieL speaking softly to her audience for she wanted to project the similitude of a working scientific/academic atmosphere. She, too, wanted a serious intent to shine through. She wanted the world to watch, to see what it was to work on, and discover, great truths.

Father Domino and Leaping Fawn watched as well, their own eyes and ears intent. An aura of silence and shimmer of study enthralled them for a time. Then Leaping Fawn spoke. It was a respectful whisper to her companion, and her gaze conveyed also the green glimmer in her eyes, reflecting the light of the deer's country.

"Do you understand, *jeune père*? Do you know what are the Giant Children? Or the people dressed in white so busy and concentrated in their labors?"

Father Domino was silent, thinking of something else, gathering his thoughts in wake of his excitement in seeing, experiencing even peripherally, such strange elements and encounters in this exceeding great vision.

Then, he said, with some hesitancy, "...I may yet speak of them. —But more—this is the underground, the earth... out of which the great monster will ascend and trample all things on top.... The top of the earth. Such as we saw being used on your people.

39

These great mechanisms come not from the creatures flying or roaming above, such as our garments are made of. They come not from the trees growing, out of which you make bows and arrows.... Of course the flints and chert you use come out of the earth, but of their own accord. Or rather, of the earth's own accord ... for you to find there."

He stopped. But she kept her peace. And, again, he spoke, "With such heavy and massive materials, cured or forged as they are with great heat, the monster will be able to crush everything on top, all things lovely and blooming, delicately flying such as damsel flies, birds that hum and dart, trees and blooms necessary to their sustenance."

"Very good, so far, *petite père*," she said, smiling. "These things you have no doubt thought of before, and will write in your parchments, books and scrolls. And you will tell, first, what happened to my people. People who refused to spare cats from their comforting vanity. But what of these various peoples? Those ascending crystalline Giants so full of love, and these underground people working?"

"These studying their findings in this cave below are the monks and nuns at their gifted labors for Good has made all sentient beings to have each their gift. These must be as parchments and as books." Here he gestured with his quill pen towards the screens. "They interest me very much. I would like to stay and learn what it is they study and I would find out many things that may be of value.... To my own fellow scholars in the Brothery north of Caht Peoples' Great Lake." Here he stopped and looked with innocence and hope upon her.

Leaping Fawn understood his hope but did not address it. She said, "Each place and time has its own knowledge and understandings, and so, for the former knowledge and understanding there is honor, because the later learning could not be but for what went before... as you have yourself learned in your studies of things former that have in large measure (but not all) passed away."

"*Oui, tellement.*"

"But what of the others, the Giants who hurt us in their passing? The scholars here have not hurt us. You no doubt will look into why that is, but perhaps you have some understanding now? Only think where we are. The Caht Peoples have lived here and have died as a nation."

"But in a different time, maiden?"

"*Mais oui, petite père.*"

"And it is our people, yours and mine of each generation, who helped these students through many times and inventions, each passing away but leaving ever more knowledge behind."

"You are wise to include my people for once your people were even as they in their uses of great nature's making. Too, the vanquished have achieved greater learning in meeting their invaders on Usi'opans' more learned instruction."

"However...." But here the friar hesitated, doubtful.

She said, "It is as THE DEER has taught me. They learn more and more of what is not most needful."

The friar was disappointed. His joy fled. He had been delighted with the new learning and was about to declare it the Other Next World—highest of distinctive phrases in his mind.

After a moment, he said, "The Giants are, I think, somehow involved in the studies of this peculiar Brothery. And they cannot be from this land and time. Are they then celestial beings? That look of love I have not seen before except in you, but only dream of elsewise. Once or twice."

"These are, as you say, what the students study with their instruments of detection, but are not seen as we have seen them." She stopped, as if listening, a look of stillness in her dark, solemn eyes. In a moment she said, "We may see them yet again, these beings that they study. Would you like to look once more upon the students' parchments?"

In his assent they move close, becoming no longer listening walls but slim gleaming lights as thrown down from illumination high above, yet clad still, in their own eyes, as ever. But, to the scientists at their screens, the two become as glimpses of inspiration, lights that shine within the mind, enhancing, and guiding (just a bit) toward some new idea, or avenue of learning not seen before.

Then Father Domino and Leaping Fawn were gone.

Where did they go, if not to chase the Crystal Giants and witness their adventures?

They went hence. To the mountains of a moon in that solar structure of their planet and universe.

Standing atop the white-dusty slopes, they watch the slow and awful moving of two galaxies, one disc-like, made of star grains; the starry other as with wings reaching far across the universe. These two giants merge in remaking, amid the flux of gravitation and shearing forces, great coruscating fountains and foundations of light. In their flying dance, transforming local heavens, two mighty colored flashing giants, *Andromita* and *Creamery Way* corresponding in their dance. Here some trillions solar systems gather in vibrant, shimmering, and colorful display.

And these two watchers stand alone in the silver mountains, with but each other, to see it. Their hearts are filled with love for all the celestial bodies, and all those souls contained therein, and for the dance itself. The mighty dance, of disc and whirling wingéd light that shone and slowly shook together. All shone as if for Father Domino and Leaping Fawn. As if for them alone.

s. dormAn

SiXPointz HiTopOLis

Meantime, what are the giants doing up in HiTopOLis, the
city neighborhood and universe parallel to their own? As these
WIMPs emerge from underground in clouds of particles too small for
surrounding eyes to see, what do they find?

—Watch this! It was, of course, expressive Jayrai saying this,
emerging into the light of SiXPointz. But then she stopped in awe of
these great surroundings. SiXPointz 1900 EE of the parallel
universe is high and densely compact of soaring massive buildings
glinting in the light of late afternoon sun. Shadows darken one side
of glassy next-door-neighbor skyscrapers. This is the deafening
concrete-and-polymer press of virtually pixilated structuring, piled
high into the air of the roaring soundscape (waves of which they are
a part)—piled so high the sky is scarcely seen except in moving
reflection on plate-polymer. The city is surrounded by glittering
suburbs and a huge athletic complex on the west side.

Next Jayrai did her best to seem to hold hands with her
fellow gang members. And at once she felt the answering press of
their psyches on her own in response. How would they inhabit any
disembodied episodes or adventures in this gleaming crowded scary
place? Pome was wondering...how to get home.... Worrying.

Now that the two witnesses from another time are no longer
there and seeing them as crystal giants, the FivePoints 2017 gang
are but ghosts. Ghosts to anyone, ghosts to themselves. Dim
clouds, but with personalities and other attributes of the human:
Able, as though with eyes to see and ears to hear, but with no body
each might in some sense *own*. What is a human being if the
elements of its flesh are scattered? Pomala, Fabian, HBBBAH, Tu,
Jayrai and Quadri might say they are alive and have *feeling*—are
possessed of emotion—they react and perceive much as always. But
with this difference: they have no bodily form to interact, or to act
upon other bodies. Even the inanimate—iron-concrete-glass—they
go right through without effect. But another conception might say

they are *part* of all.

Jayrai could not recognize, in this deafening monstrous city, the city of her own universe with its population of a mere quarter-million. It was alien to her frame of reference, her familiar and intimate neighborhood with its familiar, and comfortable, neighbors.

—Oh, guys, this is so ... sprawling cosmo— *Nandian!* Can't be Akropolis. Not even Americle.

And everybody else thought, —*Tu?!*

But Tu was overwhelmed and silent. He almost wasn't there. For once his analytical thought escaped him.

—Tu!! Tu!! They wanted him so. As each identity hovered over the sweltering pavement beneath the sun- and cloud-reflecting massive glass, their thought was united in search of him, almost with desperation.

—I'm here. He sent his thought at last.... —There's almost no me here to help, though.

—*OMG!* The soul of Pomala screamed. —Are you sure? Are you sure you're Tu?

How could this be Tu? This wuss, this emoting wimp. It's got to be someone else! Maybe another universe leaked a parallel and dumber Tu? What would they do without the smart kid? This scattering of almost nothing ... expanding all its borders as it rose in consternation among the futuristic structures of the *oh-so-alien* world. The WIMPs spread out so far and high in agitation that, while still somehow clinging in strange awareness of one another, they encompassed traffic and intersection below—*and* they met above the gigantic structures of HiTopOLis. Then, in great surprise, and still aware and holding to one another in loving consciousness, together they looked down upon their outspread and sketchy cloud of virtually invisible particles. Glancing through its (as it seemed to them) dimly glimmering vapor, they saw the intersection spread far below in glorious patterning. Like a snowflake in crystals configured with increasing complexity in spurs of walkways, streets and passages. And it was not FivePoints as they had hoped to see, but SiXPointz! A six-starred intersection! —glorious configuration of the most moving kind.

And they loved it. They loved everything. Even Quadri and Pome who wanted to get back...where? But they fell in love with the beautiful and moving scenescape—patterning shot through with moving particles of humanity far below.... Humans simply—as they guessed — going about their daily business, late afternoon shimmering gold inside the standing canyons, clad in light and cloud.

Mesmerized, they watched the traffic far below and sometimes dipped their gaze to street-level to see how six emerging avenues crossing at the intersection could route their traffic so precisely without mishap. They saw doubled tunnels for three avenues of one-way traffic, and bridges for three others. The vehicles seemed to couple and uncouple. They moved quietly, as quiet as do many electric cars in their own place and time. The deafening noise, at first supposed to be traffic alone, was simply non-point in source. It came from everywhere—the insides of buildings and underground maintenance works, the speech and shouting of pedestrians on moving sidewalks, the flying cars shooting in and out of canyons with an orderly synchronized flow. And everything was reflected in dizzying array from the vast and shining glass walls of the city — monstrous city — whose glamorous spell both enraptured and excited them.

—Look! On the outskirts! They must have the Olympics here!

When, at length, the sunlight slid away and the sky was changing, fading, there came a moment, very magical, when the WIMPs, still held the mighty intersection in loving gaze. Just then: Artificial lights everywhere shone in the deep blue and faded evening sky, and they saw within its buildings people of HiTopOLis moving, thousands upon ten-thousands moving within the lit-glass canyon walls, level upon level. But some walls were opaque—as though closed to view from other human eyes. But this did not stop the *weakly interacting massive particles* from penetrating walls. Everything, in all buildings great and small was revealed to them.

Many things they saw these HiTopOLis humans doing. Some good, some bad, some frightening and evil. Yet the WIMPs themselves, now less anxious on their own behalf, felt nothing but love for all the folk they saw—all but evildoers, who did what WIMPs knew were evil doings in the flesh of human beings to other human beings. These they could not love.

And many people they saw were hurting, or hurting one another. All the vices of humankind absorbed so many of the suffering. And yet, also many humans were there to alleviate suffering. There were offices with cubicles, and brothels, casinos, classrooms, laboratories for experimentations, hospitals—all with multitudes of workers. All were visible to the WIMPs. These young watchers were as clouds of six-pointed witness. And they were mesmerized, together.

—Doesn't this city ever sleep? HB was asking.

Pomala said, —You mean like we used to sleep when we had.... She stopped.

—When we had bodies. Fabian finished for her.

—Yo, yeah-o, we had bodies, echoed Jayrai. —We had flipping bodies!

—Bodies?

A very tiny query. It was Quadri's, the youngest of the FivePoints gang now in the alternate universe. And this was the first time his thought was felt—not as some *impulse* of a lost and little child, but as a verbal construct, a question he was hoping some one of them might answer. Not Tu or HB or even Fabian, but maybe Jay or Pomala. —Bodies? Quadri really wanted to know.

They were silent, still gazing, listening, yet attentive to him.

—I want to go back, he said. —I don't want to be a ghost.

Pomala asked, —Don't you like to see them all, Quad? She so wanted to comfort him.

—It's—it's a little like a game, suggested Fabian.

—Yeah, said HB, —One we can't control. We can't make these characters do anything! As yet unaware that he was part and parcel with all these things, he peered like some invisible giant into a building where nurses and doctors in scrubs and other uniforms went to and fro. And there were moving gurneys with people on them. HB seemed to make as part of a wall with several doors, opening his mouth very wide—as he felt—recollecting the action from his time in the flesh—and some orderlies walked a laden gurney through, its bald-headed occupant softly groaning.

—See? I can't do anything with them but watch... and maybe sniff? Maybe not sniff. Listen to what they say. It don't make much sense at the moment, but maybe if I wait a while? See if anything comes through?

—OMG, softly murmured Tu.

—OMG—is this Tu?!" Pomala held Quadri closer in her loving psyche.

—No, said Tu. —Don't you see? We are *irreducible* quanta.

—Yo, what you talkin'? said HB. —We still seem to be people, bro. You saying we can't get no smaller — um, have our personalities, um — oh shit!

But, considering, Pomala thought, —Oh good! See, Quad, it's Tu after all. He's not some other Tu. (And) *OMG!* Would you look at the elevator! It looks like it's nothing but light! There— where they put the sick old guy down HB! His gullet or whachacallit's made out of light! She thought she saw him in the building's features and lights.

—Ow-soom, whispered Quad.

Tu muttered. —HB, that's what I mean. I mean we're irreducible as both personalities and quanta.... And, incidentally, those are photons, electromagnetic radiation. They make up light.

—Don't feel a thing! HB declared it. Grinning, they were sure.

Fabian said, —I think we better pray. I, I mean....

—He means we in deep du-du. —Oh *c'mon, Fabe,* how's

46

that gone help? said HB. Then he stopped, remembering what happened in the other universe—if that's what it was. When he had started that fight in Paddy's pool hall 1900 CE—only there they said 1900 A.D. He was sorry almost a moment after he started that fight in Paddy's with those out-of-date racists. And then the whole thing changed. The fight was gone like it didn't happen. It went back to being what it might have been if he hadn't started that fight. *And no one was hurt after all.* No one was killed. Even though he had *seen* Tu getting the breath beat out of him. Maybe the whole thing had something to do with that part of his head integrated with a special eye applied science had given him? He just didn't know how all that had happened. He remembered calling out for help. And there was the big fellow going past peripherally—or in his enhanced mind's eye. Was that a prayer?   —And then everything was OK—except he couldn't figure it out. Dubious, now he said, "Maybe we need more science. Maybe that'll get us back to where we belong?"

　　—But, said Fabian, science is what got us here in the first place. That experiment down there in the big lab—after the A'ndians and the crypt and 'the little girl'. I don't think I'd trust it to get us back to what we were. Tu?

　　—So....

　　—OMG! said Pomala.

　　— ... It's just....

　　—He's got *no* ideas! said Jayrai.   —*Nada*, none, no dink. It can't have been the Native Americles. They came out of the crypt with us, just before we got here—wasn't it? They took 'the little girl' from Pome, but with science? —I don't think so.

　　Pome said, —And it can't have been 'the little girl'—even though Fabian thinks I'm responsible just because I wanted to get her some help.

　　It was true that Fabian was sore at Pomala for grabbing the little girl's hand after Tu did the calculations from *The Hadesthon*. She had grabbed the little girl away from the gravedigger's brother just as the tower clock began striking toward 11. Tu had had it all worked out on the basis of his calculations regarding Pluto's orbit from the game. If she hadn't grabbed the little girl's hand they might be back in their own place and time—still embodied people, still playing the game. But no— .

　　—Look, I'm sorry I did that, OK?!

　　He sighed, —OK, Pome, OK. I forgive you.... But still, seriously, we should pray. My great grandma would. She says it helps things. Tu? Fabian was giving Tu an extra-sensory nudge, seeing if he was still with them, hopeful that Tu was not going to fade —or anything. They just had to keep together. That's all. Just somehow keep together.

Meanwhile, the new and fascinating city was like living structured light, welling up from the ground, the street, the substratum, in solid geometric structures, processed and culled from earth's storehouse of elemental materials. And really, they could not take their eyes off it for a moment. Not with all that play and movement, deep and loving yet potentially disturbing drama, of this other place. This— ?

—Tu, how far away do you think these parallel universes— did you said alternate, parallel? —how far away from our universe are we? said Jay.

HB asked, —Would we need a wormhole, d'ya think? To get back? Like in the old SF movie?

—*Contac? ConSmack*!! That was so ow-some, agreed Pomala. —But we'd need a lot of hardware and energy.

— ... But how would we—? murmured Tu, as if to himself. His presence was scarcely discernable.

—We better pray, said Fabian.

—Pray.... echoed the small thought of Quadri. He was virtually mesmerized by the lit surroundings beneath a dark and seemingly closed dome of sky. How would he face the East? They could not even see the stars. Maybe if they went higher? Quad wondered, anxious.

—Maybe we need both? suggested Jayrai. Maybe we should pray to some deities to get the science we need to get us back?

The city seemed to swell—here gleaming, there glimmering — glowing around them. They realized that they were sinking down; or, at least, in inertia their attention had fallen. It hovered, its massive scattering of particles covering the strange six-pointed intersection, or six-lanes stretching; of commercial and personal lines toward six directions into, and away from the city center of.... They could not quite call it *Akropolis*, neither could they yet think it HiTopOLis.

Tu had been *incommunicado*, but now ventured something. —She may—I want to nuance this—she *may* be right. Maybe we need both. Maybe each one, religion and science—maybe each has a different purpose.

—You mean like the difference between a toothbrush and toilet bowl brush? This, of course, was HB's contribution to the profound conversation they now engaged.

Fabe said, —Those do the same thing—scrub. Just on different surfaces. They are virtually the same tool, HB.

—Right, said Tu. Like the difference between—. Science is a way of finding out and proving things, rationally. It uses reason, but can't answer one reasonable word: Why? Intelligent design is a redundant coupling of words and an oxymoron in this context, btw.

—So now there's a new kind of moron. (HB) Can I get in on that? Newness and all.

Tu kept on. —Why is everything, uh, here? Religion is about a god and interacting morally. Master Kung, ethics and like that. We're not sure how rational that is. Because if there's a god—. You wouldn't be able to prove god. If a god is—. Everything, all laws and maths and molecules and processes and evolution can be studied and known but their maker would only be inferred, or be an opinion.

—The reason why we can't prove there's a God is because we aren't smart enough. (Fabian) Only God could prove there is a God. Your dog cannot prove that you are a human being. He can only follow you around, wagging his tail.

—Lucky him, he's got a tail. (HB)

—Inferred? You mean *guessed*? Jay might have been rolling her eyes—if she had eyes.   —So how does that help? she said.

—So science is like the ruler, said HB, and Big Fello is the dude who thought up and made the ruler?"

"Hey, there goes one of the scientists who brought us here!" said Pomala.

—Where? Everyone was asking.

—There, where the building is streaming light and people.

—They all are, remarked Fabian.

—There, beside the taxi stand or whatever it is, where the light-copters and cars take off. She called them light-copters a term of her own invention. But she had no idea how they worked.

They looked at the streams of humans going in and out the tall, massive, light structure.

—Come *on*, let's follow him, she said. They could feel her impulse tightening and tugging their scattered attention toward this particular structure, ignoring its giant porticoed doorway rhythmically opening and closing, opening, closing, and passing through the building's elements like so much lit mist.

—They all wore scrubs, said Jayrai. —How come you think it's him?

—I was in all that gear, hoods and masks, gloves. Didn't you do it?

—Naw, said HB, we was too busy figuring out their game. Like, were we pool balls in Paddy's, ricocheting through universes, or just plain old ghosts in one of Big Fello's moth-eaten stories?

—You keep thinking about that, said Jay. I don't remember any of that happening. No Big Fello. I'd still like to know how far from our universe we are, she continued. —Look, he's in the elevator.

The man was stocky, like his name. He is Berle, the

scientific (not administrative) head of the program, has a bit of a
paunch and is clean-shaven, with reddish hair, and golden eyes full
of calm humor, when untroubled.

—Stretch your gullet, HB! said Jayrai. —Get him to the top.
Wait, he's off now. Let's go in. By this she meant filter through
walls and make themselves at home—attending only to the rooms
this particle physicist lived in. —Forget that other stuff, Quad.
That thinking about how to face East. Meediinaa's on hold for now.

—I don't think the man'll get us back without help, Jay, said
Fabe. —Let Quad go ahead and pray if he wants. BTW, Tu, how far
are we from home?

—Yeah, from the REAL universe, said HB. Not this hiccup of
Big Fello's.

The man went into a room off the compact square hall
opening between kitchen, living room, and three bedrooms with
baths.

—How many light-years will it take? Will Aunt Sissy and Griz
and the home-folk be daid by time we get back. Or what? HB said it
lightly but felt dark, sunken and glooming. ... If Fabe did not think
the dude could help them. Only the warmth of these pointillist
rooms, their steady comforting glow, encouraged him.

—It's just that—he's not God, said Fabe. If he had a look,
and it could tell, it might or might not be a shrug. Maybe a hopeful
shrug?

—Let the man talk, said HB. By this he meant Tu, not the
scientist.

Jayrai thought, —*Make* the man talk.

Tu said, —Watchit, Jay. You want smart kid or not?

—OMG!! said Pomala.

—OMG! said all but Tu. Tu doesn't say much but when he
does it is only firm, dry, analytical talk. He keeps quiet because he
doesn't like to see the eyes rolling. Which is different from the
withdrawal he's been experiencing on this phase of their dynamic
experience. This tough talk is definitely not Tu.

But HB was off again. To Jayrai, —You don't remember
wrestling with the lamplighter? —That grip of yours 'bout put him
under. HB had taken it in from the corner of his eye just as the
roomful began pummeling him in the pool hall, 1900 CE. Now he
was saying this to her, trying to figure out what she knew about that
incident in Paddy's.

—Nope. Now shut it. Thought you wanted one of Tu's
discourses? She said *discourses* with disdain and exaggeration, but
she wanted to know. Hugely.

—What are they talking about? said Pomala. The new
universe's scientist was in the bedroom with his son, leaning against

the wall by the bed, looking at the bedtable screen, talking. They could see through the walls and windows to the twilight ambience of the city, glowing and sparkling in coruscating variation. The boy was in bed with a table tray and food—vaporous bits of burger molecules signaling—plus there was a built-in screen, tilted for easy viewing. WIMPs were a part of these things.

—If we could understand that talk we could signal him to get us the shit outta here, said HB.

Tu had withdrawn again. But, while fading from the WIMPs' attention, he was contemplative, concentrating. He was ready any moment to give them his rational opinion that, if this was a parallel universe, they were about a centimeter or half-inch away from the FivePoints they had inhabited much of their lives. In Fabian and Pomala and HB's case virtually forever. But... was it the time scheme of CE 2017, or 1900 A.D.? However, that question was peripheral, not where his concentration focused. He was just trying to understand the conversation between man and boy.

Berle and his golden-haired son, named Gneis, were talking about an aspect of biology, that of transformation from one form to another—as in the metamorphosis of caterpillar to butterfly. In particular, Berle wanted to know if the butterfly retained any memories of the caterpillar. (In translation) he said to his son Gneis, "Does it recall, for instance, its last meal on milkweed? Or what it was like crawling around on all sixteens?"

The WIMPs, though not getting the conversation, were aware of another teenager moving around in an adjacent room, the kitchenette.

Berle said, "I heard it turns into soup in the chrysalis. How's soup remember anything?"

"S-soup," said the teenager after swallowing a small bit of burger. "P-pretty good, Dah — 'thinking' soup. The soup's made of ... cells called em-imaginal discs... in some s-soupy stuff left over ... from caterpillar p-parts. The important thing is those imaginal cells ... that become butterfly parts. Enzymes ... virtually digest the caterpillar."

"So soup—does it remember?"

"T-tricky, but ... yeah. Neurons survive ... soup and butterflies remember. ...M-maybe the cell soup is unconscious."

"Maybe it's enjoying its own taste?" said Berle.

—They're talking about metamorphosis, said Tu after some moments. —Caterpillar to butterfly. Like that. See the screen images? But I get the idea the dad, I think it's his dad, already knows. He just wants to see what his son knows.

—Wow you got all that? said Pomala. She meant the subtlety in Tu's surmise. It was based, of course, on Tu's own experience.

—So does the kid know anything? asked Jay. —Or is he like us? — meaning *not Tu.*

—Apparently, said Tu, meaning the kid knows.

—Will you be able to talk to him? —the dad, I mean, said HB.

—Not until I get a mouth, said Tu.

—OMG! said Pomala.

Tu was not explaining the technical difficulties. *Tu was being satirical!* So not Tu.

HB was saying, —Maybe they've got DiGiOuija to download? We'll just send'em some brainwaves and they'll get it.

—If we could send brainwaves, said Fabian, we wouldn't need the OuijaBorge.

—I-knew-that. We's bein' light here.

But then the room was full of people, other people in the flesh. Teenagers talking and laughing and wearing wee flashing colored lights—all over their bodies—almost like piercings or tattoos, but lights. FivePoints 2017 thought of the correspondence at once. These teens were tremendously attractive, brimming with energy and intelligence, apparently full of wisecracks. They wore strange gear— what looked like headsets—abbreviated helmets—with visors pushed up on their foreheads. Sheesh, Gneis's brother who had been in the kitchen, came in with them. Fabian had seen him open the apartment door for them. Or at least he had waved a hand or done something else—Fabe couldn't quite tell what—to make it open.

—Gotta be us! In this universe, said Jayrai. —Those guys are the SiXPointz kids. Gotta be.

—Tu? suggested Fabian. —See if you can get what they're doing.

While the SiXPointerz were talking, laughing, getting Gneis going on some game or other, the parallel universe from neighboring FivePoints filled all the space and objects around them with their vast attentiveness. There was no evidence of WIMPs anywhere that these HiTopOLis humans were aware of. But they were there in deep concentration. The WIMPs had no bodies, unlike these new-to-them teenagers from this strange glowing city of particular lights and various glimmerings. WIMPs had no defining flesh in vascular activity—no parts pumping blood through ventricle, veins and arteries. No nerve endings to be damaged, interfering with the synaptic, and thus motor, activity. They were almost like a soup for extraction of what they might yet become. But not quite. And no real idea of it—or where, when, how, it might yet happen. So they forgot it now, and became observers instead. *Weakly interacting massive particles* from another universe. Not so very far away.

s. dormAn

XploHding Whorllds™

Meantime, Father Domino and Leaping Fawn have nowhere to stand as they watch the smaller planetesimal Theo blindside their own larger planet. This is the beginning of all things for them, all constituents of their material being are now cycling, as they witness, into the making of Eartha, their home. Who can say what these two *humane* witnesses are made of or how they are made? In spaze, amid invisible dark matter, they witness this great collision. Their planet Eartha—molten, turning on its vertical axis—is met by Theo spinning off past Elios. Theo has been thrown from its course by the star's greater gravity ... slamming into Eartha with explosive force. Kinetic energy, energy of mass and motion in combination, frees great burning blinding bits of crustal matter and—as the two witness—these great burning chunks, coalescing, swiftly turn lunar, becoming moons beyond the exploding broken planet. Yet swiftly, as they watch, it seems the melting crust of Theo, in making these flying spinning moons, has left behind its greater body—a molten core—to meld with that of great Eartha. These two planets, the lesser Theo and the greater Eartha, become one, now tilting on its axis. The gravitational force of the remade planet's two moons dampens its wild spinning ... slowing ... slowing. Now one massive molten planet Eartha, in heaven, is, in its movement, restrained to the orbit of the star. Its own sun-star, called Elios.

The two witnesses are in no way injured. They feel not the physical force of energy releasing, except in some residual way—in some spurring movement of their soulical being. They are but psyche, *impressed*, feeling the thrill of witness intensely. Invisible Being has brought them here in this limited form, sustaining them. They know only that they are out of body—unable to experience except within the confines, each, of his or her own soul.

And now they are in Gneis's bedroom with members of the SiXPointz gang—friends of the fraternal twin brothers. Here the gang plays the game of XploHding Whorllds™ wearing 4D™ visors over their eyes—looking like insects—moving targets here and there,

53

or exploding things, with a look. But a game. The idea is to play making a new heaven and eartha, BABY™, a.k.a. the new creation. The gang's team call themselves the MACHOs. Kidz they play against, who lived in various parts of Eartha, are called RAMBOs. The MACHOs play together whenever they can—that is, in the same physical space. But often they play into the small hours in their own apartments, some under the covers (if they don't want grown-ups to know).

Father Domino and Leaping Fawn also see the Giant WIMPs, who arrived in their universe (earlier below SiXPointz, in the laboratory). The site is not far, in location, from where Leaping Fawn's clan, as part of the *Ehioerrian* or Caht People, were destroyed nearly four centuries before. It is known in Berle's time as the Lost Nation (partly through Father Domino's historic scholastic effort).

The Next World Native and the friar saw the WIMPs as materialized Giants in crystalline form. They too had become part of the structure of the apartment and were visible to the two witnesses as glorious shining structure—of windows, walls and doors, of furniture; with gigantic shimmering faces like jasper and other crypto-crystalline quartz. Their eyes shone as though emerald, golden beryl, topaz, onyx-stone, tourmaline, and mother-of-pearl. (This last would be Pomala who was albino in FivePoints Akropolis of the universe next door). The WIMPs were unaware of the two witnesses who themselves had no actual appearance during this particular visit to the time beyond Father Domino's own.

"Think you to behold the images they manipulate and partake of, *mon petit père*?"

"*Mais oui, ma princesse.* But first, tell me what we have here."

He did not like to admit that he saw no images save the people in the room, and what was on Gneis's screen. What images? Were these images she spoke of in some way like those of *le Grand Créateur* that they had witnessed—the great making and remaking of the planet Eartha? For she had him to understand what was the nature of that cataclysm.

"What have they on their heads?" he said. "For I perceive their head is not in its true condition. At least, I trust, *le Grand Créateur* has not made them so. For these have, almost, the head of the insect with its great dark eyes, mandibles and antennas."

"That is correct, *jeune père.* They see scenes, people, creatures and accoutrement invisible to their own eyes, needing the special head covering with its special eyes. In this manner they play much as you, in your world and time, have seen the masked ball, the play in the theater; and also this is like pieces moved upon the chess table, and is somewhat in the manner of frontCannon, in

54

which tokens are exchanged, signifying—whether great or small—loss and gain. And the Giants from alongside SiXPointz are curious, as are you. I might tell you the story of each person from these two separate places, yet understand we are here to find out 'the game.' Each has his or her own tale to tell, but that may be for the book of some other *érudit*, not your own."

"Say on then. Or better, *princesse*, show me the game."

Thus, as observers, they entered the gamescape in which MACHOs might help bring BABY™ to LIFE™. Each in depletion of its own energy, steps of conception and differentiation would bring BABY to LIFE. The game began with a BIG BAMM™, as the MACHOs initiated the first round. Their opponents, the RAMBOs, tried to block its expansion with various tactics. Cooling, stasis, rerouting, warping, flux and counter explosions were all tried. But when RAMBOs tried these counter explosions, all their initiatives backfired and BABY was well on its way to being launched. As a result of RAMBOs' tactical maneuvers, and with counter maneuvers on the part of the MACHOs, there was much energy-laden debris floating about in the ultimate dust of XploHding Whorllds' atmosphere—created as a result of energy loss and exchange.

Cadillalaxies had been born and were now birthing solar systems at a prodigious rate. Of course the gamescape of XploHding Whorllds included ingenious visual pyrotechnics. Sound—shouting as voluminous as a hallelujah chorus—had been added to intensify the experience. This dampened the realism for those kidz aware of its gratuitous nature—as some were aware that RL sound-waves outside Eartha atmosphere had yet to be discovered. But ultimately the hallelujah shout heightened BIG BAMM's emotional value.

Watching it all, Father Domino was enchanted. As shown, Leaping Fawn had instructed him in the real BIG BAMM. Prior to that he'd had no appreciative perception of creation beyond a few quiet but colossally powerful commands. Now, watching the game, he missed the immediate presence of Leaping Fawn. She had been with him prior to entering the gamescape but, in the game's excitements, he had lost track of her. Now—as he appeared to himself—standing a bit cartoonish and flat-footed on *Planet Genesis* (tiny, and turning slow slowly beneath him)—he watched the spectacle of spaze-time spreading and rippling before him. And, before ever truly missing her, he began to detect Leaping Fawn's presence dispersed here and there throughout the glorious elemental 'scape in all its various subatomic particles and coalescing elements, its stars and worlds. Next, but peripherally, he could see her solemnly smiling, through all—directly at him.

Leaping Fawn. Leaping Fawn.

Yes, she said, *it is I. I suggested the gamescape to Berle, the scientist, and he ordered its designing for the children.*

But how was this?! You have no doubt been consulting the messenger-tutors of le Grand Créateur, *and inspired this father on Eartha with the great maker's gift! He knew you not?*

Mais oui, mon petit frère. Mais oui. *He knew me not. But wait! This is not all. BABY is not yet born. Watch! And you shall see more.*

The explosiveness and coruscating elements, along with the scarcely discernible laws of the game's lineaments and structure, spoke to him *with her own familiar Ehioerrian accents.* Also he might, here and there, on his periphery, glance at her familiar face— if he but refrained from trying for it with his direct gaze.

Meanwhile, outside the gamescape in the bedroom of the MACHO named Gneis, the teenage gamers were shouting.

"Don't let BABY get sucked back to the ABYSS™!" (Sheesh)

"BABY's gonna make it this time!" (hipPo)

"SloTh's too slow—can't do a thing!" (biMbo)

"WarPer's just making it easier!" (Claude)

Sheesh yelled, "Watch-out-move-on-that-counter-explosion — get some of that energy! BABY's gonna make it! BABY!!"

These members of the SiXPointz neighborhood were moving about the room. Peripheral vision, in a magical meshing of headset reality and virtuality, kept them from crashing into one another and the furniture. Berle leaned against the doorframe, watching. Only Gneis, and GURlee in the bedside chair, sat still—moving their messengers with quiet, dedicated skill through the crackling, roaring flying dust and debris, momentum lit everywhere with spectacular quanta called photons. These were unbeatably swift and profuse. No member of either MACHOS or RAMBOs knew what to do about them. The photons seemed beyond controlling. But Gneis and GURlee were most adept at the eye-moves needed to order their own particular roles.

Father Domino began to distinguish, from these two players, skillful flickers and blinks along with a certain mathematical timing. He picked these two out within the gamescape and then found he was able to tag their signature moves—often artful and flawless. He also learned to come in and out the 'scape to watch the MACHOS moving about the bedroom. In his excitement and astonishment, particularly over what he saw as a possible subtext of the game, the gigantic alien WIMPs were now outside his attention. Like the MACHOS, the WIMPs themselves were unaware of these two historic observers— the only persons *belonging to this universe* who were knowledgeable, aware of them. Instead, Father Domino found himself so taken that he was rooting for the MACHOS against the virtually invisible RAMBOs. (The RAMBOs had almost no substance for his attention to latch onto *and* they were against BABY. He did not try for more. He remembered that Leaping Fawn had said something about all these participants being left for some other scribe to consider. Nor did he focus on individual MACHOS except for his brief perception of GURlee and Gneis.)

Being teenagers themselves, the alien FivePoints—the WIMPs—concentrated their attention particularly on the MACHOS, trying to distinguish (without really thinking about it) the characteristics of each. They also were able to penetrate the gamescape and watch its activity, but the game here was secondary to all but Quadri. Quadri had given himself to (or was simply psychically taken by) the events, and warfare, of the game. He desired so strongly for BABY to make it, that he *almost became* BABY in the struggle unfolding both within and before him. He was part of the game, maybe even its most ardent participant. But Quadri was powerless. He could affect no action with his gaze. That he had gaze did not even occur to him. Simply, the game was Quad and Quad was the game.

"So Dah, I s-see where this ... is going," said Gneis when the others had left ...having failed to get BABY born. SiXPointz, including Sheesh, had gone up to hipPo's apartment, leaving father and son alone, to cheer one another. Some things had got knocked about after all. Berle cleaned up the mess, straightening things, ferrying dishes to the kitchen where he left them for Sheesh to do on his return. Berle had already eaten hastily in the institute's cafeteria between glances at the investigators' findings on his laptop screen. Berle was tired, but still excited over the day's work.

"Yeah?" His father smiled. "Where is it going?"

"So, so. So far we've ... never been able to ... get there."

"But?"

"But ... eventually we'll s-stumble around ... the RAMBOs somehow and get Eartha to fly."

"After many abysmal attempts." His father smiled again. More than anything he wanted cheering for them both.

"But you know ... what I mean. We'll get a planet ... going that can s-support life."

"Right."

"So. So, so, there's just ... so much else...."

His father waited.

"Take me, for ... instance."

Berle waited. He had reddish rusty colored hair, slightly frizzly, and his eyes were warm and golden. He was stocky, not tall, open and friendly.

"You said before ... when Sheesh and I ... forming in the

womb ... not split so much as stuck together and had different genomes. And, so, so, I *really* got stuck ... we saw later. At first I was ... all right, and then ... I had to be carried, etc." Gneis did not say *and then Mam got to work on it*, because that would make them sad. "...Now other things, and... and I worry we're ... like ... binary stars and he's never going to ... get away from me and...."

"You want to know how they're coming developing experimental treatments ... so Sheesh can have a life of his own."

"No. I mean yes. Of ... course. But that's not ... what I'm getting it." Gneis was more golden than Berle. He had golden hair but it was straight. Sheesh kept it cut for him. They call it the cereal bowl cut now. Their mother had first used a cereal bowl when they were little. Sheesh did his own hair that way, too.

Gneis continued. "We ... are learning a lot ... from this game. Seeing how hard ... it ... was for everything to ... get going ... get made or make itself ... so to ... speak."

"Yes."

"But, still. So, so... it's not going to be like ... with the butterfly—is it? I mean ... for me. BTW, ...I know you already knew that stuff ... about the butterfly and chrysalis. —Even if they ... come up with something—so, so—."

"Are you still hopeful?"

"Yes ... no. You see, I want ... the experiments ... on me ... even if it won't do anything. Because."

"Because...."

"Because it won't be ... as boring as. ...As not doing ... anything. When ... do you think ... they'll be ready to try ... me?"

Berle looked at him thoughtfully. He would answer, of course. But he was sorry. Yes, there might be plenty of trials for his son. But. There was still a long way to go. They had to be careful. Very very careful. There was so much to it. And it must be done right. By this Berle meant, morally. "Checking" —at unintended sequences. He gave his son's self-risk a pass, but not the imposition of risk on others. And benefits he feared, if forthcoming, would be for another generation. Not for Gneis's. However, this was the part he would not tell. After all, it was only Berle's surmise. Maybe it would go swiftly after all.

Deeply regretting Gneis's missing mother, he spoke a few hopeful words. He leaned over and wiped his son's mouth.

Gneis could virtually move digitized things around on the screen with his words or his eyes. But he could not put his hand to his mouth. He could not lift a spoon.

Several floors up, in hipPo's apartment, there was more room for the game. Gneis was one of the best players. Sometimes he tried

58

KythHinG Sheesh on it, but that did not always work. Each MACHO had begun to see less and less of him. GURlee saw him more than anybody; he didn't seem to slow her down. She was already fairly slow. BiMbo, hippo, and Claude were more mobile — they were all over the building and sometimes roaming the metropolitan neighborhood or — never at night — the park by the crematorium. "Where they skim off the top of the milk to make ice cream." BiMbo was fond of the joke.

Everyone would take turns scampering beside Gneis giving him faux directions when he was abroad on his "eelie," as they like to call the chair with triangular wheels. But that was mostly before his mobility was curtailed by a simple lack of power to grasp the "joystick" of the eelie. Now, when his hand lost grip they had either to place that hand and stay holding till it worked, or power the stick themselves. He could give it commands but his voice was changing and he needed an upgrade. He was hoping the institute would give him an eelie he could operate at a glance as part of their work on him. The gang hoped. Small Claude thought that wouldn't happen. He prided himself on his realism.

HipPo's apartment was twice as big as Sheesh's. His mother was an administrator at the institute. "A big cheese there," he liked to say. And then biMbo would contradict as she was doing now over cracks in the universe. At the point when he says "big cheese," she says "big sneeze."

"If I'm a big sneeze," her mom would return, "that makes you a little sneeze. Maybe a cough or a wheeze. You get everything you've got from me, don't forget."

"So so someday *I'll* be the big sneeze—"

" —Big cheese—" from hipPo.

" —And you'll be a little old lady."

"Not if I can help it," her mother might say with a crisp white smile.

Now they sat in the room4living with their insect-head gameSets—complete with antennae—in their laps, drinking sodas from the kitchen beside the giant windows. "But if there were cracks, they'd be leaking dark matter?! Then there'd be practically nothing and what good's that for a game?"

"We might have to stop calling ourselves the MACHOS." This crack was from Claude. "We're actually not very tough anyway."

"Just a pile of black holes, brown dwarfs, and neutron stars, is all," said hipPo. "That stuff can't leak, little guy." As much as to say, maybe you're not so big but *I* am.

"All this means," said Sheesh, changing the subject slightly, "is that BIG BAMM's only a phase change. Maybe it didn't start with SinGuLariTEE™ ... but that might make the game more interesting.

Starting in a cloud or a sea ... or something."

Sheesh was the one with the bowl cut like his brother. He had rusty blonde hair like Dah's but not frizzed. He had freckles like him, too, only the man's were now spread out and more blended, giving him a generalized sunburnt look. While Sheesh had the tiny individualized freckles sprinkled over his face and arms. HipPo and biMbo were dark and had stylish 'do's on account of their mother sending them to the *Lovely Shop* above the lobby, on the mezzanine. HipPo and biMbo each had blue-black hair layered on top, but biMbo's also hung past her skinny shoulder blades. They had the warm dark skin and aquiline noses of their father and mother. Claude was, in fact, small, slim and pale and wore contact lenses or glasses. He was intermittently smart enough to come up with interesting ploys, plots, and pilgrimages.

"Then it all turned to ice?" Claude asked. "Is that all BABY II's gonna have to work from?"

"We'll see," said Sheesh. "Dah's got 'em working on it."

Mz. Bopoi, wearing a glimmer-grey business suit and short fluffy dark 'do framing her aquiline features, came from the kitchen into the room4living. She set her stemmed glass half full of amber liquid, on the elegant glass and gilt table—a very crisp angular low piece. She said, "He'll keep them at it because, he says, 'It'll keep the designers out of trouble.' " She went over to the great gleaming polymer wall, to glance at the metropolitan night, pale and lambent, past the interior reflected lights of the spacious room itself. Against the further, towering downtown, distant flycars moved up and down or across the sky, purposeful—specks with their own peculiar lambency like glowing bugs. She came back for her glass.

The kidz were grouped round the low table, lounging over the living room suite; or—GURlee and Sheesh—seated, with legs crossed, on the thick carpeting.

"That gets me," said biMbo. "How can grownups get into trouble—the bosses?"

"Apparently you don't watch the news?" Claude was being sarcastic again.

"Oh that," she said. Her adolescent voice was not quite the piping of Claude's.

GURlee sat quietly watching them all, glass of Kake held very carefully in her small hand. She caught Mz. Bopoi looking at her. This meant she was supposed to smile. She supposed. Smile? Was that? She smiled. So did Mz. Bopoi. *Whew.*

But the two kidz ' mother was thinking of the city being full to its quivering gills with vice ... and of the mutation of human nature (as she sometimes thought it).

Sheesh said, "You're used to being around adults who've got

60

a grip on themselves."

"Digitize it, brother!" said biMbo's mother, smiling. She drank from the long-stem and set it down; carefully, the clink of glass on glass.

"That's Dah's department. You should hear him. I get it from him. He says he's been pumping me full of antigens but I think he's got that mixed up. Aren't antigens supposed to be toxins? Anyway he wants my immune system to build up antibodies, just in case I get any ideas. I tell him, if I'm only made out of particles I'm especially gonna watch my p's and q's."

"And then what's he say?" asked biMbo.

" 'What are p's and q's?' "

"P's and q's aren't the problem," said hipPo. It's g's and q's give me fits." (These letters are translated approximations, or as parallel simulations of Akropolis Anglish.)

Eyes closing, Mz. Bopoi cupped her dark hand over a yawn. "KO, guys," she said. "It's past your bedtimes."

"Don't you mean *your* bedtime?" (biMbo)

Sheesh stood and set his empty soda glass on the table, clinking. GURlee looked at him. She stood and set down her glass likewise. But carefully, quiet.

They were on their way to the door, but Claude sat there with Mz. Bopoi's son and daughter. They were still talking. Sheesh waved his thanks and GURlee did likewise. They slipped out the door into the quiet plush passageway, receiving the last of Mz. Bopoi's smiles.

The other kidz continued their conversation, swirling ice cubes in soda glasses, taking no notice.

" 'ConDensing Worlds' just doesn't have the same entertainment value," said hipPo.

"Right. It's kinda like the gAmemAster peeing instead of sneezing," said Claude, hunching his slight shoulders, glancing surreptitiously at the woman standing by the kitchen door, hand on its frame. He looked back at the kidz to see their expressions.

The room4living lights went out, leaving them at first in the dark. Then the dimmer glow of the city shimmered through polymer.

"Uh-oh." Claude said it without turning, and ran to the door, clutching his gameSet slung round his neck. "Wait up!" The Bopoi siblings heard him call as the door closed behind him. HipPo and biMbo scrambled to their rooms.

When Claude got to the elevator his friends were gone.

SiXPointz HiTopOLis

Violence in HiTopOLis

The WIMPs from another universe encompassed the episode with focused attention. At the same time, peripherally they encompassed the whole neighborhood of SiXPointz and, fainter, beyond to the vast metro and suburban areas surrounding the busy intersection. They did not sit on the furniture or drink the sodas and wine; they did not walk through the doors or peer in the windows of the building. Rather, in some super-material way, they *were* these things and had always been so (all unbeknownst to them), even while inhabiting another version of the universe, city, neighborhood; inhabiting, also, bodies of flesh and blood. Yet now they were attending to this place, these people, these things, in a way before impossible. And they did not feel at home.

Quadri said, —They stopped playing the game.

He felt himself back in the situation that did not feel like the game. Did not feel comfortable, like he belonged. He wanted to go back. ...Where was back?

No one responded. They were aware of Claude going down in the elevator, fingering his game/headset and staring up at the green-lit floor numbers as these counted down past M to L (mezzanine to lobby). WIMPs were aware of the Bopoi siblings in their separate rooms, changing into PJs, climbing into bed, and humming separate tunes. Mz. Bopoi was reading in bed, her eyes turning the pages but barely seeing. In Gneis's room, several floors down, gentle snores escaped softly. Sheesh was in the kitchen now, cleaning up. Berle was gazing at his small vertical screen, dreaming (Tu hoped) of how to make an image-oriented presentation of his findings. GURlee sat in the ground floor lobby, legs dangling from one of the burnished heavy aluminum benches. Now Claude came out of the elevator toward her.

Finally, HB said, —Yeah, so...

And Jayrai said, —Tu?

Fabe said, —I think we should pray.

They could almost hear Tu thinking.

Then they could: —It's the mind/brain disconnect, he said. Better, the mind/brain connection?

HB sighed.   —Here we go with the unreliable narrator.

—Shouldn't that be protagonist, hero? (Jayrai)

—Tu a hero?

—Tu'd make a good hero! (Pomala)

—What was that they were calling during the game? Are we getting anywhere with understanding them? This from Jayrai again.

—Not to another universe, I hope, said HB.

Tu said, —If the scientist can make the dark matter presentable with some sort of graphic, we may be getting somewhere.

Here Tu was expressing intuition. The intuitive was the only clue he had, and he did not like it. There was no science for that.

Sheesh had emptied the dishwasher a moment before. Berle came into the kitchenette to help him load the plates and cups.

"So GURlee got home?" he asked.

"Uh, no."

"Better go see if you can catch her."

"Maybe Claude's with her by now."

"What?! That's almost like nothing!"

Sheesh threw the onion he was about to stash onto the counter. It rolled, bumping into the canisters. He tore his jacket off its hook and went out the door, dragging it on. "I thought it was still early! Thought they'd go together!" He yelled it over his shoulder.

The WIMPs watched him run down the hall.

HB said, —What, the little girl? Too late, bro. She gone.

They experienced Sheesh's running footfalls, impatience at the elevator.

—You getting this talk? asked Jay, Because I'm not.

—Me either, said Pomala. —So maybe a little. I think I knew it was about the skinny girl.

—Little girl, said Quadri softly.

(Pomala) —You got that, too, Quad?

—Oh good, said Jay, I get to be the dumbest one here. When am I gonna get my arm back? Her power arm, the synapse with hardware!

—There she is, said Pome. Getting into a lite 'copter alongside a man in a suit. The little boy is with her.

—That can't be bad, can it? asked Fabe.

—Oh yo, it can! said HB. Them suits! They tricky.

—Oh please, said Pome, My mom's stepbrother wears a suit, my uncle. My sister works as an ad min assist in the Districk of mAne and wears a suit. I'm the only one dresses like this. Er....

63

(Pome wasn't tattooed or blue or albino anymore. Just some scattered dark matter, that she thought maybe still mattered somehow.)

—We better check it out anyway, said Fabian. His attention was already given to the flying car, cramped little scene, and the way everything looked in the lit air over the city from GURlee's perspective. And Claude's.

Pome said, —I think you're right! They aren't feeling too easy.

—Maybe it's the view, said Jayrai. They haven't been in one of those flying things before, bet.

The glittering city flattened and spread quickly before them, looking so tiny and dear with its toy-like towers and fantastic gleaming gridwork, spangled with lights of every intensity and vibrating other electromagnetic fare. It was hard to focus on the grainy-looking persons in their spectacular flight over the city.

—And he must be flying on auto-pilot, said Fabe.

Suitman was speaking softly, inquiringly, and at times with a jocularity some of the WIMPs found grating—all but the youngest. But even Quad could see that the man's face was a smudge, his head a blur above his pale burnished bronze pixilated suit.

—Man's an asshole, said HB.

—I don't trust him, Pome, said Jayrai. I think he's up to no good.

—Yes—but it's not the suit.

—If he didn't have the suit he wouldn't have the lite-car, bet on it. His particles scream wealth while his talk says I'm cuddly and soft. Look at him. He's dead. Got no feelings. (Jayrai)

—He's got a feeling somewhere, said HB. —Look.

They looked.

—Uh-oh, said Fabe. When they land he's gonna hurt them. What can we do?

Silence. Tu was still attending to Berle—in the living room waiting on Sheesh's return. Tu was focused on the screen. He was trying to read Berle's mind.

—Pray? asked Quadri, now caught in their unease over the man. He a ghoul?

—Pretty much, said Jayrai.

—Verifiable zombie, said HB.

—Thing is, said Tu, science is the practice of discovering and verifying everything material down to the smallest particle. That's why this is a problem. Evidently we've been discovered and verified so we must be material. He stopped, thought:

—Hence the name *matter*, dark matter. He's engaging in the search and verification of dark matter. They *think* it makes up most of the matter in the universe. Um universes. Still, even though we're experiencing stuff only bodies can experience via senses, we've got no corporality, so therein lies the problem. Normally you need a brain to incorporate all this stuff so your mind can think of it, or be aware, plan. This is where science's at a loss. Neurons can be seen and measured and configured with diagrams, graphics—electric signals (transmissions of energy, nerve fibers, etc.). All this is studied, but are we? What are we, really? There's a kind of gap between us and the materials and how they work, cells and molecular structure—which we're used to thinking we're made of. This is all incoherent. I don't mean what I'm thinking here is incoherent I mean the fact that what we can know doesn't stick together with the we-ness of we. I mean, face it, we aren't even made out of star-stuff like these guys are. I mean we *were* until we got like, um, this. See, he's making an isometric image of what his findings tell him, but he can't make an image of himself coming up with the image—so to speak. The picture of him making a picture won't do it because that only shows him a picture of a thought, not the thought itself. Now—

  —Tu!!! Are you going to help us or not?!! Look, I've been telling them you'd make a great hero, and all you're doing is analyzing! (Pomala)

  —So, I can't think of anything.

They did an equivalent eye-roll. At least he was apologetic.

  —We better try the prayer, said Fabian.

  —OK, you go first, said HB.

I been, thought Fabian. —Quad, will you go first?

The flycar had leveled off well above the city and the WIMPs were both confined, *and comprising* the city. Even Tu was paying better attention. They were virtually the super materiality of the flycar, the children, the harmful man, and the cosmos. Nothing is solid ... the lit-night glowing, scattered uncounted particles of leptons quarks bosons gluons muon and other forces playing out of the deepest love and steepest wrath of everything, and nought. They saw packets of corpuscles moving, lines of energy and force flowing and firing along the nerve fibers, cells dividing, *the beating hearts of Claude and GURlee; fear and confusion*; the awful nonentity in the pale bronze suit, glancing sideways at the children as he touched them here and there. These children of HiTopOLis—Claude and GURlee—were themselves now seen to be praying even as they trembled. Every particle of their little beings shifting, rolling and yawing. Praying to Whomever it is children of any universe pray to with all their might.

  The WIMPs feel Quadri swelling with the urgency of Fabian's request. They feel a wind beginning, Universal, belonging neither to the particular materials (densely scattered), nor to the open many abysses, not to the problematic psyches—the souls of humans in their almost peripheral connection to personal bodies *of which they know so little.* This alien-seeming wind increases, scattering, widening, building, *breathing, bursting.*

    —It is Quad! Quad is getting ready! Quad is going to blow!

    —*Quad!* (Pomala shrieking)

    —*Hah-Laa!! Hah-La!! Hah-La Be!! HAH-LA BE PRAISED!!*
The wind of Quad's praises both draw and scatter—in ultimate tension—all lights and gaps of darkness, 3-D pixilated lights and shades: Engulfing the flycar and riders. The sick and self-begotten driver. This wind expanding to the heights and depths of HiTopOLis until ... it contracts to that final point of singularity—Quad's next, whispered, sound. A final whispered utterance of small Quadri. Small utterance, it was, so very small.

    —*death to the infidel,* he said.

    Then, the strange otherworldly wind subsiding, all seemed almost normal once more. The car a flying packet of lights driven by the smudge-headed non-man.

    But there came that small difference in the scene, revealed—but for an instant. An all-encompassing presence of that singular cloud of witness:

    People. People arrived in the air above them. Solemn people looking like flesh-and-blood, dressed in old-fashioned weaponry—feathers dressing long hair, bowstrings taut, feathered arrows, johnny-hawks with great thongéd flints, warriors standing, with arrows nocked, knives and hawks poised. And on their backs were cloaks, soft cloaks of skin scraped clean of fur and flesh, sewn together, fringed in tails. Caht-tails in rows, dangling.

    And then they were gone.

    HB was thinking about the smudge-head. —He already daid. Just don't know it.

    —I wasn't expecting him to pray to Hah-La, thought Fabian.

    —Yo, he's Aslem, what else would he say? (HB)

    —Whatever, said Jay. Did you see them? I think it might work.

    They could feel Quadri smiling.

    Tu said, —This is strange.... He appears to be playing with the SF question.

    They looked away, gave Berle a glance, there in the living room with his unscrolled screen.

    —I think he should play with the *A'ndian question,* said Jay.

    —You saw them? (They thought it together at once).

    —We all did, said Fabian. What's it mean?

    —If we all saw, said HB, it means we ain't crazy.

(Jay) —Where did they come from? Where'd they go?

— Do you mean which universe they go to? (HB)

—What SF question, Tu. Pomala was asking. —You mean—

—"What if?"

—Right.

—Like in, "What if the next universe is an inch away from us?" Truly amazing! You sure? (Pomala again)

—You got it, said Tu. Did not think you would. But that's not what I mean, the what-if.

—An inch? said Fabian.

—Come on, said HB simultaneously. —Just cause we don't actually *get* the stuff the way you do, we still know how to communicate stuff we do know—*probably* better.

—Which what if?" said Pomala and Jay, losing patience at the same time.

—Not sure yet.... Kind of out of my realm. So to speak. Tu stopped.

—Say it. We see what you're thinking, said Jay.

—What if —No, I can't. It's not testable. And he's a scientist.

—Then maybe he *wants* to test it. (Fabian)

Tu was, finally, not clueless but exasperated. —Test it when it's not testable?

—Shit! (HB)

—So—were *we* testable 100 years ago? (Jay)

This appeared to check Tu. (He knew they did not mean as in their flesh-and-blood identities. Attraction, conception, birth, life, and death of individuals had been tested billions of times, and turned out each time to be *fact*.) He knew Jay meant in their current particulate state. And now here was flesh-and-blood (the scientist) testing for dark matter and doing remarkably well. He was doing a good job of discovery, verification, demonstration.

Tu felt he himself would have to acknowledge the search— based as it was on ignorance. Honor it. Ignorance was what made science go. So now they felt the emotional energetic equivalent of Tu's helpless sigh.

—He wants to *test* the physical laws to see if there's a moral connection. Tu hesitated to say more.

They were silent. They looked back with full attention on the children in trauma and fear with their smudge-headed captor inside the small flying car (of which they themselves made a part).

—You could put that the other way, said Fabian at last. — Test the moral laws to find the physical connections.

—I don't think they're verifiable, said Tu. After a pause, he said, —The scientist is thinking.... —So, it's not what *I'd* go to....

67

He's thinking the search for cryogenic dark matter might lead to a formula to overturn vice in the city. I think. Not sure about that, but seeing some connections here.

  —Meaning smudge-head is dead, yes, but he still gets to go on doing shit to little kids, said HB.

  — I'm not sure I get the connection, said Tu. Can you define or refine that a bit?

  —I dunno, said Pome. —What about climate change? That's moral right? Or would that be immoral? People not thinking, just burning up the fossils? Greed and consumerism?

  (HB) —What do we know? We're a pile of particles, according to Tu. Everything is, even these guys. Meaning, if we were to write them out, they would be a pile of zeros and ones. Can we really know that stuff?

  —According to Tu that's what he's trying to figure, bro, said Jayrai. For a moment they all focused on Berle.

  Tu thought, Okay, but he's going to ruin his career if he's trying that and they find out. Meaning Berle's colleagues and those bestowing grants.

s. dormAn

The Police Give It a Try

Meanwhile, deputy chief Capt. Kent S. Clarke, had spent afternoon, early evening in his cuboid, studying recent data sets of crime pragmaTometerics for SiXPointz. Just in case, he sent out reports to metro neighborhood detectives and officers, an alert to the possibility of child abduction. He picked up his coffee cup. Stale.

For some reason Toesda nights were high in the meterics. Clarke thought that was odd. This type crime clustered on these two weeknights instead of, say, Frgda. Sagorda night should have been the night, he thought. Not Toesdaze, with Throsdaze a close second. In their patrol flights his men and women would peripherally scan the sets and head out from the TuBeWay or HoRT tiMons or Donken DohBits to these hotspots, looking for ... anything. He wished he was out there. Clarke picked up the cup again.

He swiveled to face the expanse of windows, dimmed lights in the cuboid, and stared out the glass past his dim balding reflection onto traffic below, above, and middling—over the dark of the ash-burial gounds across the way. In daylight the glare might have troubled such gazing, but at night it was easier ... both to see and perceive, to distinguish sounds poking through the groundswell like high points on the charts behind him, neatly blinking on the scroll. The intermittent shriek of some flying ambulance, descending toward PerSons HosPickle, passed on the opposite side of the building and softened, changed inflection, the way such sounds do as they recede. The shrieking was immediately replaced by one of the blue wails of his night patrol. He turned back to his detail-screen, next to the scroll, then to the *dadar* to check whose.

Philipa's. He still needed a report from her. It would have to wait. She was busy.

Now the phone beeped. Either a false alarm or someone was in trouble. Clarke would listen to the dispatch on the tiny speakerphone, while yet scanning the traffic, the lit windows of buildings towering round the dark grounds across the street, the pedestrians immediately below. He had to stand up, peer down through lights and shimmer-glow for that last. Across from the building, in the midst of the labyrinth was that dark spot. A gap in the shimmer of night. The park of the crematory, where by day a soul or two might be seen, intermittently, wandering beneath trees or standing in silent bereavement.

All day, and part of the night long (the watch that concerned him) someone was hurting someone else. Somebody was stealing, murdering, getting murdered, crashing into somebody, getting hit from behind. It never stopped. At least to Kent S. Clarke it seemed nonstop. *The city*, he thought. Rich yet broke; alive but dead; proud, humiliated: empty and overflowing. What could he do for it? Nothing.

Nothing.

But maybe *one* thing. Yeah. He told himself often. It was necessary. You can do one thing. You can do what's next to do. For someone.

Floreeia in dispatch was receiving the report of a possible abduction. The unexpected weekday again! A missing child, anyway. Possibly two together. That was unclear. It needed confirmation. It needed another parent or guardian calling in. Last seen together in the lobby of the new Kress Building. Everyone still called it "new" — even though it had been built three years ago. On the spot where the old neighborhood grade school, Kress Elementschool, had been demolished. Why's that spot so prevalent? They would have been more watchful tonight if they'd had this report earlier. Was it cosmic irony? Was it intentional — something to do with the site as formerly that of the school? That new building, oddly, was named for the school.

Absently scratching a speck on the glass before him, Clarke listened to the second call come in. ...Confirming the request for an officer in the second case: Two children apparently taken together. Maybe just outside the building, maybe down the block: nobody knew. A witness was to call was to call. Philipa would probably be there to take the statement any moment.

Even though he'd dimmed the lights to look out on the neighborhood, Capt. Clarke could distinguish his own muscular uniformed reflection moving back and forth across the glass, restive. Receding hair, bit of a middle-age paunch. Lit from behind by the screens and scrolls of the trade. The station, being across from the crematorium park and gardens, his view out the window was always dark in the middle, this time of year, this time of night. This multitude of small lights reflected the cuboid's scant furniture and dimensions, a desk with shoddy swivel chair, one other chair, counters lining the cramped walls filled with data and HD screens. He heard the buzz from other law enforcement cubicles, a hum of voices, the intermittent cough, ongoing talk rarely loud enough to distract from the business at hand.

Neighborhood distress. Brokenness everywhere. Shattering lives — fragile, hapless. The strength of evil like some unknown being, an entity, a hammer breaking all that was carefully structured: People, relationships, families. These were the roles of life supporting fragile beings. *The business at hand.* Lending a hand, a head, some technology *and know-how.* Too bad that last came directly from the knowledge of evil itself.

I don't *want* to know, he thought, and turned back to his desk. He sank into the chair, asked for reports. A precise wave of the fingers. "Philipa?"

"Yeah, Chef?"

He almost smiled. *Chef.* Would she ever stop that? *Like I'm some kinda gourmet guru cooking up some crime for her to taste.*

He didn't need to ask where she was. The USP symbol for Philipa showed in the corner screen above him. And he saw also those for Manny Fyle, plus Gadon and Gaddone.

"So, so?"

"It's a text from a friend. The new Kress Building."

"I'm not surprised." He saw the blip stop there on the pavement in holographic 3-D.

"Going up to the apartment now. Will get back in a few."

"Right." He picked up his cup, drank the cold coffee, grimaced.

"Too bad we can't get technology to walk kidz home for us," said Philipa to Berle. They were in the tiny kitchen with Sheesh, whose head was bowed. Philipa still had her pad out, glancing at reports she'd filed on the tiny screen. Clarke would now be reading these at the SiXPointz bureau. She stood straight, her blue-gray uniform crisp, badge above her breast gleaming in the floodescent light.

Sheesh leaned against the sink, staring at the inlaid veneer covering the kitchen floor. Words and phrases every which way— monochromatic bronzed print—veneered. Claude. Claude had once asked him how the words got there. Why the walls in this room were papered in book pages. He kept reading the same words over and over without really registering what they said. If only he could do something to fix this. He wanted to go and wake Gneis, ask if he had any ideas... but he didn't like to disturb his twin when he was sleeping. The habit was firm — No Waking Gneis; in part because it meant having to do things for him, in part because sleep was the only break Gneis had from his increasingly inert body. In his dreams he could run, he could swim, fly, *play batball!* If only Sheesh could send him out to play batball while he fixed Gneis's supper....

But he wasn't thinking of this now. He was thinking, *What would Gneis have in mind for me to do?* Wish I could kythH him better. Or period.

"Yes," Berle was saying to Philipa. "What we need are gadgets instead of grown-ups. That way we could stay kidz ourselves and do nothing but play games and eat pizza."

She smiled that gleeful smile of hers. The one that says you don't really have enough going on with that. Tell me something funny. Her eyes were mocking gray, her hair brassy, skin light and dimpled in the right places.

"You know what I mean," she said. She looked over at Sheesh. "I'm going to check with security, see what they've got in sensory on..." she looked at the LCD " — GURlee, is it? and Claude. Want to come? You know what you're looking at. I'm not sure I would."

Good, thought Berle. She knows how he feels.

The words on the floor firmed up a bit. Sheesh noticed: *go sing it on the mountain.* "KO," he said, and brushed past them both, jacket under his arm.

"That lyno is a toot," said Philipa to Berle before leaving. "All those old sayings. Liking that wallpaper, too." Pages of texts all over the walls. "Whadyado, get the book in one of those moldering shops on 2ⁿᵈ St.? Must've taken years to peel it apart and paper this kitchen in *a book*. Looks like it's got a good coat of polyurethane on it though." She rubbed her finger along some of the text there. "No grease, or not much."

"Yeah, we keep it pretty clean," said Berle. Nothing more. He did not want her thinking of other things, other missing people. Not now.

She squinted at the small black words of one page. Sections of this particular book's pages had been separated and stuck to the wall in order. They had yellowed from time and the coating. She said, "Not familiar with this one: 'Come up, Sleeping Fawn.' "

"Local history. Don't think about it too hard," said Berle. "We need that noggin for GURlee and Claude."

He stopped a moment, then asked (as she thought he might), "How comes the other thing?"

"No news yet," she said. She forgot to say, Seems like years.

Sheesh had only seen Kelso a few times since their move to the new building. Once or twice in connection with their Mam search. A friendship with the security man would develop from this. And Sheesh had never been to this level of the underground before. He'd been to utilities, washing clothes. There were lots of machines there for housekeeping (and those residents who washed their own clothes). That was where building operations, heat, plumbing, electric and other maintenance were stationed. He'd also been to the lower undergrounds, exhaust-smelling, where residents and shoppers park their cars. At first he had wondered if GURlee and Claude had got lost down there, maybe exploring.

Philipa, Kelso, and Sheesh stood close together, watching the moving 3-D images—the lithe freckled teenager with rust-red bangs, the slim but frequently competent detective, and Kelso. Security was a small whiteboard roomful of sensor-processing, including various data gathering and holo registers. On a glass shelf above them were sports trophies from Kelso's youth.

"That's them," said Sheesh. He pointed to the small pair shown exiting, and continuing outside under the portico of the Kress Building. Two views in holography, tiny 3-D images of two skinny kidz, small beneath the roof of the portico; starting out together. GURlee had taken hold of Claude's hand but—none too nicely—he had loosed hers. Still, they were together. There came a deep supporting edge of the portico, blocking the camera's field of view, and there they had disappeared.

The security manager (nights) showed a view down the block. "Right there's where they should be," he said, turning the second register, just a bit, for them to see. Kelso was an old man—or seemed so to Philipa—and to Sheesh, especially—perhaps readying for retirement in a year or two. His hair was graying, close-cut fuzz around a balding pate, his whiskers close-cut fuzz fashionable in his youth. Now they made him more grizzled than handsome. He was tersely spoken, wore wire-rimmed spectaculars. Carried a Gluk in his handmade leather holster. Sheesh noticed the holster because Philipa's was polymer, like all justice enforcement wore.

This view they were looking at included small pale night-lit images of people moving to and fro on the pavement. There was stop-and-go movement of cars, both ground-level and elevating. More of the craft-bottoms on these last, but there were images giving the higher view, if needed. These were all from two hours before. He had other kinds of data, for Philipa to download and study back at the neighborhood metro. She'd take a close look at these with Kent Clarke on her return. But the visuals were always the most potent record, especially when, like now, audio was indistinct.

"Where'd they go?" asked Sheesh, a bit subdued after his initial uplift on seeing them so plainly, both inside and just outside the revolving glass doors of the building.

"That's where the work comes in," said Kelso. "That blind spot is where they disappeared. We've always had that blind spot. Now maybe the building manager will 'manage' to get that complete

73

surveillance we need." Looking at them with bleak eyes, he said this dryly, as doubting it. The police had been here before—once?—no *twice* before on a similar call since the building opened. "Even the school had better surveillance than this. —Several years after I got there. It took a while to convince them."

"That's right," said Philipa. "You worked there—here, too."

"Yeh. Began there in 1880. The building was pretty old then but I knew every nook, room, closet, auditorium; and the basements, as they were called. Came in to security after I lost my job at the factory—Netherlands Carmakers, on the eastside. You probably don't even remember it."

She smiled that golden white smile of hers but said nothing.

Sheesh stared at the looping holo, seeing them inside, then outside — and wished Monsieur Kelso would get on with *the work*. Trying his best to channel Gneis, he said, "So, they could be in one of the cars, one of the flyers?"

Philipa's gray eyes looked encouragement at him. "Show us the cars moving on down the pavement, and those lifting. Slowly. Maybe we'll see something in one of them."

The 3D images streamed slowly. Some interiors were glimpsed with passengers; couple taxis, one sleek luxury flycar with opaque windows. The flyers had lifted or were descending, and nothing distinguishable was seen in these—just the bottoms on short wings and the faint glow of electrics from under. Few identifying numbers

"Give it all to me—I want these images," she said. "We might even be able to sift that audio. Find the numbers. Do you recognize anyone?" She knew he would've said, but asked anyway.

He shook his head.

"How about those flyers? Recognize any of the craft?"

"Yes. And that's in the first report." He pointed. "That's the architect, one of the building's owners. Flashy, dark flycar, but he's just like that. These here are the building manager's and one of the scientist's from the detection laboratory—the one further down—your dah'd know him, I guess," he said to Sheesh. "And there's the car belonging to the owner of the *Lovely Shop*. She had a long day, looks like. Longer than usual."

"Four distinct possibilities," said Philipa.

Sheesh said, "M. Puce." He thought, *If they didn't do something like jay through that traffic.* (Just there, in the perspective, the burnished support hid the street and traffic.) Where they might have crossed. He didn't think they'd do that, but those two were not exactly predictable. "Would there be cameras on the opposite side?"

"Of the street?" said Philipa, smiling. "Good catch. I'll check that out."

FivePoints 2017 CE—from the other universe—had not been focusing on what passed in the building since Sheesh first rushed after the children. They knew only some of what went on because, as *weakly interacting massive particles* capable of disbursing far and wide, they nonetheless tended to stay with GURlee and Claude, where their chief interest lay at the moment. However, they managed, also, to attend somewhat to detection efforts ongoing in the building, and to the studies (Tu especially was interested) of the particle scientist, Berle.

The blur-head in the car seems to have no destination in mind. He is speaking friendly to the children, sporadically. And harming them. They are by turns confused, apprehensive, and crying. His talk is meaningless to the ghosts who are from somewhere else—a place an inch away from his nose had he been able to detect it. He could not. Smudge-head (as he was also known by them) had no idea his every action was been watched and commented on, weighed in the estimation of beings with understanding. Beings more moral than himself.

The WIMPs discussed his morals or lack of them among themselves, with the detachment of serene beings that nonetheless had some interest in seeing the plight of the children eased. They were not, generally, emotionally involved in this version of reality — except for the outcome of their own predicament in it. This predicament is what involved their emotions. The seeming haplessness of GURlee and Claude's distress provided not even the vicarious experience of an action movie or role-playing game. Neither was it, for them, as the detached observation of those who study statistics, robotics, or natural phenomenon; those scientists watching for outcomes solely vested in the thrill of discovery itself (without thought of its consequences). The WIMPs were, instead, disinterested in a way that only spirit can be. In this crucial matter they seemed—even to themselves—divested of the soul of their kind.

—Is it just me—or does it seems odd that this monster doesn't know he's a monster? In this special disinterest, Jayrai was asking.

—Maybe he's got some missing genes, suggested Pomala. Say, one sympathetic to other human beings.

—I don't think he's—it's—human, said HB. You always think people can be fixed. That's how we got in this "fix" to begin with, girl. Now, pay attention. Things ain't fixable, you getting?

—But, she responded, I'm counting on Tu. Don't discourage him.

Fabian said, I'm counting on the Native Americles to bring

him down. They are the answer to Quadri's prayer. Seems they have them in this universe, too.

—Tu? (HBBBAH) —Tu, what thinking? Think that man at the 'puter will find that god particle you always talkin' bout? That's what might fix these messes? You said he's looking for connections to laws, physical to moral laws, etc...?

At last Tu entered into their speculations, surprised with himself that he cared, even in this disinterested way, something about GURlee and Claude. Clearly it was *wrong* what this thing driving the car through the air was doing. Tu felt *wrongness* in a way he could not articulate. Yet, underneath, he felt surprisingly unperturbed about this wrongness. *Wrong.* He said to himself. *Gravity.* He said that to himself. *The graviton.*

—So, don't be just saying these words, said HB.

—No. It was as if they heard Tu shaking his head. —No. It's got to be the genes. The scientist should be looking at genes, not particles. For his what-if.

—You mean, said Fabian, they need to isolate the right sequence? And besides what'll they do then? Give'em therapy through more wrongness? Sucked apart embryos? Fabian was not for culling genetic materials unless the process conformed to morality. Actually understood in all its ramifications and consequences. Do genes have particles? This business of particles was too.... —So, look—*we* are particles now! And we can't really do anything except pray.

And Father Domino (who meantime had been lost in wonder of that great shimmering city of HiTopOLis,) was now seated in his cave asking himself, quill-pen in hand: *Here may we have a dialogue in the formal sense of the word. But have we* a vision *if what we are given is people arguing with disembodied others in a nether-world of mist — or even in a world of light? If vindication through argument is the sole purpose, of both vision and the creation of character, can it be truly visionary? The people in the city do not know the giant children are here. ...But...perhaps we have here one of the Spirit's manApean satires?*

Yet, (as his thoughts continue in this vein) this ghostly expression is how they experience life in *this* world. This expression is not *complete*, as made in heaven. Even so, whether ghosts or giants, they can affect no thing in this place, for 'tis alien to them.

These are people from another part of *la création de grand créateur.* They are as giants in our world. He wrote, his pen scarcely scratching over the smooth surface of the valim: They are tall, made out of great crystals, various and shining; multifaceted and vari-colored. They are full of great glowing power and love. We

76

here in this world of blunder and bloodshed and woe have never seen their like. Where do they come from, I wonder? Truly Great Maker's works are past discovery for very fullness and complexity. Even in *nos textes sacrés* we find no giants made of adamant, made of stone. Within *l'Écriture* we find beings not of our world—but they are spirit, they are lights.

And the good friar bethought him of the scientist—the natural philosopher and meta-physician as he was wont to call him. Berle was of the friar's own world. Berle was of the friar's own *place* in the Next World. (As the First World liked to call the continent of colonial- steam and sailing-ships' discovery.) *He lives in the further time from my own time of slaughter and annihilation, my own time in which the Ehioerrian are destroyed by destructive weapons, en masse.* While I do nothing, nothing, nothing but watch. Berle, as he is named, will live not too far from this cave in which I sit writing down these words in valim now that they are slain.

Yet this friar did not look about him at the standing scroll racks, did not make himself aware of scented smoke drifting up from the small bowl on the mantelpiece. It wafted through cracks in giant ice-brought mica-stone, which had been melted and recrystalized in earlier ages — earlier than those of the massive sheets of ice. These mica-streaks were half a'gleam in the tallow candlelight.

And Father Domino began to weep, tears falling silent as he wrote. *Raison d'être, Raison d'être....* (Reason for Being, Reason for Being.) He looked to *le grand créateur* as he worked and wept. He looked, he looked and looked for what he could not see. It was that quiet presence ever so small and slight that came to him, now, with comfort ... even as the friar's quill-pen flowed slowly out its words, and his slight hand dipped its nib into the vial for ink. It was no giant, no great overwhelming force, this quiet presence, but a respectful love. Then the friar wrote: Berle, the scientist, as these are called of 1900 EE, searches for physical forces, *materials* made of law. A made set of instruction, to preserve all and ourselves in creation. A way in which we may forsake the trap of our own minds and self-will, so that we may humbly receive the world of creation which we ourselves have not made. *Car tu as créé toutes choses, et c'est par ta volonté qu'elles existent et qu'elles ont été creéés.* (You have made all for your pleasure.)

Thus it remains to be seen if in HiTopOLis questions of good and evil — so long in care of the brothers and sisters and higher authority — might cede such stewardship to the sciences. Is conscience to be guided by forces they may learn to know, not by faith or trust alone, but by proven standards? Can it be so?

The friar wondered, thus amazed. He thought, we have seen other laws yield knowledge of themselves by such studies, experiments as they are called in future time. Can they be tested and shown to exist?   —Is this what the world comes to in future time? But how will it help the children when not all believe? Science, they may say, can prove—but what is that to us—what is the language of numbers to us, who will go our own way? And again, he wept.

Heedlessly wiping eyes and cheeks on his doeskin sleeve, he dipped pen again, moving now away from these speculations toward the strange appearance in heaven of the armed A'ndyan clan of believers whom he himself had converted to faith. Among their number were Antipatihee, Tumbling Beaver and old Horn-in-Morning—who however was no longer old, as Tumbling Beaver was no more a child. Yet, though they looked so different, it was impressed upon the friar's spirit that these last two were the selfsame persons he had known.

He wrote, *I saw them whilst standing on the second moon with Leaping Fawn.* 'Twas as though air and clouds and distance were collapsed and our gaze beheld our warriors who were slain in battle. From above we saw them surround the craft of the wicked, weapons poised for battle and to slay the evil one. They had both spirit and corporeal being. But a voice from the midst of Elios — our own fat star, and closest in the spaze-time void — spoke: a stern, bright and radiant prohibition. And turning I saw that Leaping Fawn had heard it, too. Her dark eyes were very bright. Not as though reflecting our great star, out of which this great voice spoke, but as though both brightness and radiant voice were inside her own being.

"HOLD!"

The voice was powerful, bright like Elios, strong. "Hold your weaponry at the ready, *Caht People*, until war in heaven is fully prepared."

Then Leaping Fawn and I looked upon them and away from Elios. And we saw these warriors become as clouds, dark with thunder and reversed lightning.   This lightning was turned to darkness with black jagged forks, very potent and patient, passing back-and-forth in their clouds of witness — as though from one being to another.

And the voice said, *This is the forbearance of those who obey the tout-puissant. Who were slain and yet live to obey for evermore.*

"There. Now wasn't that fun?" Smiling, blur-face said this to the children as he dropped them off on the far side of the dark elegant burial grounds of the crematorium. "Follow the path, go through the gate." Still smiling as though to assure them, he pointed to where the tall wrought-iron palings met gateposts in the distance. There they'd find a gap just big enough for such skinny kidz to slip between palings and post, and so enter the thoroughfare to the SiXPointz intersection. "Slip on through, and go home." He did not add that they might do this again sometime. He counted on their relief and silence. Blur-head felt quite safe.

To Claude and GURlee he was not blur-face, smudge-head, or any of that spiritual reality glimpsed by WIMPs, for whom things in this city had the look of dust held together by other information; had the look of pixilated people, recognizably individual but cobbled together, loosely. Pomala had taken to calling them pixie dust. The others went with that sometimes, too.

But to the little SiXPointz kidz he was a man with spiked hairs seen sometimes in the building, sometimes in the skatePark or getting into and out of cars, always shiny and luxuriant. They were so relieved he had let them go that Claude, at least, whooped his joy. He clutched his game set extra hard, glad it had not been taken away by the rich monster-man.

This nice man-turned-into-a-scary-man. This is what GURlee, wondering, thought. She too held close her game set and ran after Claude. The awful and confining flycar had slid up through dark trees into the pale but dimmer-dark sky, then slipped between the building tops glimpsed beyond the wall of above on the right. Traffic was still rolling-flying-stopping-starting.

Will I get home safe? she wondered. Will they have to see him yet again, maybe coming out of Lovely's shop or the cafe on the mezzanine? Isn't that where she saw him before?

But, inside, she felt the edges of the deep dark hole, and a black scary place edging close. Tonight she would sink down, way down, hanging tight to its edges; and legs dangling, toes pointed quiet toward the dark. The void as it was called in the game. *Oh baby!! Oh baby!!* Baby!! Baby's gonna make it? Or — sucked back into the abyss.... (*Shiver whimper*)

The abyss, wrote the friar. Hence silence, hence unmaking dwelt.

"She won't say a thing about it," said GURlee's big sister, Gorgeeous. "She doesn't want to talk. I can't even get her to nod her head.

This was said to the detective, Philipa, in the kitchenette of Gorgeeous's bohemian flat—some studio corner rooms of Bleak Watch Building, not far from the Kress.

GURlee was in her bedroom with lots of small stuffed fishies, birdies, mice and moles piled all around her, softly, to keep the creepy-crawly cruelties at bay. She had prayed her prayers and when the two women left her in the dark, hung there, silent. Silent.

79

Oh Baby, she thought, in the silence. Unspeakable to others.
Are you gonna make it?

Claude was in his mother's basement bedroom, with its
windows at street level up above him. He looked up there, his round
round eyes seeing, and not seeing, hundreds of legs go by. When
will they stop? He forgot them. In the silence he thought of how to
escape the evil man. If only they could catch him. But how will
they? Who will find out the truth about him? Maybe I could
ixelPink his picture, put it in a bottle. Lower it in the sewer by the
curb. Someone might see it bobbing in the sewage department, open
it, and guess what happened. Yeah. But then what? I don't want
anyone to know what happened. It's bad enough it happened.
Happened. GURlee knows.... Is that bad? Maybe not. Maybe that's
kayOh. What if I had been alone?

Oh, why do grown-ups get to be grown-ups?! I was gonna be
one! Couldn't wait! The sewer! Yes, the sewer.

Claude did not cry. He shivered. He shivered.

s. dormAn

A Reverberator Tries It

Meanwhile, having seen that the kids finally got not-so-safely home, the *weakly interacting massive particles*, having expanded, look down on the city, and suburban surroundings, from high above. They had seen the flying car go on its way and land on the roof of a distant tall glassy building. But they were now high high above, looking down on HiTopOLis sparkling in the night like gold... and higher they went, rising. Seeing many such intersections aglow. Shimmering, loosely blanketing, as though crystalline snowflakes, handknit together. Rising, spreading, WIMPs saw the great deep of Eartha expanding before them in pulsing bright spots, connected with threads of light. And these threads were themselves lit with bright spots, more delicate, in tune with the pulsating threads. Now, oh so remotely—as fireflies stitching the deeper darkness in dainty flashes—cities were as though signaling one another in a great and darkly burnished dance.

If Gneis had been with them to see this great and lovingly made pattern, he might have said it looked like a far more brilliant and fantastic connectedness of ... of great glittering chunks of fungal bodies, reaching toward and touching one another with delicate filaments. Filaments of life neither animal, vegetable, nor mineral. Life, he might have said, in a very basic form.

But these particles of dark matter, these WIMPs kept rising, spreading in slow and stately wonder. Further and further spreading as the solar system of which Eartha was member shone full of Elios-lit debris: not gold but silver the asteroids and moons, moonlets and planets, planetesimals, dust and dwarf planets, the flashing of cosmic rays and particles. Until, spreading again, the WIMPs saw (and were become themselves) this solar system of the alternate universe—now but a tiny sphere of light scarcely lit by a far far far and minutely central fact of that star—*There! No there! Where? Oops. The sun is gone, gone into tiny mode.*

All lights and shadows of the system were now engulfed in the great web of lights—the galaxy. A great web with its own centers

81

of brightness, its own connecting filaments, particles upon particles of light.... But, this now gave onto the universe itself... They zoomed into great color-lit clouds of dust played upon by gravity—the dust's own gravity and that of other, massive bodies far and wide, streaming in brightness, and spiraling outward; mysterious and shadowy and darkly lit. No longer could they speak of it, but *must* wholly live henceforth only for it. Only. Only. Only be engulfed in the marvelous makings of which they now seemed such a part.

A part.

—A part. A bunch of parts, HB said it at last.

—A part. Said Fabian, echoing agreement.

—A part. Said Jayrai. Girls! A part.

—Particles. Said Tu.

—Am I a particle? asked Quadri.

— 'Fraid so, lots of'em, said Pomala. Here, give me your hand. When you get big enough for astronomy class you can tell them all about it....

—But we're lost. (Quad)

—No we're not. We're right here. Pomala sought to reassure him, and herself, and them all.

And. —They were back, witnessing the distress of GURlee and Claude, each as they lay abed in separate apartments. And, peripherally, they joined the slow and stately dancing of the universe, found the detectives working the case (Pomala and Jay especially interested), watched Berle late into the night as he calculated, theorized, read. They were also aware of Gneis asleep, Sheesh lying there wide-eyed in the next room. Of Father Domino, or his guide Leaping Fawn, they were unaware.

—What a mess. (HBBBAH) Yo; shouldn't The Universe be fixing this? It's got laws, forces, makes more sense than—than I can get out of it. All them formulas and maths and—*Got its own bliss!* Or am I getting' it wrong? —Can't be, girls, can't be wrong about this bliss!

—Dude!! ...Not bad like man-monster. Man's a monster of the universe. You see anything like him out here? (Jay)

—Pray, I'm telling you.

—To the universe? (Jayrai again.)

—Look, he may be getting close, said Pomala, shifting her focus toward Berle.

—No, it's in the DNA, said Tu. But he watched, with most understanding, the numbers, thoughts, drifts and dreams of the particle physicist. —If there's a moral law it almost can't be proved, *and* it can't be a physical law ... unless in the genetic code.... *And* it's irrational.

—But that doesn't mean it's not real, said Fabian. Irrational

82

just means stuff doesn't seem... isn't... well, normal. Look every culture had or has morals.

—Except probably our own, said HB.

—Yes, said Tu. There used to be so-called natural law that was believable, then. In Americle—I mean our own universe. The *chao* my ancestors said. This is in terms of cultural imprint but is discredited... in the West. I Think. Materialism, latest in a sting of isms, has no moral law.

—Not discredited in the religious West, said Fabian. The knowledge of good and evil. Only in government it's not allowed because they say it's unproven and law can't—

(Jayrai) —Shouldn't that be the knowledge of good and bad apple pie? And the judicious, system not the government? But you know, where we came from (by *we* Jayrai meant her family) there was the *charma*. Like, "say nothing to wound." Or, "the cruel are like cats." Or, "When asked, always give."

—What about PC, though? That's a moral law. (Pomala)

—They made some of it civil law, Pom. (Fabian) You can be arrested for some of that incorrectness. Also, it was like the old red-letter purity people. Popular opinion can hurl tomatoes and put you in stocks.

(Jayrai) —They should put the big letter A on abusers' foreheads, said Jay. Tattoo the A! Then little kids can tell who the monsters are. Advertise on kids websites and TV.

—No, I mean we got no morals, said HB to Tu. Does this actually *disprove* the law — or is that what you mean by unbelievable?

Jay said, —There's got to be a law that says a monster is a monster is a monster. Maybe it's in those fancy symbols and numbers on the display, Tu?

Did she make Tu smile? (Yes.)

—The detective is talking to her boss, said Pomala.

—What we need's the DiGiOuija, said HB. The spirits talk to them through their virtual hands in the OuijaBord. That's us. If we can tell them where he landed, where he is mixing that drink there seventeen blocks away or whatever (they all look briefly) — maybe if we can just get'em to look out the window down at the cemetery. Get'em to think of it. The whole city is spying. Maybe the cemetery entrance is on there somewhere. They got cameras everywhere. (Except where they need them like the entrance way.) HB cast thought toward the Kress Building.

— Yay! said Pomala. — You're good, HB. Look, Quad, they're focusing on the gate! They must have picked up HB's vibe! There's the vids of the girl and kid on the sidewalk from the cemetery there. Now there's a view at ground level. Can HB really get them to read his mind?!

Philipa and Kent S. Clarke were now looping the views of GURlee and Claude. The *weakly interactive massive particles* shrank into "the chef's" tech-loaded cuboid. All but Tu, whose attention was still divided toward Berle in his apartment in the Kress Building. The others could find no interest in watching a man think.

"Can they have been there all the time?" said Clarke speculatively. He rubbed his face, balding head with its few crisps of sandy hair on top, getting rid of that late night weariness.

"You haven't got one of them going into the grounds? Check that?

They scanned back quickly through the hours, shaking their heads at last.

"If someone dropped them off there, or even outside at the other gate, they aren't saying," said Philipa at last, smoothing back a strand of her sleek brassy hair. "We've got to look through the other cases. ...And there was one — which one back in the early summer?"

"Frankos — the Frankos kid. Never came back.... That we know of. Have to check with Gadon and Gaddone. They're working on that."

"That might have set a precedent — maybe sending the perp over the line. Turned some abuser into a killer. In that case, he would have killed these kidz maybe? (Or she?)" The thought gave her an inward shiver. "So so," said Philipa, "these cases might not even be related."

"Funny why kidz don't talk."

"I don't think that's so unusual." And Philipa was thinking. He let her think. He watched her.

At last she said, "You know these kidz are probably being sexually abused. Maybe even used for pornography, who knows? And kidz are silent critters, anyway, when something scary upsets them. And I don't think they would talk with their peers, even the teenagers. They don't talk these kinds of things over. They talk about everything under the sun but their personal lives and personal happenings. They'll talk over grand ideas but not their parents. Everything is watched and absorbed in silence, even what goes on at home or school. For one thing, if you talked about what went on at home ... anything you say ... some brainless bully will pull it out and use it on you, nakedly. You don't even say stuff to your friends because of real or imagined shame." She stopped.

He let her think. He looked away.

"I've never told anyone this, but I think my foster brother may have been molested. You grew up around here. Couple decades older than me." The reference was an exaggeration. She

84

grinned. He was relieved to see that grin reach into the great gray eyes.

She asked, "Did you go to Kress Grammar, I guess you called it? Kress Elementschool."

All of a sudden he could see where she was going with this. "Someone was accused of sexual abuse, someone who worked there. After I left for higher school. —He was murdered, I think, when one of his victims grew up. They caught the murderer not too long after. There may also be a murder-suicide related to all that. Not sure." He started tapping in search terms. "So it couldn't have been him, anyway." He looked up, then went back to scanning department files.

"Yeah, but that's not what I'm getting at. Remember, the neighborhood has been aristofied since then. You were looking for tie-ins. The Kress Building is on the same site as the school. Has the same name. If more background is needed that might be one place to look. Stuff is ancient history. But you just pointed out how these things can linger and, well, fester ... without counseling. Not sure how much faith I have in that, either. This could be a kind of perverted vengeance."

He looked up at her thoughtfully. "Not even vengeance. Plain old corruption. One perp turned some kid into a perp, years later. Here, look at this."

He turned the screen. "See this? The stain seeps into the present."

She scanned the page with info on the murder. One of the victims was in prison for murdering his abuser. Apparently he'd located and murdered other unrelated sexual predators.

"There's where I'll start," she said. "I'm going to read up on all that. It didn't happen in our neighborhood, but apparently it may have started here — at the old school and migrated with the abuser and then his victim widened the scope of vengeance from there.... Says he's in prison on the lake. The Ehioerrian Island Prison. I may have to talk to him."

"What about your foster brother — was it?"

"Hmm. So, so, I wouldn't know where to look now. Haven't heard from him in years."

"Your parents take in many state kidz?"

"Enough to cram the house full. You wouldn't believe...." She saw him waiting to get more without asking.

"Yeah, they needed the money — but they loved it. In fact, I think they needed the money because they had so many kidz."

"The neighborhood has changed since then," he said, smoothing what was left of his hair, absently.

"Yeah. All these rich people, professionals, high-toning the neighborhood, bringing everybody else down." She smiled. A smile tinged with sadness.

His eyebrows went up.

"Heart," she said. "It ain't got the heart. Berle says maybe that's next door. In some other universe." Her smile came back with a little light.

—See, said Pomala. HB's been working on'em. Huh, Quad. They know we're here somewhere.

—Oh, what? —Like *we* got the goodness? said HB.

—Oh what! You getting their talk!!? (Jayrai) Oh please get me a translator! I'm missing out, yo. Girls, you better tell me what's going on. Pome! You be my translator. You got us into this — taking the little girl's hand.

—So, but, see. And I do apologize. Patiently Pomala was going to explain that the little girl in their universe needed their help. —You see we had all the know-how in 2017 to help her. And that was 1900 CE, and then we were going back to 2017, and I thought if I brought her with us... she could get help.

—And just why was that again, y'ol li'l white thang? asked HB.

While HBBAH had been a tall slender black youth with big broom-cut, Pomala had been an albino in body—in their own universe. She had face and upper body tattooed blue.

Now explaining, —She'd been raped! And no one was getting her therapy. They didn't seem to know about that in 1900. They didn't seem to know she was autistic, either. I thought if we could just take her back with us she'd get counseling, therapy. They might teach her to talk.

Fabian said, I get it now. But still.... It keeps looking like *you* did this. How did you think an extra person would fit into a different time without disruption?

—Her and that scientist, said HB.

—Forget that! said Jayrai. Forget about the little girl that can't talk. Help me to *hear*. I want to understand them, too, if *you* can. Did detective lady say something about our universe? Do they know about that?

—Can't be ours, said HB. It's no good, either. Our Big Fello's moral particle's missing there, too.

—He doesn't think it's missing, said Tu, referring to Berle. He's trying to *locate* it. *And* it's not the god particle. The HiggsBosson is what allows for equivalent particles happening simultaneous — same place, same quantum state. *And* it's unstable with no identifying features. It's not like gravity, not some moral law, some moral particle, some universal god.

The WIMPs are in the material things, including the breath moving in and out of those in the flesh. They are part of police deputy chief's counter (made of composite materials) at which Father Domino stands, writing about A'ndyans in heaven preparing their attack on evil. The WIMPs are unaware of him working there. As the scene progresses in the police cuboid—full of technology and several minds working—the friar is to one side writing down observations, one ear listening toward heaven. For those with eyes to see him, he wears buckskin and dips his feather quill pen into his ink vial, standing, head bent, at the counter just to one side of the two night-detailed detectives.

Fragments of the friar's visionary work would become part of the local history and end up translated and transmuted in old manuscripts, books, and on d-readers for those in the future to look into. Translations, especially of contemporary surroundings and mechanisms, would not be precise using Berle's language and terms of his day. As these things go, details may be lost or transformed, and also each succeeding copyist or printer might or might not use creative license, adding their own cultural touches to material given into their charge, so readers might understand better. Early on they tended to copy precisely, and add their own thoughts in the margins. Berle the physicist, and his biologist spouse, had read in print many of these things earlier in life and had introduced the children to some of these materials. But Berle had been inspired to collaborate on role-playing games with it. Historically, such had gone all the way, over land and sea, to Frankè, from Father Domino's brothery. From the land of the deer, Leaping Fawn was even now telling the friar of difference in the universe but a few millimeters away. But not in those terms. In simplest language, far removed that it might give but shadows of things seen here, he transcribed these peculiar declarations without the current HiTopOLan detail of understanding.

To wit: In that other place-world, wherein the WIMPs had had their bodily form, there were many corresponding and historical differences with his own. Slavery there had been relatively recent, where in his own world twas more anciently pervasive. In his and Berle's universe the A'ndyans had not been enslaved or concentrated after some initial skirmishes, but (more or less) assimilated. Revolution and the violent overthrow of "authority-as-birthright" were both actual and fairly recent phenomena in the WIMPs' world. But here revolution had been peaceful. The aristocracy had initiated a vision of democracy, choosing its own assimilation in consequence of consumerism. There'd been no horrific massive wasting of plagues, so that population, progress, discovery, invention and production had gone apace—even as the friar had surmised. The diversity of culture had rapidly homogenized under pressure of migration and materialism. But, absent massive warring and pestilence, debauchery and depravity have flourished instead. Hence, Berle and others (with skill, education, sense and sensibility for such work), are searching for answers among the stars. To realists, mystical observations of material shown to Father Domino by Leaping Fawn are romantic interpretations. Yet others, such as Berle himself, did not color it so. His answers, while derived from the stars, would be factual in tone. If he succeeded, his work would be free from the taint of romance, mythology, and the outright charge of falsehood and lying. (Or so he hoped.)

Philipa said, "What we need are droNes."

He gazed back at the screen. "I'll click on through and order you up a fleet ... you want 'em scrambled or fried?"

"Serious here," she said and did not call him chef. "DroNes are smart, they know what looks questionable, out-of-the-ordinary, *and* immoral in the way of abuse.... Probably why the current admin doesn't want — ... to pay for them." Here she was stepping around the subject carefully, smiling. With the fiberboard half-walls, it was, after all, an open room. Atmospheric hints suggested that some unknowns hereabouts were in the pockets of city elites. She went on. "With even just a few in the neighborhood looking through walls and all that, we might get to the bottom of it and clean the place out. Make it safe for little kidz. Teenagers."

He looked up at her again, face lit by the screen. The nightwatch: His cuboid was almost always dim, lighted by these displays, and giving the place and his deadpan look a gentle subdued quality.

She stood straight, uniform trim, the brass badge over her breast glimmering.

—Why do detectives here wear uniforms, I wonder? (Pomala)

—Maybe they just don't know any better? (Jayrai)

—They don't want to go around naked? (HBBBAH)

The deputy chief said, "SiXPointz needs better wardens for parents. These guys have got to keep their kidz close and let'em speak and deal only with those they know. Hand kidz back and forth, literally. Trading off with people they trust. There's no other way now. Probably had his nose in those subatomic particles of his. —Your friend Berle slipped up. Or the kidz' parents. Now get on back out there—look at those encrypted links I sent you." He looked at the dispatch screen. "You ride shotgun with Fyle while you look at that stuff."

Clarke was shaking his head over what great cops they were—*got to be careful what you say in the stationhouse?*

The WIMPs were together, yet everywhere at once. When

s. dormAn

Kent Clarke's office was void of Philipa they withdrew focus from there. They might have spread out to the reaches of this alternate solar system, the galaxy, and beyond again—but they were concerned with self-recovery, with getting back to their own. And, if truth be told, they were still in that state of disinterested suspense about how smudge-head might be captured and made to pay for his evil deeds. First and foremost it was: *How we gone get back where we belong in alt FivePoints 2017—with bodies!? If we do will we know ourselves? Remember this? Recollect this place made of pixel-dust, zeros and ones?* Or, as HB put it, —Will it be six of one or 0011001100 of another? —You mean 0000110, said Tu correcting him.

And secondly, *Let's keep up with these girls and see what they do.*

However, and attending from one place to another, they found, in succession, sleeping households: Claude in his basement room, talking it out in his sleep. GURlee in her room, breathing gently behind piles of stuffed critters. Mz. Bopoi and hipPo and biMbo asleep in their respective bedrooms of the elegant spacious apartment. Sheesh lying several floors below, facing the ceiling. Gneis unconscious of anything, but dreaming himself walking, flying, swimming. Even Berle had gone to sleep, though his displays were still lit with numbers, symbols, graphs, diagrams, graphics—by him on the couch in the room4living.

Tu was transfixed there but could scarcely get beyond what was visible, even while joining himself as much as possible to the constituents of the software and machines. He might have effervesced an invisible quality of muttering to himself. But Tu had better control than to express it. Had he been in the body, his friends would have seen only his blank stoical look, symmetric Osiian features, and a black bang straight across his forehead just above his solemn eyes.

But, the night long, the others stood watch over the gallantly lit neighborhood, recording its ways and doings of people and vehicles, including Philipa and Fyle flying patrol, answering calls. To themselves they were not as dense as clouds. But to the glance of Father Domino, Leaping Fawn and the taut A'ndyan warriors, above, WIMPs are as great crystalline giants with future potential to smash everything to bits if they will. These heavenly recorders, these people from an historical time know better than anyone, far better than the WIMPs themselves, just how monumental they are. The MACHOS, asleep in their respective places, and resting — from suffering, RPG's, and schoolwork—are of A'ndyans' own kind, of their own universe—not thundering giant aliens.

SiXPointz HiTopOLis

The *weakly interacting massive particles* sojourned the night overseeing this neighborhood of tall buildings and aristofied brick and stone mansions, apartment houses; jiving and jibing with one another; trying with increasing flippancy not to worry about getting home.

At last there came a lull in traffic, above and below, a brief cessation of pedestrian ingress and egress ... before the giant Eartha spun around into sunlight and the edges of everything glimmered then glowed, in response to the outpouring of Elios' energetic life. Eartha's great sun. The air was first pinky, then golden and bright. People and things sped up with a different kind of verve. A bit more wholesome and sensible, if more hectic, than what was felt in the night life of HiTopOLis.

WIMPs watched as their new friends went out their respective buildings and, holding hands now (perhaps for the first time), climbed aboard public transportation for school. There was much almost silent movement, sudden stopping and starting, takeoffs and landings of invisibly powered and directed vehicles—following, HB surmised, some kind of hidden network, signals or grid. The transport of school kidz did not fly but went underground through tunnels and came, at two stops away, to the school some could see from their apartments with no trouble; on the west side of Kress Building.

—What wimps, said Jay. Can't even walk a block or two. Is this place so unsafe, like we saw last night, *all the time*?

—Guess so, said Fabian. —It's worse than FivePoints by about ... to the power of what do-you-think, HB?

—Don't ask me, ask Tu. I can't even count to half dozen in binary.

—I think Tu is back down underground in the lab with the physicist, said Pomala. Looks like the little kids are going to the same school as the big kids!

—No, they're splitting up, said Fabian. See, the squirts are going on that side—off the great entrance. They turned down that big corridor. Look at these tiles! What glitter and glam.

—Those ain't tiles, I'm sayin', said HBBBAH. It's pixilated, granulated, mural of some kind—I'm saying again. Yo, pay attention if you want my respect.

Fabian snorted and would have kicked his butt (if he had one). — I'll respect you when I'm a person again.

—Stop! said Quad, who was sick on the night-long bickering and sniping.

—Watch it, said Pome, or you'll have *me* praying, Fabe. — See, you're scaring him, she said.

They weren't too successful at shaking the sarcastic nite-jibes.

—Look, we've lost our police officers and don't know who's on duty today, said Jayrai. And if we don't stick close to these kids we won't find out if they help get man-monster. I think Blondie in bed or on that tractor of his might be thinking about this. There's something about him, yo? But we got to keep up with these kids in this crowd, see what happens till Tu gets us sorted out.

—Making him do all *the work*—I mean magic? Likin' it! said HB. Let the brain-boy figure it out, and we'll play Sherlock to the Chef's Watson, since we know where smudge-face lives.

—The *what's* Watson? exclaimed Jay. OK: We get him to look at the gum on his shoe after he stuck his foot in it on the pavement where he tricked the little kids into riding with him. BTW, where *is* the sarge or whatever he's called? We forgot to keep track of him.

—Forget it, said Pome. I'm going to school. You shadow Claude and I'll take GURlee.

—Meaning the little boy and girl? See, I'm not getting all this.

The school was built around a great courtyard with portals and gaps to let in light for play and trees. It was an immense elegant structure with glass walls and iron supports — struts and beams — a great superstructure to hold up the transparent walls. Some walls were, here and there on various floors, opaque (the lavatories). The four sides of the building were roofed in dark solar arrays, edged in shining metal frameworks. There were cameras in every angle of the building at various heights, along with deVices for audio surveillance and other documentation. Everything, as always, seemed full of minute interstices. The WIMPs called it low-rez. They saw all the holes, gaps, spaces, pits in everything made.

Thanks to the trust of Philipa, Gneis was looking in applications holding various files relevant to last night's abduction of the children. The police were not one hundred percent certain they had been abducted because the little kidz weren't talking about what had happened, or where they'd been. They didn't know the particulars. All the bits and bytes of secret scary experience. How to piece it together, when nobody was talking?

"That's what guidance counselors are for," said Philipa to Gneis as she sent him the relevant links and files.

Gneis was all head-shot on her screen. His thin wasting face, beneath golden bowl-cut hair, was looking at her. But he looked rested, ready to roll. He said, "Unless ... it was one ... of the guidance ... counselors."

"Whooo — you're good," she said to his image.

In fact, Gneis was rolling about the accessible apartment. His fraternal twin Sheesh had seen him safely deposited in his chair, via robotic mechanisms interfacing bed and eel-chair. Sheesh checked often around the apartment to make certain things were working right for his brother. Rolling was perhaps not the right word. The eel-chair had versatile treads, almost triangular in shape, able to negotiate small impediments, differences in surface and height over floors. In this way Gneis *could* go all the way out to the portico on the ground floor in his chair. Then there was a ramp he could use if he felt good enough to handle the congested sidewalks with voice activation only. Most days he did not, and in wet weather never.

"Yeah." He grimaced. "...Good."

She knew the grimace was actually a grin. He was ill, he was dying, but he was one of the good ones, one of the smart ones who could put bits of things together and come up with a new thing altogether, something no one else might have thought of. He'd done it for her before now and might do it this time for the good of them all... and the neighborhood.

"So, so," she said brightly, "I'll leave you and the VRS to it! Talk to me again...."

She was gone. Gneis began speaking again to the screen. He had moved over by the window in order to glance out there now and then; but his real concentration was focused on the files and moving data-stream she had sent — her files put together for deputy chief Kent Clarke and others, detectives peripheral to the case.

One thing made it harder for him. The rate and way his voice was deteriorating. It seemed he had to retrain more often. It was not keeping up with changes in the pattern of speech. He was hoping for an upgrade, but did not like to ask for one. Berle trusted him to go into the account and pay for upgrades, but his son knew it was getting difficult financially in Dah's world.

Enough! He thought. *Get on with Claude and GURlee. Find out what's going on.*

He looked at GURlee's phone data. Nothing for last night after the game. Claude had no phone. He was lucky to have the game-set — a gift from Mz. Bopoi along with the occasional supper. Gneis looked at the satellite images, the street grid for the time in question. Philipa had isolated specific cars, but they were all from the wrong angle for identification. Not too well defined. The city, with its sparkle-lit pinkish-golden nebulae, was impossible. He wondered if she had asked the Federalaze for better images (if available), or corrective software. He then added that as verbal notation to the file.

He stopped, addressing the eel-chair. It turned slightly and he gazed out the window. From here, at an angle, he could see the tops of the trees in Cremery Park. Some were dark old green, but many would change color vividly. Dah's lab was far below the grounds. He could even see a cornice on the police station across from there. He checked back to see where he got the idea they'd been in the park, the burial grounds for the crematorium. *Creamery Way*, people joked in the neighborhood. Mostly teens and old people joked. He didn't mind the connection, but had noticed some middle-aged people did. ...He wouldn't mind being up there in the stars.

... You could, he thought, go all over the multiverse when you went back to nature. Your body went up in a plume of smoke and just some bits — some flakes of ash — were left for the eartha to remember you by. In the old days his ancestors had gone to make up nutrients for the people to come — maybe members of the same community. He smiled, unseeing anything but that plume and those star particles... and... and this great big goofy loving face in the Cadillalaxy. Looking back at him, winking.

His eyes were barely open. But he saw its face, tricked out in stars, bluish inside its spume of star particles. The huge features looked strange.... A friendly face. Like it knew him. But it was blue along with whit sparkles of varying intensity. Its hair kind of went upward in a plume, blue-and-white sparkly like images in XploHding Whorllds, which came from telescopic BubbleImages™ of the miraculous OutThere™. It was kind of girlish, too.

—Hi, kid, it said. —I'm Pomala.

He smiled back.

—*This is so neat, kiddo.*

She didn't say it ... exactly ... but he knew what she meant. He had to agree. *Neat.*

—It was smudge-face that did it. GURlee and Claude.

"Mmm?" Gneis hummed his musing aloud, unaware.

—*He lives over there.*

The face began to fade. Gneis started awake.

What was that?

"You ... won't believe ... my dream," he said to Sheesh.

"I'll believe all your dreams, brah," his brother said that afternoon when he got home. Sheesh stood by with treats

Gneis told him the dream. "... And her hair was ... like a blue flame. It went up like a flame ... full of dark ... blue stars. She was HUGE." He had to say it twice so that his brother would understand.

"That's a toughie. What does it mean?"

"Smudge-face ... or ... smudge-head did ... something with

GURlee and Claude."

"That's it? What's a smudge-face?"

"Donno."

"What about 'over there'?"

"Don't know ... that either. What's an ... over there ... in spaze?" He thought for a moment, then said, "Maybe ... approach it gently. Just ask G&C about ... smudge-face."

"You mean, like insert it into a conversation — or something?"

"Yeah. ...Something ... like that."

"It might be worth a try," agreed Sheesh.

"You're face ...looks so—. The freckles ... on your face ... really popping ... in this light, brah. At least—we'll see if the dream has some ... probably miniscule ... significance ... if we talk to G&C. Beyond just making ... me feel good." He smiled his pathetic wasted smile.

"That's good right there. 'Nother bite of cookie?"

"What do ... you think?" He said it twice as a matter of course.

Sheesh did not exactly get that, but he knew what was meant. He fed his brother more cookie.

"Also, what's a Pomala?" he asked.

"Something ... we saw in XploHding ... Whorllds, in the ... Cadillalaxy, I think. Maybe an ... asterism or ... constellation in a nebula."

"Look it up," said Sheesh, nodding at the display. " — Or I could?"

Gneis grimaced, letting him turn the screen. "Check for a ... girl nebula ... called Pomala."

"What? How's that spelled? —A Girl?"

"Female, teenager ... like us. Try different ... spellings."

Some key taps and pauses followed by more taps, more pauses, colorful images expanding and contracting, coming and going on the screen.

"Try some ... conflations," suggested Gneis (twice).

They did this for a while, then Sheesh said, "Could it be... supposing...?"

"Another universe altogether," suggested Gneis. "You're taking this ... more seriously than ... expected, brah. Anyway, we ... got no way of ... finding out."

The WIMPs surrounding them sank. The scene defocused a bit.

—That was cool, said Jayrai, getting it. While it lasted.

—Wait, listen! said Fabian.

"Maybe we should talk to dah," Sheesh was saying.

94

"Of course," said Gneis with a slurr.

—My girl! said HBBBAH. Now all we got to do is squeeze Tu, see what he's got. Forget the little kids, man, this might be getting us home. We was never gonna ruMble wit dees MACHOs anyways.

—MACHOs! (Quadri)

—MACHOs!! (Pome and Fabe)

—The other dark matter, the kids playing the game. (Tu)

Pomala said, —But, HB, I wanted to help the little kids.

—Whad I tell you bout that?

—He's right, Pome, said Fabe. You're gonna mess us up again.

—How's come I'm the one? Maybe it was the A'ndians. They took "the little girl" from me didn't they? They virtually pushed us out of that 1900 CE crypt, HB. She's still alive in our universe somewhere, living way back in primitive times maybe! Why don't you blame the A'ndians?

—Yeah, said Jay. What makes you girls think we won't be living like *that* if we go back? I mean — how are *we* going to live like our ancestors? The civilization of mine, IIRC, goes back a bit further than yours. So HB will carry fire better'n us, yo. In fact, if yours hadn't been enslaved by Fabe's ancestors you'd still be — uh-oh.

—Undercutting your argument, Jayrai, said Fabian. And besides, mine fought for the North. They had no slaves and were dirt poor to boot.

—Stop!! (Quad)

Pomala said, —Quad's right. What good will we do our universe or Akropolis or FivePoints if we do get back? Without the girl even.

—What *good* will *we* do?! Whad I tell you! It'll do *us* good, everybody we know. Okay okay, I'll stop now. I hope. ...I'm just looking for *my* good. Okay *okay okay*! Tu?

—He's still working on it, said Tu, referring to Berle. I tried to nudge him off that moral particle thing and they're still working on the dark matter, but I think he's too preoccupied with the other thing. And they need that funding. But I can't do anything with him but watch.

—Pome's the only one who seems to get anywhere. (Jay)

—What about me? said HB. I got the cops thinking about our universe, too.

— BTW, said Jay. Remember that scientist we saw with him? I think she's a scientist? Pome? The one making notes in the lab when we came? She's not there in the lab anymore, and I saw her with Claude.

—Reporter, I think. She tried to get somewhere with

95

GURlee—couldn't. (Pome)

—Let's focus on that. There. She's with Claude in the basement. (Jayrai)

The WIMPs filled up the place where Claude lived—the basement rooms and materials, the smell of fish and fries. There were only three rooms, excluding the shared bath in the hall, but they were comfortably furnished. Claude's mom was a prostitute but she tried to keep that away from Claude. She didn't "work out of the house," but what was going on he had an idea from what kidz said to him—taunting. And he was alone a lot because of it. He didn't think kidz' sarcasm was fair. He said back that their sisters and brothers were prostitutes and they didn't get paid. Why was that better? Claude's mom (whom he always called by her name, Pegmo) was home with him this afternoon. She knew something was up and it wasn't good. But she was not concerned for herself and her work.

ShieL, the reverberator, who had spoken to an audience of lay people and scientists while down in the lab, was sitting across from Pegmo. In addition to *Virtual Futures* and *BalOnion Nation*, shieL worked for any outlet hiring her stories. And of course she worked for THVR, The HiToP Viral Reverb.

She had heard that Pegmo was a prostitute and knew how it went in this city. Betting, booze, and brothels drove the city, as Berle put it. The physicist was actually trying to figure that scientifically, but she was the last one to mention it. As a reverberator, she knew of stranger things. She kept notes on his hints, the numerical, and modeling, fracTils, but that was it. No talking about it. For now. If something came of it she'd be ready with all the reverberation. Till then, quiet. The lab did need that dark matter funding. Because it would have been speaking to the situation, she had not even reminded him that some of the exorbitant taxes service workers like this paid went into such studies, as well as infrastructure and everything else, including the pockets of the administration: only the elite of industry (the service and what was left of city industry) were exempt. It was on the backs of these people. The more you had of power and wealth the less you paid percentage-wise. One thing they didn't tax in this profession was for healthcare. If Pegmo wasn't healthy a lot of important people might suffer. There was still work to do on these diseases and more viruses kept mutating all the time. ShieL knew that was one thing the Mayor and friends would see to if nothing else.

They sat together at the table. The skinny little Claude, his brown hair long with fringes across his brow, was eating the meal of fish sticks and fries his mom had spooked for him in the micro-freakquency. Pegmo sat close to him with her hand rubbing his neck while he ate, sometimes scooping a bit of fish whitesauce onto his plate. He'd shrug her hand off his neck, embarrassed, or irritated. He dipped sauce away on a forkful. And then wished he hadn't shrugged. After a bit her hand came back to start rubbing again.

Pegmo's hair was tangerine-green, with spikes of flaming orange. She had long long dangly earrings like seed pods on some exotic plant. Sometimes, especially while working, she wore chartreuse contact lenses. No one was really sure what she looked like under all that. Her body was sparkling with lights, had one massive tattoo—some images (in those places covered by clothes) out of *samakutra*. Claude had never seen them. In fact, Pegmo herself sometimes thought the other kidz didn't exactly know much, though they talked loudly in their absurd ignorance. Tonight she was ready for work, wearing seven-inch heels that flashed and glittered purple lights. She rarely left for work until after Claude was asleep. Last night, of course, had been different. Claude had been with the Bopoiz, and after that.... That was why the reverberator was here asking questions.

Pegmo had inquired about shieL's current recordings, and been assured that all deVices were off.

ShieL keeL herself was rather round, dark, with flaring nostrils but large luscious lips. She was short and overweight. She was saying, "I heard you and GURlee went missing for a little while last night." ShieL keeL raised her eyebrows innocently and smiled shyly. This was the look, a sort of helpless look, inspiring confidence during awkward questioning.

Claude nodded and dipped his fish stick in whitesauce.

Pegmo rubbed his neck. Softly. She curved back his hair behind one ear with her finger. Claude was saying nothing. How unusual. It was almost like he was chunneling GURlee.

Mz keeL said, "You know what works (for me) when I want to talk about something I don't want to talk about?"

Claude understood perfectly what was meant by this verbal paradox. But he waited, spearing a fry as Pegmo poured out a bit more catchup.

Don't mind the police for not thinking of this, came the stray thought from somewhere. ShieL said only, "I draw pictures. Look."

She brushed away stray salt that had sprinkled the table when Pegmo missed some of the fries. She got out her pad and drew a stick figure falling down stairs. The staircase was a simple contour, a zigzag line, and the stick figure was flailing as it tumbled down. Then she did another with stick figure. A pile of crumpled lines at the bottom of the zigzag. Claude smiled.

"That's me." She pointed.

97

"...That's all I'm saying...." She raised her dark eyebrows innocently.

Claude smiled bigger.

ShieL turned the pad, and placed the pen beside it

—*Care to give it a whirl?* This, from the soft drift of late afternoon light, shot with dust motes pouring through the windowpane from the street above. This from the furniture, inaudible.

ShieL herself said nothing.

Claude chewed his fries, looking at the stick figures. The stairs, zigzag from top to bottom. He chewed more fries, he did not reach for the pen.

Pegmo picked up the pad and looked at it. "That musta been some spill." Her voice was unexpectedly deep. It was a bit rough, like there was something in the back of her throat, a bit of crushed peppermint.

—*Just a flying stick, maybe?* Suggested the micro-freakquency, the humming frudgerator, the plate, the fries, the dusty light.

Pegmo stood, tore off the sheet and lay it aside. She went to the frudge to get Claude a glass of milk. She took a long time. It was like slo-mo, only very very colorful.

Claude picked up the pen and drew a flying stick. He chewed on some fish, considering the drawing. It was a horizontal line with shorter swept lines, slanting a bit on either side. Pegmo was pouring milk, very very very slowly.

ShieL nodded when she saw the lines. Like a twig drawn on the page. "Pretty good. Better than mine, in fact." She glanced at hers: "It's kind of hard to tell what that is at the bottom of my stairs. ...Anything else?"

Claude swallowed and looked around for the milk. Pegmo handed it to him. He set down the glass, wiped at the moist mustache, and picked up the pen. He drew three circles on the flying stick—up front.

"Any arms and legs for those?" asked shieL.

Claude attempted the arms and legs, but was soon giggling and scribbling over them. He made long sweeping scribbles, ending furiously.

"Can't do it," he said. And swallowed the milk, small adam's apple bobbing in his throat.

There was silence.

"Oh yeah," said shieL after a bit. "I know how you feel. I should strike out those stairs, those crumpled sticks there." She did this, slowly, then rapidly, and crumpled the paper, looking around for the trash. Claude crumpled his in a tight ball and threw it into the corner bin between the counter cupboards and the door. His didn't miss; but, following it, shieL's did.

"No fair," she said. "You've had practice."

Claude said, "I'm good." He grinned.

"The Bopoiz want to MACHO tonight," said Pegmo. "You OK with that?"

Claude hesitated.

"Sheesh called and said he'd bring you home or you could spend the night."

"KayOh," he said. "...Which?"

"Whichever you want. You could wait to make up your mind."

They talked of what he might bring, Pegmo and Claude.

ShieL was making notes on the pad as Claude cleared the table with his mom. When Pegmo had mopped and dried it, shieL turned the pad toward her, and Pegmo scanned it with chartreuse eyes. She nodded as she did so. ShieL showed the pad to Claude, but he couldn't read it. He nodded as well and went to get his stuff.

"Want to come with us?" Pegmo was asking shieL.

"Yep." She raised her eyebrows and smiled shyly.

—What a great outfit! (Pomala referring to Pegmo's dress.) Remember how they dressed in our solar system in 1900 CE? Long dark skirts, cinch waists, long puffy sleeves and prim hats?

—Our *universe*, said Jayrai, correcting, proud of herself. Got that part anyway.

BABY™ Get Born!

Leaping Fawn had shown Father Domino many things. She was as a delicate flower of jewel-like transparency, toward whom it was impossible not to feel worship. Yet this was forbidden. Leaping Fawn worshiped THE DEER. Many things she had shown, each more glorious, mysterious, and wonder-making than the last. And TERRIBLE events had occurred. More TERRIBLE events were to happen. But her splendor sustained him. T'were impossible to feel such terror without the deepest unhappiness. Yet was grief hopeful of assuagement because of glory so promised in the splendor of her quite pure spirit, and of her sublime jewel like appearance. She was splendid more than fine gold once given to knights in service of their bounden royal lord.

However this was, and however he saw these many mysterious events (whether in or out of the body) he always came to himself here in the cave (far far from the brothery) — in the land of battle-wood and bogs and among ledges where the nation was destroyed. THE LOST NATION. Sometimes he was outside the cave. Sometimes burning bodies that had not sunk in bogs. Sometimes gazing on the heavens through stems, calm stars shinning without discernible movement until next he looked. Then he would think of sublime and unspeakable, paradoxically dense and diaphanous, movement and spheres he had seen in the heavens—*these*. These very glimmery seeming-innumerable-immovable stars!

And however much he saw of the vision *past-future*, however his time spent with her, or seeing only in glimpses (her face shining and smiling or solemn and shimmer-dim), Father Domino would wake, quill pen in hand, at this work. At work on illuminated manuscript of scraped hide he called valim. Geagosasa—who was even now becoming a great tribal lady among clans of the conquerors *Haudenosuni*—Geagosasa had, as it happened, left behind good valim for his use. He would use the rags on his back if need were.

So hard was this ink, this valim, this script to make! So thin and so cold was the friar! He was always so lonely without her, without them. His life was unendingly lonely. In visions, in the writings, he forgot this.... But then he had to forage in winter, he had to wash, he had to walk and see creatures unlike his kind.

Raison d'être, Raison d'être. Father Domino wept.

Often 'twould seem there was no one. No one to read these manuscripts in *sometime-to-come.* But—how was this to happen?—things he wrote would they indeed be for Berle the Claric to find in various scripts—imprecise first in transcription and translation; then in facsimile of future times when all things are different? Berle the Claric would have nesting shapes and lines to work with in configuring. Like the snowflakes, ever falling, into which he'd been driven at her biding. Crystals nesting within crystals within crystals of glorious symmetry.

Such configurations, he thought, were needed of the aristocracy to forge heavy industry; for which they give up serfdom to get many workers and make themselves rich. For patterns are always used in human life. This was the nesting pattern: Generations, nested within generations of Peoples of whatever kind, would always need food, rest, clothing, shelter — however achieved. Bodies would need bones and flesh and blood and *crevelle.* Folk would always need *La Grand Créateur.* He was *life in them*—He who devised figures, patterns, pieces and laws. And the friar knew also that Leaping Fawn was walking and sharing with Berle the Claric, but Berle had no understanding of that. Berle thought the thoughts were his own. She had shown him mysteries: patterns and formulas in strange juxtapositions—of numbers and letters and figures—of which Father Domino had little or no comprehension. He had no time to learn of these and they must ignite their ways through the folk in time.

The floor of the cave was cold, hard, and damp. The light was scant but here things he needed were safer from elements, animals, enemies, strife. Striving is what Berle would call ambition. The friar would be without ambition but solely to be lost in these visions, waiting for all coming-to-pass. Here he could work in peace and be lost to discomfort if only briefly as he watched and saw all. Watching and transcribing the visions for some unknown length of time.

Now once more, the quill pen taut in his hand, he feels himself drawn into visions, dissolving. Falling upwards into the snowfall, fragmented, yet paradoxically Father Domino — whole.

"Come up here with the braves encircling the city," he hears her voice say. Her voice lights in his mind, reminiscent of that of The Deer's. THE DEER had called her that way: "Come up here!" —

at the destruction of the clan in the swamp land. She had gone up the hillside, up the hillside, bloody, she had gone. But recently on the hillside in thickets he had found and heaped her body with stones.

Now he breathed her name. "Leaping Fawn."

"Yes, Father Domino! Come up here!!"

The snow was thickly falling. He fell in with the fall.

He saw the blue light descending through snowfall. Or was it ascending? Father Domino could not tell. He was part of the snowfall and could not tell up from down. He had not the pull of the earth upon his senses to tell him. But, through dense scattering, he saw a blue angel moving swiftly, an angel of angry blue light. Wrath was in the face of the blue angel—falling, ascending, he could not tell. Swiftly, swiftly past him—angry. The personification of wrath. The snow did not quench him. He, THIS WRATH, did not quench the snow. But, as he passed, his blue light mingling with that of the snow, Father Domino was aware of changing hues. This angry blue being transforming snowfall. Snowfall blued and darkened, the light going with it in passing, and the symmetrical flakes—as these fell in the friar's gaze and on his frail shapelessness—were become darkness. The darkness of which he himself was a part. Darkness and pieces and falling and settling. And Father Domino was once more in the city, and HiTopOLis in darkness. The small hills on which it stood and which surrounded it—darkness the hills, darkness the structures, darkness and ashes and dusting. All its lights quenched. And light shone nowhere in particular, yet he could see the shades of the drift and dense scattering. Layers of movement, infilling him, absorbing him. And people walked down there, covering their faces, some huddling together, but multitudes drifting apart. Coughing. Pressure of the dense fall muffled every moving thing. All machines stopped. There were only people, half-guessed forms in darkness.

He wanted to call out to them, but something stayed him. He watched instead. He did not think how he was able to watch. Later he thought perhaps he was in the cave all along and seeing only because it was what she wanted to show him. He watched.

Thick darkness. Everywhere.

Drawn, he went higher. He felt himself now looking downward, through dust and darkness and unmaking. Darkness was thick over land of dust and dimness, and the city now nowhere visible in darkness. He felt his field of view expanding, and yet it was but dust and darkness. Now, in descending a bit, layers of hills he discerned.

Here and there Father Domino descried thin spires, thin streams — of smoke ascending. These scattered smoke spires were paler than the thick dusty darkness (of which he still felt himself a part).

What are these smokes?

He wondered. Before he could think to wish she might be here to tell him, a voice said,

These are they who survive. These are those the A'ndyans teach to survive.

A'ndyans?

Yea. These are the ancestors of everyone.

Father Domino was sitting in the cave, these words now distantly echoing in mind. *These are the ancestors of everyone. Once upon a time all survived as you do. They will survive that way again when HiTopOLis is gone.*

Smudge-head stood a moment looking at the Lovely Shop. He did not exactly see the lovely things shining in its windows off the lobby of the Kress Building, the garments displayed and clientele wandering inside awaiting appointments or fingering items of elegance, tasteful jewelry and blang. He had seen it so many times, had had a hand in devising both structure (the building) and complementary features, including the business itself. Instead of seeing, he was thinking. Thinking of the possibility of being murdered one day; of where he would be dining with the Mayor tonight and of conversations there; of how he was going to "see" Claude and GURlee again; of his probable murder; of the next real estate deal; and of finding out more about the many kidz he'd seen so often in the Kress Building.

The WIMPs, watched him from the constituents of the shop, the draping colorful garments and bizarre hats on the heads of mannequins, the flashing of blang. They scarcely noticed their progress in mind-reading because of what they were in fact reading. It was scary. Smudge-head wanted some teenagers rounded up for stem-cell matches to reverse aging—through medical channels, *all proper and legal of course.* Now he was thinking of his latest project, the tryogenic institution. With its absolute zero of suspended animation. He wouldn't be murdered so much as becoming a "patient" until they figured out a way to bring him back to life. Suspension — in more ways than one. They'd hang him in a bag full of liquid neatrogen upside down. That way if a leak developed decay would begin at his toes until—an alarm sounding—they discovered it, with time to spare for repair. The whole setup for patients would be continually monitored to minimize things like that happening.... And that meeting with the Mayor... the policy discussion.... The kidz in the Kress Building. Wasn't the boy's mother—? It might be fun to check that out.

The WIMPs got sick and disgusted; so they focused on the upstairs apartments instead. Both Claude and GURlee had come a bit earlier—in time to escape Smudge-head's notice, though this was inadvertant. Now the WIMPs' attention was split between Gneis's bedroom and the spacious Bopoi living room, several floors up, with its grand view of HiTopOLis in evening light.

Mz. Bopoi did not look long at GURlee tonight, but said right off directly to her with a kind smile, "Maybe BABY will make it tonight."

GURlee glanced away. GURlee's sister, Gorgeeous, had come with her and, in a bit of hidden awe of the elegant rooms and the view, and of Mz. Bopoi herself, she hesitated, then ventured to speak for GURlee. To GURlee, but with an eye also on Mz. Bopoi: "Do you think so? That would be nice."

Claude also said nothing. The Bopoi children, hipPo and biMbo, were silent as well, fiddling with their game sets. Claude? Being silent not clever? This *must* be serious—whatever it was.

—Whew, said Jayrai. There's more action going on in paralyzed boy's bedroom. If they don't pep up, BABY's *not* gonna make it tonight.

—Dunno know about that, said HBBBAH. What are they up to, Tu?

Gneis and Berle were conversing in low voices, reddish and golden heads bent slightly to the screen of the bedtable tilted toward them. To one side was an uneaten burger. Berle would finish it off after Sheesh got done making some soup in the kitchen for his brother.

—I think he's got the particle question mixed in with the two little kids, said Tu referring to Berle, to Claude and GURlee.

"While we're waiting for Sheesh to come up, we might have some pops-n-pies. That sound KO?" Mz. Bopoi sent a hopeful glance toward Gorgeeous.

She squeezed GURlee's hand and jumped up. "Can I give you a hand?"

"Hands are excellent things," said Mz. Bopoi, smiling.

They went into the kitchen through the doorway next the grand view of cloud-and-sun burnished HiTopOLis. The city was lively with vertical, diagonal, and horizontal movement.

"I think the RAMBOs are ready," said hipPo, looking at his slim deVice with dark eyes.

"I'm putting on my headset," said biMbo, flinging back her headful of dark wavy hair.

"Better wait. Sheesh said he'd be here," returned her brother. "We need them. Gneis might even come."

The dark eyed girl shrugged. "Wha'd *you* do last night,

Claude?" This was said low, with quick calculation for the earshot toward the kitchen. Clinking sounds and murmurs came from the doorway.

Down in Gneis's bedroom they were getting him ready for the road, meaning the apartment, hallway, elevator, and so on. From habit, it was not so much arduous as tedious. Lift him onto the eelie, take off the pj's, fit on the street clothes, lifting butt, arms, and legs, patch in some tubes, a line for medicinals, and fix the head brace. While they worked they talked about Gneis's dream.

"I have no idea what a smoke face is," said Berle, squatting, smoothing the boy's blond hair. "And I don't know of an asterism or nebula called Pomala.... But that's an interesting guess about an alt universe." He stood up. "I'm going to think about that one. It's a toughie. But you think of it, too." He said this, gazing down on his son with a smile. He looked at Sheesh.

"Ready to roll?"

Sheesh gave him the thumbs up.

"By the way, I think that's a pretty good idea—asking them about the smudged face. Dreams aren't always just detritus chucked up by the psyche. Sometimes they are... zonal. When you're in the zone, sometimes things come to you. True things. Gifts you are given on the way...." He looked at them quizzically. "You believe that?"

Sheesh smiled. Gneis drooled from the corner of his lopsided mouth. His twin handed Dah a crumpled napkin from the tray with plate and bowl, on the table behind him. Berle wiped the drool with it.

FivePoints was watching.

Claude said nothing. He looked at biMbo.

She said, "Your ears stick out funny." His face was small and narrow, dimpled at the chin, big-eyed, and, yes, his ears pointed east and west, or north and south, depending.

He was thinking, looking at her. Slowly, very slowly, he said, "So does my tongue." Slowly... he stuck it out at her.

Claude slow? But she was quick. "You're making me barf."

Claude smiled. The MACHOs were pepping up a bit.

"BABY might make it out of XploHding Whorllds tonight," said Mz. Bopoi coming in, carrying the tray, with uplifted voice. Gorgeeous was behind her with another, bearing dark fizzling Kake™ in glasses, with also a long-stemmed glass full of something light, sparkling, for her hostess.

—Tu, have you got this BABY thing figured out? Fabian was asking.

—BABY needs born, said Quadri.

—So, said Jayrai, all babies need born, Quad. What's it got

105

to do with stars and big bangs and singularities? It's only a game. Tu, we got to get back to that half-inch away. I want my arm. I want my job.

—You *hoping* for that job. Remains to be seen if you get it, interposed HB.

—Okay then, mom's waiting. Bros, sisters. —How about dat, yo?

—Some of us haven't got—

—Stop! (Quad) BABY's gonna get born! —Who is BABY? (Quad)

—*What* is BABY? (Jay)

Sheesh and Gneis came in from the foyer. They were in the spacious room.

"We've got pops-n-pies," sang hipPo.

"Hope you've got room for dessert," said Mz. Bopoi.

"Got your setz?" asked biMbo. "Get out of here, if you don't!"

"We do," said Sheesh, displaying the two game-sets. He put one over Gneis's head and let the dark virtual reality mask sit, for the time being, across his brother's wasted chest. There was a moment of awkward silence as the others set their pops-n-pies on the table. Mz. Bopoi had gone into the kitchen and now came back with a tall travel-mug complete with straw, handing it to Sheesh. "Hope you like this, Gneis" she said.

Gneis slurped at it, trying to suck. He pretended to get some and pulled back. "Good," he said, as she leaned toward him, smiling. Sheesh put it to his lips.

BiMbo actually knew better than to say anything.

—Smudge-face is in the physicist's apartment, said Tu.

—*OMG*! said Pome and Jay together.

With an incurious glance and nod at the computer on the coffee table, there he was, sitting on the couch across from Berle.

Quadri shivered violently. His subatomic particles danced and dissipated away from there. He tried to compress into Gneis's travel-mug on Mz. Bopoi's coffee table.

—He can't get you, Quad. There's no fear, said HB.

—Of course there's fear! said Pomala. We'll keep you safe, Quad. And GURlee and Claude.

—How you gonna do that, Pome? Fabe was about to challenge, thought better of it but, of course, it was *out there*.

"Your reputation in fracTils is growing in HiTopOLis, Dr. Quarts."

Then they saw Smudge waiting for some kind of response.

—What's his *Real* reason for coming, said Jayrai.

Berle's response was very slight. A sort of nonresponse. A light—now gone—in Berle's eye. Smudge-face did not recognize it.

106

s. dormAn

Maybe he did not see. Maybe he saw a non-comment, a sort of
stonewall or surface like stone.

—He's not so good at seeing, Smudge? said HB.

—He prides himself on reading people, though, said Pomala.

—Like I said, said Jay. You're good. Think his head'll ever
get de-smudged?

—Just don't please try to help here, Pome, warned Fabian.

Smudge-head said, "I've heard it's possible to apply a sort of
geometric or visual approach to the numbers crunching we do in the
markets. Very beneficial. A better graphic look at the pattern than
what we've got now; some generated visualizations to map
emergence—should give us something to sink our teeth into...."

The WIMPs started booing and hissing.

"... Something also to smooth the complications, and give us
a condensed view."

—*Boo. Hiss.*

—But see, said Tu, you can use that for all kinds of science.
Fractils can simplify things studied. In our universe this method
was discovered by Brotmantle, following Peppler's model of thinking
outside the sphere. Or the circle. You see, Peppler made that
historic leap from the circular orbit to the ellipse. That was a
geometrical insight inspiring to Brotmantle. He began looking
carefully at shapes and patterns and physical objects — even
gigantic things like coastal outlines, and penetrating deeper to find
the same pattern in smaller and smaller fragments of the self-same
coastal material. Take blood vessels—

"Doesn't really interest me," said Berle, thinking with regret
of Gneis. "I'm sorry you had to come all the way up here for that
answer."

"So, so... we'd be prepared to offer—"

"I know you're a busy man," said Berle, standing, holding out
his hand.

—*No-don't-take-his-hand!* said the WIMPs, all except Tu who
was still in the middle of his info dump:

—Mathematics in the Euclidean model couldn't handle these
patterns—like what you find in ball lightning, galactic arrays, and
pigeon poop parts—not with the simplicity of this fractal
visualization—

—If he could visualize the pictures in Smudge-head's mind
he'd go to the cops NOW and have him arrested, said HB.

—You can't arrest people for what they're thinking, said
Fabian.

—But what you said about prayer? This was put in by
Pomala.

—They got to do the deed, said Jay

107

—And get caught (Fabian). But I see what you mean, Pome.
That prayer's a form of thinking... but it's for an action you hope for.
Not evidence in a court of law.

Quad was still hunkered in the Kake cup, waiting. Hoping
the game would begin.

—That means he's got to do it again, get caught, for justice to
be done. (Fabe)

—What about Pome's dream? Gneis had it, heard it. That's
eyewitness evidence. (Jayrai)

—You've been smoking ffuts, said HB. When's the last time
they used dreams as evidence?

Tu was saying, —I think the physicist is considering the way
wealth is distributed in comparison to housing starts. He's already
working on the fundamentals using fractals! Look at the screen.

—Even though Smudge-meister is going out the door. (Jay)
Holy—Cow, she finished. Whoops—not supposed to say that. I
thought he wasn't interested in Smudge's plan!

—Are you getting stuff, now, Jay? asked Pome.

—Not so much. It was more what Tu said with the evidence
of my own—

—Yeah, we get it, said HB.

—Now he's looking at patterns in the housing market, said
Tu. From 100 years ago, and now graphs in decades, years,
months—I think. That last one's today ... I think. See that? The
pattern's pretty much the same no matter the time increment.

—Shh. (Quad)

—They're playing, said Fabian. (The kids and adults had
darkened and cleared the room of small furniture, dishes.)

—Yo, will or will not BABY make it to-NIGHT!? (HB) I'm
going deep. Y'all can hang out here talking fractions or whatever,
but I'm inside these Gneis-goggles. If 'n I be the goggles, maybe I'll
get his attention. Oh shit man! This game is amazing.

They all crowded into the game, Tu still with half an "eye" on
Berle's screens. Now they were in the game's incipient universe,
feeling the simultaneous, remote compression and explosive forces
battling it out. There was nothing here but the struggle — RAMBOs
vs. MACHOs — which the game measured and portrayed along with
a combination of tingles, jerks and full starts, with lapses of futility
impressed on the psyches and bodies of players. Through a series of
rhythmic percussive beats coupled with a throbbing point of light
and other electronic stimuli, they felt all in a united nervous system.
They were surrounded in an ominous sucking darkness, impressing
their emotions and nerves to replicate the VOID™. The WIMPs felt
the presence of RAMBOs, but would not otherwise experience them
at this point in their alt experiences—not as they did material

108

objects and people in the apartment; and in HiTopOLis at large.

RAMBOs were compression. Their intent was to quash the explosive welling contained in the SinGuLariTEE inhabited by the gangs. MACHOs, with great dexterity, by a series of gambits played blindly on their finger-pads, or with the occasional glance, are struggling to be the superior power. There was a component built into the visors providing for rapid eye movement and directional gazing that allowed players to shift power pulses wherever they could—provided a RAMBOs failure in that area. Thus Gneis was playing as well—often much better—than hipPo, biMbo or Sheesh. And Claude and GURlee were playing better than usual tonight. They seemed to have a fresh acuity, more energy, as though themselves an element of urgent explosive force.

Mz. Bopoi, still wearing her business attire, and Gorgeeous in T-shirt and naejs, watched from the kitchen doorway, imagining the universe, struggling, unfolding, based on the shouts and movements of the children. Under their breaths the women began chanting: "BABY's gonna get born, BABY's gonna get born. BABY's gonna get born...."

Meanwhile the WIMPs were into it. Quad was feeling breathless, like BABY. He was closer to GURlee in playing and began to feel her movements and flashing eye-patterns. Excited, excited, he lent full attention and actually tried for the first time since his shout-out to Hah-La to effect some kind of action. Sort of riding shotgun with GURlee. He was so coordinated to her moves, pulses, evasions and pushes, that even Tu was forced to look full on their play.

—Quad is not working against her, noted Pomala.

—As you might expect. (HB) He moved from Gneis to hipPo's POV

—Yeah, said Fabian. Usually two people working on the same problem together will approach it in different ways, enough to make the whole thing fizzle or at least take longer than it might have. I'd like to play with the guy in the chair but I'm afraid to mess him up. I felt a couple moves wanting, held back, and then he just blew a couple of the RAMBOs apart. There's a lot more debris going out, *sparkly sparkly dusty dusty!*

—Ow-soome. (the WIMP chorus)

Tu's attention had gone back to Berle. *It's big and instructive but it's only a game. This is the real stuff.* He watched Berle standing in the kitchen gazing at the wall. Gazing at the floor. At first Tu thought Berle was daydreaming, seeing nothing but the what-if question, or the application of fractils to the data on dark matter. Then Tu noticed Berle's golden eyes begin to read.

—Phooey. He's only reading the wallpaper and the floor.

It looked like the walls had been papered (probably by the twin?) in printed pages from old books. And the kitchen floor tiles, though scuffed, and shiny only here and there, were pieced together; and inlaid with words.

Berle went back toward the computers, now staring at them. He went to a cupboard in a bureau with printer and digitizer on top; opened the cupboard and pulled out some booklets, reading. Then he began scanning pages from one booklet, and then another. These pages were already on the kitchen walls, but now he wanted them here, too. He left this and went to the left-hand computer on the coffee table to check on it. He clicked open other folders and some files and entered these in. Now he was crunching the words.

—Yes! said Tu. He's got these histories or whatever and's looking for some sort of pattern. I guess the what-if is dead in the gaitorade for tonight. Man's got too many interests.

—What about us, though? My job, my arm, said Jayrai, momentarily distracted from the question of—

"BABY get born! BABY get born! BABY get...." The chorus was shouting from Bopoiz' kitchen doorway. (The kitchen was dark.)

—Why can't that be one of his interests?

—You and that arm! said HB. Is that the sum total of your existence?

—So what about you? You keep imagining me doing something with my arm at FivePoints THAT I DID NOT DO. I did not crush the Lamplighter's hand, HB. That's only in your imagination! You did *not* get beat up at Paddy's Pool Hall in 1900 CE! Yes, we are trying *even* to get back to 1900 CE if we can't get home, but that stuff there just did not happen. Srsly, girl. DID NOT HAPPEN.

She felt him glaring.

She said, —So okay,— *I* didn't see-feel-hear it. Maybe you did, but I did not.

HB said, —Maybe it was another alternate universe and just sorta slipped me into it and I saw you there? Briefly. I remember calling Big Fellow—the Grandmaster—remember the show-master?—and then it changed back to-to... nothing much going on at Paddy's. Just the usual early 20th-century racism, that's all.

Grandmaster? For some reason this recitation of events shut her up.

"BABY! BABY! BABY!"

The darkened room was rocking, kidz playing off furniture and walls. Like pool balls ricocheting off the rails. Yet there were elliptical and circular movements, circlings back, attractive like binary stars. The city of HiTopOLis glimmered and gleamed into the living room, a massive moving backdrop to this explosive play, this construction of the universe, the cosmos. The BABY!

—I think he's got you, Jay, said Pome. And, HB, you can't blame that on me. You probably got yourself into that universe? Confess? What actually happened?

HB was silent, thinking it through. Riots. They had been having labor riots. At last he said, —So I called'em a pile of fucking racists, and they just piled on me. Yo, they were beating the shit outta me, outta Tu, Fabe, and everybody. I saw Jayrai out the plateglass nearly breaking the lamplighter's arm off. Even the bartender was brawling—which in FivePoints 1900 woulda got him kilt. He be blacker'n me you recall.... I remember starting it that way and then just didn't want it to keep going.

—So what happened? asked Pomala. How did you get back?

—No idea. (Was he shrugging?) Plus, we don't know if it was an alternate—whatever. *This* is an alternate universe. It was me calling the show-master. I remember seeing him, or somebody HUGE going up the street on a HUGE horse. Somehow... somehow I knew that was him.... I'd have to say he brought us—me out of it... somehow.

—Srsly, said Jay. I'd say you were magic, but what does that mean anymore? Tu says we're practically stardust. I'd like to think that. But my—

—We know, we know—your arm.

The WIMPs Give It a Try

Meanwhile, dark hefty luscious shieL keeL, Philipa the trim uniformed cop, and tired old Kelso looked at the loops again in the underground Kress Building security suite. They were looking for possibilities. On the wall was a small shelf of burnished colorful trophies, some from his younger days on the HiTopOLis team, minor leagues, his game being ratball. Otherwise, the walls, tables and desktops were crammed with gadgetry and screens, some of it very old, some of it useless. One of the computers, from the old school, was on the floor at their feet, under a table.

Kelso squatted down, groaning. The groan was nothing compared to what it would be when he got up again. He turned it on, waited for it to boot and listened to them talk above him.

"See, here's what I got from the wastebasket," said shieL, after describing her methods in Claude and Pegmo's rooms. She smoothed out the crumpled scribbles on the desk in front of a monitor.

"You guys are good," said Philipa, meaning the reverberators. "Why didn't I think of that?"

ShieL looked at her innocently from under her brows. "You will."

"Next time," said Philipa, smiling. "In the meantime you wanna use my badge?"

"I heard that," said Kent S. Clarke from her QuipPad.

"Sorry, Chef!" She said, pushing a button. "Hoo! When am I gonna remember to switch this thing?"

"You *could* get into trouble," said shieL.

"Yeah, any number of ways."

"Can I see that?" asked Kelso, reaching up for the wrinkled paper. His hand was lean and knobbed. He did not turn to look up at her. Probably wasn't flexible enough, especially squatting like that. She looked down at his fuzz-trimmed light reflecting pate, and handed him the drawing. She could feel his knees hurting.

112

"I've got a digital if you want to load it," said shieL.

He scanned it with his gaze, said "sure," and Philipa said, "I'll have that evidence," and took it back. Floodescent lights buzzed overhead. "You need better light. That one's going dim. Can't be good for your eyes having it flicker like that."

"You wanna get down here, look at this, or not," he said testily.

One hand on the table, shieL went down on her knees like a small mountain, Philipa nimble beside her, and together they peered at the screen in its ugly big pale plastic box. Neither one remembered that this particular kind of computer had formerly been the slickest thing going, that its looks had once been awesome, had struck its users fatuous, and was actually worshiped in other parts of the world. Kelso had been looking over the rollcalls relevant to the case at hand, names of the children, now grown, in classes at Kress around the time of the then unknown predatory behavior — which had since come to light after the murder of the alleged perp. Plus the Sgt. had since uncovered a murder-suicide possibly connected to the apparently on going and historical sexual abuse.

"I don't think that's legal," said shieL keeL, gazing down the roles.

"What? That paper?" Philipa was reading them, too, but asked without distraction.

"Right. Inadmissible, and all that."

"You do want this badge, don't you? I'm beginning to think I'm unworthy."

"Good thing you shut off that QuipPad."

"She messed that up, too," said Clarke from the deVice.

Kelso, who had yielded up his groan getting to his feet, merely smiled inside. He was too tired to grin.

"We've got the stuff here, chief," said Philipa. "Can you handle a floppy? Kelso says it's all he's got for you to copy."

"We'll send someone over," said Clarke. "He'll get what we need. Freddie the FreakinTech they call him, Kelso. Got it?

"Yeah, I heard."

"He's clear. You might hire him—do some of your stuff. A freelancer."

You guys are really cutting back, aren't you? Kelso thought this but did not say it. Too tired. Humor just wasn't worth breath anymore.

Pomala was trying to get Fabian's attention. —I think the basement security man was praying just now, Fabian. Between groans.

—Fabe's busy getting BABY born, said Jayrai.

—Tu interrupted his observations of Berle in order to correct

113

Fabian. —It's got nothing to do with the subatomic array, Fabian.

Fabian came out of the zone. — Why not?

—You're over-thinking the game.

Fabian appeared to be speechless.

—Yo, the appearance is a figure of speech y'unnerstand, Ms. Story Writer, said HB.

—Please not the alt alt, yo? They are not *real!* Don't start talking to them, said Jayrai. It's complicated enough. And I just—

WE KNOW! said HB. Then, throwing it away, (—your arm.)

—Tu is talking about over-thinking stuff, said Fabian. Tu. Can you believe that? OK Mr. Under-thinker, how's that over-thinking the game? Isn't that what we're made of? Subatomic particles?

—But this part of the game has to do with forces, with heat and intensity, with winging it. Expansion with cooling must first be established in order for the energy to convert itself into particles. Sort of precipitate out.

—But what about gravity? That's part of it. You said not too long ago it was a particle. Couldn't all that fall back into the nothing, the ABYSS, without the what'd-you-call-it—the graviton? If we force these bits just a bit, not too much I understand, we'd be more on the way to BABY.

—Tu hesitated.

—Tu?? (HB, Fabe, Pome, Jay)

—Let me... let me think about that, said Tu. As though recollecting a daydream: *...Gravity is what pulls everything back....*

—Don't go over-thinking it. Pome, security was praying? said Fabian. How could you tell?

—I seem to be turning into a very distinct mind reader. Some of us are. Remember Smudge at the shop window?

—Maybe security's a better target than Eelie? suggested HB. You didn't quite get who Smudge *was* into his dream.

—The problem was looks, she said. Smudge's got no looks. He's just a smudge. The old files, the class rolls don't mean anything to me.

—Rolls? asked HB.

—So look at that! said Jay. *Smudge is in the basement with them!* Pome, see what they're saying, quick. Help security think! Give him a dream!

—But he's not asleep.

—If (HB) we could just get that shelf with those sports trophies to kinda slide onto the floor. What are these sports, btw?— If we could to get that to drop on his haid he'd be out like a light. Then you could, you know....

—Oh please.

114

—If we could do that we could lift smudge's finger to point to himself. (Jay) —Except I wouldn't touch him for all the tea in Osia.

—Yeah. It seems we can be part of the trophies in the shelf but we can't budge'em. What's the point? (HB) That all looked so easy in the beginning.

—It did not. Your memory's full of holes (Jay).

—Holes?

HB was grinning his diabolical grin—if they could see him, not just intuit his presence. The one he used whenever he recollected out loud (not often) that his mother had died.

—Stop, said Tu. At this, he seemed almost a placeholder for Quad who was deep with GURlee and probably wouldn't want to be in the basement with Smudge right now anyway. But Tu continued. —We need a better understanding of the nature of reality.

(Groans.)

—You're sounding like security, said Tu.

Joking? Tu?? (More groans.)

—Come on, you aren't old like security.

—We respect the elders in our culture, said Jayrai, forgetting her familial claim on complete Americalization.

—Mine, too, but some of them just aren't—there yet.

—Tu. said Fabian. The guy was praying and now we are paying attention. How does that fit in with your nature of reality? And if you say, *coincidence*. Well, you're reality isn't so—

—Encompassing is the word I think you want, said HB. You probably can't even stand that particle/wave thing, Tu. I mean which is it? Are we particles or waves?

(Everyone but Quadri and Tu.) —HB! Is a physicist???

—Just what in hell are we? Try to tell me yo' haid is wrapped round this thing and I'll kiss yo' face when you get one again.

"I came down to see how it's going," said Smudge. "Just for a minute. I've got a meal with the mayor in another few." Smudge looked at his watch, unconcerned. He meant, "How's the allegation of child abduction coming? They're not really going to find anything? Just a couple of kidz ignoring bedtime." But he didn't say it.

He glanced at the wrinkled paper from Pegmo's wastebasket spread out here. "What's this?" He said, offhand. "Childish."

"—Scribblings of my granddaughter's. Cute kid. Lives out in Lost Angels." Kelso looked him square in the eyes.

Philipa stopped, realizing how much she'd been about to say. It was the architect and an owner and he *should* know about getting better coverage on these building façades. But Kelso was right, he was a suspect. Everybody was suspect until there was only *the*

115

suspect.

ShieL thought, Maybe Kelso knows something we don't. Maybe he saw something in the rolls, and just hasn't spit it out yet.

"So there's nothing about the wayward kidz yet? We need to get that straightened out." said Smudge.

"Working on it and will let you know if something specific turns up."

"You need more coverage out front," put in Philipa.

"We'll have to see about it." A glance at the watch.

When Smudge was gone and having learned only that Kelso's granddaughter lived 2000 km away, the QuipPad said, "I didn't know you have a granddaughter out there."

"I don't," said security.

"Nice work," said Capt. Clarke.

"You going to share Kelso's files with me when you get them?" asked shieL of Philipa, as they were going out the open steel doorway into the concrete passage toward the elevators.

Philipa said nothing. She looked at the QuipPad. Definitely off. She checked it again. Yep, off.

"I'll let you know."

"Noncommittal, then?" said shieL with her innocent glance.

"Yep." Philipa smiled, and reached out to summon the lift.

Smudge stood under the portico with his deVice, sliding through and auto-setting the options for his apartment utilities, HVAC, window shades, music; then timing an auto-text to his libidinous fare. He was activating his evening for after the meetings. Smudge did not waste time marveling over this gadget that anticipated all his fleshly desire. In fact sometimes it was a nuisance to activate and trim his sails. Let all of life anticipate him. He simply wanted to be the grand master of everything. Not even have to point his finger. With the advances they were making, if he lived long enough, he might see it happen. And there were contingencies for that living-long-enough, too. Litigation for human gene patents on-going right now. Yes, let all of life anticipate him, and he would just *go.*

—*Go?* Wish we could send him back to the ABYSS, 'stead of BABY going back. Send him back to nothing, said HB.

HB had spread his attention just far enough to be in the pixilated deVice, the pixilated corners of the portico under-roof, and the sidewalk carrying its moving pixilated populace—these live souls embodied for a few years in the myriad makings. In the mind of some great seemingly unknowable extra-cosmic artist who sometimes seems fixated on subatomic particles.

116

—But shouldn't we kinda wish that Smudge be fixed instead? asked Pomala.

—*Fixed? Him?* What-you-talkin'? (Fixed?)

—You know, remade?

HB said, —That's what happens when he goes back to the ABYSS. He'll start all over again, maybe be better. Like BABY. BABY II. I mean, really? Particle or wave? Oh don't You roll dem Big Fello eyeballs?? Please, if You are making us, can't You just get us on back there? Please. FivePoints 2017, that's all we ask. The *other* universe. The *other* one.

—Real solid bodies, and good jobs, said Jayrai.

—Without evil perps, said Fabian

—A decent library with fiwi. I'd even take the soup kitchen 'stead of that 1900 pool hall. (HB again).

—Yes, said Pomala. No evil perps. No evil anything.

—No evil! (Quad).

The game, obviously, was over. MACHOs lost. And BABY never made it completely free of the ABYSS.

Stars before bodies, thought Tu. Those are the rules. Those are the parameters—a quantifiable temperature, determining the result of the experiment, which if altered would vary the result.

Father Domino was in the cave, rapidly writing down their prayers. *"Et la fumée de l'encens, qui est venu avec les prières des saints, monta devant Dieu de la main de l'ange."*

"So, Dah. Where... does... the... SinGuLariTEE... come... from?"

Gneis was asking. Sometimes it takes a while.

The two were up late, talking. For some reason Gneis could not sleep tonight. His twin was in bed in the next room. The room4living had virtually become Berle's room. The bedroom off the hall had a bed loaded with books and Berle's clothes...and surfaces covered in dusty chemical and biological equipment—a nuneson burner, microscopes, beakers, conical flasks, mortar and pestle, probes and the like. He had removed the room's computers and put them out here with his own, sometimes scanning through the genonoMetrics and other biological data. He seldom turned the couch into a bed but often shucked his clothes down to his underwear and slept on the cushions with a blanket, no sheets. Or he might fall asleep dressed, just pouring himself onto the couch to doze after deep thinking or surfing the day's findings. Tonight he was fairly awake—enough to spend time with his bed-bound son.

"It's a design spattered against a nonexistent wall, the SinGuLariTEE. Some of us—scientists—can believe in Cogmos from

117

nothing. It's harder that way—belief is. To believe all made by someone would be easier because you've got a design. Is there such a thing as *unintelligent* design? If you've got design you've got encoded intelligence. Splatter paint on a wall and it looks chaotic, it's not. From its raw materials and formulation in the factory, cataloging, shipping, the make of the brush splattering, the trajectory, adhesion, all in accord with laws, designs. According to this, things that go wrong aren't really going 'wrong.' "

He went on. "What if you only had sensors for molecules? You didn't have five senses, but one—the ability to recognize molecules? Take the instance of the A'ndyan paddling his canoe upstream, with the breeze ruffling water currents and the leaves in overhanging branches. Your mother might've been able to take that simple description and give it to us, verbally, in all its many—in its molecular structure and movement, with synapses firing and chemical reactions, etc., and it would be reality, and true. It would also be complicated and take a very long time. And for us not be nearly so pleasant. —So so, maybe it would be for *you*." He smiled.

My mother. Gneis was so glad to see Dah's smile.

"Laws that underlie everything are designs, everything made is underlain by laws of its making, decay, remaking, etc. from its molecules and atoms and—need I go further? It's good you can't see or prove this someone because you'd be forced to worship — where's the humility and that? No joy for that someone. But where does it come from, the SinGuLariTEE? That's a toughie," said Berle. "Maybe It takes it out of Its pocket from time to time to play with it — Mind does."

"Like in Fodder's papers? You... think... there's... his *Ground Crater?*"

"We're talking here together, aren't we? Don't you?"

"Some... times. From... time... to... time." Grimace. That would be with a smile. Berle leaned close to wipe drool pooling on the corner of Gneis's mouth.

"How many space-times can Mind dance on the head of a pin?"

"...You... don't... know?"

"I'm learning as fast as I can."

"... In... case... it runs... out?"

"Time?"

More drool.

"Now... now... now... I'm learning."

Berle waited.

"About... about. The moral... molecule."

"You mean the possibility of?" Berle glanced at the screen tilted toward Gneis in his bed table. There were graphics of

118

molecular chemical interactions, a blue and green backdrop with other colors, red and brown lines—and corresponding sparkly electric signals modulated by chemicals triggering neural-transmission of correlated outputs.

"Why... why don't... you... start... there?

"You mean on the moral question? The moral particle? The what-if? —Let's be frank about that. The *what-if*."

Gneis was exhausted, looking at him. He said nothing.

"Of course it interests you. You are bio-man. You are BABY's man. I'm still hunting through the ABYSS. There's a long way to go to BABY.

"Would... science... really... be able...."

"That's why it's called 'what-if.' But don't get me wrong. A chemical cannot absolve autonomy. Integrity would still be integrity. A choice. Things will be more mysterious as we go along. Not less. The mystery will always deepen. Think about how little we knew eons ago... and yet (of supreme importance) the big mystery then was, 'Why is that piece of meat always faster than me, and how am I going to slow it down so I can get it?' We forget that that's still potentially a BIG question. And it's a tribute to them that they figured it out. Or, much later, 'How did that seed get all those apple orchards inside it?' If I find the moral subatomic particle what will it signify if I still can't love that silly old pretense of a neighbor down the hall? If I've got to pretend kindness or courtesy every time I see him? But never mind. I won't care... as long as I got something interesting to pursue." He grinned, plump red face framed in ginger hair—Dah. "KO, I was kidding—sort of. But you see what I mean. In some degree or other *oixtosin* is not going to take my choice away from me. Just like I'm not gonna let my take on cake make me fat...er.

Gneis (faintly) nodded. "G'nite, Dah."

Berle stood and pushed the table away, but not too far. His father did not lower the screen, but put it to sleep. He brushed Gneis's hair with his hand and kissed his head. Then, gently, he lowered the bed flat, and went to turn out the light. His own screen gleamed from the darkened living room into the tiny hallway. He did not close Gneis's door. It would not be one of those nights where he poured himself onto the couch. There was so much to do. Now he was on Elsewise's trail. The Fodder would have something for him. He just had to look carefully. Something was there. He could feel it.

Feel it? No really? Chemicals? The synapse were firing and chemicals at the bottom of these thoughts?

Naw. I'm convinced. Mind came first. Had to. Not the brain, but the other way round. ...Sometimes I believe it. Sometimes I don't. Like son, like father I guess.

—Aw right! said HB. You gettin' that? He's got the mind all thought out!

—Rub your hands whyn't you? asked Jayrai. Next you'll say yours is the mind's gonna tell him.

—Or Pomala's, maybe (HB's return).

—Who's Elsewise? asked Fabian.

—Tarned if I know. Who's the Fodder?

It was late, very late. They'd all be going off duty. Clarke stared off at the dark leafy treetops of the crematory burial grounds. *They came from down there*, he thought. It was an absent thought. He moved on. Better let shieL have the Kress security info. Something might come of it. The architect of the building was one of the kidz in Kress school from the old days. But there were other such in the new building, too. ShieL would have the worst of it. He might not talk to her again. But they had to try something. His was another of the vehicles on the security loop. And he was stalling on needed security image gathering... according to Kelso. Even though it was the building manager's job, not the architect's, the latter could do something. ShieL would have to let us have her encounter with him.... And, after all, she *was* really good at this sort of thing. Worlds better than Philipa — who had her own strengths, and, who just would not work for this, cop that she is. Visualizing Philipa's strong displays of martial arts, a gleam entered his eyes. He could not picture the hefty shieL doing any of that. His focus shifted and he saw his own reflection. The gleam passed and he turned back to what he'd been considering.

"You can have that talk with shieL before you go off if you want, Phil."

No answer.

"You there?" He looked at the deVice.

Nope. She was off. He sent her a message.

Tomorrow would do. But, yeah. Just on the face of it he was the primary. The best suspect they had solely on the fundamentals —evidence. No one else came close...yet.

He tapped in some notes for Kirby, who was on next. Some very careful notes, drawing no conclusions whatever. Just bare facts. And nothing about Phil or shieL getting together. Kirby was an unknown. Just why that should be in this work was a sorry business. But there it was. Some people had deep pockets... full of other people. And *sometimes* — no matter how good you were — you couldn't say who they were. You could only have your doubts. Kirby was one of them. A very big doubt.

Berle was reading a translation of a translation. He thought

possibly he had everything extant. Fragments of the original were in
the HiTopOLis HistoricaLSociety. The whole, though, had been in
Latinum and then Franké, once upon a time, but there'd been a
Franké donation of the least important fragments, in honor of some
monument, anniversary, something. Oh yes. It was during the time
of a dedication of the statue—the Lost Nation Brave in bronze,
standing straight, poised with his canoe and cape fringed with cat
paws. Tails? The Franké loved the Lost Nation. It now stood in the
park of the crematorium grounds, moved from where it stood watch
on the famous Paths Portage. The statue's original foundation had
to yield when the place was obliterated for the intersection, the
underground or something.

All these documents had been digitized—like the whole
world—and now he could rifle them looking for clues to local history,
to the universe, and life. But the original language, he knew, was
not today's or his own. The Fodder had written the living pictures
and happenings out in words, words commiserate with the He-suit's
own time, language and understanding. The illuminations were
lovely but not very instructive. *You have to exercise your
imagination.* Elsewise and the Fodder, and all the natives must have
had other names as well. Sleeping Fawn was obviously Elsewise.
But things the He-suit had experienced needed sorting: some were
historic, and some visionary. And even with these definitions
knowledge could never be precise.

Take the heavenly warriors. That was visionary, mythic.

(Fabian was wondering.) —What warriors? The A'ndians in
the sky surrounding smudge and his victims?

Berle sat and pondered if the visionary warriors were
supposed to be the same warriors killed in the last battle with the
Birdfeather People. Seemed so. The Birdfeather People destroyed
the Catclaw People, of course, but did they then become a sort of
universal or cosmic force?... Is this what Fodder the He-suit means?
And what are they doing in the sky overwatching what I can only
think of as HiTopOLis. Surely, from his description of the shining
stone city we are now looking at *us* — because he had localized
visions—*as I interpret it. That could be wrong, but I don't think so.*

*... However, the most interesting thing — those crystalline
giant kids. That's a puzzle.*

— Giant crystalline kids? That's a new one! (HB)

The WIMPs were convened.

—What is Hesuit?

—Who is Elsewise?

— This is too much for us. We're never gonna get through.
They might as well start up the game again.

—Just let 'em all sleep. Don't be trying to put any dreams in

their heads. We got to get him concentrating on the particles again.
The WIMPs. The dark matter, the next-door universe.

—If only there was a nice garden path and some hands to
hold. Look his hand is so full of holes— I can't lift it no matter how
hard I try! Looks like it slops around a little but otherwise does not
move.

—That's what the holes are for: So we can't lift it. And don't
say we should be his milk and spoil it. It won't spoil. We got no
agency. We're WIMPs.

Berle continued reading, but now on his flexible scroll. He
was spread out on the couch, pixilated, full of holes, turning
occasionally, completely engrossed in the visions. He could see it all
in his mind, just as words of translations from the Fodder described
it for him. The words: War in pale atmosphere above the mazes of
the world. A world dense with corridors, rooms, and halls, stadiums
and auditoriums, and vast networks of arteries. The words describe
things sometimes alien to the Fodder's imagination. But Fodder
would have recognized correspondences, and read of ancient
cultures and far-flung isolated cities. But the world Fodder is
describing is far more compact and dense than what Fodder could
have known or read of. Something this He-suit would never have
seen in his time and place. Fodder may not have imagined it
without help, without that muse he called Fawn and Elsewise. He
scarcely had words for it ...but probably used words from older
stories....They were as ancient myths, describing in extrapolation of
their day. But more and more, each time Berle read, reread, these
manuscripts and books... it had become more clear to him what the
He-suit was giving to the world.

The Fodder's antiquated words showed people made out of
dust, dust from the stars exploding. This is what the He-suit meant
when he wrote about humans coming from dust and heaven. But
first he showed the big event, when all was, immediately after,
compressed —plasma of 10,000,000,000°K where unclear reactions
between neutrons and protons bound and broke apart in collision
after collision, and thus the light elements *were*. Photons are
elements, particles, pieces of light with radiating force, the duality
particle/wave.

How could the He-suit have known of this? Of course it was
brilliantly visionary and there were no right words for it. And it took
us—how could we not have guessed (until so many hundreds of
years later) that this was what he, in his meager hut, had been
describing? —But of course people—in general—still don't get it.
They are too busy living, playing games, tormenting one another,
being slaves to their greed, libidos (here he wondered what had
happened to GURlee, to Claude, that they were so silent). And then

he wondered why he should see their silence and perturbation in connection with it. But— yes—it had to be something of the sort. Either that or some other sort of violence, violation. For the libido was governable. Happily so... though others... he stopped a moment. Others might think this an unhappy truth. Or maybe—by now, for many, control *was* no longer true.

In Berle's mind rose an image of a great dark smudgy, oily, greasy, filthy cloud pouring furiously from a crack in the earth — in the midst of vast labyrinthine cityscapes. He looked back at the words on the flex scroll. Yes. In *the vision*. Berle looked at it. ...And those insect flying things with lights in their tails—uplifting flying craft fueled by energy found in the earth....

—Over here! The po-lice. Get wit my program.

—But Berle's getting warm, HB. We got to stick with him.

—OK, yeah Fabe, but at least give me Jayrai. Okay with you, Jay?

—Sure. I mean Pome's doing good without me —*of course.* What's up with the police station, HB?

Tu was thinking, The man's doing his career no good with this. A physicist can't be interested in visions and myths if he wants funding and respect. Plus, it's only his imagination. He should leave it to historians and literary scholars.

—Stick here, Quadri, said Pomala. Stay away from the police station, okay? But, Tu, don't you think he's getting closer to us with this?

—No.

—But Tu, what are you doing about it? (Fabe.) You know more than anyone but don't seem half as good as Pome at moving him along, or even HB. If you can't put some 21st-century alt univ equations in his way, get him thinking of what it might take to draw dark matter back through, through, well, that steel tube of his—

—Kinda like an umbilical cord—only metal, suggested Pome. Maybe suck us down and around and through—and there we are put back together at FivePoints.

(If he had a head Tu would be shaking it.)

Fabe: I'm checking on HB and now Jay, but I think Pome's right, Quad. Better stay here with her.

—S'up guys? he said to them. It's the other chief's shift, right? The questionable one? What's HB so intent on here?

Every screen in the chief's office was lit, and the ambient glow in the dimness suffused them.

—Tarned f i know, said Jayrai. Can't read these people worth beans. Coffee beans. Which I notice they go through a lot in this office. Look at the brew-cylinders and cups. I think I'm turning into coffee here, wafting around the cubicles and sucked up these nostrils.

(HB) —This chief is scanning the stuff from Kress security. He's been on the phone to somebody —unauthorized, I think. Look —yeah —here's Smudge interrupting his scheduled icky seduction on the 17th floor of the HiToP labyrinth. He's got himself in an uproar. *Smudge is boiling over.* Look! Don't get too close. His whole apartment is going nuclear, his head is a mushroom cloud. We better stay here. This chief is grinning and probably thinking about his wallet.

Kirby downed his coffee, smoothed back his longish dark hair, and was reaching again for the carafe. He set the phone screen down on the desk and let Smudge rant. Then he picked up the phone, said "yeah," and put it down again. This happened several times. He was as cool as if the AC was cranking, his hairy forearms relaxed on the desk, hairy knuckles at ease, cup steaming in his hand.

Finally he picked it up and said, "Won't do any good. You'll have to deal with the original. I might wipe this, but it'll still be in the other deVices and Clarke's head. Too many people have seen it. The best you can do is look out for the reverb. She's a friend of second watch. Don't let her baffelow you, get you digitized saying something. Why do you care if they know you were in school with the murdered perp? He's dead and so are a lot of other people. Just go back to your fun and we'll keep it low-key on this end. Wanted to let you know, that's all."

Kirby's grin was so big his black mustache stretched to the max. Its follicles looked—to the WIMPs—like potholes on the side streets of Akropolis.

—Back to the bottom, square one, the abyss, said HB.

—NewsLady don't stand a chance (Jay).

—I'm not so sure (Fabe). We aren't done praying by a longshot. The good guys are going to win.

—Get out the worry beads and prayer shawls! (Jay) Where's my buddhe when I need 'em?

—Buddhe? Thought you were—what's your religion again?

—Its freedom! Freedom from religion. We meet once a week in somebody's basement on a rotating basis, and whisper a lot.

Meanwhile, back at the apartment, Berle has dozed off. Gneis is fitfully sleeping in the next room, off the cubic hallway, Sheesh's door ajar opposite; the bathroom door open between, its nightlight gleaming into the hall. Pome, Tu, and Quad are part of it all, and of these bodies with respiratory gently flowing in and out.

—How did we get here? asks Quadri. He is apprehensive.

Somehow they know Fabian is focused here with them again. The breath is going in and out, the rooms full of oxygen and carbon dioxide (as they *suppose*, the next door universe being a bit iffy — did people dwell in these gases?) In and out. Room full of gas. The WIMPs part of it all.

—God created us in the Garden of Eden, Quadri (said Fabian). I'm pretty sure your ancestors believed this, and I don't see a need to get rid of it now. We were just some dust lying around— Suddenly HB was there breaking in. —Big Fello created the dust first and then he, he what they called half-baked it with a lot of finessing and fussing and forming—

—And he breathed into us and we became living souls—only there was just the one of us at first. (Fabian again.)

—Quad, please don't listen to that. (Tu) It's the Western/Middle-East storybook version, and we've gone past that. *OK?* (He is definitely directing this more to Fabian and HB, before continuing.) —In simplest terms, think of it like in the game. First came light elements from the BANG and then the stars and galaxies with the force of gravity. And then the stars themselves forming and unleashing heavy elements and these coalescing in earth and dust. And then condensation, then lightning electrified cells. And biology started extrapolating life and after trillions of so-called years we grew up into us. Then Steinein came along and began making sense, and Darnwin. And until that we were pretty much storybooks all the way down. Storybooks deep into history. Tu finishes, wondering if he has simplified enough for Quad. He thought, I'm never going to be a teacher. I've got to concentrate on research if we ever get—

There was silence, except for the breathing in and out, and— in Berle's case—the snoring.

— But how did we get here? asked Quadri.

(Jayrai in bland satire) — Is this what you call a loop? She was over the spectacle of Kirby and Smudge-face, having gathered that Kirby was playing both ends and Smudge was going to have to shell out a whole lot of money. She said nothing about this but it was in the air all the same.

She continued. —It was that underground lab, Quad. Remember? That cold place, that tunnel. Those burnished hockey pucks. We came on them. We're trying to get this snoring pixilated whale to recognize we're here so he can do something to get us back to our own universe! In case you haven't noticed, we ain't got bod. No bodies. They're inside the graveyard or in the crypt we ran into after Pome grabbed the little girl's hand. Or someplace. The UV next door.

Pome said, Do you remember that Quad? We hid from the grave-digger in the crypt? We fell out and the A'ndians were there?

125

—I thought we were outside the Library. At the cemetary. (Quad)

—It's complicated. (Pome) That was in 2017. Yes, we were outside the Library™ playing the Hadesthon, but somehow suddenly we were in 1900 CE. Or A.D., they called it.

—But where is FivePoints? Our neighborhood.

—In the next universe. See, we are particles now. Dark matter. WIMPs, I think it is. And we're trying — Yes! We're trying (he'll get this, guys!!) We're trying to get born again like BABY.

—But who is BABY?

—The Cosmos, with Humanity. (Tu)

—Us. But we aren't quite human even when we have bodies, said Fabian. And, if Pomala hadn't grabbed the little girl's hand we wouldn't be in this fix.

—It was the game, I think, said Tu. The Hadesthon, not the girl. I had the calculations all worked out according to the UTC. We may have been about to be transported back to 2017 but....

—L'il ole white thang ran off with the little girl so we lost our place on the transport and ended up dust in the next universe. Unnerstan? (HB)

—Do you think they'll start the game again soon? asked Quad.

—Your attention span leaves a lot to be desired, said Jayrai.
—Do you mean BABY's or The Hadesthon?

—Either one? (Quad)

"I had the strangest dream last night," said Berle. Night had faded but morning was not brightly shining off the many windows outside the Kress Building. The atmosphere was lurid and murky.

"I had... one...."

Sheesh said, "Remember? We told you he had one the other night about a smudge in the galaxy, an asterism? A nebula?"

"Let... Dah..."

"Go on, Dah," said Sheesh.

"I dreamed the walls could talk. That is, I dreamed I could understand walls."

"You mean understand how they came into being? asked Sheesh.

"No. I knew that before." Berle rarely smiled when he said such things. "Something thought up particles and set them loose. It must have been excruciatingly hard just getting to aTomic superstructure, and then there was molecules, cells, and differentiation etc.. Seeds, trees, or was that trees, seeds? How about concrete? Makes more sense to work on that first, coming from rocks. Yes. Start with the magma."

"We've been over this. The dream? It'll take you a half-hour to work your way through evolution, the Stone Age, cultural history and workmen getting up in the morning to make sure everything gets built and keeps working," said Sheesh.

Gneis watched them, gleam in his eyes, drooling.

"The dream, yes. It's got something to do with the dark matter experiments. But you know how dreams are. It was somewhat chaotic. Mystifying.

"So... so... was mine."

"Dreams can be important though," said Dah. He was thinking of the Fodder's papers, musing.

Sheesh asked, "What was it about the dark matter experiments?

"On background?"

"Better let me finish making breakfast first."

Sheesh came back with a power drink for brah, some scrambled eggs, juice and coffee for dah. Berle said, "Theorizing wasn't enough. We needed experiments to expose dark matter. We don't look far off to find these particles because they are right here with us, awaiting detection. And, if we get it right—discover its nature—we can do the calculations to figure out how the universe comes to an end. More to it than that, of course."

Long inured to the conceit of why anyone would want to know about an end-time event, Sheesh said," And if we are a curved universe, a sphere?"

"In that case all the matter, including dark, would collapse back on itself, reversing the BANG. A loose analogy—on a smaller scale—you see it with compact or degenerate stars. But the density of galactic clusters is actually much more dark matter then light."

Gneis watched this back-and-forth, willing his questions through Sheesh.

"And the end if we are a flat universe?"

"Seems to allow for other alien particles not found in the universe curving back on itself. Dark matter isn't electromagnetic in action, like cosmic or light rays. Being weak, we look for them underground where interference from the stronger brighter particles is lessened. By recreating the beginning conditions, we try to discover its amount—how much—if not what it is. (It's not enough to just say it's "matter.") Even so, by our experiments, we find there's much more than can be accounted for otherwise."

"So what was it about dark matter experiments in the dream?"

"Long story short, we may have some dark matter from another universe here. We may have *drawn* dark matter here."

"You... you told... told...."

"You told us that theory before now but don't you think that's why it turned up now? Just because there's some theory? I mean how could you possibly know? ...It's not in Fodder's parchments, is it?"

"I don't know if it is or not. I'm not through analyzing them yet. It's a hard go. They're all translated in our tongue—as he would say—but still needs thoughtful interpretation to understand."

"But you've been looking at those things for ages. Ever since we can remember." He did not mention mam, but glanced bright-eyed at Gneis, and slowly wiped some egg from his mouth. (He had been spooning some down as they talked.) "I mean, the walls are papered in those pages and even the floor is tiled with their words. How much longer do you need?"

"No, I haven't been at it, Sheesh."

"Maybe... maybe...."

"Maybe that's why you dreamed this?" Sheesh said it rapidly. Maybe why Pomala was seen by Gneis?

He looked seriously at his son. "Back to that, yes," said Berle.

Elioshine was absent, no shimmer on windows and frames of solar arrays at various heights across the buildings of SiXPointz. Specks of small flying vehicles, like bugs glimmering with lights of their own, were floating, diving and lifting.

"You want to know how my dream relates to the alternate universe as a possible source for *weakly interacting massive particles*, and—." He stops, quiet a moment, looking at them.

Gneis looks more like a skeletal little boy with a messy mouth, the cereal bowl haircut. His brother is tall and strong, slim and lithe, hair straight and longish. The teenagers nod encouragement.

—This is it! (Half the WIMPs, minus Quadri.)

—Shh! (The other half, minus Quadri.)

"... Wish I could say...."

—Shit!

—Shh!

"It's more of a feeling, more a sense than a concrete understanding. It's like the walls and furnishings and even our breathing, the life of HiTopOLis, the stars and galaxies are telling me in this dream. The dream is not mathematical like the analyses we are doing in the lab and on the screens." He gestured toward Gneis's bed-table display.

"And, like dreams, it's kind of... I said it was messy, mystifying, but there's a quality about it that isn't. This quality is hard for me to define. Like qualities themselves. There was something crisp or clear or pure about it. Like these things were, in

128

the dream, more real than we usually take anything as real. Furniture and walls talking, that is. I don't know. ...Anyway. There were no words I recall in the dream—except—for one phrase. Something to do with money. Instead—the everything—was having a conversation with itself, and could understand what it meant. No words, but what words *meant*. Or a better explanation for it: meaning shorn of words."

"In other words?"

Berle smiled. "In other words, I knew they were here and that we'd brought them. And that they wanted—I'm pretty sure about this part—they wanted to go back.

"You mean to its own universe? Like as if these were *people*? On a trip to Laska or Merbuda, and want to come back to HiTopOLis?"

Berle had to smile. He had to. "I feel silly to say it. But, yeah. Like people who want badly to go home."

"But... but... that means...."

"Doesn't that mean the furniture wants to go home, the walls? The stove, fridge, the planets and stars? Gneis's PJs?" He wiped some yellow drool from the pajama collar.

"Not exactly. Maybe. But if this is true (and I think it is), there's dark matter out of place—so to speak. And I don't know what if anything to do about it. The odd thing is.... I care. It's one of those unintended sequences of experimentation and application. I care not only as a scientist but as a human being. The latter condition came first, after all. I'd better not let that get away.

—*He knows!!*

—But looks like we got to get used to being scrambled eggs. (Jay getting and not quite getting it.)

"I don't know, Dah. You've talked to us before about rational and irrational. And you know what this sounds like."

"You mean, am I talking real people instead of mindless particles?"

Sheesh shrugged. "Yes. Gneis had a talking nebula or something but we don't think she's...."

"But remember it's a dream. Dreams are symbolical, full of images. It doesn't mean they aren't true. This is not science but a rational perspective on dreams. And you know my thoughts on mind."

"Mind... mind...."

"Mind came first. Brains afterward."

"Right," said Berle, "brain is something science can study."

Berle had gone off to work in the underground lab below SiXPointz.

Sheesh had got Gneis dressed for the day and seated in the eelie with its electronics hardware and screen before him, his head supported on either side by a brace. Modification, donated by MediCorpo, had proved Claude wrong about the glance-activated eelie. A completely new chair had not been needed to supply Gneis's hope for continuing to get around. Now his twin came back into Gneis's room, pulling a longsleeved T-shirt with logo over his head. He smoothed it into place over his torso, asking, "Did he say anything about a smudge in his dream?"

Gneis merely looked his negative at him. Then he looked pointedly at his screen. Sheesh came around to look for himself.

There was a message on the screen from Dah, saying, "First, I've got to learn if this really is WIMPs from 'elsewhere.' Second, is it important to gather (somehow) and send it back. Third, how?"

"Donno," said Sheesh, standing back. "Looks to me like he's already gone to number three in his head.

Gneis was tired already. He merely looked agreement at his twin. Then, pointedly, he wrinkled his nose.

"Have you been smelling something funny, too?"

Again, the glance of agreement.

"Wonder what? —No, actually I'm afraid to ask. Can that be—sewage? Smells like a sewer?"

—Don't look at us, said HB. We is getting the hang of the virtual DigiOuija but, still, that ain't us spoiling any power shake.

—Well, said Pome. We're part of smells, gas, stuff, aren't we?

—If it's in the air, agreed Fabian.

—Bad enough being it! Good thing *we can't smell*, said Jayrai. I mean smell without nostrils, not our butts!

—Good? Not to have noses or butts, girl? What be de matter wit you? You Jayrai, you somebody else?

Sheesh stood back, letting Gneis angle the chair out the door with a glance at its virtual controls. It would have been easier for Sheesh to do, guiding from behind, but he knew better than to let the other lose an ounce of agency over his deteriorating form.

Exiting together, standing in the hall, he said, glancing at his phone, "Looks like I got one now. "Guess Dah forgot he said before he was going to think about your dream." Sheesh read the message aloud: 'Did Gneis say there was smudges in his dream?' "

—Oh will you look at it?!

—We are 2 for 2!!

—We are definitely going home—

—And the cops are going to get Smudge-head!

Tu spoke up finally. —You may be getting somewhere with that. But the first, I think, is very iffy, if not an impossibility. There is a lot to consider here. When you think about it, the search for matter needs geometrics for gravitational dynamics of galaxies and clusters. But it's debatable whether this is possible. It would actually be better to measure the universe instead. (He sensed a certain derisiveness but of course went on.) If they can measure microwave background radiation, or residual shine of the Big Bang, they can look backward in time and practically see what was there before even the atoms were built. Or let's say that stuff was very very hot—something like 3000°K—so our atoms at that point were shredded. Radiation was the thing breaking it all apart. So the BANG can't even be seen, really, though it would be cool if we could have seen the singularity itself backward in time. There's just too much of a barrier at that point for us to penetrate to the singularity, or anywhere near it, even though at that point you're closer to it in light-years than you are to us, um, to earth. At that point matter was neutral, and it means radiation comes from everywhere because of the shape of space-time. Everything has expanded tremendously since then, about 1000 times, actually. But back then it was only 300,000 years old.

—Tu, what's that got to do with us getting out of here? (HB)

—Admittedly very little at the moment.

—The *moment*!? Has it got *anything* to do with it?

—Well, we're talking about everything here —

—*You* are!

—So of course it's got something to do with it. Something like us has *got* to fit into it because it *is* everything. But I may be getting to that *us* at some point.

A virtual derisive snort passed itself around.

Tu continued. —Steinein said the speed of light is the fastest speed information can travel.

—I wish someone could even send us to that inch-away called FivePoints in a snail right about now, you gettin' dis info?

—No bit nor byte could travel along that afterglow faster then 300,000 light-years. So you see that any smaller than that and the whole thing would collapse under its own weight, the gravitation of its mass. Unless of course it was bigger than that in which case it couldn't figure out what to do with itself.

—But that's next-door!! (Fabian)

—Honestly, Tu, said Jay. This almost sounds like you were getting ready to play BABY instead of figuring out how to get us home!

—Well, I have thought about it.

—What!!

—Will you lookitit! Tu's getting ready to play BABY against RAMBOs with the MACHOs!

All this had taken almost no time, as they went with the two boys toward the elevator, Fabian pointing out the logo on Sheesh's shirt. It was a black longsleeved T with golden words in glitter, sparkling: "Lost Nation." (Interpreted)

HB made like he was a gullet for their use as the doors closed, and the twins sank past the mezzanine toward the lobby of Kress Building. The two HiTop boys agreed that the sewer smell was on the increase as they went down.

As Sheesh left the sheltering portico for the already puddling sidewalk, Gneis watched from his eelie through plate-polymer, ignoring school studies on the screen before him. The downpour had begun. Rain poured down like bullets across the view where these great windows rose to peripheries of the surrounding mezzanine above him. He thought, *If I'd been here I would have seen what became of Claude and GURlee.* There must have been other witnesses... but it was dark out... with ambient light shining from here and above... enough to see with — if you were paying attention. Unwittingly someone may have taken a picture of them, at least enough to show that single moment in time when they "disappeared."

It smells better here than it did in the elevator. He wondered what was going wrong and if they were fixing it. But here it smelled like all the nuanced pleasant artificial almost blossomy stuff coming out of the Lovely Shop, and other stores like The Gag, Pot'sBarn, and the Christmas Pup Tent. Food smells at this time were small — coffee, and, he thought, cheese pockets, croissants.

But the street and sheeting rain held his gaze. Pouring rain in unrelenting waves. It wasn't raining that night. He tried to visualize them. Sheesh says they must have got in some vehicle or other, probably a flyer.

He backed away a bit. His gaze went to the revolving doors where the reverberator was stepping out, plump, dark, and well-dressed, tie and patent leather shoes. He'd seen her plenty of times on the screen. She must be the one, he thought. Claude had ventured to brag about a reverberator stopping by his basement apartment. But that was all Claude said about it. Apparently he wasn't going to be taped, appear on the news, or anything. There just wasn't enough to the story yet, thought Gneis. Now she was shaking out her brumella and turning to wait for a businessman coming through the doors. Wasn't that the owner? The man responsible for this whole bang-shee? These shops, this building?

Gneis's gaze went round the place and he recalled how the old school building was here long ago — so, so maybe it *wasn't* long ago, depending on your age. The reverberator was talking to the architect, actually holding a deVice out to catch his words and images. He seemed glad to talk to her. Animated. Gneis wished he could be animated like that.

For some reason the owner had all his attention. Just for a moment. He really was interesting to watch. Now why was that? Usually he was very boring, hard to notice; just some well-groomed man in immaculate business attire, powering through his many commitments and dealings with city high-ups, and other well-groomed men and women of business. Showed up on the visionary screen all the time. Usually Gneis paid him almost no mind. *Probably because he pays me no mind.* Gneis was in a charitable mood today.

Gneis liked people. He liked to watch them going about their business. Sometimes it was fascinating — there were so many of them. So many kinds. Yet, he thought he could detect types and patterns in both people and movements. Oh those precious movements. Some days he would be here from morning till late afternoon when Dah or Sheesh came, whichever came first. Usually Sheesh. The people streaming about, going in and out, carrying stuff, talking in twos and threes, laughing — he hardly ever saw anyone crying, maybe a little kid throwing a tantrum, howling, whining. Not the same as crying. Gneis sometimes wished he could howl and whine just for the opportunity of *keeping himself* from doing it. Yes! All this movement. It's weaving the living pattern. Loving it. Loving us. Making a massive moving something-or-other. Gneis sometimes caught a wave of something while watching all this activity: A wave of something he had never heard anyone else mention. He wondered now, for the first time (remembering it) if others had this experience and just didn't say anything. Or if he was sort of alone in it, like being alone in most other—more physical—ways.

Look at that rain pouring down. It was amazing. Sheets and waves, yet he could almost see individual drops but they weren't like drops... they were like... like... like a blizzard of stars? Some wet hard stars falling in plenty to earth. Only doing no harm. Like an envelopment made of, of everything. Everything. In bits and soakiness and caring and love, showering and bucketing down!

And, and, he knew that the wave had gone past again just now! leaving everyone as is. Revelatory, but gone. Again. Ah. Yes. Mind. That's what it was. Some of that Mind Dah talks of sometimes (not very often, but enough). Funny, I never thought of it when he said it: *Mind* is capitalized. Mind is love.

And the rain was still bucketing down on the city. The traffic stopped or slowed through it, and no one was taking off swift into the shattering air today.

The Lovely Shop lady was there giving him something,

putting it under his nose. He sniffed. A thinned-down power drink through an extra-long bent straw. He gleamed and drooled up at her as she set it on his tray-table, telltale sparkle in his eye. And when she walked away he glanced back at the reverberator and owner.

Fabian and Pomala were paying a lot of attention to Gneis, but Tu was still dumping about the universe.

—There's too much matter unaccounted for when looking at everything detectable—stars, galaxies, signals, structures, everything. The visible—*all* the other electromagnetic stuff too—is not nearly the whole story and other faculties and tech don't touch it, so—

—But that's— (Jay)

—Yeah? (HB, continuing her thought) So? We live in a different universe, Tu! How does that work? We are here and don't really know *what* kind of place this is. Except for everything being made out of pixie dust, it *seems* like ours. We had a joy ride to their outer-space and even so that's still a mystery! How does it all work? Our universe got so full we slopped over into this one? There wasn't enough dark matter here so this one just grabbed some out of ours— grabbed us out of the burial park? Are our bodies still there—just dead bodies? Or are they alive—in some kind of coma in the burial park?

—I understand your consternation, HB, but this really is beyond any science I know of. Theories there are—

—*Grumble grumble grumble* 'consternation.'

Meanwhile, Gneis was watching the businessman and reverberator converse. The back-and-forth. Gneis was a bit shy, reticent, but decided to ignore that and approach, see if he could overhear them. (He liked conversational snatches, but felt better about it if others just happened to be around him.) They seem to be talking about the need for more security tech.

She was telling him how some kidz had gone off somewhere. He said he knew about that, didn't she remember him being with her and the detective officer on the lower level in security recently to check how the investigation was going? So, so, did he know about the series of child sexual abuses, historically, in relation to this site? No, he hadn't heard about that. Maybe there *was* a need for more auditory and visual technology here—*If*, as she was suggesting, it was current as well.

He glanced at Gneis and frowned. ShieL also looked over at the boy in the eelie.

"Oh hi!" She gave him a big smile. "Berle's boy?"

Gneis nodded slightly. He looked back at the Kress Building owner. Then Gneis closed his eyes. He opened them again. The man looked—. Almost like his head had disappeared. He closed his eyes again. *There's something wrong with my vision!* A couple tears welled under his lids. *Another thing.* Another thing was going wrong with him. It was like demoneos. One fell, knocking over the next, and then the one next to that, and another and another and another, until the whole string of them was down. He blinked and shieL knelt beside him.

"Will you be KO?" She asked kindly.

Her face was in front of him. Except for the blurring of his tears, her kind smile and dark eyes, full lips and hawk nose, were normal. Maybe it was going to be all right....

He smiled back. The drool fell with the tears.

She stood, still smiling down on him.

The owner said from behind her bulk, "Are we through?"

"Just one thing more, since you are so patient."

The voice had not seemed quite patient to Gneis. ShieL turned, stepped back to him, and Gneis saw that his head was no more. Just a small dark-blue cloud in the air, like something out of a factory on the visionary. He tried to look round at the people moving in and out. No one else looked like that. How can it be?

The two had moved off a bit, the reverberator seeming to prefer it and so did the man. They were standing out of the busy concourse, over by the plate-polymer running with silvery rain.

Gneis was no longer worried that his eyes were collapsing along with the rest of him.... But maybe—he now feared—his mind was? —Or would that be his brain?

Apparently it was going to be a long day.

Gneis was still there, and it was still raining, when Dah came through the moving doors. It was that time of day when masses of people hurried in and out. There'd been no rain when he started: Dah had left his brumella upstairs and now he was wet through. Gneis drooled when he saw the plastered hair, clinging clothes, and the way Dah hunched forward, trying to protect the Tech in his pocket.

"Your face is wet," said Dah, deadpan, though he did not eye the drool.

"You, you... you're... a p-p-puppy, D-d-d...."

They started toward the elevators, Berle's shoes squeaking over the polished marble floors, people grinning at them as they passed. On reaching the elevators, the two were given a pass by others to ascend alone.

"So," said Berle as they climbed. "Sheesh says there was some kind of smudgy thing going on in your dream? I'd forgotten about that."

"Sm-smudge-face."

"Was it anything about the police or someone having to pay money?"

"No... no... it... it."

The elevator doors opened.

"Listen, it's been a long day. Kinda wet." Berle grinned. Water was still dripping along his neck from strings of rust-colored hair, as they advanced down the hall. "Tell you what. Try to work out a report with Sheesh sometime? We'll get back together on it."

He pressed the combo and the apartment door opened.

Sheesh came squishing down the hall behind them. He too was wet but less so.

"Hey," said Dah. "How'd you escape the deluge?"

"The underground isn't flooded—yet" said Sheesh, smiling. "But it smelled pretty bad. He made of face and held his nose— awkwardly—trying to hang onto his d-reader and books.

"Yeah?" said Berle. "What is that? We had it in the lab—very remotely."

"So so, it's the sewer, isn't it?"

"But why? That's what I want to know."

Sheesh dropped his things on the coffee table and went into the kitchen, aware that Berle wanted him to think about it.

—Bet we could find out about that smell, said Pomala.

—No! No! No! said Fabian.

—A sewer is a sewer, said HB.

—Now doesn't this prove something? asked Jayrai, suspiciously.

—About the alternate universe you mean? saidTu.

—Exactly, said Jay. We've got sewer problems in Akropolis. They even had 'em in 1900. Remember?

—Here's a thought, said HB. Maybe the multiverse is Big Fello writing his own fanfiction. He liked the first one so much he went outa control.

Fabian said, —And we couldn't do anything about those sewer problems either, Pome, so what's the point? There are people whose job it is to see to that stuff. And it's their responsibility and we've got too much on our plate already! If you want to fix sewers wait till we get back and then run for mayor or something—OK?

Berle had moved Sheesh's things and opened all the display screens for the evening. He was on the couch with everything spread out around him, and an empty plate and glass at his knee. The two boys were in Gneis's room, working on the dream report. The shade was up. Outside rain poured down on the city, showing lambent and diffuse buildings, windows, roof arrays in glistening mistiness; shadowless.

They worked a long time. They were getting virtually no homework done, but reportage with speculation had high entertainment value tonight.

"KO, said Sheesh after a bit. "Let me read it back to you: 'Pomala is not the smudge. She is the blue-and-white nebula pointing out the smudge. Or smudge face (we don't know what that means yet). We thought maybe it was an alternate universe because we didn't recognize the nebula or whatever. No other proof, though. No furniture talking, but like with Pomala in your dream—the WIMPs, that is—this provides some sort of evidence for it, we think. If the two dreams can be taken together.'

"That good, brah?"

Gneis said, "So so so far."

Sheesh continued reading: " 'Pomala is in your dream as dark matter, if we remember right. So she must be the WIMPs. This is speculating. What is not speculation: Pomala says smudge-face did something to GURlee and Claude. Also, he lives somewhere. We think it's a him. We aren't sure where, though.' That it, brah?"

Gneis nodded slightly but gazed off a bit. He thought of his hallucination in the lobby this morning but said nothing. He had nothing to say yet on account of his fear.

Rain

Time passed. It kept raining. Days passed, raining.
Meanwhile, several floors up from the physicist's apartment, the
Bopoiz had the gang in to play. Ostensibly it was to be XploHding
Whorllds (otherwise known as BABY); and now Tu was all set to play
this time round, surprising them. He was planning to match wits
with FivePoints, playing with RAMBOs against the SiXPointz
MACHOs.

It was a spacious elegant apartment, often lit by the
neighborhood of SiXPointz and the city of HiTopOLis itself —
especially when the game was on and interior lights turned down.
Mz. Bopoi never seems concerned about the glass and gilt furniture,
or what the MACHOs might do to it. Berle once opined that it could
do more harm to the kidz than they could do to it. However, she
said it was so rugged ("not in the least cheaply made like most stuff
around this town") that they'd have to break the plate-polymer
behind it (also rugged) with an I-beam, and shove the furniture out
onto the sidewalk far below, to do it damage.

GURlee was already here, sitting in passive observance of the
high spirits of everyone save Gneis. She could not tell yet what
shape his mood was in, his head slouched against its brace. Once it
had been easy, but not lately. Not that GURlee was deliberately
thinking of it. GURlee did not seem to think. She absorbed without
much thinking. She was a walking zone-out. Claude was not here.
There was no attracting her attention with Claude. GURlee zoned on
the roughhouse play of MACHOs as they shot lip and tumbled over
the furniture. BABY was on hold till Claude arrived, and Kake had
been spilled twice. Once hipPo had to clean it up, and once biMbo.
Their own Kake had not been spilled but each had been the party
knocking it over. Sheesh was cross-legged on the floor, sometimes
beside GURlee, sometimes shooting an arm out to capture the lit
bubberBall they tossed around and batted off the plate-polymer and
walls. Once, making a grab for the glowing ball, he shot over the

138

leather couch, teetering on its back.

Suddenly biMbo was shouting: "Quiet! Quiet! They're talking about it!! The Visionary is talking about it!" They all turned to stare at The Visionary.

From where she'd been talking in the kitchen doorway with GURlee's sister (the casually clad Gorgeeous), Mz. Bopoi (wearing business attire) upped the volume with the remote. Reverbs were on:

The anchor, friend and colleague of shieL keeL's, was giving her intro, saying, "The Confederate mandate for improvements to the sewer system had been overturned last year in the privatization of the citywide utility. Having formerly studied the problem of overhauling the sewer system, the city of HiTopOLis is now reeling, under the malfunctioning of combined storm and effluvium sewer system. ShieL keeL, what can you tell us about the latest Confederate investigation and what it means in light of these persistent rainstorms we've been having. Any letup or curtailment on the flawed CSO tunnels we've been hearing about? For our viewers, CSO stands for *combined sewer overflows*."

"Foo-yee! Foo-yee!" shouted biMbo. "We want to hear about the storm! Will we be trapped here, or not?!"

Someone was pounding in a small way on the door off the front hall.

"BiMbo, be quiet and go let Claude in," said Mz. Bopoi sharply. "I want to hear this reverb."

The reverberator was saying, "CarlE, there's been no real fix on those tunnels." Giving her reverb an arresting touch of realism, shieL keeL was standing in the rain under her black brumella, ankle deep in water. "We now know that the mayor gave the KO to downgrading criteria needed for tunnels holding sewer water overflow, in concession to the privatizing policy he said was needed to bring costs and safe operations under control. E-mails between him and SewerCorpus executives show that he guaranteed them lower cheaper standards than had been demanded when public stewards were in control of the system...."

"I'm here!" announced Claude as he darted, slim, small and breathless, into the room4living. "Mz. Bopoi, Pegmo wants to talk to you!"

"CarlE, in one of these e-mails the mayor responds with glee to these headlines quoted by his liaison with city councilors." She read from the deVice, and the text was also televised for viewers. "'Hedge fund leaders lobby for privatization of public trusts as private firms compete for public utilities....' These e-mails show that safety regulations have been shaped in order, not to reform standards and construction safely, but to expand profit margins for investors."

Pegmo, not liking to embarrass the Bopoiz by coming dressed for work, had never gone beyond the elevators in delivering Claude to play with his MACHO friends. Parti-colored, garish, wearing trippingly tall red-winking steeLtos, she came into the well-appointed room and Mz. Bopoi drew her into the kitchen, with a brief word to Gorgeeous, asking her to keep an eye on the kidz and an ear open for TV reverbs.

The anchor was saying, "Does this mean, shieL keeL, that policies are in place guaranteeing that public health and safety concerns are subject solely to the making of money for nonresident shareholders of SewerCorpus instead of—so, so, the health and safety of citizens of HiTopOLis?"

"My Mom wants me to stay here!" announced Claude to the kidz in the room, who were now getting out their gear for the game. "The basement apartment is flooded with sewage!" He let fall his backpack.

"No kidding?" asked hipPo. "For real?" He looked at Claude's wet bedraggled clothes.

"Come to think of it, the smell is worse since you got here," said biMbo, holding her nose and coughing hysterically.

Gorgeeous, in naejs and T, had been standing near as The Visionary gave its report. She caught shieL's response to CarlE's question: Some of the investors were HiTopOLis residents. ShieL keeL proceeded to list them alphabetically—one of which was identified as developer and an owner of the glamorous Kress Building. "The way Bill Blender, spokesperson for city council, sees it, CarlE, they have to be accountable to shareholders before 'customers.' They don't call them citizens, CarlE, but customers."

HipPo shouted, "Claude, Claude, what's it like to wade through sewage?"

"We didn't. We escaped up to the landing and didn't get in it. You shoulda seen it rising!" He grinned, a brave show. Peeking out from the kitchen doorway Pegmo saw it, some relieved.

"What is so defective about these tunnels, shieL keeL, that they can't carry the load? We understand them holding without treatment, that's the purpose. They should be of a size for the job. So what's wrong?"

"CarlE, before I answer that, I should tell our viewers that these tunnels are supposed to have a capacity for the city's overload—with this first untreated part containing the highest levels of pollutants—during storms. Viewers, these tunnels fail even to hold it when there are no storms—as the residents of the neighborhood of SiXPointz can lately attest. They live directly over some of the tunnels. And the CDMS lab, where particle physics experiments are ongoing, is right next door deep under them. Fortunately, that lab is built deeper and in a manner to exclude and/or isolate even the minutest materials down almost—or seemingly—to atomic levels. They can't confirm yet how well it's working, but so far the flood hasn't penetrated. Not so fortunate the higher basements and other lower levels of businesses and residential areas of the neighborhood."

The MACHOs, lounging over the furniture, were quieted, geared up in their BIG BAMM headsets; intently playing the game against the invisible RAMBOs who lived all over the confederated country. The GPR (GamePersonaeRoles) were intent: stern personae commanded to engineer and build, or destroy, the new universe according to animistic, incipient—sometimes seeming irrationally oppositional—laws and principles of design. Now XploHding Whorllds had got to that 300,000 year point—recognized by the WIMPs from Tu's impromptu lecture.

—Tu, please stop!

—Tu, it's not fair—

—This helping the RAMBOs this way.

—The RAMBOs always win! Stop infiltrating RAMBOs' thoughts.

—Tu, the MACHOs need you; C'mon stop it.

"CarlE, it's the cement. Viewers, don't confuse concrete with cement. Cement is the binder used in the making of concrete. You can have cement without concrete, CarlE, but you can't have concrete without cement. And this is where the contractors for SewerCorpus did the fudging. Concrete (along with iron and steel) is the developed world's infrastructure, the basic construction material. The cement content determines a concrete's strength and therefore it's particular use. For instance, in nonhydraulic use, cement using slaked lime will harden in reaction to carbon dioxide— incidentally, that stuff we breathe out, CarlE. Not good enough for $H2O$ holding tunnels."

"So shieL, that means it does not make for the hardest matrix needed to bind a mineral aggregate essential for sewer tunnels— which hold water and may themselves be under water?"

"That's right, CarlE." ShieL looked down for a moment at her deVice, checking notes for the reverb. Rain sheeted across, and the wind blew. Tilting her brumella against the wind, she persevered.

"CarlE, apparently SewerCorpus should have screened contractors better—or else they purposely hired contractors who did not use the more costly hydraulic cements. This is the kind that will harden in strong chemical reaction, resulting in durable non water-soluble construction. Combining this stuff with concrete constituents makes the tunnel—so necessary to infrastructure of

141

this type—able to withstand the severe test to which storm water and human sewage can put them."

The kidz playing the game were now active, hollering and bouncing on the furniture. Her face a mask of make-up, tall shoes winking, parti-colors flashing, Pegmo hurried up to Claude and squeezed him; kissing him, saying goodnight. He shrugged her away. BABY was in a difficult stage of development and the RAMBOs had just about sucked her back into the SinGuLariTEE. But then Claude jumped up, and, as Pegmo reached the door in the hall, grabbed her around the waist, squeezed, then rushed back into the room4living; game headset a bit lopsided. Mz. Bopoi had joined Gorgeeous in front of The Visionary.

XploHding Whorllds' electronic voice announced a dramatic turn of events through minute speakers in the visors.

"BABY!" Several MACHO voices joined a shout. Even Gneis raised his voice in *huzzzzA!* GURlee was the only one silent—but smiling. Seemingly she was contributing most to the play, slowing particles by interacting with the HiggsBosson field, which had been so contained till now by the opposing RAMBOs. The field was not known, however, as HiggsBosson, as Tu was bound to explain.

—I knew it! (HB) —Tu, I knew it was you! Girl you stuck by us, gave scope to that girl GURlee or whatever her name!

—According to the physicist's notes they call it Beauregard Higgsson, said Tu. And we don't have it yet in the FivePoints Akropolis universe.

—How can that be? said Fabian. What's making our universe happen, if there's no Higgs field or particle or whatever in it?

—We do have it. We just don't *know* it yet, I mean. I mean we haven't *proved* it.

—It looks now like BABY's gonna make it this time! (Jay) Thanks be too Tu!

The kidz were all over the living room, knocking into Gorgeeous, sending Mz. Bopoi into the hallway where doors to the study, bedrooms and baths ranged out like spokes on a bicycle wheel. Empty Kake cups went flying, and Gneis glanced his eelie off to one side. Then he slid into the kitchen. Safer there. And it was dark since Mz. Bopoi had switched off the kitchen light.

—Tu you de miracle! —how'd you do that?

—The RAMBOs had always been successful in suppressing the field, said Tu. The physicist could have given his kidz a tip but evidently decided against that. You see —

Gneis was in the dark, looking out on the play. In his virtual visor he also saw the success of the MACHOs in slowing things down. The MACHOs had had it wrong, he saw. *The whole time we thought the Beauregard was the bad guy.* Simultaneously, Gneis watched the play in the luminous living room along with the gamescape's unfolding universe in his visor.

"Viewers, the complex matrix of sewage water is a mix of many chemicals, including concentrations of ammonium, phosphorus, nitrate, with lots of conductivity, alkalinity with pH ranging possibly between 7 and 8. And because of things such as bleaches used in cleaning sinks, tubs, and toilets, there's a presence of trihaloMethanes always present in these waters."

"ShieL, shieL I understand this is a substance chemically precipitated to bind the clastic material of concrete?"

—Tu we are SO glad you switched sides! (Pomala)

—BABY, BABY. Quad was singing it.

"BABY's gonna get born!"

"BABY get born!!"

Tu gave credit where it was due, saying —This is the unity between the electromagnetic and weak forces. The weak is massive and slows the protons, neutrons, and electrons down just enough— and they are actually expressing the same underlying force. So now they are slowing to amass, or at least behaving like it—which amounts to the same thing. Mass. Subatomic particles that make up everything can now combine to make atoms—of which people and things are made. Or, if it's a photon, it doesn't act at all. Photons just don't act with the weak force, therefore don't get mass. *Mass,* fellow WIMPs. That's the thing.

—Plain as the nose on your face. (HB was grinning.)

The two women were again by the The Visionary to hear shieL keeL say, "That's right, CarlE. Calcium and clay combine to adhere and solidify. The aTomic mass of calcium, for instance, is 40.078 amu with a melting point of 839.0°C, a boiling point of 1484.0°C, protons/electrons, 20, neutrons, 20—with a cubic crystalline structure, that is classified as alkaline earth, along with magnesium and other metallic elements in group two of the periodic table. In short, CarlE, the concrete of these sewage holding-tunnels is made out of some of the same stuff we are, but we're better made."

Meanwhile, Gneis sat braced in the dark kitchen. Looking out on the hopping, energetic dim luminosity of the great room. He was also watching the universe unfold. Evidently, at some point soon, BABY would get born. He could not help tears falling. And he could not even brush them back. It may be happening—all joy. But here he was in the dark with pangs of pity. Pity for himself and his plight. It had been he and *not* GURlee who most aided Tu in the event. *Who-in-the-Kake is TOO, anyway?* Gneis couldn't help but wonder. Apparently Pomala was TOO, as well?

So, kid? It'll give you something else to work on. That's good isn't it?

—Rejoice, kid, rejoice! (Fabian)

Gneis had taken to calling himself "kid" lately. And kidd-O. Maybe ever since the dream. He kind of liked that. Kid.

—They look like—we all look like—kinda like the pool balls in Paddy's! (HB)

—When they break them apart? Like with the—what they call—the cue stick, cue ball? (Jay).

—Since we are essentially all these things here, yes. We all look like those pool balls breaking. Everything in the universe being made. (Tu)

"So far, no official warning off." Deputy Chief Capt. Kent S. Clarke leaned back in his swivel chair, hands clasped behind his head, a gaze through pale virtual spectaculars—where he could see her talking—and also gaze out the windows of his cuboid. "One or two of my fellow "lowers" have hinted that it might not work — pursuing this thing. The intimation is there's nothing 'in it,' nothing to go on, etc...."

He was talking to detective officer Sgt. Philipa over the thin deVice clapped to his head — ear-and-eye spectaculars that let him gaze, as well, out rain-streaked glass spread the length of his rectangular cubicle. It was a large cuboid, befitting his rank; lined with various screens, monitors for stats and visuals necessary to the crime detection work he headed in SiXPointz on second watch. It was also Kirby and Bart's cuboid, 3rd and 1st watch, respectively.

It was dark out there, that dim luminous rainy sort of dark you find at night in this city—except for the dark hole surrounded by edges of this wet luminosity. The whole scene looked like some picture of the dark framed in a suggestion—the notion, merely—of light. There was light at the edges of every dark thing, giving both the monstrous dark and the light itself away. The suggestion or delineation of some sort of ... revelation of these seeming polar opposites. Clarke could be turned to this sort of reverie when it rained on watch. His windows overlooked the crematorium park at SiXPointz HiTopOLis. He glanced back at one of the screens behind him. There was the timeline for the missing kidz.

Clarke paraphrased the official buzz. " 'Just a couple kidz playing around, driving their adults crazy'. No need to ask, Phil, you know what I think. Has keeL got anything for you since the impromptu interview she did with him in the lobby of Kress?... Really? ...She got it from—? That's interesting. And the kid also— at Bopoiz? KeeL thinks he may be ready, say a couple things. Good. So, get on over to Bopoiz and see about that! It's not late, not likely to be past the kid's bedtime. Putting those two things together along with that snooping you did on the murder-suicide.... You'll get something out of this yet."

He glanced from the screen with timeline, out to where the dark was visible in its dimly lustrous frame. "Before you go—how you doing out there? I've never seen it like this—going on for so long. The reports are for more of the same. You should see the satellites. Amazing breadth across the continent."

He listened to her, still watching the dark. "Yeah, I knew that about all basements in this part of this city. Yeah, I can smell it from here. No need to tell me about it. Kitty is fit to be tied. She wants to leave. But she's always wanted to leave. This is a pretty good excuse.... But how are *you* getting along?... At least you've got a croozer now. Try to keep that thing in juice. I know it's hard.... I know it's no fun being grounded, I know that. But think if you worked in a cuboid all day surrounded by screens? How would you like that? Sure I'm not getting wet. The grid is barely working, though. Sometimes there's a glitch and a switch while the generator comes on. They had to move everything—I think you saw— everything they could into the lobby. They've got electricians and even mechanics working the load centers, locking and tagging, trying to get utilities secure in the neighborhood."

"Right. I'll let you go."

A bit chagrined, he turned back to the weather reverbs; switching back and forth between them and those about the citywide utilities, and patrol contacts. He should not have detained her. He had to take Kent S. Clarke in hand. The less Kitty liked him the more he thought of Philipa. And that was bad. Bad for the Kitty-Kent union. Bad for the work. Bad for him and Philipa. —And there he was, doing it again.

He swiveled, looked once more at the timeline and trail of evidence. The graphics were excellent, including visuals of the children meeting up in the lobby of Kress, exiting together through revolving doors ... and reappearing later outside the crematorium gate and walls. And it was all going to converge... somewhere.... He just didn't know where. Or who.

More, detailed, evidence. *Proof.* That's what he needed.

—Girls! Down here! Look at it!
—No. Don't come down here!
—The sewer tunnel?? OMG!
—Quadri! Don't go with them! Stay with me!

Clarke looked at the statistics, the pragoMetric points of reference in child disappearance and reappearance cases. Then he stopped, thought about the peripheries, even irrelevancies. Math is

145

never enough, you need the imaginative leap. All that math they bring to anything—inert mathematical structuring, pile of numbers, webPatterns, no matter how elegant, you need that thinking, that imaginative connection—. He switched to confirmed missing persons—all adults—last known locales and residentials. Then he noticed a new one, checked the date, and again the residence and last-seen. Wait a minute. Says Claude Troy couldn't get her to call. That's the kid's—. Kent Clarke looked back at the screen where Claude's timeline showed, then at the new missing person stat: Pegmo Troy, prostitute. *Only now they call them sex workers.* This isn't what Claude was going to be about at Bopoiz. ...Who called this in? ...Someone named biMbo.

"Phil, you there yet?— Listen, why didn't you tell me about the kid— Claude's mother." He waited while she checked her deVice. "Not on your watch? What kind of answer is that? Not on mine either. But guess what— she *is* indeed missing. Talk to the Bopoiz about this when you get there. I don't need to tell you to be thorough. —Yeah, I know I just did. Get back to me... Yeah, I know you won't skip town, don't have a date, etc...."

He took off the pale spectaculars and leaned back, hands clasped behind his head. Then he swiveled and leaned back again, put his feet up on the long worktable facing the framed dark.

Sometimes these coincidences stagger me. The thought process ferrets connections from minutia. But sometimes they aren't so minute.... She works independently, but will contract now and then. Clarke began thinking of Pegmo's business. Its legality set her free from contractual work, from serfdom, but made it hard to trace. The thing was to see what Kirby had. That was the watch for this new missing persons report.... and this series of incidents. Is the missing Pegmo Troy now the ignition of contact? Starting this thought train? Connect these temp child disappearances with a possible parallel track — the SiXPointz unsolved missing persons? It all looks so coincidental, until you start to think of tuning it with diverse pragoMetrics ... seeming almost to *push* you toward.... The mere idea of coincidence—dailiness shrouding thought—. But it's there all the time to be considered. Theories of probability—a pattern revealed under scrutiny, invisible to a mind clouded in randomness. Because the missing data is—missing until—.

...What I'm thinking is no preternatural belief. Things can be modified but solely according to the law of their making. Initially, all physical and mathematical laws embrace future contingencies. Because the laws themselves are always *now*.

Come on back, Clarke, thought the 2nd watch deputy chief; now seeing his own reflection in the dark hole represented by the burial park below. Framed in the dim wet luminescence of the

s. dormAn

HiTopOLis night.

Candles flamed, here and there, in the apartment because power was out on the block. BiMbo and hipPo were confined to their rooms, aglow with their screens and deVices on battery. Mz. Bopoi sat on the massive wraparound leather sofa, her arm around Claude. She knew about another mother missing in this building. Missing from the lives of her children's friends. The wife of her friend, Berle. *Mary Bala Jones.*

The smell of melting beeswax was heavenly, a relief from that sewer reek to the nostrils of the detective sitting across from them.

He looks so small, thought Philipa, glancing away at her tiny recording deVice. *So small.* She looked over at him, gently, speaking gently. "Yes, Claude, it might really help us find her... if you can tell us what happened to you and GURlee that night. I'll help you? You just answer questions? One at a time. Maybe nod, or shake your head?"

Claude has not taken his tawny gaze away, as on the former occasion. He looks at her. Slowly nods his head.

But will this work as yes-and-no, thought Philipa. If it's not to be verbal...? She propped another deVice, the QuipPad, on a low glass table between them, to record audiovisuals of the small, seemingly mesmerized boy. In fact, she knew him to be paying the keenest attention. Now, it was going to happen. Now they are going to find out.

So that's done, thought Kent Clarke as he put the two-way audiovisual spectaculars into the inner pocket of his Macintosh. His spectaculars held the recording of the interview at Bopoiz. He heard Kirby stopping by the next cubicle but one. Shifts were changing.

He set his handheld deVice face down, with care, beside the digital rat they used for half the screens in the deputies' shared cuboid. Kirby came in talking, sluffing his deVice next to the rat as usual.

"What a stittt-awful place this is." He said it, grinning under that black mustache. "That mess of equipment down there when you came in?"

"It was," said Clarke.

"Wonder when we're all going to be sick? Anything else going on? How you coming with those kidz?"

"Still working on it."

"Nothing," said Kirby, with a lift of his brows, eyes gleaming a faint taunt. "Nothing there."

"You got something on a *bigger* something, I hear. Quite the coincidence."

"That will turn out to be nothing, too. Seems to happen to these workers all the time and then come to find out they needed a little break and went off somewhere with a big spender. Those guys are always incommunicado or something like it. They 'go hiking in Siboria' or 'sailing to Barnia' or someplace. Can't be reached by man nor woman-beast. You know this."

Clarke gave him a conspiratorial grin. "Yeah. I do."

Kirby reflected a bigger grin. A leer.

"See you," said Clarke, still grinning, picking up and pocketing the QuipPad, Kirby's deVice. "Let me know if you need anything. Otherwise, I've plenty of z's stored in me I'm about to spend." He walked out and down the passageway between partitioned boxoids where chattering and endless work were ongoing. He got into the stinking elevator.

It wasn't that much of a trade. Kirby would try to reach him before too long but Clarke would manage to be to be incommunicado himself. Clarke had changed his password and, as an extra precaution, neglected to store anything from the night's work there. That was what lockboxes were for—only Kent S. Clarke was holding all the keys now.

The plan was to crack, upload (debrief), re-encrypt, and return Kirby's Quip apparently untouched—with apology. He ended staying up half the night ignoring Kitty's absence, consulting with code and encryption cracker, Freddie the FreakinTech.

During the tedious course of virtual instruction, which Freddie FreakinTech was putting him through, and, over the increasingly tedious cups of coffee Clarke brewed for himself, the two chatted back-and-forth about this and that—mostly about the weather. The weather was no longer commonplace conversation. The weather was the most interesting thing going. The stats on this weather were groundbreaking (so-to-speak). Hyperbole was as dense as the rain itself. People vied for hyperbolic descriptions of it. This was *all* the rainy weather that had ever been since the beginning of time. Mind or the universe or somebody was reusing every drop ever produced and recycling it all at the same time on Eartha's seven continents. There would be no more rain, ever, after this. People in other universes had sent out pigeons only to discover that rain had fled their own planets, solar systems, galaxies and etc. to take up permanent residence in this one. In short, it was going to rain for ever. And Ever. There's going to be an Ever. It was to be nothing but rain.

The police detective and the young consultant entertained themselves like this, back and forth, for some time. At one point Freddie mentioned the friendship he'd struck up with the old guy—Kelso—who worked security in the basement of the Kress Building.

That is, Kelso had been in the basement before the rain storm of the millennium. This millennium, during the first part of which, Freddie had said, A'ndyans had kept track of rainfall on rocks, on stony ledges, chiseling in records, and laying antlers of varying length to harden in clay.

During their conversation (yesterday in Bone's Bar), dry old Kelso had said, at some point, that it was a sad thing A'ndyans had all intermarried, being completely absorbed in the Usi'opan peoples who came here. Kelso claimed that as part of his ancestry. "He said he could make bow-n-arrows if he had to but he couldn't make bullets. Look Chief, I'll message, see if he wants in on this? Kelso's got some pretty interesting stuff to say about it."

Clarke said, "On the case, or the A'ndyans?"

"The last, the ancient tribes."

"Don't bother messaging. We're working, remember? Just tell me stuff as we work along, if you want."

"One thing he said was it's like they're extinct now. That they'd be *distinct* if that hadn't happened. That, if they'd been shunned, ill-treated, mocked, congregated, nonPC'd—that kind of thing—that, so, so, they'd be something special. Have some sort of special place, special thing to do. Something like that. You'd be able to tell there was something to them."

"Not like us, you mean?"

"Like that, only (he said), they are us now, so there's no difference."

"So what would be so important about a difference?"

"When I brought that up—. That's when he went into a rantzypantz over the state of things. He calls that the 'moral state of things.' "

"You mean the immoral state of things."

"KO, if you want."

"What'd he say?"

"He says you guys wear uniforms because people want it like that ... so they'll know when they're being spied on by the law. You know he's old, KO? They call him Kelso the Koot. —He says, You know we didn't have massive tech surveillance like this in the old days. That sounded like a contradiction to me. But he said, not if you're the mayor. No? says I (like, please go on you dyno-sour). Ever wonder why? he says. Nope. Never. So then Kelso says, It's because we're an unscrupulous, unfaithful, adulterous, evil corrupt greedy unfeeling wicked debauched—you understand any of that?— society. And I says, Maybe, what's adulterous? *And*, he says, we deserve everything coming to us. All. Except the children. (He cut me off before I could ask that. We were in Bone's Bar—it was quite the conversation.) And *you*, he said to me. 'You're also the exception.' There was that look in his eye."

"What'd he say about the basement at Kress?"

"That it was a sewer. He said rats had been floating in dead from somewhere. He tried to figure that out."

"Anything?"

"Maybe from the piping. Those rotten tunnels of SewerCorpus. Apparently the piping was done by them, too."

Before morning, in the quiet dark, murmuring rainfall on the window panes of his flat, Kent Clarke found his jackpot—a total surprise. With the virtual help of Freddie, the deVice—the QuipPad, the thing he held in his hand—had turned out to be not Kirby's but the architect's! Apparently Kirby had done a similar switch earlier in the evening on the corporate guru himself.... And—Clarke was willing to bet—for an entirely different purpose.

Oh, but this town was something else! And there was horrific news Phil would want to put off having to break to her friend Berle. Well, she could. This was only very suggestive on that account. Wait for corroborating. He thought he was going to be sick. He was the police, thought he had seen it ALL before. He had not. Clarke hated uploading this stuff. It made him wonder why anyone was alive. Why are there people? Why not just animals? No, he thought, animals are better than this, purer. They might be brutal, fierce, knowing no mercy, their victims just as injured, dead—but at least they were pure. Morally pure. Even *orangutans*, he thought. Even *orangutans* would not be true murderers. *And we are supposed to be the sole being with moral agency.*

Next night, the screen in Gneis's bedtable showed the mayor of HiTopOLis, live from the mezzanine two levels below them, promising that a new company or two would be forming to handle cleanup and repair once the storms passed. His face—sandy and pasty but handsome in a blonde kind of way—was a political head talking, inserting his 2kPax into the swollen debate about what to do.

In his seat next to Gneis, Berle thought, *How can I get us in on that cynical profitability?* Its name won't be SewerCorpus, of course. It will be CleanReliefCorp or other nonsense.

"...We can take comfort," said the mayor, "from the latest of these weather experts' projections. Worldwide warming trends will diminish the likelihood of monstrous atmospheric extremes now driving stuff over this continent. Trending will be influenced in such a way that it will factor out the 700-year trend as a matter of course. The bend we've all seen in satellite pictures since the, so, so, so, since the advent of satellites 100 years ago, will gradually disappear.

This wall of high-pressure, generally happening once or twice a year, is predicted to be moving further north from us, so it's bound to deflate in frequency—permanently—over the next couple years."

Berle shifted in the chair. And, listening longer, he now thought that... *He seems to be reaching into other areas of town discourse with some of this speech.* Berle hoped there would be questions afterward. He hoped someone would ask pungent penetrating questions. The kind to wipe that solemn reassurance off his bland face. Maybe someone would upend him into the basement of the Kress Building—the mayor was making this reassuring blather downstairs, for viewers, and those in the lobby.

Berle turned his head away from the screen and hoped Gneis could not read his mind. "Hey Sheesh!" Standing, leaving the room he called, "Trade places! It's my turn to make supper, anyway...."

Gneis watched him go, wondering over the abrupt departure.

Sheesh came in and sat in Dah's place. "Anything interesting?" He didn't expect an answer but gave his brother a look to let him know it, before glancing back at the screen. "Hope he doesn't overcook the fish cakes like he did last time. That the mayor—again?"

They watched the familiar face. They listened to the familiar voice. The mayor was on a lot lately, since these days of rain.

He was saying, "The sensational media has too much influence, so convinced is it of its own importance. It has to appear knowledgeable in its exposes and investigations... but in fact, these tend to be sensationalist, all over the speculative map. The opinion-makers speak of conclusive opinions but, it seems to me, that these bod-casts have more zeal then conclusiveness. Bear in mind that the object of the reverberator is to create a sensation rather than bolster the cause of truth. Truth is only boosted when it creates a sensation for them. This is their business. So please, consider well, debate within yourselves, and determine and understanding, one which builds up the truth, instead of tearing it down. Remember, they want to keep you on the edge of your seat, not necessarily inform you."

Sheesh sensed, rather than saw or heard, a sudden disturbance in his twin brother. He looked over at him and saw a truly scared face. A terrified, deeply concerned, face.

"Brah," said Sheesh, standing, looking concern toward his brother. "What's wrong?"

Gneis looked up at him from between his head braces. *How can I tell him? How can I get it across?*

Gneis had seen that cloud of soot again. The head talking was a dark cloud of smoke with a voice. A veritable black blast from a mini volcano.

151

SiXPointz HiTopOLis

How can I tell him? How can I get it across?

Berle had been standing in the door, listening. The smell of
burning fish came through the hall from the kitchen—the kitchen
papered in facsimiles, translations, of Fodder Domino's manuscripts.
He was aware of both sons' distress, and didn't quite know how to
address it. And, with another, smaller, part of his mind, he was
thinking: *Sensation?* You mean rain and floods and broken sewers
aren't sensational? Exactly, what do you mean calling on our senses
this way? Are you going to tell us these facts are dull? That we're
dying of boredom? Need something to make our lives interesting?
That we aren't more alive in all this than you with your suave
intelligence?

Downstairs, on an elegant mezzanine overlooking the busy
lobby of the Kress Building, reverberators were grouped round the
Mayor before dim upper-level shop windows. Most electric lights
were out in the shops, but, sparsely, people went in and out. He
stood in his long stylish black TxGore (thrown open), with his back
to the lobby below, wrought-iron railings shaped like tangled
branch-stems twined with leaves behind him. A few aides stood with
him. Down in the lobby the crowd went about its business, blown in
from everywhere, hoping for some comfort, maybe coffee and flowers,
clothes (however unlikely in prospect). But coffee? That would
always be, would it not? Some were scattered in groups, hearing the
speech over speakers dotting the public space, looking up at the
knot of reverberators; at the Mayor's back, and his assistants and
security, some of whom faced them. This scattered audience below
also had their QuipPads and other deVices recording the mini event.
Not once did the mayor mention that the sub sub levels had movable
utilities removed to higher basements in the building. This could be
assumed. Some cars were still floating down there, or submerged.
There was plenty of disruption in the city and surrounding
neighborhoods. And enough left over to leave stories behind for the
great grand generation to follow (should any survive either this, or
its own peculiar disruptions).

"Mayor," Mass Moss, broad-shouldered and dressed in black,
shieL keeL's black colleague, was asking, holding out his deVice.
Mass Moss wore a waxed leather raincoat and stylish fedora.
Behind Moss and keeL and other reverberators, camera people with
tiny hiDif imaging, bod-cast the streaming reverb. "Mayor, we've
heard reports that some child abductions have occurred in this
neighborhood; and we've also heard of images confiscated from some
deVices, or maybe one deVice in particular, to bring lasting shame
on big figures in this town—one in particular. Enough in these
images of children to make the hair stand on end if these came into

the public sphere. Such a turn of events may not be unlikely, we're told. What have you got to—"

"That is what I mean! Exactly," said the Mayor in rapid response, instantly turning his broad back on Moss—spontaneously (as it appeared) to address clustered groups below. The response there was sudden, rapt, deVices held attentive, high—to capture his performance.

In apartments overhead, where people watched on their battery backup Visionaries, Berle, Sheesh, and Gneis, saw the back of his head and shoulders. It still looked like smoke to Gneis. He stared and trembled.

"This pointless sensationalism and charge-worthy libel— slander—denigration of character. I've heard of these allegations, and they are baseless and disgusting. Let me remind you reverbs that theft is no upholder of justice in our city. Stolen goods are no evidence—no use for any purpose except blackmail—also illegal and immoral in this town. In our courts of law!"

Dah! I want to ask you about dark matter, I want to ask you about dark energy, about photons, about—. Dah, I want to ask you about reality, about mind! Dah! I want to ask you—what's real? Are some of us *not* real? Which ones are real?

Emergency power was on in the lower utilities levels. Earlier, Kelso had been chatting with BruceE, custodial maintenance, in BruceE's office. "The tenants giving you a hard time what with being in the dark?" asked Kelso.

"The 'residents' you mean. Not too bad. It'll get worse."

Now Kelso sat on the stairs below that level, mesmerized; watching a colorful scarf float in with the filth from somewhere. An isolated bit of bright red-orange, snakelike, a bit metallic. Now it lay dead in the water about 5 m away. Kelso could not reach it without... something. From his perch on the metal stairs he looked around for what to use. Below him filthy water with bits of brown or black debris sat stinking around half-submerged metallic control panels and heavy motors—equipment of miscellaneous sorts, crammed into this sub-basement. Things not to be moved in the emergency, most of it disused or useless, off-line anyway for one reason or another. Below this level was all underwater, but here, in this upper basement was now the high point of the flood as far as the Kress Building was concerned.

He hauled his arthritic joints and bones up, climbed these stairs to the next level, located the custodian at his desk and asked about the broom closet.

"That the fancy name for it?" asked BruceE day watch head of maintenance. His feet up on the metal desk, eyes staring at the

Mayor on the screen, BruceE was middle-aged, desultory, unsmiling, redhaired (what there was of it), and pointing down the hallway.

"Whatever," said Kelso in passing along what appeared to be freshly waxed linoleum, and the white-painted concrete walls of the corridor.

"On the left!" BruceE tossed the direction over his shoulder. "Do you believe this official ratsstittt?" He called down the hall.

"Neither does anyone else," came the words remotely back to him.

"Nobody's gonna believe it. One cynical city we are."

Kelso came back through with a couple push brooms and a clamp. "Going to sweep out the stittt with that, the flood? What? Got to keep these brooms clean."

Kelso just kept going. The stocky BruceE heaved himself to his feet and followed along behind him.

Turned out Kelso did not need the clamp for the second broom. The scarf had almost reached the stairs. They stood staring as slowly it came to them, seemingly of its own accord. There was definitely current here? Imperceptible, by bits of stuff appearing to sit there, but apparently not. If so, that would mean it was still rising?

Kelso lifted the scarf out on the bristled end of the broom.

"Hate to think where that came from," said the other. It hung dripping, limp and smelly, stained with skuzz. "Maybe a car or something?"

"I think we need to call the cops," said Kelso.

"Just a scarf," said BruceE.

"Yeah. And that's just a glove," said Kelso pointing. "And that there's just a stocking. Used to be quite the glamorous stocking, glittered when the lights hit it... before the sewer got it."

"Maybe it's from one of the shops," said the custodian. "The Lovely Shop."

"Why don't we let the cops tell us?" suggested Kelso. Dryly, with a lift of his sprouty overgrown eyebrows, gray, above his wire-rimmed glasses.

"KO," said BruceE. *Kelso the Koot.* "Cops it is." He felt for his phone. Not on him. "Got your phone?"

Kelso said, "Lost in the flood. A relief actually. Might not be getting another one."

BruceE stared at him.

Kelso propped the scarf up to dry against a wall of the stairwell, still on the broom brush; and reached out with the other one, raking in glove and stocking, and now panties.

"Gag!" said BruceE, tongue out, screwing his face up. "It smells like rancid meat in here. We do need police!"

154

s. dormAn

He turned back up the stairs, calling over his shoulder. "Better c'mon. That'll make you sick."

Kelso propped up the other items in the same manner, and caught up with maintenance at his desk where he'd left the phone. "Can I have that? Or your Quip or something? I want pictures in case something happens."

"Yeah, if you promise to get one," said BruceE, detaining him also to ask, "So what do you think? Where'd that stuff come from? Same place as the rats?"

"Looks like," said Kelso, about to walk off. "You got any other ideas?"

BruceE tilted back, put his feet on the desk, looking at the screen. "I hope it doesn't relate to the Mayor's ratsstittt, that's all. You hear about that stuff the reverb's asking?"

"Which watch you get at the station?" asked Kelso, meaning the police. "Morning or afternoon?"

"Still morning," said the other, glancing at the round black-and-white analog on the wall.

Kelso was wishing it might have been Clarke's watch. He did not trust Kirby, but first watch Bart, also, was a cipher.

DeVice in hand, he went back out to the stairs. "That linoleum's looking good," he called back. *Nice job. Almost gives me hope. Almost.*

Meanwhile, golden-haired, wasted, Gneis has spent the morning communing with Sheesh, whose own hair was rusty blonde above crisp freckles. Gneis finally told him about SmokeHead.

They came up with the name at the same moment, according to the light in the former's eye. Gneis could not say it right off but the word came from his twin's mouth, predictably, in the same flash of an eye.

"And since no one else has smokeheadedness—that you've seen—we can safely assume that the architect is the only one. According to the abducted reasoning of Burdock Bolms this might be a backward prophecy of solid probability. Or, as Dah might say, as solid as anything can be which isn't saying much. (Since, he says, we are all full of holes or other imperceptible stuff.)

There was one point on which Gneis wished to correct him.

It was still raining, the room was dim though it was late morning. Elevators weren't working, nor plumbing nor lights. There'd been a run on water jugs in stores so Dah had them on rations — both on bottled drinking water and battery power. It had taken Gneis the whole morning, working comprehensively with his brother, to divest himself of his terrible burden of trembling and fear. There was no downside to the process because of this great

155

relief. Coupled with the activity of wise use of — or obliteration of useless — time. Sheesh has noted to himself before now that brothers are good for wasting time with, and for knowing how to read your mind. Gneis was thinking the same, in addition to: Brothers feed you cheese hamburger. When you could eat it. He was wishing for one, but under these conditions, that did not seem on offer.

"Again," said Sheesh, "we must resort to Burdock Bolms. Bring into the light of our abductive abilities every single trifle we know about the Kress Building builder. Number one." He looked attentively at Gneis. Then he said, "He bought the school, tore it down and built this risehigher with glam shops on the mezzanine and ground floor."

Gneis looked his agreement.

Sheesh said, "is that a trifle?" He looked at Gneis. Then he said, "recall that observable regularity 'arises' (as Dah would say) when we have massive numbers of trifles...." He hesitated. "...So so single random resulting acts cancel out each other... making everything predictable and stable."

He looked at the ceiling, then at the rain-running windows. Gneis also was looking.

"I think we can safely say that a lot of trifles went into this predictable and stable risehigher."

He looked at their empty glasses on Gneis's bedtable where Gneis was also looking.

"Maybe not so safely. Or at least abduct that the sewer system is only stable at the molecular level.... That is... the various molecules of which it is put together are probably stable but they aren't put together in the right quantities or right way. If reverb reports are to be believed."

His gaze, Gneis noticed, withdrew into itself on the slow absent look of abstraction.

"It would work only in terms of correct concentrations of various stuff. Concrete is not about making sure one particular mineral does the job right. Concrete is about making sure concentrations yield the right structural integrity.... Have I got that right?"

"No-no. Al-almost." And Gneis was also still thinking about his missing point.

"KO, they've got to be the right elements in the right quantities. Onto the next trifle. There's got to be a formula for determining smokeheadedness... even though we've only encountered it once. Once? No wait—you said *the mayor had a smoke head, too.*"

Point absorbed. The light in Gneis's eye was exact.

156

s. dormAn

"Another thing I just thought of," said Sheesh. "SmokeHead number one—that's the architect—gives kidz choo-choo's and other goodies. We don't get any because we're teens. And besides what do we want with goodies?—except for right now when choo-choo's would be an excellent thing to have. —So that's trifle #2. But not sure we can add that because we don't know about the mayor giving out goodies. Also, the mayor did not build the Kress Building."

He looked at his brother. "He might have invested in it."

"I didn't want to have to tell you this," said a voice from the doorway.

Gneis's eyes turned, and Sheesh looked over his shoulder. Berle Quarts was standing stocky, rust-colored frizzy hair sticking out, against the door-frame of the dark hall. Dim diffuse light from rainy windows showed an inscrutable face. Evidently he had been listening to this one-sided conversation.

He said, "I'm sure he thinks it a trifle, the architect. The mayor, too. Like I said, I wish I did not have to tell you. But you should know. The SmokeHead is a child molester, a child pornographer, and possibly a child rapist. These things aren't actually trifles. They are the destruction of the universe. My sons, in order to salvage creation we need to discover the moral particle. Pronto."

The first part of what he had said made them gape. The second part made them wonder: What good will the moral particle do? The two boys stared at him.

Inwardly hurting. Berle the physicist was in pain. But he looked back at them, inscrutable.

Sheesh felt he had to do something. He didn't know what. Gneis, utterly helpless and broken, felt it all. Terrible, exhausting.

After a moment, considering Dah's inscrutability, dimly aware of confusion and pain, Sheesh spoke. "What's that mean?—Pronto?" He thought he had not heard that one before.

—You been awful quiet. You here?

—I went to church while you were in the basement.

—Church!? They got *church*!?

—I don't think they call it that.

HB has started a conversation with Fabian.

—God knows they need one. In this neighborhood—in this universe, Fabe. Seriously? You better show me.

—I think it's gone. I mean, they went home? The ground floor was underwater but they had something upstairs. They got into the back, through an upper window, on the second floor where the embankment abuts.

—You mean they have Hah-La, you call God, too? asked

157

Quadri.

—If he's the same one, said Fabian. I don't know. Can't tell.
But—Look if it's the maker it *has* to be the same one!

Jayrai piped in. —As far as you are concerned.

—Nope. As far as everyone is concerned. Look, we're here.
Who else can orchestrate all this? You think there's one over here
doing all this, and another that brought us here from there? How
does it work? It's got to be the same, otherwise there'd just be chaos
instead of design.

—This isn't chaos? (Jayrai) The sewer, bogus cement— the
decaying bodies? Not chaos?

—Not if you are Jayrai and I'm Fabian. This other stuff's
tricky, but it all works according to laws, doesn't it? Physical laws?
So it's not chaos. For instance, if we don't know the difference
between right and wrong—Ms. wannabe barista—we don't know how
to make coffee. That's why bodies in the sewer.

—Eyes rolling all over the place, said HB.

—Only I think here they've got it—xianity—mixed up a bit.
As best I can understand. It's still us trying to understand their
minds, basically. I mean, we are part of their brains, right?

—And their chairs and refrigerators. The sewer water,
decomposing bodies.

Tu said, —But that's not their brains your understanding is
coming from.

—Or their refrigerators, said Pomala. How is it we can read
their minds... and even give some of ours to them?

—*You* can give some, I think, said Tu.

—You helped with BABY, said Pomala.

Tu continued. —But there's a whole lot of mind in
everything. I seem to understand this more. Not sure where that's
leading.

—They've got religion either backward or inside out. Maybe
upside down. It's hard to describe, said Fabe.

Jay said, —You're going to have to explain that. And
remember, this is *your* religion and not everybody else's. I'm still
leaning toward lots and lots of gods.

—That might syncretize better with science, said Tu.
Polytheism. The way they make the world is magic...and so is the
vision of Fabian's religion. In the early 1900s people once did think
science would provide a synthetic basis for magic. Magic was
science we don't get yet...they rather mistakenly said. Also, Fabian,
your comparison between kinds of law, physical-moral, may be
apples and oranges.

—But it's not mine. I mean, xianity isn't mine, it's what I
believe that's been passed down. Remember, I said I don't see any

need to get rid of it.

    —Just because it's old? That's bogus, said Jay. Why did it start in the first place? That's the thing. Just because "it's always been done that way," is not a real reason.

    —Right, said HB. We've always put food in our mouths since the beginning of time. —Oh since the beginning of mouths; but that's not why we do it. We do it because we're hungry. BTW, you been hungry since we got here? Me either.

    —It started because they killed X and he got up from dead again to save us.

    —But why? Everybody else still died anyway.

    —Because we are dinners. Keep breaking ourselves on moral laws. And now we are going to not be dinners, and rise from the dead, too.

    —If we ever get that far, said HB. On the other hand, maybe the Grandmaster's A'ndians killed us with their tommyhawks and we just don't remember. Anyone recollect that? Maybe it *wasn't* the Hadesthon *or* the little girl.

    —But why are we dinners? said Jayrai.

    —We just are, OK?

    —I thought you said it was because Evan and Adan ate the pear, said Pome.

    —They made a choice. They chose and so we are dinners.

    —But I didn't choose to eat the pear, said Jay.

    —*Everything* fell because they didn't believe their creator, said Fabian.

    —Everything? What does that mean?

    —The humans were like their creator, who wanted them that way, said Fabian.

    —So God fell, too?

    —That's what I've been trying to get at. About the xianity here, said Fabian. —They think their maker thinks a lot about nature and creation and they're supposed to take care of it. Only they call Maker *Mind*. They seem to think Mind fell, too. But I don't see how a perfect Mind could fall, so that can't be right.

    —Have they got X? Did he die on the cross? (Pomala). Does he redeem everybody? How can this be the same God if he or she fell? Wouldn't that make him/her a dinner?

    —X suffers, too. That's it! Yes, I think I see. Their X is like ours through a body, conceived of Mind, the God of their alt universe. Like Mind sparked X. When he died in their torture chamber he didn't say, "It's finished," he said, "It begins." Like something was going to happen next on his account. Everybody—the authorities who did it to him thought he was nuts. But these present day HiTopOLis believers don't. In our universe we believers say that humans have a god-shaped hole in our hearts, here they say Mind has a man-shaped hole in his heart. That Mind is crying for Man, for humans beings.

—Then how do you know it's the same Big Fello? said HB.

—They cry and pray a lot, for one thing. And both Mind and their X—they call him Jobe—which I thought was curious because we've got a Jobe—and theirs sounds a lot like ours—except the torture chamber and death and resurrection (not in our Jobe's book). But both Mind and X and this other one—you see the three-in-one thing here—the other one—they call It *The Comfort Zone*. That's why they cry. Because It comes to help them.

—Anything else different in that mish-mash-up? asked HB.

—Yeah. They think subatomic particles are Mind's body that broke and got put together to make everything, including them and their brains. Almost like he made everything out of spare parts ...because there was so much overflow. And they seem to think it happens again or will happen again—to fix all the dinning, the fallenness.

—No shit?

—I think. Not sure.

They all "looked" at Tu. Even small Quadri was wondering what Tu would say to that.

—First, said Tu. Crying and praying is *human*, that's why they cry and pray. Uh, if they are human.

—That, too, agreed Fabian.

—Anyway, I was with the physicist and his moral particle just now. They are still trying to figure out Smudge. So I wasn't there while you were all at church. (Tu)

—Fabe went, I didn't (Jay). HB and I were in the basement attending to Kelso and BruceE.

—Is there a mosk? asked Quad.

—But, continued Tu, it sounds to me like a blatant attempt to schematize particle physics with belief in God—which I don't think will work. For one thing.

Tu stopped. He tried to start—they could feel it.

Jay started laughing. —*Lookatit! He's thinking, It's never been done that way!*

—It's not real science, he said. If we could submit God to the numbers we might have something.

—Oh, said HB, like you mean Big Fello's not observable because trying to measure him would somehow change him? Because we don't know if he's wind or matter?

Pause.

—No doubt you would like me to admit something along the lines of: In the interaction between us and—or what used to be us—

that is, classical objects—between us and God; interaction would cause some sort of changes. So it won't wash because—

(Jay, still laughing.)

Tu finished, —It *just can't be.*

Laughter all around. Quad joined in even though he did not know why they were laughing.

—Besides, Tu went on, this is a category error. Fabian's idea about right and wrong for making coffee is, to use HB's term, "bogus" because so-called moral laws and physical laws are not in the same category.

—They are the same if breaking them is like breaking the law of gravity. (Fabian) We fall off a cliff and break. We do the deed and something breaks. Those bodies would not be there in the sewer if some laws did not get broke—the moral laws.

Tu was thinking.

—Very sad, said Jay. Fabian is making Tu think.

—You are actually saying, said Tu, that the laws don't break. They remain in place and everything material breaks—while the laws stay whole.... I guess I can concede that. Not without reservation, however.

HB tried to comfort him. —Don't worry if you're not getting everything right. Be like me. Be an unreliable character. So—did you pray with them, Fabe?

—Of course.

—Do any good?

—We'll see.

"Don't go, Dah," said Sheesh after moment. Gneis lay back, his head flopped against its brace. Rain sheeted over the windows in gusts, everything interior shone gray, a faint glim-dimness. A few floors below them, on emergency power, Kelso and BruceE were alerting police to discoveries in the basement.

"You think the—er—maulester architect is Pomala's smudge-face? You know, the blue-and-white nebula in Gneis's dream. Your dream, too. And does this mean the walls and furniture and particles and stars, and stuff, know stuff we don't? I mean, I'm not sure I see what you mean about the moral particle, but maybe I'm getting warmer? Colder? What?"

"I wish these damn lights would come on," muttered Berle. The hardware he'd been using remotely to view the condition of the lab was now off. He spoke up impatiently. "I'm sorry, boys. —I'm frustrated over these brownouts, blasted mess. I just want to get to work and we're all busted. —Want some tuna-fish?" He grinned.

"Nuts would be more fun." Sheesh turned to his brother. "I can mash some up for you. And make you a shake—don't worry a thin one—canned milk, though." He started out of the dim room past Berle.

"Berle said to them, "Again, I'm sorry. I am thinking about it all, believe me."

"No doubts!" called Sheesh as he passed through darkness into the faintly glowing living room. The screens were all dead dark but there was a candle and he took its brightness (held in a cup) into the next room. Floodescent lights not working in the kitchen.

Sheesh was disturbed and stood preoccupied in the doorway, candle in hand. He thought, *that must be what happened to Claude and GURlee when I blew it.* The candle's glow shed over the cupboards and appliances. No electric for the opener. No cans with ring-pulls. Slowly, absently, he went and fumbled in a drawer for the mechanical can-opener. He picked it up and sniffed to make sure it was clean. There was no using the dishwasher these days and he'd been getting a bit careless in the cleanup. And his hands weren't clean. City water *might* be kayoh, but the electric to pump, no. *Claude and GURlee.* He felt a strong wave like wet gusts on glass—deep regret coming through. Chilly, mourning, sad.

He sniffed again. Dah was going to get tuna-fish, but there was no mayo.

Oh! Yeah—mustard! He saw mustard in the cupboard next to stacks of canned tuna-fish. He worked the can-opener, but it had no purchase. Oh yeah, the broken one. " 'Slip-shod, slap-dash' he says." He rummaged for the new opener, wondering what would become of them if this one broke, too. Cheap junk, Dah said. BalOnion is "the sHoDDylAndZ," he says.

KO! Tuna-fish!

Now he was looking at pages—the papering—glossy on the wall above the counter beneath cupboards. An oily fishy smell wafted up from the can.

"I saw thin spires," (he read) "streams of white smoke ascending through heavy darkness. Paler than the surrounding thick smoky darkness, of which I still felt myself a part." Sheesh paused to read the words which he had seen hundreds of times. He had stopped reading these texts consciously, but was somehow often aware of them even so. Maybe because of the hand that had put them there.

" 'What are these?' "

" 'They are survivors. The A'ndyans teach them how to live.' "

" 'A'ndyans teach them?' "

"Yes. We live as all ancestors of everyone live."

After a minute Sheesh realized he had stopped making tuna-fish. Then he finished it up in a bowl, still reading, and reached into the cupboard for the colorful cardboard can of mixed nuts. *These are going to need a hammer.* ...And the only way he's going to get a shake is my shaking the can, pouring, and stirring in sugar....

No hammer. He got out the cutting board, poured nuts on it and began mashing with the bottom of the skillet (after checking for cleanliness).

This is not how our ancestors lived, he thought, grinding away at the nuts. He popped a filbert into his mouth. "But we're getting close," he said out loud.

"This is nuts! Sheesh announced, coming into the bedroom with the tray. "Want me to get you some canned milk, Dah? I forgot to bring you something to drink."

Berle was rather thirsty, but he said, "I'll just have a sip of yours if you don't mind."

"I think Gneis wants you to have some of his, too," he answered after a glance at his brother. He handed it over.

"So, so, so, have you got Smoke and Pomala figured out yet?" Sheesh could not help but be interested. However, he wanted badly to go play the game with the MACHOs but that was on hold no doubts. (Hopefully no worse than on hold.) "You were of course sounding off with Gneis on the particle in my industrious absence, correct?"

"No. I—we were talking about vesicles moving molecules to necessary destinations at the needed time. This all happens so minutely, yet it allows everything we—and our bodies—say the bloodstream, neurotransmitters, everything—to happen."

"Oh yeah. The 'our bodies are like cities and infrastructure waiting to happen' kind of thing."

"Exactly. Sort of. You've heard this before," declared Berle. "So, so, no bread happening around here?" he asked. He wolfed a mouthful of tuna-fish.

"Not lately, Dah. Did you get any of that molecule stuff from Gneis?

"The conversation was necessarily one-sided, but I think I did before. Get it from him...or someone."

The boys got the reference to their mother immediately.

Sheesh said, "Will the MACHOs be getting together for another go at BABY, do you think?"

"Not tonight, anyway," said Berle, hedging toward the bright side. Away from thoughts of Mam. "I hear your last go-round was better."

Because of nebula TOO, thought Gneis.

Berle was abstracted. He had watched a loop of lab doings, from before, of suited technicians, GeesliE helping Puce torque the rod clamped to the six-sided stacks in the super-cooling chamber.

But he was thinking now about his last view of the SiXPointz

163

lab. It looked KO. The CDMS detector (for detection of cryogenic dark matter) in the underground laboratory looked fine. The laboratory, in which they worked, cavernous and agleam with monitors, cables and heavy equipment looked fine. The super-cooling shaft in the floor for experiments on liquid-helium-cooled crystal germanium and silicon—all fine.

Everything looked fine. He just didn't see how to get there now.

Saying he wanted to give the Bopoiz a break, Claude came in later brightly dressed for the weather. Berle was KO with it; silently. Identifying who really was wanting this break.

"Have you eaten? We have tuna-fish and nuts," said the physicist.

Claude had fared better in the apartment several floors above, and so shook his head. His hair was longish, girlish-seeming, because he was so skinny and small. He asked Sheesh to help him go look for his mother.

"Outside? In the rain?"

Claude nodded. "Why I'm dressed like this."

"KO, fellow MACHO."

Sheesh looked at his twin lying back in the bed. "We'll tell you our adventure on return, M. Bolms. This will be known henceforth as the Case of the Missing Mother. —Is that good, Claude?"

But he sensed his brother wincing. He did not look at his father. Sheesh groaned but not aloud.

"Once we find her that will be KO," said Claude in his high piping voice.

"Yes. I know about that," said Sheesh. Claude's response was a relief after his painful blunder. "M. Burdock Bolms will be sifting the matter. It's our job to bring back more clues." He led Claude into his own room to don his knee-length rain jacket. "The more clues Bolms has the better. See, even any negative clues, meaning clues that don't exist, don't go anywhere, can be used in a process of elimination. Inspector DeStrade, where shall we begin," he said, throwing on his best Englic accent.

"Our apartment. It was flooded, but she may have gone back anyway."

Sheesh had his doubts but decided to say nothing and adhere to his own stratagem. It would give him time to come up with something. Not for the first time in the last several days he wished he could channel Gneis, whose abductive faculty was far superior.

GURlee was standing outside the door as Berle opened it

onto the corridor for them. She had not been about to knock, but was apparently just standing there—colored lights on her winking.

"Where's sis?" asked Berle, looking down on her. Meaning Gorgeeous. He looked past her toward either end of the hallway.

GURlee looked up at him. Her hair was stringy-wet, hanging in her eyes. She had on a bright green-and-yellow rain jacket but had neglected to cover her head with its hood. Her legs, clad in purple cotton, were soaked.

"Sis?" prompted Berle, moving back as she came in.

GURlee walked past into the candlelit living room. She stood still, then wandered into the tiny hall leading to Gneis's dim room. "Hello!" They heard her say, remotely. Berle shrugged and followed the other two along the corridor toward the elevator.

"Was that 'hello' for us, or Gneis," asked Sheesh after his father reminded him to go along to the stairwell at the end of the passage.

"Us, I think," said Berle, wishing she had not been alone... but it might be all right if Gorgeeous had gone upstairs... or something.

When the three got down to the level of the mezzanine they exited the stairwell and went to overlook the lobby. Shops were dark below and behind them, but people hung about, hoping for something or to get out of the rain, glaring at their devices, or clicking along, talking desultorily to whomever they could reach. Some even spoke to a person nearby, animated, but as often conversation was taciturn, morose. There were small children who ran about screaming gleefully, popping about, occasionally reprimanded by the distracted adult. Tall polymer windows let in light from the gray windswept downpour covering the urban neighborhood of SiXPointz.

Berle was going to leave, go back upstairs. He handed Sheesh a brumella and talked a bit with the teenager to get a sense of his plans.

"Limited." Sheesh's reply was cryptic. Then he said, "We'll just check out Claude's apartment first. Don't worry. We'll try not to do anything stupid and will stick together like butter-peanuts and jam.

Suddenly Berle spied Kelso below—gesturing slightly. Bespeckled, balding, in his security uniform, Kelso stared up at them quietly. He stood by the faux-paneled stairwell door, on the edge the dim-shiny lobby, looking up at Claude.

"Wait, guys! There's Kelso. Stop a minute." The escalator, to either side of the wide stairs, wasn't working of course. The boys were already hurtling down, self-propelled.

When they were all down, Kelso came over, thinking of

165

missing women, wondering what to say. To Berle he said, "Can I
have a word?" Obviously he did not want the others to hear just
what that word was.

"Sure," said Berle. "These guys were going out, anyway."

Kelso yelled as they hurried off to the revolving doors.
"Push hard on those doors!"

"What a mess," muttered Berle by way of opening the
conversation when they had gone. Kelso looked toward the
windows, rain sweeping over. The two men stood a while, watching
the boys standing under the portico. "There they go," said Berle at
last. "What's up?"

But just now the police were coming through. "The police!"
he said. Philipa, in regulation foul-weather clothing, was among
them.

"Yeah, that's what I wanted to talk to you about. Was that
the kid—Claude—I think his name is? —His mother's missing?"

Upstairs, GURlee sat with Gneis, staring at the gray rain
sheeting and blowing across the windows. Drooling, Gneis stared at
GURlee. From the corner of her eye she caught a glimpse of drool
sliding down onto his neck. She smiled back at him, hardly moving.
They both turned gaze to the window. Tiny lights, stationary, were
in the air across the way above, and on their level: Two glass
buildings visible from this part of the Kress Building. Those tiny
lights made it interesting. They could see mysterious dim glows out
there, some of them moving. But no people. They did not need to
see people for window lights to be interesting.

GURlee's wet sneakered feet and thin cotton-clad legs
dangled from the chair beside Gneis's bed. He lay back quietly,
reclining, not quite supine. They began kythHinG back-and-forth in
wordless mind-meld. Their kythHinG was more potent than what
usually passed between the twins. (Sheesh had to keep checking
with Gneis to make sure he had the right thoughts.) Now, for half
an hour the room was filled with eerie silence, while rain would
sometimes swoosh across the window, sometimes patter. Had the
exchange been laboriously filtered through word, it would have had
sounded:

*I've been in touch with strangers from another world. They
live far away in a nebula, I think it is, called Pomala-TOO. They know
things about us we don't know.*

That's interesting. Wish they'd contact me.

*They may have and you just don't recognize it. See if you can't
think about it sometime and try to kythH with them.*

What are they like?

Not sure. Sometimes they argue. They seem kidz like us only no bodies. They are awed by HiTopOLis— or they were. Now it seems to creep them out. They like playing BABY.

Yes. I think I know that. Yes. Didn't they actually help us get past the RAMBOs?

See, you do know them. Don't give up. Keep trying to understand them and you will.

A nebula? In our universe? The blue-and-white one with eyes you are showing me now?

That's what I'm wondering. You are getting some intelligence but I'm thinking— and even Dah may have had a dream about them or even from them—

Wait— what was his dream like?

[Gneis recounted for her how the items of Eartha had been conversing in Berle's dream.]

They seem to be part of everything. They know stuff. Like if something's going on in the hosPickle or the school or grocery store— and we have no idea — they know stuff.

Do they know we are kythHinG?

I'm not sure at the moment. But I think they can kythH with us. In fact, I think my kythHinG's improved since I became aware of them. I'm considering all possibilities. Maybe that's how they got here.

My kythHinG's better too lately. They seem... nice.

Kind. But I think they have a problem.

What's that?

Somewhere along the line there's been a mistake. They don't want to be here.

Why?

[There was a pause. They did not look at one another while kythHinG but out the window or at the ceiling, the walls.]

I think they have bodies elsewhere. Or something. Not sure. Maybe they want to get back to them... or in them or something. One of them has this job. TOO wants to be like Dah but thinks the moral particle is bosh.

Bosh.

Bosh.

I like that word.

If it's a word. [Gneis]

TOO thinks there's no such particle?

That's right.

Is there?

I don't know. Neither does Dah. That's why he's looking.

Why's it so important?

No idea.

Can BABY get born without it?

Don't know. But—

But?

KO. Morality is important.

KO. Claude and me are scared.

You didn't kythH about that.

I know.

[Gneis did not prod her. Without knowing why, he's known all along she was scared. The MACHOs and their families knew it.]

One of them, called Fab — short for Fabulous, I think — believes in Mind, kinda like Dah.

Does it have any meaning in our language?

Yes. I think Fabulous is related to fable.... In our language. Don't know if I have this right of course. You can see how difficult it is to understand what we don't know.

Who else is there?

J., who wants the job, and Brother Blake. And there's a little kid with them, maybe about your age, maybe younger. They watch over him. Especially Pomala. He scared too. Quadrangle I think he's called.

Do you think they'd watch over me?

They might. I don't know if they have any power to do that. They seem pretty powerless to me. Not like HatMan or SpriderWoman or TheFantasSeventeen, or anything. I think they are subatomic particles like us, only not put together. Extremely weak. We've got atoms, molecules and cells and synapses and stuff.

But you said they were everything.

But they aren't bodily coherent. Maybe they aren't a nebula here, but from another universe. That's what Dah thinks. The Pomala-TOO universe. That might explain it. Fit better with the physics. It may not be possible, but maybe he can help them get back.

It seems like the more we kythH... the more we learn about them. Does it seem like that to you?

Yes.

[He stopped kythHinG and looked at her. He started kythHinG again.]

Where's Gorgeeous?

I don't know.

[Gneis stopped again. He was not looking at her. He thought Dah should know this but he hid that thought. Again he began kythHinG.]

BABY will get born. If protons were even .3% bigger they'd be so unstable they'd decay out of being protons. If gravitons were even a little more powerful stars would be gone in an instant and life wouldn't have a chance. The force holding nuclei together? Any

stronger and there goes hydrogen, waters, stars— everything.
    BABY? The new...?
    Creation.
    Everything?
    Yes. And BABY will *get reborn.*
    [GURlee went round to the end of his bed and looked at him through strings of wet hair. She shivered. Except for the protection of her colorful jacket she'd been entirely soaked on her way over. Her eyes were gigantic, looking at him.
    Strengthless: Helpless: He frowned. He could only think of his mother, of Pegmo ... and now Gorgeeous. He hid his thoughts.
    GURlee began kythHinG. *It will be KO.*
    The eerie silence continued. The rain.

SiXPointz HiTopOLis

El-Chinso HosPickle

Before the arrival of the police, as Kelso and Berle waited for them to leave, Sheesh and Claude stood under the portico watching it drive down. Bouncing like bullets, rain swept across pavement, a few passing cars sending up breakers of spray. Sheesh looked back into the spacious dim lobby. Its light came from out here. He saw stragglers, estranged huddles, and Dah standing with Kelso from security, watching them. Sheesh wondered briefly what that was about. He looked down at Claude.

Claude raised his piping voice above the sounding wind and downpour. "I think that was maybe, maybe a blind."

"What was?" He looked again through the gloom at Dah and Kelso.

"My plan." Claude stopped.

Sheesh glanced at him quickly. "Explain."

"See. I don't think your Dah'd like us going where I really want to go."

"Which is?"

"So so I do want to go to the apartment. But *after* we go...." Then he said in a rush: "To the crematorium park."

"What!? What for?"

"That's where the bad man dropped us — me and GURlee. See, the police officer said it might help find Pegmo if I told her what happened. And that's how it ended." He looked up frankly, eyes tawny beneath his hood and fringe of bangs. "He flew down there and we got out. It was scary. We ran for the gate. I can't go back by myself but thought maybe you'd help me."

Sheesh looked away from Claude's inquiring gaze at the sleek petrol/electric car slowly passing.

"I'm not sure we should go there without telling Dah."

"Please."

A calm *please* from Claude was unusual.

Sheesh looked back into the dim lobby.

170

"C'mon, Claude. You don't know. Maybe he'd help us." But he thought Dah would not leave Gneis and GURlee. "He might take you and leave me here. What about that?"

Claude shook his head.

"Come on."

Claude looked determined, small dimpled chin out. "I can't chance it."

A passing car splashed them. Sheesh turned toward the door. Claude darted left into the rain, running down the sidewalk. Sheesh hurried after, hollering for him to wait, but Claude did not check his rapid, splashing scamper toward the intersection of SiXPointz. Sheesh caught up and grabbed his thin arm.

"Don't Claude. Don't. We'll do it together."

Cars passed slowly, slowly through storm water and sewer pools. Everything in HiTopOLis was slower; its cars sparser, its days darker. At the moment, there were no streetlights coming on like usual in the rain, no lights to the underground escalator, no lights to stop traffic. The electric grid in the city was operable, but power was rolling with periodic brownouts, blackouts, in neighborhoods. Drivers sought when and where to charge—but it was anyone's guess, save the infrastructure managers... who were not always trustworthy. Stewards of the grid were privy to information about when and where there'd be power; helping their friends and families with this knowledge.

Through hesitant traffic, Sheesh held Claude's hand as they crossed the intersection. At a stopped up sewer-hole beneath the sidewalk, they jumped a last puddle and Sheesh began a conversation with the little boy. He began a running pitch to ditch this plan. But Claude was walking up Change Street—no matter what—toward the crematorium gardens. When they got to the gilt wrought-iron fence and gateposts, Claude was about to slip through the opening between gate and palings. Then, hands on the palings, he stopped.

The pavement was slick, greenish, slimy underfoot. They both stood on the sidewalk staring into the murk. Beneath tall scattered trees—all within was gloomy and gray, thick with swiftly pouring rain. Brown wet grounds leaked streams through gray grass down onto the walk. Claude stared, hopeless. Then Sheesh felt some faint hope himself. This place, full of the running ashes of the dead (as spookily he thought it)—this place might conceivably squash this bad idea.

"Look, Claude," he said, tugging the boy's hand. "There's the police station."

Claude turned to look up at the building across the street. Behind long horizontal windows they saw ceilings reflecting dim

171

lights from screens. There were power and lights in the building. There on that floor, up there. Sheesh pointed.

"See, Claude. They will know better what's going on. You said yourself the police think you might have helped them."

The cars were slowing past. Sheesh continued. "What if we go over there and ask what they found out?"

Dah said Captain Clarke was good, but Sheesh didn't know if this was his watch. They looked up at the long dim horizontal windows from which Kent S. Clarke sometimes looked down at the dark spot surrounded by the lit sections of SiXPointz—lit on one of its better days. The little boy was shaking his head. They stood gazing only a moment, Sheesh in his gray kneelength rain jacket, Claude wearing more colorful gear. A gust of wind blew the brumella inside out. Sheesh turned it the opposite direction and it blew open right-way again.

Claude said, "They don't know anything. They told Mz. Bopoi so on the Quip. That's why I'm here."

"You don't want to go in there, do you? Not really. Be honest." Sheesh gestured back into the gloomy expansive park, shivering. "I'm telling you there are no clues in there. No one would set your mother down there, and she would have walked home if they did."

Claude looked up at him, suddenly hopeful. "That's right! She'd go home like I did. We can go there now. Thanks!"

Thanks from Claude was also the exception. Sheesh grinned down on him, relieved.

After the talk with Kelso and arrival of police, Berle trudged back up the stairs. He stopped once, peering down the spiral stairwell at uniformed comings and goings far below. Echoes, rumoring, came upward to his ears. Was it overkill? Was it real? Something in him quivered but he gave no outward sign. *First they pick up the clues, then equip the sewer crews to go down and bring up bodies from—wherever.* One thing was certain. The body-search crews would not be coming through this commercially prized glam building. Bodies would be brought up through some humanhole in the street, or some derelict building with tenants barely holding on to some roof, some shelter, and no heat, no lights, no—

He went on up the concrete stairs, trying to think, trying not to think. *Let's see. Yes. GURlee and Gneis.* Probably staring at the ceiling together. They do this thing. That something. That —

Don't be down there, Pegmo. Don't be—. Sheesh and Claude. Sheesh and Claude. Don't be down there, Pegmo. Don't be floating in your basement apartment. Be outside on the stairs, waiting.

172

Mary Bala Jones?

Ballerina! Oh Ballabeano! Princia-mia. The screens are dark! I've got to go read your walls all over again. Got to find the words: Pick up those threads once more. Those filaments, like mycelium— Eartha kept fertile. Filamentary neural networks, lit with electrochemical signals. Filamentous galaxies, cluster-bound, weaving the universe taut. *Mind thought about you and you were!*

Mary Bala Jones.

Berle yanked on the steel handle. *Oh my darling!* It broke off! clinking bits onto the concrete floor. Damdd steel handles not supposed to break! How would people get out of here? *My darling!!* He looked at it in his hand. At the holes for bolts and nuts. At broken bits on the floor. His face was wet. Wet. He stuck his finger in the side-hole and, curling, drew out the latch. *People need to get out. Get pipeduct tape. Prop the door till then.* Thankfully, there was the rubber wedge. He stepped into the carpeted corridor.

The universe is breaking. My darling!!

He was hearing Bala say the words: *The moral law is not superfluous but integral to infrastructure. There is no infrastructure without it, as necessary to it as gravity, in which force it also is bound. It is as necessary as all the physical laws so pertinent to our maintenance and well-being. Every human is a steward of both morality and his or her own particular—often by necessity ritualistic —duties. "Breaking" the moral law breaks everything in connection with it. The moral law itself remains, in the event, unbroken. But everything else falls apart. Or. —Will, beginning at the moment it is broken. Sometimes there is no evidence, maybe very little, at that moment. Repair at the moment of offense against this law is crucial and can prevent great damage.*

He heard Bala's voice saying this. His own Mary Bala Jones. She'd said it to him before. They'd had many conversations. Many conversations lit with her appearance. Her face serious, or smiling at the sticky polyurethane on her hands. The paintbrush thick with it. A wipe of her face with his hand, sticky. Getting it on her cheek or chin, she was. "These words must be important to you." He had laughed, just a touch mocking. Just a touch. Oh, he hoped, it was just a touch.

"You see, Claude," said Sheesh as they waited in the doorway of the El-Chinso HosPickle. The fix-it shop in one of the old buildings still standing in aristofied SiXPointz. Mz. Bopoi had opined that it would soon be gone. There was one block to go in the downpour, and then they'd be at the basement apartment of Pegmo and Claude. What was Sheesh going to do then?

But Claude had turned away from the rain and, face against

the dirty glass, was staring into the dark interior. Here's where GiZmo, the friend of Claude and Pegmo, worked. The little boy pulled on the handle, rattling. He peered into the gloom. Not open today. He wanted to ask, "Have you seen Pegmo? I only gave her a hug the other night."

"Claude," said Sheesh, raising his voice a bit. "Claude, remember what I told you?" Here was something to think of before they got there.

"Told me?" Claude turned and looked up at his face—gray, shadowed, mute, dim. "What?"

"You asked how the words got all over the kitchen and I told you?"

"You said your mother put them there?"

"She did, Claude. Our mother put them there."

"I almost remember her. She gave us choo-choos? She made them herself. But where is she? Pegmo told me not to ask."

"That's just it." Sheesh had never said it before. He had heard it. Dah had said it. Very fast: "We don't know."

"You don't?"

"What I'm trying to say...."

He stopped a minute, trying to channel Gneis.

"She had to have put the words on the walls and floors before she left," said Claude.

"They mean she didn't leave us on purpose. Let's think of Pegmo's words. I mean, let's think of stuff she told you."

"Will that help us find her?"

Sheesh frowned. His gray-glimmering hood was dripping on his face. "It might not. But so, so. I think.... Maybe it will bring her near. Maybe it will feel like she's here. That might be good, wouldn't it?"

Claude was silent, looking up at him.

He turned back to pull on the handle, stare into the brown gloom, seeing almost nothing; the corner of the counter where people would talk to GiZmo, put broken stuff for repair.

Flooring of the El-Chinso HosPickle was ripped apart, board by board. Bodies were being brought up—decayed, piecemeal or whole, some fresher than others, decrepit with chemicals. The count was being tallied, but this gruesome event was ongoing, and likely to take several days.

Kent S. Clarke had been working on the case. But he had not been informed of the imminent arrest. He would understand the reason why when he learned of it—which would probably be in a few moments because of the light-shining presence of shieL keeL, investigative reverb for *SpittinImage* and other reverb outlets.

Having conferred with shieL keeL, and acting with select members of the force on her own authority, Philipa charged through the Kress lobby and up many flights into the offices of the architect on the airy jutting top floor of the building. ShieL keeL (who had advised against the arrest as precipitate) was with them. Up here the architect came and went through an exit at the top of a short private stair, onto the rooftop where his vehicles were parked—always in readiness to take off. Here, high above HiTopOLis, was the glassed-in station with charging availability and his chauffeur ready (if desired). The architect would have been gone by the time these uniformed officers of the law had emerged into his suite if ideo in the stairwell of the building had been working. Or if the lock on a private stairwell door leading to the office penthouse had not been shoddy.

Philipa nearly screamed: "**[Name redacted]**, I arrest you in the name of justice for the abduction, torture and murder of Mary Bala Jones."

This news was not now unknown to Berle, Gneis, or any of the MACHOs and their families. Before all else, before any other source could expose knowledge of this atrocity, Philipa had told her friend Berle in private of its possibility. And he shared the devastating news with his loved ones and friends. They were avoiding all media for now.

There were of course other bodies, and perhaps other murderers. But Philipa was at pains *first* to make known, both to this city and to the great confederated continent-wide City of BalOnion, that the physicist's spouse was an innocent victim of kidnap, torture, and brutal murder through corrupted libidinous desire.

He sat tall at a polished granite counter where he worked simultaneously on several computer-aided designs and graphics, spread on gigantic screens along the wall. The architect jumped up in surprise, knocking over his tall red-leather upholstered chair, shouting at corner ceiling mics. "gOD™!! Come up here! gOD!!'

"gOD evaLL™ is being detained in his office as an accomplice, **[Name redacted]** (you BLANK-IT-EE-BLANK!!), and the world sees the arrest of you both. Remember that anything you say can and will be used against you in a court of justice!"

"If you get that far!!!" The architect had gone fuchsia-faced, sweaty, his outgrown spike-cut sticking out like gold quills on a hedgehog. He was in shirtsleeves rolled up, wearing a blue velvet tie clipped with gold and emerald clasp, winking. Making a vivid image in shieL keeL's QuipPad as, casually with a broad grin, she aimed it at him. He almost succeeded in wresting himself from the arms of the officers in trying to get at her. The grin, however, was almost entirely false. Put there for the purpose of enraging him. Of showing the watching world of SiXPointz, HiTopOLis; and the swollen great City of BalOnion, reaching its vast intricate tentacles of light into every corner of the dark continent over which it had spread... much as Father Domino had seen in his visions long ago in the wilderness of the Lost Nation.

"Cuff him! jeEves. Kristi Saaaers stay with me while we look around. Get them both up there—you and Worchester, WaTSon, get the chauffer to fly the big one. Nothing but that E-jet will go in this storm. Don't let them out until you land on the roof of SiXPointz station. I doubt he's got the basketballs to take a header into the city between here and there, but you never know. And keep those polymer pistols on him."

A moment they stood while—struggling in the arms of police officers—streams of invective poured out of him, fulminating, furious, impotent.

"There's no proof—NO shred of evidence against me! You'll be sued for false arrest and lose your place in the City. You and that thieving clown Clarke with the lot of you! Images he found are none of me! It makes no difference if sex or murder or whatever is on the deVice! I'm not there and never have been! So don't give me this, you **[invective redacted]**."

Philipa looked as shieL keeL, and then put out of hand to stay jeEves and the others a moment. ShieL keeL had nodded that it was KO to proceed: Her deVice was off. She laid it on the countertop were all his tools and gadgets were spread. Officers still held him, struggling, by his arms.

Her eyes hard and shiny as mica, Philipa could barely resist the energy in the room. In a small voice, she said, "I don't care. You're a predator. You turn sex into an atrocity." She got into his sweaty raging face and said, very quietly in a whisper he quieted to hear, "Maybe you did no torture, murder. I don't care if you are proved innocent or guilty in court. A lot of kidz are going to see, at least, the kind of monster you are and keep well away from you now.... And you can turn in your friends — whoever they are who did these evil things.... A ploy, maybe, yes. But effective. (You **[explicative redacted]**.)"

"Take hands off ME, **[redacted]**!!"

Hers had been a quiet answer, but his frenzy accelerated.

Claude and Pegmo, GURlee and Gorgeeous: They sat together in the latter's apartment—cuddling, each with his or her own family member. They had all been brought together on that fateful day when death and its evidence came to light in the Kress

Building. Pegmo and Gorgeeous were found by the boys on a
landing below the sidewalk on the basement stair outside Pegmo's
flat—huddling together under the metal awning, deep in
apprehensive conversation. Pegmo was injured. They looked up
through swift rain and yelped for joy on seeing the two boys. These
two young women had made determined and successful escape
together from the neon-lit *HouzzEz Of illRePute* in the next quarter,
LandLo cirCle. There was a chain of these brothels in the Great
City, and HiTopOLis itself had several, a few of which were tied to an
anonymous but infamous worldunder figure. Gorgeeous herself had
not been a worker. She had gone cover-under in search of Claude's
mother and there found Pegmo and two others; and together they all
escaped. That harrowing tale was told by them to police, but—more
potently—all over the media. So far major arrests were thwarted—
abortive, and miscalculated. Morale was either low or lying low at
area police stations. The hoped-for trial of the murderer of Mary
Bala Jones was not yet forthcoming. And the architect, falsely
arrested, was free.

"You're off the force, Phil," said Kent S. Clarke as she stood in
the cuboid on 2nd watch talking with him. Rain ran on its long
horizontal windows, nearly invisible but for the reflection of the
cuboid's screens—owing to the black hole in the cityscape made by
the Crematorium Garden Park across from them. Sparse lights of
SiXPointz lit edges of its dark, framing the pair in dim reflection as
they stood talking together.

"Yeah," she said looking at him, then away.

"It was all premature."

"Yeah.... Issuing my own warrants.... You knew you had a
boZo on the force."

"So it's my fault." He smiled.

"I'd do it again." Her features were dark. Baffling. "Chef,"
she said. No smile.

It was his turn to look away. Then back. After a moment he
said, "You'll keep your weapons license." They both knew why she'd
need it.

They stood for a moment looking at one another, saying
nothing.

At last she said, "I need a recommendation for the
consultant's license."

"I can't do that."

He held out a white envelope.

She stood staring at him. Then looked absently at the
proffered envelope. "What's this?"

"My recommendation for the investigative license."

Slowly she reached out, took it. "I thought you said...."

"That was the 'consulting.' This is for the straight private investigation."

"I didn't think I could *get* that one." She opened and glanced over it."

"There's a file in your messages, too. But yeah, depending on who's examining applications you may get that one. It's in the covering file—when and to whom you apply. ...But you've got it backwards—as usual. Now, shieL keeL. I'd give her one for the consulting, but you—you'd do fine in straight private investigation. Especially if you consult shieL keeL."

"I see," she said, chastened.

Then, "You know I'm glad to have it, chief. *That's* the work I need."

"You'll do fine."

"Like you said."

"—So it'll be my fault if...?"

She grinned. "ShieL keeL's not the only one I'm gonna consult."

ShieL keeL had stopped using side-by-side interview clips of the architect. It was global viral now. Her independent status had facilitated this showing of the arrest coupled with their previous interview—witnessed by Gneis in the Kress Building lobby. But she wanted to keep her contract with *TrivialTryst* and other news outlets. It would run viral for sometime. Every time some parent worried about their offspring—there was another hit. Somewhere. And another. The monster wasn't vanquished, but he was known. Everyone looked away. Or stared. And gave him a wide berth. Even changing his jewelry and 'do did not completely disguise him.

The chain of *HouzzEz* was said to be under investigation, but it would take time before anything came of it. In the meantime, workers were considering their options, and meeting regularly. They spoke of ionizing. However, they are cautious. The worldunder would try to infiltrate any such ion, and seize power if they could.

It was probably there in Fodder Domino's manuscripts, said Berle. DoomDaZe were on their way, but.... On their way, he said.

s. dormAn

WIMPs Discuss Their Lost Bodies

The WIMPs were concentrated in the crematorium gardens. Site, in the other universe, of the graveyard from which they had vanished.

—Now what? Physics doesn't seem important to Barrel anymore. (Jayrai).

—Review, suggested HB. How did we get here? Get out our nonexistent fingers and count the ways. Ways we might have got here besides that detector thing. We had bodies, right here, only in the opposite universe. But where'd they go? We daid yet?

In their parallel home universe, persons of Jayrai's ancestry, believing in reincarnation, were yet (in many places) cremating familial leavings under the open Nandian sky. Although the WIMPs were unaware of their alternate universe Western history of this practice, some of them — Pomala and Fabian (the only members of the FivePoints gang of Western descent) — were later to learn that, historically, a political struggle was in process around the time of their own 1900 CE. In which, persons wanting to cremate loved ones were at first prosecuted, then set free as law caught up with demand for established practice. Hence, in the Akropolis universe, the *Act of Cremation* was codified into law in 1903, and safety requirements for this process imposed. At that time, members of Fabian's faith dominated the culture and made complete use of the rationale that God, upon the resurrection, could raise ashes as well as dust from dissolution, bestowing new life. Pomala's ancestors also believed, being of the Orthofax faith. The great-great grandfather of the WIMP whose real birth name was Blake Griffin (HB) was saved from the rioting mob, and unjust execution, by the Papist prayers of family and friends. Or so, after overhearing their hymns, he found himself believing. These ancestors, therefore, also believed much as Fabian's and Pome's.

179

SiXPointz HiTopOLis

It was raining, dark, and spookily numinous for anyone in the SiXPointz neighborhood brave enough to enter these dark grounds. It was a sodden foliaged grassy space; lambent with scarcely lit dimness from remote edges of the park. WIMPs combined also in hulking, hunched black shapes called trees—now mere shadows.

—Right. We had bodies, at the Glimmerdale Cemetery—probably on this spot in the alternate, said Fabian. But I don't think we died. However, one of those bodies had a hand, holding onto a little girl's hand because—Why did you do that Pomala?!!

Jayrai said, —HB seems to think—*I* think he thinks it had something to do with the Grandmaster, or Showmaster or whatevah, from the 1900 CE traveling show. Why do you think that, yo? You're not actually sharing anything about it, HB.

—But you see, Pomala said; the little girl couldn't possibly get the help needed in 1900 CE because they didn't know about autism then. They didn't even call it CE but A.D. (whatever that is). They also didn't have rape counseling which she badly needed. But, again, I regret it and apologize, and wish I could do it all over again... I mean *not* do it all over again.

—Because (HB) —Big Fello completely renovated a very bad situation, like a good showman would. They'd been having riots, iirc. He'd be good at fixing these flubs. Good at incorporating them into the show. I was brawling in Paddy's and they were killing us, remember? (He felt their negation, them shaking their heads.) And, I don't know how I knew this, but the Big Fello went by outside in the gaslight on a gigantic white horse and changed everything back so we could get out of there and nobody was hurt and—

—But why did he change everything if he did? (Fabe)

—Because I called him. I didn't even know the man but he was coming past and heard me, I guess. I may have seen him out the corner of my special CossycSystems eye? Actually, I don't know how I knew he was there. He's Magic, you-hear-what-I-say.

—The Hadesthon? suggested Tu. It's on the list. Remember, we were playing the Hadesthon initially in 2017 right outside here (Tu indicated the glimmering palings out by the street where, remotely, a few cars slowed by, wipers swiping).

—The Hadesthon, said Quad quietly. He was longing to play that game again.

(HB) —Still magic, Tu, Dr. Scientist.

—I was trying to fix that, doing calculations before time ran out—11 p.m. 1900 CE by the clock.

—And you finish the calculations just as the battery ran out. And we were all situated on the stone wall right out there (Jay)—

—Right where it should be FivePoints Akropolis in the home

180

universe instead, and Pomala got off and grabbed the little girl's hand. Yes, you had a reason, yes you regret, yes you apologize but. Why did you do that?!! (Fabe)

(HB) —Here's something: maybe it was Pluto. Remember they downgraded Pluto when I was a little kid. Maybe he was mad, the god of the underworld, and since we was playing his game he tricked us — it was those guys in LA we were playing. Sort of a devil in the machine. How about that?

—Oh please! How far are we getting with any of this, asked Jay. *Because we could go on speculating all night.*

—And, (Tu) keep extending the field of cause-and-effect exponentially, *ad infinitum.* We can't know what's going to happen by a particular choice acted upon. Even a small one. Apparently every time a person does something the cosmos is changed.

(HB) —It's not easy finding our universe again even though it's only a couple millimeters away—say you.

—I wish I could say I don't care anymore, but I do. If only.... (Pomala) One thing we forgot was the Native Americles. They were the only ones who seemed to fit in when the city was gone. Remember that? Outside the tomb? It was right before we got here and the A'ndians were in the tomb, too. That must mean something. Then they ended up with the little girl, after all. Weren't they in the traveling show?

—Twice right, said Jay.

—And they couldn't help her in the Stone Age or wherever it was. They just seemed to think she belonged to them. She wasn't an A'ndian, though.

—It's beyond us, said Fabian. The whole thing is beyond our capability and *that's* why I say,

—Get down on our knees and pray, I know, said HB. But I got no kneecaps anymore. Maybe it's too late for that.

— We *can't* give up, said Fabian.

Quad whispered, Don't give up. His small thought was coming from everywhere. The battering rain, the shadowy dimness, hulking shapes, flickering residue of city lights in a tumultuous, chaotic time, an alien place.

— On top of all this, said Tu, the south solar pole was to change polarity next month. In the Akropolis universe.

—And Fabian wants to blame me for taking the little girl's hand! —It's like we can't do *any* good.

—Seriously, said Jay. Please don't try to tell us what the polarity change means in any of this, Tu. —A.D. or CE? No— stop! But look, we helped people here though, didn't we? We helped them with BABY. We helped with creeps and criminals. We helped people bond. Maybe Pome wasn't so far off with her help. But really, I want someone to help *us*. We've got to try budging the physicist out of his funk —

—Funk!? You're choos-choos, Jay. *That's grief.* (Fabian) What are we going to do about that? I'm still saying, and I think Quad will agree with me, that prayer is the answer. Okay maybe not prayer, but God. We've got to ask God to help us.

—Oh no... (Pome). I just thought of something.... It's bad, too....

—Worse than this? (HB) I don't think so, white thang.

Pome said (slowly, thoughtfully), What if—say—we do get back. It might be... —What if it's at the same point in time as when we left... and... we don't remember any of this and... I make the same mistake...?

—No worries! (HB) Do you see how sunk the Barrel-man is?—WE AIN'T GETTING BACK!!

—Pome, Pome, said Fabian. I take it all back. Forget what I said about the little girl. I mean it. I repent and apologize. I'm never bringing it up again.

—Pray, said Quad.

—But, said Jay, where are our bodies? Are they just lying there outside the tomb in the Stone Age? In a coma? Which time frame—CE, A.D.? What?

Tu said, —There are enough of body particles right here as an alternate. But I think that's something we can't deal with in this universe. So the main point now is the physicist. You did some good earlier, Pomala. Maybe try something like that again.

HB groaned. —What do you mean—enough body particles here? From the cremations? Is that part of us now—I mean us part of that, burnt bodies?

—In a way. Forces moving interactions of elementary particles—. If there's dark matter—this has not yet been proven—it's abundant enough to effect waving but possibly never enough to make protons and neutrons. So that is theoretical and debatable. Mass between galaxies far outweighs their visible materials. Something like 40 times as much, something like 300 times more than what's in stars, total, and the rest of visible matter is gas so WIMPs dominate but aren't confined to —

— Oh-no-the-info-dump-head-back-to-the-bleachers.-Get-off-the-field!

Over the course of the next hour they heard the Teenage-Mutant-Ninja-Giraffes' version of dark particle physics (during which HB wondered how it could then be called physics), ending with Tu's reminder that theoretical science was not trying to find explanations for undiscoverable unreal things, but to discover and formulate real things for human understanding.

—That's reassuring, said HB when the dump was done.

—So all this HiTopOLis people-ash here has nothing to do with us? asked Jay.

—It might. If we were next door, said HB, but we're not.

(Fabian) —So science is God's info-dump on Creation. Except for the unproven stuff that moves things around — It's all dust like you said, Tu, or I think you said. Just like in the Garden of Eden.

—No, said Tu. That is a *story*. Therein lies the difference. Science is not a story. Science is systematized knowledge comprising testable explanations, predictions, and applications, aided by mathematics (also a science), incorporating logic, statistics, thermodynamics, continuum mechanics, plasma and atomic physics—

—And another data dump is launched! (HB) *Zzzzzzzzzz*.

(This dump cataloged and subdivided, and sought examples and attribution for various branches.)

Meanwhile Pomala and Jay (like the others) were only half-listening. These two were considering the little family huddled in the candlelit room4living partway up the Kress Building.

Father Domino and Leaping Fawn stood in the dim smoky cloud above, dressed in robes of pale chamois leather, looking down on the gigantic alien crystal children—as these sought to understand all they were part of and wondered how they would get home. Back into recognizable bodies. From where the priest and the maiden from Lost Nation stood—gazing with love and respect upon them— the Giants looked colorful, faceted, shining, with various distinct crystalline colors, glowing and flashing as they moved. The WIMPs were as immortals, lounging and at ease.

At the behest of mindful forces toward a sector of the great *City of BalOnion*, this maid was gathering rain, rain glimmering with subdued light. As each individual droplet spun from her fingers (held each to its spherical form by sturdy bonds of attraction and atomic interweaving): glistering torrents lashed downward, composed of pre-materials, according to laws devised in *Mind* forever beyond comprehension of peoples, however mindful; peoples made almost solely of cosmic dust. Created from self-Sacrificing and no other force. The *exNihilo* from which all other laws, forces, particles, babies, and bodies derive.

Jayrai and Pomala focused in the apartment of the physicist, completely engaged by script on walls and wooden flooring of its kitchen. The polish was off, but the floor was more of a designer experience. Letters and words had been cut from veneer, inlaid, and arranged to attract the eye. However, by such designing, they were harder to read—of various size, font design, and configuration. The color scheme was virtually monochromatic in bronze on beige background, in shades of each. Jay, especially, was fascinated by these floors. Pomala looked intently at sections of the wall, making neither heads nor tails of plain print.

—It's all geek to me, she said. She kept at it, however, so interested was she to see that people had bothered to exert such effort at communication.

—They must mean something. They *must* be words, whatever their meaning. I think we got that the boys sometimes read them. We saw Sheesh reading aloud that time.

—Sheesh? (Jayrai)

—The one that walks. He's not as good at E.S.P.-KyThingg as his brother.

—Aren't they the Fodder's words? asked Jayrai.

—They are, declared Pome. I think his Dah's got them in the digital memory banks, too. The screens in the living room. They are supposed to be historical documents, or copies of historic docs, maybe inked on pigskin or something.

—So they played football back then? With the First Peoples?

—Hoho.

Pomala tried reading another wall. —Stuff here I don't understand about under the city.... Don't think the Fodder gets it either. Lots of works and busy-ness way way down there, remember? We saw way under the sewers and outskirts? Maybe he doesn't know how to put it. Can't tell.

She came back to the first wall. There was silence as the two scanned and considered.

—This is odd, said Pome after a bit. ...I think I'm actually getting some of it.

—No! Really?

—One is starting to read like a primer for primitive living.... Here's how to catch and prepare something. Porcupine, I think. It's prickly whatever it is.... Tells how to approach... flip.... Takes two kids or one adult with a heavy stick.

—Way! you got all that? Amazing.

—Supposedly it's delicious in maple syrup.

—No!

—This Fodder guy is something. He makes his own clothes out of skins.... But he has to take handouts. Doesn't like dealing with them.

—With critters?

—He's got this friend. Dancing Deer, or something. Or is it Sleeping Deer? She helps him a lot. Sometimes she's called Elsewise, or Elsewhere.

She was silence again, reading.

—Over here he's talking about the stars.... This is really weird. He's talking about a star cloud or galaxy or something called—guess!!

—Jelly bean?

—No.

—Pajamas?

—No.

—George W. Q. Barbesque?

—Pomala!!

—No!!

—Yes.

—No!!

—Yes.

—No!!!!

—Pomala. For real. But looks a bit different from my name, except the description is sort of Gneis's dream-me, like blue and white clouds studded with stars. So that's how I know.

—We gotta tell somebody! HB! Guess what?! Fabian! Pomala says she's in this wallpaper!

—I thought we agreed on us being wallpaper already, said HB. He was bored of the ash-yard, bored with the info dumping, bored with himself, but willing to be excited if possible.

—No no. I mean she's mentioned in *words* on the wallpaper.

—It's not me—it's the dream me. Like in the dream I gave Eelie only a bit different. Here it's the name of an actual something or other in space. See, it was written hundreds of years ago by the Fodder guy. The physicist should reread some of this stuff. It's almost prophetic. Like with *Madam Swahili of Astonishing Supernatural StagePlay*. Remember that?

—Kinda. I was hoping it might be real, though, said HB. Like the *DigiOuija*.

—HB, that's not real either, said Fabian. I think even Tu will agree with me on this.

(Tu) —Yes, but I don't agree with you on the other. Both solely stories, neither is science.

HB stopped. He said, —I think you both should consider that we—what-I-been-sayin'.... We. Are. Supernatural.

Dead silence.

After about an hour, Tu ventured, —Maybe sub-natural.

—So so so anyway. Infra-natural or ultra-natural—how is my Dah going to help? He believes in Mind but I don't think he gets this other stuff. People as dark matter? Weakly Interacting Massive Particles—people? He thinks you're furniture.

Live silence.

185

Everyone together: —Who said that?

—Thanks for finding her, said the thought.

—Should we tell him we didn't know she was one of them?

(HB)

— One of the sewer bodies? (Jayrai) *Who* was one?

(HB) — His mother.

— *Contac,* said Jayrai. I mean, *ConSmack.* How 'bout that,

Tu?

s. dormAn

The Mediums

—Girls, we've got ourselves a medium. (HB)
—I don't think we should call him that. (Fabe)
They were "looking" at Tu.
—Uncanny....
—Uncanny?! That's it? What kind of science is that? We're looking to you for the science, Tu. (Jayrai)
—Are you still with us, Gneis? I'm Pomala.
Silence.

They concentrated on Gneis' bedroom. It was silent now, but for the lashing of rain on the windows—by the bed with its small shriveled form. They were silent. The room was filled with silence. And the family of Mary Bala Jones. GURlee and Gorgeeous huddled quietly in a corner, sharing a chair, trying not to take up space in the small apartment bedroom. Dah sat beside Gneis's bed, the tray-table pushed off to one side by the window. Tears fell slowly from Berle's eyes. He blinked them off, head down. His big freckled hand, lit with a few reddish hairs, gently clasped that of Gneis. A frighteningly withered hand, thought Gorgeeous, looking full sadness on them.

—I guess there's nothing more I can do for you, Dah, said Gneis.

No response. Berle the physicist didn't seem to hear him.

Gneis seemed still with those in the room. There were long moments of silence.

"Sheesh, Sheesh," whispered the man. "Gneis...."

Sheesh stood tall and lithe, rust-blonde hair, crisp, fresh and young; close beside his father. He moved closer, leaned his thigh and torso on the man, reaching out to cover the two hands with his own. His father's big hand. His brother's was like bird's toes but it's flesh was silken.

The FivePoints Akropolis neighborhood gang went back (in mind) toward the kitchen.

—Let's wait in there a bit, said Pomala.
—What'll we do now? (HB)

187

—What's wrong? asked Quad.

—"He ain't daid yet," said Jayrai, quoting HB.

—Are we daid? asked Quad. He did not know. —Was he supposed to be scared now?

—I can't tell if you're dead or not (Gneis). Maybe you *are* sub-natural WIMPs.

—Does any of this mean you won't be our medium? (HB referred to the grief and separation.)

—I'd stay and talk but *this is joyful.* We've got somewhere else to be now. But, so so, you *are* misplaced. You've been a big help, though. Thank you.

The room was suddenly empty, as though a big blow from the storm outside had swept life and everything away. They felt it all pull apart, vanish, emptying.

—What happened to everything?! said the WIMPs.

—I'm told it'll be back again, said Gneis remotely. And he was gone.

—Uncanny. (Tu) Everything is gone but we're still, we're still ... we're....

—Some scientist, said Jay. *Now* what do we do?

—We can't go back in there once it all comes back, said Pome, referring to the bedroom. Too much sadness, grief there.

—They'll be paralyzed. (Fabe)

— Uncanny, said Jay, echoing Tu. He isn't paralyzed any more but now *they* will be. This is crazy. Crazy.

— Here it is again like he promised, said Pome. And she was reading the kitchen walls once more.

The "work" of the crematory was ongoing even in these times of storm. A history of the HiTopOLis world (reported on by shieL keeL) showed cremation performed upon a pyre under the open sky, or amid primal woodland by settlers from over-the-sea, who learned it from ancestors and their great myths. Ongoing storm over BalOnion (a continuous 39 days altogether) did not dampen the burning of dead bodies in commercial furnaces. To transform corporal leavings into particulate and vapor, an equivalency of $3m^3$ of hydrocarbon gas is used these days. Thermally designed to maximize consumption and repress emissions, smoke, particulate, and odor are minimized but not eliminated on the memorial grounds (especially beautiful in former days), for the quiet meditation of mourners. However, in these days of rain, few came here to mourn. Most were content to remain at home, and dry if possible, during cremation of loved ones.

This was shieL keeL reporting in her feature on the subject sometime back. Much energy, she said, is consumed in vaporizing the water content of bodies. A body of medium build, or 68 kg of flesh, has 65% water content, requiring 100 MJ of heat energy to combust. According to shieL keel's report, in which the viewer toured the primary and secondary chambers to watch an anonymous body being burned, combustors are shielded in refractory ceramics. The first chamber burns hot enough, between 760 and 1150°C, to vaporize the body's water, drying the organic remains. During transfer to the secondary chamber organic leftovers are oxidized in the higher range and it is here that pollution controls deal with smoke, particulates, and odor.

ShieL keel was a while in the production and showing of her feature on cremation. *Virtual Futures* feared for its advertisers until the SiXPointz Crematorium Association itself stepped in to subsidize, on its advertising budget. It was thought a familiarity with the process might ease people into it, promoting its popularity. Evidently the grounds were formerly a cemetery and bodies yet interred remain 6 ft. (as it was then called) under the immaculately-tended surface. Those wishing ash-burial in the new park were placed in small golden, silver, or brass containers just beneath the surface. Or scattered from blowguns as dust on the lawns. In the process, however, it was well-known, virtually nothing remained for these containers. Heat recovery networks throughout the SiXPointz infrastructure economized the process.

Today, only a few come to mourn. The little family and faithful friends of the physicist stand in the storm beneath the furnaces to witness, as is the custom, the joint scant material passage of their loved ones. Above, on the wind—young Gneis and the murdered Mary Bala Jones.

Berle, head bowed beneath the brumella he shares with Sheesh, does not look up as electronic bells signal the passing of these remains into the elements of earth and sky. And his eyes are wet. Wet. These beloved materials. Materials of a species' making and remaking, since the BIRTH OF BABY™ —as the process of cosmic evolution was known in the game of Berle's devising.

If only I had studied vesicle traffic, the genetic material required; disentangled protein information for vesicles to fuse and transfer; the neurotransmission from one cell to the next. Why physics? The useless quest, the frivolous, the worthless. How can it matter?

—"Matter." Ha-ha. Gneis laughed. The glowing flashing crystalline giant. He had been revealed to some in the Crystalline Universe as Gneis the Crystalline Giant, but not to them here in this basin of tears and groans.

Berle, head bowed beneath the brumella, went on grieving.

Biology. Biochemistry! I might have helped him. Deliver. Fuse,
nerves firing. Trigger enzymes and hormones. Oh for precision,
control that cellular cargo to reverse, block, truncate! that disease.

The little dark group stood small beneath the massive,
minimalist, boxy, top-heavy structure of the crematorium. Covered
in dark waterproofs and big dark brumellas, looking at their boots
and sodden sooty grass. All the MACHOs and their adults, grieving
the loss of their friends on the margins of towering black drenched
leaves, limbs and trunks of seemingly careless trees.

Sheesh said, "Yeah, Dah, it's true that mutant genes cause
pile-ups in cells, and proteins bind with precision... but Gneis is
still, so so, *Gneis*, right?" At the stocky men's elbow, Sheesh said it.
This fodder looked up at his son. How did he get so tall? When?

"How did you know that? I mean I thought you didn't go in
for it?" His pale eyes were wet, looking up. They gleamed in the
glimmer of vapor and rain. Falling. Falling.

"So so, Dah, Gneis told me of course. I still don't go in for it.
You don't need to either. You're into something else.

How'm I doing, Brah? asked Sheesh.
—Not bad. Better, I think, said Gneis.
Where are *you, anyway?*
—What do you mean? I'm right here.

The WIMPs were too sensitive to join them in sympathy there
beneath the architect's dream of top-heavy building, great dim trees,
the smoke and rain. Grieving was for others, not themselves. Time
passed.

—Gneis doesn't grieve either, said Pomala.
—But, unlike us (HB) he's like—
—Like hugely *happy*. (Jayrai)

They had decided to wait it out in the dim kitchen, where the
only light was rain, rain-light. Just barely light. There was one
window, not so big as in other rooms of the physicist's apartment.
The WIMPs focused themselves there, not concentrated in any
particular *thing*. They were not, for instance at the moment reading
the walls, or aware of the stinky bacteria of food preparation stations
not quite clean (to a sense of smell. And of course, the smell, say of
bodies or kitchen bacteria, was lost on the WIMPs because they were
but part of that smell themselves without the mechanism of
nostrils.)

After a bit Fabian said something to Tu. —Science has given
me no reason not to believe in God. It's shown me designs and laws
and stuff. The ultimate mystery—? Science can't answer that. Tu,
don't think I don't appreciate your science lectures because I do.
What I can get from them, that is. I learn something every time you

talk, but details sometimes get lost afterwards. Anyway, I've got one for you. It's evidence (not proof, I know) of God. What does science have to say? Or can it say, about this evidence?

—What's that? (Tu, but he saw it coming.)

—Life. What's science say about that? You know. The breath, breathing in and out of us, comes and goes. And don't ref the mechanics. It's not just that, and you know it. So what is it? Gone from those bodies, those ashes, that dust.

HB said, —Maybe life's like spontaneous combustion. You know, like when your grandpa or somebody forgets they got a pile of rags with paint thinner on them closed up in the back alley shed, and, ba-Boom, no more shed. Or alleyway. But plenty of life hopping around trying to put the fires out. How 'bout dat?

—No no. (Jayrai) —It's when a lightning bug lights on some amoebas or molecules or something ... and there's another lightning bug and they hump and have a high old time.

—They're already alive, though, said Fabian.

(HB) —You're turn, White Thang. More on life. Quick before Tu dumps his load.

Pomala was reading again. She said, —Here the Fodder has long poems on the Great Maker breathing into them—Evan and Adan. This is like our xianity only they got emotion, intellect, and will—no souls or psyches or whatever.

Finally Tu said, —Those could be the same thing.

—Which? she asked.

—All of it. All the same thing. They became people — with psyches—in the story, that is.

(Fabe) —So we say God's breath made dirt live after it was shaped into people.

Tu said, —The great evolutionist said we needed to think of matter's origins first. And we've been doing that. (Yes, he did leave room for a breather/maker but we're pretty much past that). I don't say there can't be, *can't* be. We aren't there, however. And, like I said, a story is not even evidence.

Fabian "snorted." —A story is evidence of a storyteller.

—Yes, but not a story-telling god.

—No-no. I mean there are no stories without *some one making* a story. Out of stuff already in existence, yes. But my point is *something has to make*! The chair can't spontaneously come together! Even a molecule has—

—Stop! (Quad. Evidently he thought Fabe was shouting.)

There was silence. Pome was reading.

HB said, —I think they came in and went to bed.

Jay said, —Who? the grieving? The breathers?

Tu continued. —We do have believable—I mean plausible—

191

chemical operatives which might *conceivably*— (snort from Fabian)
—permit of biomolecules—even RNA—to bootstrap naturally. When
chemistry established self-replicating cellular metabolic energy-
capturing....

(Dump proceeds.)

When Tu paused, Fabian said, I almost wish I could talk like
that about Life. But you're actually showing us—

—That science ain't got the same *umph* as story, finished HB.

—I was going to say it's got *nothing*, said Fabe.

—But (Tu) at least it's willing to start with that.

—OK, that's good. (Fabe was mocking, just a bit.) It's where
xianity starts if you think about God's sacrifice.

—If you've got something to sacrifice it's still *something*, said
Tu. I don't mean—I mean in this it's not *nothing*.

—And "Two negatives equal a positive," said Jayrai. So you
need another negative to add to this, Fabe.

—If you're God you're everything, and if you self-sacrifice,
everything including yourself becomes nothing. But let me ask, Tu,
if it will be evidence if we end up back home?

—Of God? Evidence for me? We got *here* (sort of) and that's
still not evidence.

—When you say "me"—that's subjective! You admit—

—Nothing. Yet.

(HB) —Which nothing you talkin' about? The nothing you're
not admitting, or the nothing everything came from?

—Know what I just noticed? (Jayrai) Fabe, you never use to
talk like this, while you, Tu, talked like this—if you talked, which
wasn't lots, but y'know. I mean on all this heavy-duty believing
science, believing prayers and stories.

—Maybe because we've never been in trouble like this,
suggested Pomala (still reading).

—They been undergoing personality change (HB). I heard
this could happen under drastic measures—like being super-
naturalized overnight.

—Overnight! Like in an instant! (Jay)

—Sub-naturalized. (Tu)

—Sub, supe, no dif, said HB. We in the soup sure'nuff. Have
you got it figured out yet, white thang?

—What figured out? asked Fabian.

—The Fodder's got some clue? (HB) Just let us know and
we'll shoot the words straight into his haid.

—The physicist is busy, said Fabe. We need the Real Fodder.

—Seriously, Fabe, he's got some stuff here. (Pomala) I think
he might've had a direct line. OTOH, I don't know. Sometimes I get
confused, seems contradictory in places. Like under the window,

where he says the Maker carries everybody around with him in his pouch and that's why he made people — to be carried around with him. But then, over here under the corner cupboard, the Fodder has him saying people have to carry him around with them — and *that's* why he made them, so they'd carry him around. Or here, where religious A'ndians called him "killer god," but over here they've got all these loving poems about him and what he's like. Like he's got two different characters, almost like different people are telling different stories about the Maker. —I mean, see here where they say the *Ground Crater* is called the Maker, and here he destroys what he's made. And look—well—some of its not so serious ... like what things are made out of: Here it says threads from cats, and, over here, everything is made out of stuff that has disappeared.

HB said, —So apparently books are unreliable narrators. Even history books.

(Tu) —Stories all the way down. You can expect that from stories, but not science. And, btw, a lot of that is because the compilation has different tellers; and things being copied, passed around, copied again by others, translated into unstable languages — languages are always changing via inputs and corruptions. You can't expect a literal unerring meaning out of all these old things. You've got morphology, inflection, phonology, semantics and syntax. Things change from tongue to tongue, then you don't always know what you're getting.

—Fabe? Everyone focused on him at once.

—OK, OK you got me there. But.

—But? Everyone focused on Fabe.

—I'm saying God is a person. We're persons made by God, and can ask God—who greater?—for help. You know we need help. So let's ask the greatest Person there is for help.

Tu said, —I could bring one good argument for this but then you'd say, "the fall," and we'd be back at stories again, deadlocked.

—Yeah, but I'm saying we aren't, and haven't even *ever been*, humans *yet*, and you're saying—

—We're only human. (HB) Being bad is what it means to be human. So forget all that 'n' let's concentrate on FivePoints, getting back to FivePoints. I'm tired of being a bad smell, you-hear-what-I'm-sayin'? I want to actually *smell* instead of being a nothing that's part bad smell. C'mon, Pomala. Wha'cha got?

—Not that, I guess. Not yet. I looked at the *Pomala* place a couple times and can't quite figure her, or it, or them, out. I mean, she seems to be saying or doing something important, but I'm not sure. Or *what*, even. OTOH, I think there might be something for the physicist on the "what if" question. If that's true, we might be able to use it for bait to get him thinking of other realms—I mean *our* realm. Akropolis, Americle, the other universe.

—Bait? "What-if-there's-a-moral-particle"—*as bait*? Jayrai was a snort.

—Yeah, anybody can see that what-if-moral-particle is way better bait then fresh food, heat, lights, ice cream, and sex, said HB.

Jay said, —How bout fame 'n' glory? Anything bout that in there, Pome? Maybe there's a fame'n'glory molecule or something. If I remember biology right, molecules are part of cells and cells can work themselves up into muscles and stuff. That might interest him.

—Sex, said HB.

—That's not quite as great as you might be imagining, Jayrai returned with what he could think might've been a particular challenge in her nonexistent eye.

—What do you mean? How else d'we get here?

—Here? By Magic.

—Both. Wrong. (Fabian said this.) The man is dead to the world. None of that will work.

But Jay was not letting it go. —You're really thinking the purpose of BABY is sex. (Sarcasm)

—The purpose of sex is BABY, said Fabian.

Reading the walls, Pomala murmured agreement.

—His "what-if" is covered over in grief and grief is not even a thing. (Fabian)

—It is an emotion. (Tu)

—An emotion is no thing.

—It's caused in the psyche by things. (Tu)

—No, it's not.

—Classical, or natural, events impact on corporeal functions, producing grief, for instance in neurological and pulmonary associations—

—Tu, I'm not going for another dump on this. Just cut the info! It's a spirit, grief is a spirit!

—Emotion is part of the psyche along with intellect and will. The human spirit, OTOH, is made up of intuition, communion, and conscience.

—Tu! You don't even believe in spirits, the spiritual!

—Stop!! (Quadri)

—OK, Quad, I'll stop, said Tu, mellowing. After I just say, If I believed, that's what I'd believe. It's the best I've read on the subject.

—You mean, answered Fabian (also mellowing, but now curious), that, if you *did* believe in the spiritual, that's what spiritual being would be, Tu?

—If I believed, yes.

—I'm afraid, almost, to ask.

—Go ahead, said Tu.

—Do you believe now?

—No.

HB said, So you don't believe in us?

—I would have to apply us to the rigor of scientific investigation first. And then it would not be believing, would it?

—That was fun (HB), but I think he's moving again. Look, that pile of dim pixels we be part of is moving here in the kitchen. What's he doing—staring at the walls? What's he thinking? And his son is just sitting here staring at the floor.

(Pome) —I think they are sleepwalking.

—Is that the real them, or the dream them?

—They're still in bed over here.

—Now's your chance, Pome. Segue their idea-land into that part of Fodder's thought-land you think is where we're at.

Pomala hesitated.

—What? said Jay and HB together.

—So, I'm a tiny bit scared.

—Yeah? (HB and Jay)

—If I say it you might be scared, too.

—Nevermind, we scared, said HB. You're thinking what if we get sucked into the abyss.

—Or worse, said Pome.

—Oh that? said Fabian. Yes, I see the concern.

—What's wrong? (Quad)

—She's afraid that if we get back it will be to 1900 CE and not 2017.

—I'm afraid, said Pomala, that we'll make the same mistake, whatever it was that got us here, and we won't remember any of it and will end up at the underground lab and it'll start all over again.

—You mean we'll be in a loop and never get out and won't know we're in a loop? (Jay)

—And guess what? said HB. We might be a loop right now, people. Maybe we've done this all before?

—But, perhaps a bit differently, maybe ever so slightly different. Not exactly. (Tu)

—I don't care!! Jayrai was virtually screaming. Try it!! Try anything!

—But pray first, suggested Fabian.

—Pray first, said Quadri.

—Oh OK, said Jay, but I'm praying to *Newfish*. You can pray to yours and I'll pray best and we'll see who wins.

—We won't be able to tell—or, that is, *you* won't, suggested Fabian again.

—Stop, said Quadri. It is Prayer Time.

195

SiXPointz HiTopOLis

The two HiTopOLites, Fodder and son, were staring at the walls and floor: their eyes like pixilated glimmers, in pale shades.

—I think they're getting this, said HB.

—Maybe they'll pray, too. You know, to that Ground Crater Pome says they got here. (Jayrai)

—In X's name, God bless, Fabian began.

—Us, said Quadri. —Hah-Lah.

—Amen, said Pomala.

—OK, get to work, suggested HB. What's next? Where's the right writing for them to read?

—See here, said Pomala, focusing on words by the door.

Slowly, very slowly, almost too slowly to notice them moving, the two bereaved HiTopOLites moved body and gaze toward the door where Pomala, almost as slowly, drew them.

Downslope of his orbit, over 250 years ago, Otulp, also called hEll, began his descent. Father Domino sat on a woven mat on rock in his cold lonely cell, a cave or crack in steep stone walls clad in trees. Nearby—where now is HiTopOLis—the Lost Nation perished. Light fell in from that direction (sparing his beeswax and tallow candles). Father Domino's hand moved slowly, drawing the quill-tip along, feather scarcely astir. His gaze barely upon the words as he wrote, it was also entranced by the vision above him.

At first he was writing of primitive explosives falling from colorful aerial balloons, the fiery bombing of Lost Nation, *Nation du Chat*. He felt very anxious, deep in some trauma, unaware of it as recollection, while slowly he wrote.

But as he gazed upwards, and then looked deeper, he saw a gap opened in starry heaven, and closer he looked, and deeper; and he saw what looked at first like another heaven beyond, multitudes of shimmery white and blue stars, and then many and unnamable colors; emerging and spreading through heaven. And the air, blue and white above land, whereon a great city was spread. And, as he looked upon the city, he saw now it was glimmery-spreading beneath him, and he saw that he was in the midst of a divided firmament, and found himself far-gazing with wonder, with reverence and speechless awe. Looking both above and below.

What is this, Leaping Fawn? he murmured. For with part of my mind's eye, or (it may be) my own eye, I see the Ehioerrian suffering and dying as they fight with bow-and-arrow and with stone-hawks against the superior force of Bird-Crested people. Whose arms are from Usi'opa; and from Franke, the world of my kin. While, with other sight, I see the world opened before me and multitudes of heavenly lights, stars, and beings, active and at gaze upon these warriors. Then, too, here is the great city on which all gaze, and, there, the Lost Nation braves, revived, to wait upon the execution of heavenly war.

Yes, Father Domino. Write, in the parchment of THE DEER, all you are seeing, with quill pen and inks.

— The more I look at this, said Pomala, the more I think it's maybe wrong for us.

— Wrong? (HB) Say again?

— You're right that it's not going in the right direction, said Tu. This is about *them*, the HiTopOLis people, not us.

— But, said Pome, it does refer to us. See where it talks about Pluto and the Pomala? We are in the stars and lights and beings. We do have, we *are*, as what's called Pomala, a part of it and you can tell because....

— Because we have a part in it! said Fabian. We would not be here with them dreaming these dreams if we had no part in it.

Pomala said, but that doesn't mean our part is to get us back. What if we are part of something bigger? Something here in this universe we aren't even aware of?

— Oh please, don't even *think* it! What're you talking about? said Jayrai. I just want to make cappuccino at FivePoints or out at the Sharon Road Rotary. In 2017 C.E. Or, at the very least, be reincarnated as a President's daughter, not as chairs and rainfall.

—She's right, even though these aren't exactly flesh, these things we're part of, said HB. We've done our share here. It's time to go back. Barrel's got a job, a responsibility here. The scientist got us into this fix in the first place. If he hadn't been so interested in the supernatural—

—Sub-natural, said Tu. Weakly Interacting Massive Particles.

A giant groaning echoed through their beings as these last statements were made. They focused quickly on Berle. He gazed slowly, helpless and hapless, about the kitchen, too distracted to heed them any longer.

—See what you've done? demanded Fabian. Now we'll have to start over.... Our Father, he said.

—Hah-Lah, said Quadri.

— Help, said Pomala.

Berle is talking with Sheesh about his dream. "The stars will be falling. As The Fodder puts it, falling from starry heaven. But we call it the stratos, and they fall on the City, on BalOnion, as we call this nation. Ours is a truly Lost Nation." He pointed to the words. "Pomala is a sign from — again, as the Fodder puts it — from heaven. Remember, there is some verbal confusion between our time and theirs. For instance, he did not know about the stratos, and had to rely on the way things looked in his vision, without relevant verbal precision such as we have. Nevertheless, it is an ultra-nature, some might say infra-nature, war focused here on Eartha. The natural elements have spoken to us in these dreams, but these speakers are not themselves natural." He paused, to see if Sheesh was with him.

"You mean invisible particles?"

The two had been comparing dreams, and going over their readings of facsimiles, with which wife and mother—Mary Bala Jones—had papered walls and decorated the floors.

"Dark matter. The things that speak to us have become part of classical elements of creation, elements put together over vast lengths and depths of time and ages, always in some state of rearrangement, decay and renewal in other forms. Some would call these remakings sub-creation as opposed to strictly "creation" (making something out of nothing). In The Fodder's time these happenings were indeed understood, believed in, received by thinking men and women of that day, as ever they have been since Mind came to grace and gather created beings. —Us. But now the *Us* is understanding creation in a more detailed and comprehensive manner."

Long-legged Sheesh stirred on his stool in the kitchen. He had been leaning against the words beside the door, the important ones. Or so he thought at first. Dah was standing, leaning against the none-too-clean counter near the none-to-clean sink. The stainless steel sink was stinky and bone dry. He continued.

"The stars spoken of as falling from Fodder's heaven will fall as he perceived, but, in the nature of things—that is, in this material existence we are undergoing—the falling stars do fall through the stratos but, according to all current material understanding, they are launched *in this material world.*"

"You mean," his son looked earnestly at him. Slowly, almost imperceptibly, shaking his head. "You mean, aTomic weapons. Bombs. —Through that really high part of the atmosphere, where temperatures are actually warmer in its outer part than its inner?"

"Yes."

There came a pause. Then Sheesh said, "I think Gneis agrees."

Berle looked at the floor, murmuring, "You talked with him about this? When you were younger? And... and he got around then, read these walls — or was it after that, when he was reading documents on his screen." But, as Sheesh hesitated, he went on, raising his voice.

"What does this have to do with us? You're probably

wondering." Berle looked directly at his son. "In practical terms. ...Remember the reading. This is all city now and it, especially, is one target for the stars. There are military and metropolitan targets all over the world."

"Has it got something to do with the Fodder's other pages or parchments or documents or whatever—talking about how the A'ndyans lived. You're talking about survival."

Berle looked away. Then back.

"Very good. We are on the same screen."

"Why is that? Last time I was able to check the screens, everyone—so so not *every* one was saying the raining just enforces diving into the wrack."

"Think about the word."

"Diving, enforcing, rain, or plane reck?"

Berle actually smiled. "The last. It means or relates to recklessness and reckoning."

"What's that word for the divers? Big intellectual word. Gneis would know. —Oh yes, *negator*. Not so big and intellectual after all.

"What they mean negates morality. Eat, drink, etc.—and that word for them you want is nihilite.

"That. Too."

"Our way of life is a giant religion of materialism. Like religion, it changes how the world is perceived. People now are so far from seeing what The Fodder and his world saw. —That magic is everywhere, invisible and beyond control. A rich man can only order so far before coming against the limit of his power... before which he is powder — and does not see it. Those who think they see the invisible and try to control it have no humility before it. Humility is acceptable. It conduits aid. 'Diving into the reck' is arrogant. If I did that it would take away my opportunity to help someone. Like ... like you helped Gneis..... This arrogance turns everything, even persons it sees, into meaningless "data," which can be ill-used and deleted.

"Magic? But you said magic is a word we use when we haven't learned enough about something."

"I've been thinking about it. For a very long time. And I'll never want to stop thinking, learning. Truth is, it's engaging. So I'm very glad about something else I've learned."

He stopped.

Of course, thought Sheesh. He said, "Is it ... that you're— that *no* one's going to learn everything?"

They were quiet, then, looking at one another.

Berle was amazed at how well Sheesh seemed to be taking everything. He had expected much sorrow. In fact, he doesn't seem to grieve. Of course, Berle thought in a vague way, there's not as much work—under trying circumstances—for him now. "Besides all this, you miss your brother," he said. Then Berle felt troubled for bringing it up. Perhaps he was somehow trying to mend his own psyche. He wished he hadn't said it.

Sheesh was silent, wondering what to say.

—Try to tell him, if you want. Mam would like that too.

"So so. So so. ... Dah ... you see, Gneis has been talking to me all along, so how can I miss him?

Stittt! *Now this. Worries on worries on worries*, thought Berle.

The kitchen expanded in silence.

After a pause, Sheesh said, "We'll help our friends survive?"

"...Yes. Beginning will be hard."

"Right. It's raining. Cycling through the stratos, falling on Eartha." Slowly he grinned.

Another pause.

"Honestly? —I've no idea so far," said Berle. There followed speculative back-and-forth on how to begin preparing for survival. On being without. Cold hungry shelterless naked suffering. Outlawry.

Finally Sheesh said, "Do you think they'll believe us?"

Pause again.

"We'll find out," said Berle.

"But," Sheesh asked. "What about the experiments? You've got funding to go on. And what about the *Pomala*? It wants to go back. And the what-if particle?"

"I don't know. Maybe that's not so important now."

"But it — the *Pomala* thinks it is. Thinks some of it is important — that part about it/them. According to the dreams, anyway."

"I think they'll survive."

—What?! (Almost the entire kitchen was indignant, but the HiTopOLites never knew.)

Except for Quad, Pomala only did not feel indignant.

—You did to us again! said Jayrai.

—What? (Quadri) Did what to us?

—White Thang done her good deed helping Barrel on us and now we're toast again, said HB.

—Does this mean we won't get to play The Hadesthon?

Pome said, —How do you know, Jay and HB, that it wasn't The Hadesthon to begin with?

—We just *know*, 'K? You have specially toasted us this time. (Jay)

s. dormAn

Visionary Reverbs

All the SiXPointz gang and adults were gathered in the Bopoiz apartment as reverbs ensued. The Bopoiz room4living was crowded, each viewer intently watching batteryPowered Visionary. ShieL keeL was bod-casting for *Virtual Futures* on the storm, exchanging question-and-answers with CarlE, summarized here:

Coastal areas on three sides of continental BalOnion are evacuated owing to record storm surges. Martial law is in force. Until the storm clears (weather reverbs to follow news, said CarlE), there is no way of assessing damage, but reports of fiscal discouragement on the prospect of salvaging these properties for future use are circulating. —Where immediately before had been demand for exclusive seaside homes, expensive frontage has vanished into the seas through force of catastrophic erosion.

"Martial law!" yelled hipPo and biMbo in unison.

Sea levels, in many coves, reaches, and inlets, will see a permanent rise again as current coastlines shear away. Elsewhere, on promontories and mountaintops wind farms are coming into their own, as energy funneling through turbines. Latest estimates show production of electric power equivalent to 150 unclear plants, a dramatic increase of the country's total farm output over the course of the storm.

"Martial law!"

Meanwhile, in HiTopOLis itself, two score houses on formally desirable properties above the Lost Nation River fell downslope of ravines; some completely toppling into the river, choking and damming; causing water to back up and flood suburban blocks.

MACHOs and adults in Bopoiz' apartment gazed mesmerized at toppling houses.

And what had been merely level housing tracts were now flood plains. The creative historic Living History Center, featuring A'ndyan villages, were blown flat in wind gusts. But neighboring hilltop colonial log-built encampments and fortresses have so far withstood. HiTopOLis traffic is virtually nil above, street-level, and

201

below ground; every public conveyance canceled along with many inner-city connecting lines, including those north and east out of HiTopOLis to the cities of Old Yak and Daytonian D.C. HiTopOLis has enforced martial law.

"Martial law!"

"CarlE, that is how the troposphere is currently punishing us." ShieL keeL was delivering with her usual ironic smile. Her sleek hair curved smoothly round her plump cheeks, and shieL's dark eyes twinkled. "In other news for us benighted souls today, on the national and international fronts several sources report. International Physicians for Social Responsibility and National Physicians for Prevention of Unclear War—the IPSR and NPPNW respectively—say hundreds of thousands of unclear weapons, both technical and those with larger payloads, are in continual state of maintenance, readiness, and also newly processing, as we speak, CarlE. These physicians' conferences, in consultation with unnamed experts, are calling not just for curtailment or even moratorium but for a slow and complete drawdown; a careful incremental dismantling that would make the world safer in the event of conventional conflicts and war. (By saner standards, CarlE. As we both know, war is never sane)." *Twinkle-twinkle.*

The svelte handsome CarlE, ever penetratingly astute anchorman, said, "But how would that help in the event of unclear attack, shieL keeL? (We know that such research and underground work was to have been part of local history, but—viewers will recall—HiTopOLis withdrew from the proposed program.) If other nations failed to abide by the IPSR and NPPNW 's recommendations then what? If codified into law, wouldn't dismantling entirely in BalOnion put us at tremendous risk? What's the deterrent if BalOnion, the greatest nation that ever built itself from scratch, relinquishes the unclear field? What then would deter our enemies from destroying us?"

"To answer that, CarlE, we go now to my recent interview with the head of ClimAte SciEntists UberNationale, Dr. H. Icup."

The scene on the Bopoiz visionary changed and, from their couches in the room4living aglow with candlelight (owing to limiting brownouts brought on by the storm) the MACHOs and families stared at their friend as she spoke with Dr. Icup via satellite strype from her office at home.

"Dr. Icup, how do we answer the most persistent argument against disarmament, seeing that others may disregard or dissemble their disregard of your group's recommendations?"

Dr. Icup was a serious sensible man who did not quite like shieL keeL's typically flippant, and what he regarded as grossly unprofessional, tone. He therefore deployed a mild light manner in counter to it, where, if her manner had been more serious and deliberate, he would have been quite stern. Thus, he hoped to avoid an exaggerated contrast during the discussion, and let the singular truth of this message drive its point home.

In the Bopoiz room4living every child's adult was present, some sitting on the floor, including Philipa, Gorgeeous, Pegmo, and Berle. Kelso and Philipa were also present. But the children, instead of playing games, or whining because they could not play games, or bouncing on the furniture—even hipPo and biMbo— watched this news transfixed. For Berle had invited them all to consider the very possibility shieL keeL was pointing on the *Virtual Futures Newsday.* He had not hidden it from the children. But, had it not been for recent catastrophes, and these reports, it is doubtful whether Mz. Bopoi would consider the wallpaper in Berle's kitchen of any import.

"Ms. keeL, in some small corner of the globe, even a fractional unclear payload, say, 0.01% of current international weaponry, if launched, would result in worldwide devastation. Consider the competitive and comparatively small nations of BorpIs Tan and HanDistan, along with the real possibility of such launches in that localized region alone. It would be enough, given their arsenal and intent, to destroy the growing season in all northern latitudes for ten years to come, leading the world to beg sustenance from Southern countries for decades after. Smoke and ash from burning cities, burning desert minerals, and surrounding sub-tundra forests would live in our atmosphere many years, lowering temperatures and covering Elios, while beneath the benighted cities of BalOnion would have to survive.... How? How would they survive, Mz. keeL, given your dependence on food? On meat and vegetables and fruits, dairy product?"

"How indeed, CarlE?" asked shieL keeL with a smiling eye as the image of her plump face streamed across the screens of HiTopOLis. "What we need to do, what our representatives need to consider now, in light of these reports, is whether or not the cost is worth the currently sustained illusion that the world is safe in deploying (in such array), and holding in reserve further stockpiles of weaponry designed specifically to turn people, buildings, and supporting infrastructure into atoms and particulate lofting busily in the atmosphere, for a generation after even limited strikes."

"But, shieL keeL, what do military higher-ups, into whose hands we so hopefully yield the stewardship of our security have to say about it? ShieL keeL?"

" 'No comment!!' " ShieL keeL smiled. "No comment whatsoever, CarlE. We can, however, go to our *retired* military leaders, and *retired* secretaries of defense and state for their comments, now that they are no longer in position to do anything about what before they boosted or acquiesced to. But, CarlE, remember, *we should be grateful for their speaking even now.*

"Tomorrow night," she continued, "I hope to have interviews with the last two distinguished former high-ranking officials, but I'll close now with words from Gen. P.A. Cartright, former commander of BalOnion's unclear forces:"

Gen. Cartright appeared from his consultant's office in BetHel LandMerry, seated with hands folded at his desk cleared of every article and gleaming dully in the LED lamps. His glasses also reflected somewhat their small array. Solemnly he answered shieL keeL, saying, "What are we working so hard and spending so much to deter? No doubt your listeners would like to know."

He paused, and then, as shieL keeL waited, he said, "Now that the world is as it is, I, too, would like to know what we think we deter. There is no national security in all these weapons, Mz. keeL."

"And there you have tonight's reverb of ongoing conditions, from the national, international and local interest POV, the *Virtual Futures Newsday* in brief, CarlE."

"Thank you, shieL keeL."

Mz. Bopoi, who was sitting between her son and daughter with arms about them, turned off the visionary, leaving silence in the reverb's wake. They looked at one another. Even hipPo, biMbo and Claude said nothing, but looked at Mz. Bopoi and Berle. GURlee, sitting between her big sister's legs, was of course staring at them.

—Nuclear winter is not that bad — y'all could, for instance, be *toast!* (HB)

—They don't *need* to survive. Look at us! We're proof of that. (Jayrai)

Without, the rain was misting, not the driving force of recent days. Here and there, faintly glowing, light showed over the dim monochromatic mistiness of the metropolitan neighborhood. Those shades of gray they'd been so wrapped in for so long...with solar arrays slackened. Ah for that great bright spot: Elios was out there somewhere, still hard to configure except in dreams. *If it should show through now*, thought Berle, *we'd see it as the perfect circle of light it is.*

—You girls are cold, said Fabian in response to Jay and HB.

—Yes, agreed Pomala. Think how they feel. They probably don't know how to survive. Even with the Fodder's help. If you had a body you'd be worried, wondering what to do.

—Oceans of depression, yes, said Jayrai. But I can't sympathize. If *you* do, I think we'll be getting toastier. Please think of us Pomala—you've got the most pull.

—Right (HB). He's got some little corner of his brain left, and last time we checked his deep-underground particles detector equipment wasn't flooded or cooked.

—Drowned neither, said Jayrai. —Tu? What about you. You are the one who understands this stuff. Didn't you help with getting BABY born? Can't you infiltrate his brain just a bit?

—To be precise, no, he said. Brain infiltration will not work. It's his mind that needs changing.

(Jay) —I think this author's unreliable. I'm not sure I want to be in this story if they can't get you right, Tu. Here you are talking about mind like you believe in it.

—Well I do. To a certain extent. This has not been corroborated but I, we, appear to have minds here in this 'Verse— without brains.

(HB) —Yo, Jay, I thought you said not bringing the alt alt into it. Thought you said they weren't real. We got no author, etc.

"So so so we can't just sit here," said Mz. Bopoi. "We've got to develop a plan. —If we're agreed to commit to it. So far we may be motivated because of this experience with the rain, the depression, chaos. How do we avoid the—let's call it—loss of interest once this blows over. It will, eventually, and then we'll be back in our techno complacency and just trying to right life as it is—or was."

Philipa spoke. She'd been sitting crosslegged on the floor next to Kelso, who leaned against the couch side on his skinny butt, forearms on his bent knees. He had on his work shoes and security uniform like always. Kelso had made a special effort to get them all up here in the elevator. "Better just start," he muttered as Philipa said, "So so so, Berle, I agree. We're serious, and I think if we even research how to go about it, and maybe look for a spot—or find what's out there. Some cabin in some woods? But that's probably tame. The thing is, start learning. What's out there.

"Yes," said Berle. "Here's where you're highly touted investigative skillz come in." He lightly grinned—lightly.

She smiled. "Yup, I'll look into rural places. BalOnion cities—tentacles throughout but we've still got wooded lots and farmlands. Not my usual beat, but."

"Don't forget, the Fodder lived in a cave. He learned from his benefactors and—that particular cave is out, of course. It was protected for a while along with some later settlers' homesteads, but unlike those was taken off the list and blasted, leaving a crag. And some now completely-out-of-date *autres cachet* of a MinsTerBuck Ruler mansion. Big enough to house the entire Ehioerrian nation. Changed hands several times over the past sixty years."

"Digression alert," said Sheesh, looking at him.

Philipa glanced at Kelso, saying, "Right now, what I'm thinking is country land. Abandoned farms. What do you think? —

M. Better-just-start."

"Speak up," he said. "I can't hear you."

"Your sitting right here. How loud do I have to yell?" Nevertheless she raised her voice. "I said, *farmland. Abandoned farmland.*"

"Better buy it if you can find some," he said. "And I was kidding. You don't need to talk loud. That loud," he said under his breath.

"It's so much easier and intellectually interesting to talk; talk of subatomic makings, of morals, politics, the effect of technology on the changing intellectual culture. At least for me that last is challenging. But when I think of you," Berle looked at the children in the room, and back at Mz. Bopoi, "when I think of these kidz... I want to do something. To make a place, possibly for them. Some sort of way to go on. To develop a possible life when — if the infrastructure — material political and moral — of our society goes...during their time."

"If? When." said Kelso. "It will go. It has to. Even an old-guy like me—I'm learning to stick-fight."

—This is boring," said Jay.

—Right. (HB) Now that we know there's nothing in it for us.

The others couldn't quite tell if he was serious or not. Probably some of both: serious—not serious. Boredom has that effect on him.

Berle said, "Again, how to live, survive. Not the kind of thinking we want to do. Much more interesting to think how, on a supposition, say... to transfer dark matter from one universe to another."

"Or perhaps," said Mz. Bopoi dryly, "trying to find a moral particle among the minutia, the RAMBOs, MACHOs, the WIMPs."

In a moment the roomful was not so gloomy. (Kelso being the exception.) *Things, people,* even, were suddenly not so glum. Glimmering went round the edges of the room4living.

"You know about that?" asked Berle.

"Kidz talk, don't they?"

"Yes, we talk." Claude piped up, grinning, from between his mother's knees. "And I know what to do and can tell you. In school we learned—"

Berle spoke—not quite out of character—but running roughly over Claude's chirruping as he said, "—Did, did you inform the committee? Sorry, can't help wondering."

A slight shake of her head. "I don't take it seriously," Mz. Bopoi said. Again it was dryly put.

Berle smiled. Only Sheesh recognized his great relief.

"Does that mean you told no one?"

"That's what it means."

—For all intents. Gneis said to Sheesh and GURlee. —And for the purpose of keeping him out of trouble.

—Is that him again? said HB.

—It is, said Pomala.

—Ask him how to get out of this universe, 'K?

— He's busy, I think. Not sure if he's aware of us. —Or cares, said Tu.

—What do you mean? (Jay) Because now we don't care about them? So now it's *verse-vica*?

—You are gonna make one clevah barista when we get back, said Fabe.

—What kinda moral get-up is *that*? she answered. That's not moral, *You didn't do it for us so now we don't do it for you*?

—What was it you said a while back—about your relatives' moral code? "Speak no wounding evil?" Or something? "Cruel persons are like cats playing with mice?" (Fabe)

—Maybe he's right, Jay? said Pomala. —If you want your body to survive and be a barista maybe you do or will care about their survival?

—Grr (Jay). How do you care—when you don't?

—Pray? suggested Fabian.

—Your answer to everything!

—For the time being.

—OK, I'll pray—to the *trimurti*.

—OK, I am ignorant, but that might be good.

—Its three: BrahFishSheev. That should cover all bases for now, though the ancestors might disagree. (*Materialism is so much nicer than religion.*) This last was but a mutter, a small thought from Jayrai.

Meanwhile Berle had apologized to Claude and asked him to continue telling what he'd learned in school about survival, saying, "Helping my friends survive is more important than subatomic particles."

"I was going to say, getting food was easy. Colonists got great lobsters right out of the water. Colonists was what they called survivalists back then."

"Easy-sneezy—except there's no ocean here, you bweed." HipPo's tongue was loose again.

Mz. Bopoi, who sat with her arms round her son and daughter, said "What else, Claude?" She gave her son a warning glance.

"So so so there's honey in trees from bees they had, and sugar if you boil sap enough (that's the blood of trees). And turkeys were everywhere! In forests you find this stuff."

"Have you even *seen* a forest, Claude?" It was biMbo's turn to sneer.

"Go on, Claude," said Mz. Bopoi. "So far so good." She glared on the other side, tightening her hold on both.

"So so so you can gouge out a log to make a bucket-like thing—a trough they called it to put the sap in—"

"How'd they keep the trough from burning while they boiled it, bweed?"

"Go on, Claude." Mz. Bopoi continued with dogged persistence. "So far so good."

"So so so they used hot stones. They actually came for furs. They came all this way to get clothes. You can get these from trapping animals, see. So so," he cut off biMbo as she opened her mouth, "we need traps or snares to get animals!"

"Very good, Claude!" Mz. Bopoi said this quickly. She looked expectantly at Berle, keeping herself ready to speak next moment if Berle did not jump in.

He said, "It might be good if we all made lists; especially lists of what we have or need to get; and keep thinking what to do to prepare. We might explore on the investigations of Philipa, begin to figure out how to pool our resources. I don't intend to back off this. It will be worth something.... One very important thing is to keep together on it. We will keep at it together, keep checking back on progress, making plans, and so so—be a community."

Sheesh said, "Maybe we should have a name?"

"Good one," said Berle. "Any ideas?" He looked first at Sheesh, who hesitated, then around the room.

There was an uncanny silence. Then Sheesh said, "How bout WIMPs? —You know?"

"Not MACHOs?" said Berle.

"Especially not RAMBOs!" said biMbo emphatically.

"No," said Sheesh after moment. "Because we aren't really very strong."

—But you're interacting and you're massive, said Gneis.

Sheesh snorted. Everyone in the room laughed. Certainly they weren't strong.

The furniture was strangely but not abnormally silent.

Low enough (only biMbo and hipPo heard), Mz. Bopoi said, "No butter-peanuts for you two tonight."

Later, after Kelso had dropped them at their floor, they were alone again in the apartment. Apartment doors in the building were no longer electronically locked, or monitored and activated. Once the city and its well oiled infrastructure with electric grid got up and running again—*if it did*, as some cynics opined and the fearful

worried—Kelso and staff would reactivate. Thank Mz. Gad for fossil
fuels, said the optimists. Too bad it won't last, said the pessimists.
There's always elios-light, solar! the former would return. Now that
the rain's almost gone. —But when it comes back.... And so on,
back-and-forth.

For some reason Dah and Brah had gravitated to Gneis's
room. It had been straightened and cleaned, but looked ready to
receive him again at any moment. They stood together in the
doorway, Berle pudgy and shorter, Sheesh tall and lithe; glancing
over the furnishings, bed upright, the bedtable pushed off to one
side. The eelie, dully metallic, upholstered, with rubberized
triangular treads and voice-activated (also manual) joystick. Outside
the brightening mist was still thinning, city lights a-glimmer in the
diffuse dim light of day.

"Someone's going to need that chair," said Sheesh.

"Ye-es," said Berle speculatively. "Not just yet, though."

There was a pause.

Sheesh was kythHinG.

"But soon," returned Sheesh.

Berle stopped seeing the chair, stopped seeing the room. He
was thinking.

Abruptly Berle said, "Have—have you been... hearing...
things?"

"I've got ears." Sheesh smiled down on him, clear eyes and
fresh face framed in the do-it-yourself cereal bowl style.

"That's not what I mean."

Sheesh became thoughtful. "You mean—voices? Hearing
hallucinations?"

Berle waited, looking away. Then back. "Yes, I guess that's
what I mean. I mean—you are too old to be having invisible friends.
Even if they are your brother."

"So so. It's—hard to explain. Short answer is, no."

Berle was deeply relieved. "Let's have the long answer?"

"My brother is really here. Not always, but sometimes."

Berle was less relieved. "How do you know this?"

"You already know how I know it."

"You mean that thing you used to do... with... when he was
... with us?"

"Yes. And we still do it."

"But how do you know?"

"So so you are the scientist.... But you believe in Mind. How
do you know *that*?"

"I don't know it, I guess."

"Dah—you guess?"

"KO, I *believe*. Is that good enough?"

209

"Dah, I'm not the scientist. No doubts, it's good enough."

"But please explain it," said the physicist.

"Without the science?"

"Yes."

"That's good because I don't have any. So so, here goes from a not-even-an-amateur." Still he hesitated. Then he said, "I guess you just have to experience it."

"Can you describe your experience?"

He thought about it. "Best I can say is, it's not even belief, really. I just know. I think it's what you call—intuition."

"Are there words involved?"

"It's more like like like—an impression. I think GURlee does it, or has it, too. But you'd have to ask *her* I guess.

"Some kind of—impress, inward pressure?"

"That's maybe too strong, that word pressure.

"Pressure implies force... of some kind."

They were silent then, gazing at Gneis's former stuff.

"I'd like to ask more."

"I don't think more would work," said Sheesh.

"Work?"

"It would be too many words. I don't think it's for science, either. Look at me. I'm doing it — it can't be scientific."

"But you ride a cybickle — and you don't know the science of that."

"Plus I've got no words for that, either. That's something I do with my body. But this isn't."

"That's a very good answer."

Silence.

"Just one thing more?" asked Berle.

Sheesh said, "No doubts."

"Is there anything you can compare it to... that I might—or anyone—might recognize?"

His son was thoughtful once again. "I guess... it's kinda... like my conscience. It's something I just know."

"Hmm. Could you ignore it—and it will go away?"

"That's more than one thing, Dah." He was smiling down on Berle.

"KO—more than one."

"Yes, I think so. But I wouldn't want him to go away, would I? I'd get kinda lonely, wouldn't I?" His tone was slightly anxious. He did not think Dah would ask him to stop. He hoped.

"Have you been doing it — now?"

"Right now — while we're talking about it?"

"Yes."

"No. Maybe before, though."

"So so, not your conscience but... a similar ...impress."

"Yes, and that's about it," said Sheesh.

Pause.

"KO.... So so, tell him I said 'Hi.' Sometime."

Sheesh grinned. Hugely. And they turned, knocking into each other: Berle's portly belly still much as it was before the grief, and Sheesh stepping lithely backward into the room.

"Also," he said, "Gneis says the bed's got to go. It's for someone else now."

"It shall," said Berle. "How about next week?"

"KO but I'll be watching you on that."

"So so I hope you do." Dah returned his smile.

Gneis said, —*That biology equipment in the bedroom has to go, too.*

Berle had gone into the kitchen. Thinking. *That thing about the conscience. Now that's interesting. Will this be going somewhere?* It might confirm bypassing the body, biology, evolution, social theory, psychology, the lot.

—Here comes the "what if," again, said Tu. It's a good thing he's got funding.

—He's got funding? That went right by me. (Jay)

—It sometimes happens. (Tu)

—What's that supposed to mean? Mr. Knows-everything. If you're so smart, what makes you think it's the Hadesthon got us here? Or there—or anywhere? Isn't *that* magic?

—I don't know that I did think it. It was an experiment on my part. Besides, the game—and z-pod—are still lying there where we left them when the A'ndians came out of the tomb and took the girl.

—And our bodies'n'all still there. ...We hope. (HB)

—So you need science to help you prove a *story*? Prove that *magic* exists? (Jay) (sarcasm)

—What I've been saying.

Fabian said, —Getting back to where life came from, Tu, not including StinkenFrine, science has not proved a thing about lightning giving us life. So that *has* to come under the heading of story.

—You mean science itself is a story? Tu snorted at the thought. (Tu snorting?)

They all did.

—Of course it is, said Fabian. The scientists are story-tellers, very careful story-tellers. I can see how careful The Dah is. You are. But you haven't actually tried much yourself. You've only been reading and thinking. What do you really know for sure except what you've been told from sources you trust? —And this is all, btw,

211

belief.

—Consensus is very important, said Tu.

—Just like all the regular people used to trust the church higher-ups. History shows my stories were consensus for couple thousand years. Everybody in Usi'opa, Americle, believed them. And now *more* everybody—at least in our part of the world—*believes* in science.

—This is all sloppy thinking, said Tu. Historically, everybody was believing the wrong stuff. That doesn't make it right.

—*Stop!*

—Tu, said Jay (sweetening her psyche). How do you know he's got funding?

—I think she said she did not take his "what-if" seriously. I'm surprised, actually, that she's listening to him about survival. Seems to be.

—She may or may not be taking him seriously on the what-if, said Fabian. Remember what Eelie said about for all intents and purposes.

—What do you think about the brothers calling them—the survivalists—WIMPs? (Pomala) Maybe it was to encourage us?

—Maybe, said Fabian. We helped them. Maybe they'll be some kind of answer to prayer?

—Yo, think about it (HB). The two bro's get together and talk him into it! Next thing you know we get sucked back into the tube and out we go! Back to FivePoints! The REAL universe, none of this low rez flimsy stuff.

—Not 1900 CE! *2017!* (Jayrai)

—2017!! (All)

—See, it's working, said Pome. We are encouraged.

s. dormAn

The Refuge

The two men stood outside a stinky dilapidated hovel just on
the western border of partially wooded Tecumsee InterNational Park.
They had parked a couple brooms, two buckets, and their tools
outside along the wall by the door. Hammers—ball peen, sledge-
hammer, and claw; two saws of different size and configuration; a
couple coffee cans full of nails; and a few other tools—all for repair,
refitting, make-shifting. Now, holding off till the last moment, they
peered into the fetid gloom. Between gaps in the dark horizontal
wallboards they saw daylight. Droppings on the floorboards.
Rafters above on which probably were droppings. "Some sort of
animals have been at it. Possibly under the rotting floorboards.
Bottom edges of wall boards look like they been chewed. Probably a
porcupine." Berle said this to Kelso when they saw the gnawings.
      Sheesh was out back somewhere in the misty woods. He had
Kelso's book on edible wild plants. They had been tromping around
for hours, beginning in the dim a.m., but he was still at it.
      "All this will be a long-term process for mastering skillz, with
long-term preparations. A lot of time, extra work and energy. Forget
boiling water just to heat for baths—we'll have to boil it to drink!
But we've got to keep the purpose alive," said Berle to Kelso.
      And, "Even though you've got the least energy of any of us, I
think you may have the most endurance and can keep us on
course."
      "Don't mistake me," said Kelso. He had two leather-sheathed
knives on his belt. There were odds and ends for contrivance in his
vest and camo-pants pockets. "I consider it an outside chance—not
that this place'll be needed, but an outside chance that we can
succeed. You should know what I think. And that doesn't mean get
all discouraged. It means do it anyway. Also, the others need
encouragement, so f'gourd's sake change that name. Call'em the
MACHOs. (They're used to it, anyway.)" That last was under his
breath, one of his curmudgeonly mutters.
      The twilight trip out in Berle's solar flycar was encouraging
because now there was real, if dim, daylight again. The world was
soaked, almost glittering. The sun they called Elios shone its disc

213

through overall mist. The air they had breathed, walking around the property, was like heaven, not fetid, stinky or dank as it had been in HiTopOLis.

The real WIMPs had gone out into the universe to revive from boredom, and to experience the astonishing vividness, color, array and power of billions of galaxies and suns. Often they cared for nothing more. The 'Verse seemed more real than the pixilated BalOnion. Sometimes they didn't even see anything in going back into their own, probably by-now strange, universe. But then it would come to them. They didn't belong here, either. Where—where *did* they belong?

—Together, said Pome. We belong together.

—Together, said Quad.

—But I miss my sister, said Pomala.

—My big brother, said Quad.

—Yo, I miss getting beat up, said HB. And they all knew what this meant and that it *wasn't* the transfigured episode in Paddy's Pool Hall, circa 1900 CE.. (They still thought that had not maybe happened.)

—Oh please, you do not, yo, said Jayrai. Besides, you were little then.

—I still remember it.

—Nothing is forgotten yet, said Fabian. Look, that's them walking around in woods far from the city.

—Where?

—Here. Security and The Dah.

The WIMPs focused on low-rez Kelso and Berle.

—A huge pile of shit under there, said HBBBAH.

—We're particles of that, said Fabian.

—It's part of us, said Tu.

Behind the hovel stood neglected misty woodland full of blowdown. The flycar stood off, small, dully gleaming in a clearing beside an otherwise seemingly empty field of flattened and rotting corn.

—Field's full of snakes and slitherers, said Jay. Ugh. This is us? Snakes and eels and eyeless tadpoles?

"Let's set the kitchen up here," said Kelso. With a grunt he flopped a sodden board on the ground, splashing. He bent, opened a kit bag.

"Can we move away from this place? It's wretched." Berle heaved up the board and trudged off.

Kelso had grabbed the bag and followed, work boots squishing through waterlogged flattened weeds and brown wildflowers in ruins. They were going to inaugurate the place with a meal, and then set to work cleaning and mending the hovel. Each had become depressed after their initial exhilaration on walking the property.

"This is suckerly, "said Sheesh, coming round the hovel through mist to join them as they moved toward the field. "The woods back there are pretty decent, though. All those black trunks in the fog. How much would we own?"

"Already put money down on it," said Kelso. "Weren't you listening?"

Sheesh grinned. "To you? But this is so co-ald! We need to live here!"

Clearly he was not depressed. Berle did not return the grin. He frowned. "A hundred forty yacres," he said. "Including parts of the wood."

"We'll get the little kidz away from all the bad stuff in HiTopOLis," said Sheesh. He was buoyant, squashing in rubber boots, hands in his pockets, backpack full of food.

Kelso had four big empty cans and several candles. He was about to place metal lids along the board, set candles on each.

"Cooking on aluminum cans! This is great. Can I do that, Koot?"

"Sheesh," said Berle pointedly, in words and tone. "Have a little respect." But he was smiling.

Kelso the Koot was not. He said, "I'm used to it. Pile it on." He handed Sheesh the big cans, two at a time. "Have at it. See if you can figure it out." Surrounded in damp silver fuzz, the Koot's pate shone faintly in the mist.

Sheesh removed the backpack, squatted, setting each can on the board. He opened a small matchbox and struck a match, staring at the flame. Moving it slowly about in the mist.

"For lighting the candles," said Kelso. "You're wasting 'em. Set that stuff up since you're so interested. Lids *underneath* candles. Better put that hair behind your ears — don't want to set your teenage head on fire."

Sheesh arranged the candles, lit each one and topped it with a can. Kelso had cut holes in the tops round the edges, assuring airflow.

"This is scary," said Sheesh when he stood. "Matches can run out."

Berle was placing pastries full of pre-grilled beef and onions on the oiled tops of each can.

"And for dessert, *Monsieur* Koot," said Sheesh, "there's apples and pastry with cinnamon!"

"Are you just going to forget about matches running out, then?" The grump wanted to know. "Where do you suppose they come from, anyway? Do you even know?"

"Chunkwoods? Chunkwoods make'em out of those big things growing over there. Maybe whittle them down with their teeth." He pointed toward the woods with his fork (where also he supposed the critters lived). Sheesh was ready to dig in before even a whiff of pastry, beef and onions, hit the air. "Do we own them, BTW?

"Yes, but where is the chunkwood factory? Do you know that?" Berle said, peering beneath as he slipped a spatula under the pastry at the end of the lineup. It would be a while.

"Claude will be doing back flips off the downed branches back there when he sees this place. He'll think he died and went to the place where the A'ndyans live—Kelso's ancestors, that right?"

"Some of them, yes."

"Match factory?" said Berle.

"What is this? Studies in Society—Civilizations—Shop-class?"

"It is your semiannual lesson in reality," said Berle. "You've been living in game-land, magicCloud, too long and have forgotten what reality is."

Sheesh stopped. He had been tossing his fork into the air. Repeatedly. "I think I had a pretty good dose of that lately. Can't recall the last time I thought food just magically appeared."

Berle was still squatting, peering under the meat pies. He winced.

"He's good," said Kelso.

"He does seem to be getting smarter," said Dah, thoughtfully. He looked up at Sheesh. Who was now towering over him, saying, "Wouldn't it be weird if all that rain came in winter? Would it have been snow?"

"What do you think?"

"I think that field would be a glacier."

Peering under a meat-pie, Berle said, "Should have wrapped them in foil."

Kelso reached into the kit and pulled out folded squares of foil. "Sorry," he said. *Always forgetting something.*

Berle handed the foil across the can lineup toward Sheesh, who took his hands out of his pockets (reluctantly). Sheesh squatted to drape little tents over the pies. The tasty scent now wafted abroad.

"But would HiTopOLis freeze?" he asked.

"Yes, there'd be the question if they—we?—could keep everyone warm enough.

"Do you think we could?"

"There's backup generation, but that's individual buildings and campuses. Discrete backup, also requiring fossil-fuel."

216

"But what about everybody else—regular people?"

Kelso said, "Depends on how deep and far the corruption is in that town. Town really hasn't even been tested yet."

"What's all this been?" said Sheesh gesturing around, arms wide, taking in the pellucid mist of woods and fields. "All the rain, brownouts, blackouts, stoppage? Gneis sitting in the dark and unable to move?"

Kelso said dryly, "It wasn't winter."

Berle said, "Let's talk about something else — and I don't mean the weather."

—How bout the "what-if" question, suggested HB. "What if I can get the WIMPs back to FivePoints?"

—Altogether now, said Jayrai. Give a giant shout!

—WIMPs! (All but Tu and Fabian)

—WIMPs to FivePoints!! (All but Tu and Fabian)

—Why aren't you shouting, yo? (Jay)

—Maybe it's too—began Pomala and stopped. Just *too*.

—Yes. Too pushy. (Fabian)

—It's got to be subtle, understated. (Tu)

Fabian said, —Let's phrase it as a request. It will be humble.

—Yo, how do you get important attention with *humble*. (HB) Look how much attention I gave those guys who beat me up as a kid.

—Didn't you say you stayed away from them after that? —As much as you could? (Pome)

—You have to be on the alert with that. Notice where they are, before getting practiced enough to stay away. They had my complete attention until well after the swelling went down.

—Let's go back out to the universe, he said. Did you notice they have a Hades or Pluto or some block of ice like that? ...Right out on the edge... as you get to the pebble-sphere out here.

They were now focused out on the periphery of the Elios alternate solar system, a network of planets, planetesimals, moons, asteroids, meteors and other bits and pieces. Debris surrounded the system like an outer crust—called the Croupier Belt in WIMPs' own solar system. Space was at once dark and shot through with lights of varying size.

—Pitz and beezes of stuff. Now where is he—that bastard that got us into this fix. (HB)

—It's not pebbles, HB. It's gases and pieces of solid gaseous materials, said Tu. Ammonia, hydrocarbons, water. It would all be gas in our atmosphere, or at least that of planets nearer the sun. See that bright star way over there?

—I know, said HB—The sun. Like nothing but a star in the middle of nowhere. Maybe if we went down and took a dip in that—

big as a lake of fire when we get there? Would that get us back home?

—It might be worth a try if we get desperate. (Tu)

(HB) —If I were home this cold edge-full-of-stuff would be giving me the *heeBjeeBs*. But where is that shortcake monster? That Hadesthon bit-player? You know I call him this to cut him down to size. His real size.

—What? You don't worship? said Jay. Maybe we better rethink this.

—No, I'm not about to bow, raise my ass, and got no plans to ask nicely. Look. It's a piece of ice. I'd piss on the thing if I had a thing to piss on it with.

Jay was skeptical. —You don't worship ... after all this time playing the game?

—Where you been? You never caught me doing it. HBBBAH escaped every time.

—Oh wow, said Jay, feigning alarm. We are in for it now.

(HB) —There, dim. ...This Pluto is *different.... Look.* It's got abandoned buildings all over it. Looks like some people in this UV had inhabited it. IT WAS CIVILIZED, JUST LIKE IN THE GAME!!!

Tu said, —Must have got thrown by some catastrophe out of another solar system into this one. That's the only explanation.

—Which game? (Jay) We didn't get that far with BABY? — *The—*

—Our universe's game—*The Hadesthon.* The one we were playing when etc..

Then, right out of the black and blue, of which they were now a part, Fabian said, —Which would you rather be, Tu, a story or science project? (Actually he'd been thinking of it ever since Tu defined the pitz-and-beezes belt for them.) Are we a scientific experiment? —Or characters in a story?

He waited for it.

HB said, —Do we have a choice?

Silence. Deep, without intent. Silence. Massive, vacuous, impersonal. Massive astronomic spheres turning at deafening rates, without acoustical atmospheres to carry hopeful waves of sound.

—But that's not exactly what I asked, said Fabian finally.

"Next time I'm going to bring sausages and pancake batter," said Sheesh. You precook the meat and pour the batter on the cans — slowly, so it cooks as it flows. Then put in the sausage bits. That'll be yum?"

"No doubts," grinned Berle. Talking food was always better than talking weather. To Kelso he said, "So how's the strength and energy holding out? We going to do anything to that hovel? Tear it down, for instance?"

s. dormAn

They glanced back at it, small and dark against the misty woods. Like a spooky disagreeable hole to where? in an otherwise mysterious but not certainly inhospitable world.

Gazing at him through fogged glasses, Kelso said, "When I need energy I pretend I have energy. Doesn't work that way with strength." He thought, *Sometimes pretending works with memory, sometimes not.* He took off his glasses and rubbed them on a shirttail hanging below his jacket. His nose was running, but he seemed not to notice.

"Interesting," said Berle.

"So what's with the moral-particle thing, anyway? Not that I'd get it. But what is it? —That your boss brought up at the survival meeting? She didn't seem too impressed."

"That may have to do with the machinery. Maybe not. She's got her hands full already with that."

"Machinery?" Kelso wiped his nose on a sleeve.

"It determines what you can know."

Squatting, Sheesh lifted a ballooning cover of foil to peer beneath. He picked up the spatula from the board were Berle had set it. Then he put it back and grabbed tongs to turn the pies.

"We investigate what the machinery is designed to investigate. And if you're after something for which there's no machine then you've got to go with that. Until then it is theoretical. I happened to get lucky with more funding for the CDMS detection. Forthcoming, and still seems to be. For now.... Take the neutral who discovered aTomic structure. Very rudimentary making-do machinery. S/he had to improvise that but the theory came first. Of course you stumble onto things, too, with your machinery. S/he wanted, further, to know if peculiar particles spit out during fade were possibly helium uncleri, and got the idea (from Mind-knows-where) to blow glass thin — extremely — for the test-tub. At gas-exchange into ions, light emission proved he/r theory. That extremely thin glass was key. It passed light needed (so-to-speak) for the reveal."

"So... you need a new machine...? Modify what you have? What."

Berle smiled. His gaze was all for the mist, everything quiet for the moment, an atmosphere to swim in. The meat pies were sputtering. All three hungry now. After a moment, Sheesh used a glove to scoop them off the cans. There were four. Sheesh was going to give Berle the extra.

Kelso reached out as the teenager handed him one wrapped in foil, taking it in his shirttail. "That's not exactly what I asked at the start, though," he said. "Is it?"

—What is this, an echo chamber? asked HB, still gazing at

219

icy, lumpish Otulp. —With us as the experiment? And he's still at that blanKetyBlink what-if.

—Maybe the whole universe is? suggested Jay. An echo chamber, I mean. So *not* a chamber, the u-v. *Sheev*, I hope the whole universe isn't an experiment!

After a pause, Tu said, I'm starting to be impressed, Fabian. I thought you were childish, literal and dogmatic. But you are actually thinking.

—Stalling, said Fabian.

—Maybe, said Tu. I've got to think.

—Tu's making a joke, everybody, said HB. So it's not an actual choice on our part. Way out here in the *heeBjeeBs* you kinda wonder if anyone's here to choose whether story—or science project. Are *we* even here?

—Don't be scary. We're talking, yo? (Jay)

—Holding hands. (Pome) So to speak. Caring about it—us, everything.

—Holding hands. (Quadri, sounding a bit anxious)

—If we *are* an experiment (aside from the physicist's experiment with us, that is), there would still have to be an experimenter, wouldn't there, Tu? (Fabe) Just saying we could be God's project.

—Oh please. (Jayrai)

—OK, I see what you're getting at, Fabe. (Tu) You are trying to do my thinking for me.

—Need help?

—Now don't go making him mad. (HB)

—Tu doesn't get mad. (Jayrai)

—Tu is a very staid sort of person, explained Pome.

—If we can't be humans—persons—maybe we become impersonal experiments—go into the fire as failed experiments? (Fabian)

—And you girls think Tu is cold? (HB)

—But fire? Doesn't sound cold. (Jay)

—And this block of ice isn't getting anywhere near it, you note. (HB, referring to Otulp's distance from the fat star)

"I've got a little bottle with me," said Berle, licking his fingers. He had offered the others a share of the fourth pie, which was declined. "We'll get some of that brookwater back there, take it in for testing."

He gestured toward the woodland where a stream ran through.

"Be better to gather some from the spring," said Kelso.

"Spring?"

"That gurgling patch back there under a rock, where the

220

leaves are extra puddled," said Sheesh. "That's the spring."

"I'm impressed," said Kelso, wiping his nose.

"I am, too," said Sheesh (to Gneis).

"So so, verdict on the hovel?" asked Berle.

"I think it's going to destroy itself," said Kelso. "Rotting timbers will collapse under the weight of the first snowfall."

—The physicist is declining to correct him, said Tu. There's a lot going on there—not just the surface stuff. Forces unseen.

—He's forgoing the boring info dump? (Jay) Not a bad thing.

—What do you mean, Tu? The atoms will still be there, right? Even the molecules won't be going anywhere? (Pomala)

—Of course they will go *somewhere*, said Jay not withstanding her objection to the dump.

(Tu) —The porcupine will keep eating, the woodpeckers, bugs will eat it, the fungus keep rotting—all of it, yes, but that will take a very long time. Then it'll be soil with nutrients, and seeds will grow... the hovel will help segue new life.

—Where, again, did you say the life will come from? asked Fabian

—*Not* from a storyteller, Fabian.

—Right, said HB. The experimenter breathed the breath of life and it all became a living experiment. Or story, depending on your POV. In the meantime... do we jump or not?

—Meaning the sun? said Tu. I haven't given up on the physicist, since the lab is still good. Also, I now think a wormhole may be a better bet. Although these are posited intra-universe, not necessarily extra-universe. For instance, I'm inclined to think a wormhole funneled us initially—bodily reconstructed—from 2017 to 1900 in our own universe. Or even the central galactic black hole might be the better bet getting back. We've been avoiding that...with good reason. But, if the wormhole *is* responsible for bringing us here it would be because the universe of origin—our universe—gave way to this as a time-parallel universe, in a short time-jump... which I think is why the time frame is more like where we stopped temporarily in our 1900 CE. So locating a wormhole might be the thing.

—*Locating??!* What's wrong with the sun? Not that I'm liking it my own self. Uh-uh. I wouldn't mind giving Pluto a shove out of its orbit in that direction. If I could *give* a shove, but like with the other S-H— word, I can't. Apparently I can be shit, but not give one.

—What's going with Pluto, HB? (Pome) What harm has Pluto done? I know he's in the game and all, and has to be defeated—but that's The Hadesthon. This is real. Tu has not even proved that the game had anything to do with it.

—According to him he hasn't proved *any* of this is real either.

"There's no use trying to burn the hovel," said Berle. It would take a lot of energy and combustive power, but I'm for starting over, not taking it apart."

Kelso put his greasy crumpled foil in the kit and held the bag out to them. "If we build bigger, stronger, and away from it, the critter (or critters) will still have this, and be a source of food if we get hard up."

"Do we build in the woods?" asked Sheesh. "Or the clearing?"

—*Phlap*! said HB. I wanted to test myself on that fire, see if we could get back on the flames of hovel-torch.

—We've been candle flames and nothing happened with that, said Jayrai.

"We need a design," said Berle.

"A bunkhouse!" said Sheesh. "A barn with a loft!"

"We might want to think about burying it," said Kelso. "Put the new place between some of those big rocks back there." He gestured toward the woods, then knelt on the sodden board to stow what was left of the candles and cans. Berle, a bit sheepish over his own slowness (he'd been abstracted), helped him stand up. Kelso groaned. His knees were wet. Arthritic knees, Berle supposed.

—Look at the old guy—Security, said Jay. Why doesn't he just give it up?

—Look at us, said HB. We haven't even got knees, let alone bad knees, and we ain't given up.

It was late afternoon. Still considering, these three generations were talking, packing up, reluctant to leave. A sound, indistinct, then distinct, came toward them, high, through the mist beyond the field. They looked toward the east were HiTopOLis was hidden in distant folds of the rolling landscape rising toward remote eastern mountains, out of sight.

"Someone is coming," said Kelso, who though harder of hearing spoke first in recognition.

"More than one," said Berle as they gazed. Behind them the Elios was high, a westward disc.

"Three of them," said Sheesh as flyers came small through the mistiness, droning like insects.

They stood watching as the silvery insects grew larger in the mist and took on the shape, still small, of their intended design. Car-flyers.

"One of those is Bopoiz," said Sheesh, whose gaze was most acute. "The other is Sgt. Philipa's. Ex-sarge. Don't know the third one," he said. It enlarged with the others, and, (after what was perhaps a visual search for Berle's machine), circled over the woodland of misted treetops behind the hovel; solidifying, switching to solar, no longer droning. In a moment or two the three now silent

222

flyers grounded near Berle's own on the edge of the field.

"It's happening!" Philipa cried out she opened the driver's hatch.

"What's happening," yelled Berle, hands cupped to his mouth.

Pegmo and Claude climbed out the passenger side. Pegmo looked a mess, Claude looked as usual. Berle, Kelso and Sheesh saw the Bopoiz emerging, and were surprised to recognize FreddieTheTech—tall, wearing an earring and techGlasses— approaching from the third vehicle. GURlee and Gorgeeous were with him.

"Uncleri are falling!!" yelled Philipa, hurrying through sodden weeds toward them, her hair fluffing, faintly a'gleam.

"Where?" said Berle: he was calm, but feeling a small peculiar jerking in his chest. He looked toward the east where HiTopOLis was hidden among hills in mist, toward the greater invisible distant mountains. He saw nothing but mist.

"On the northwest coast," she said, coming breathless up to him. Her gray eyes were wet, she reached out to squeeze his hand. It came out uncertainly then firmed in her grasp. "Also the Acadian Interior northeast of there. Bombs are falling. It's real, Berle. We saw it on the visionary after shieL messaged. She gave me the streaming and I watched the initial reverberations on my way to Pegmo's and Bopoiz. *O Crater! O Mind! Berle, you should have seen it!* The sky—full for years! That weather will be *here*! It's coming!"

"What weather?" said Sheesh. He thought it odd that satellite stations still worked, could bring reverbs, if it was so. He stood stolid, to the ground, but Claude came running up and began cranking the teenager's hand, his arm. Sheesh did not pull away but kept letting Claude pump it, up and down, up and down. Oddly, the boy said nothing but just looked from one grown-up to the other. Grown-ups! They take care of us! They take care of everything!

—Oh girls—will you look at Claude?! He's going to take off by himself any moment now, said HB.

Tears washed Philipa's pale face as she spoke. "The oilFRactures are going into the air on 'shroom clouds! *And they did not ignite in the sky. They went into the ground for impact*, and the whole infrastructure and everything underneath is coming towards us, and shieL's been saying it all, and says more may be coming *here* for the direct hit—on HiTop, because of our uncleri industry—or what enemies think is uncleri. Is it Berle? Is that still going on here? *We did not allow the unclear labs and weaponry!*"

" 'Fraid so. Yes. My boss knows all about it and, if allowed, could have confirmed it to you. There is all kinds of work going on under our city."

"Then won't they counteract, bomb them before they get us?"

"Our program wouldn't be that far along. Theirs would be a pre-emptive."

"But how can enemies know about it and ordinary people not!?" ecjaculated Sheesh. "Why's it known to our government and enemy governments but not to us?"

"The mysteries of espeedonage. Governments know stuff citizens don't." It was the first time anyone had heard Kelso speak with genuine bitterness.

"Radioactivity, the works, will all be coming out on top," said Freddie, approaching, holding hands with Gorgeeous and GURlee. Gorgeeous, wearing T-shirt and naejs, GURlee in colorful rain gear, hood nearly over her eyes. Tall, tech-spectacled, the earring— Freddie wore what looked like pockets full of everything, bulging.

"Hozit, Fred," said Kelso. Kelso did not hold out his hand.

"Koot!" said the other, who dropped Gorgeeous's hand and reached for it.

Mz. Bopoi approached with laden arms, biMbo and hipPo lugging bags in either hand. So loaded, the kidz did not move with exaggerated grievance as under normal conditions. They took long strides, energetic, if a bit bemused. The heavy bags were getting wet, dragging and dropping. Some stayed were they fell.

"We brought supplies," said their mother, looking around for where to set them. "Steel-cut oats and various kinds of dried beans, dried tomatoes, cans of stuff. Salt! Cooking pots, plates, stuff, in the vehicles." Berle lifted boxes from her embrace and indicated the vacant board to the children. Kelso was still holding the kit, Sheesh his backpack. Seeing the sodden board, gray-green with mold and age, her expression fell. She looked about then, and took in the hovel, with tools leaning by the door. She had not noticed on first alighting.

—Dame's depressed, said HB.

—Blame her much? asked Jayrai.

—Could be worse, he replied. Could be pedophiles on the way. Look at this.

The HiTop people, in mist, gathered together round the unhappy board, now turned toward a sound, the same as Berle and Kelso and Sheesh had heard on their friends' approach—coming from the same direction.

"Someone else," said Berle. "Could it be Puce—a colleague— or maybe Capt. Clarke, Philipa? He looked back toward the approaching flyers.

"He's staying. Wants to help. Says it's his job."

"Job!?" said Sheesh. "To get killed?" Gneis said, —She meant duty.

"So so he's got a place, on the outskirts," explained Philipa. "He might make it yet. We'll see." Tears were washing, washing continually out her eyes. She was trying hard. So hard.

"Not near the stadium, the racetrack, Olympic venues?" Berle realized he should not have spoken.

"Yes. Not far from the stadium. Why didn't they scrap the work when they said so—when they said the games would go there instead?"

Berle said nothing. Mz. Bopoi spoke. "The work was ongoing, building. The silos are hidden under those Olympic complexes."

The flyers came on, switching to solar—quiet—and circled, landing near the other machines.

—Guns, said Fabian. Here are guns. Some funny looking weaponry.

No one moved. They stared as the architect climbed out and stood watching them, his hair tinted brass but not now fashionably spiky. It lifted in a faint breeze. The children looked up at their grown-ups, took hold of their hands. He looked at them all, as if to say? *I'm still here.* His driver started over toward them. The lawyer. There were no service workers, no chauffer as in his usual employ. The other flycar hatches opened, and men got out, a woman. One of these was Bill Blender, spokesperson for city council. These did not come forward. Berle, his face blanched and stark, freckles standing out, immediately stepped away to meet them. Wearing suit and bowtie, the driver stood out, lean and lank like a cadaver. The physicist saw that it was the architect's lawyer whom he'd seen crossing the Kress Building lobby, and on *Virtual Futures.* goD eVal—or so they called him. He had no idea if that was his real name, had never paid much attention.

Kelso advanced toward them with Berle; and Freddie, long-legged, splashing. Kelso had his Gluk but was thinking he would not be wasting lead on them. *Not to eat the architect and his friends.*

—Doesn't like the hovel, does he? (Jay, referring to Smudge)

Sheesh had stayed with the others. Claude had stopped pumping, but still gripped the teenager's hand. "O Crater, o Mind," Philipa said softly, over and over.

"The deVill!" Mz. Bopoi powerfully said. "The deVill! The awful nerve! The deVill!"

The children stared, GURlee. Gorgeeous stared.

Pegmo, parti-colored and bedraggled, reiterated foul exclamations in her deep rough voice. She muttered, and gripped Claude's other hand. He did not withdraw it. "The idioTs can't stay here," muttered Pegmo. *HaSoLes. HaSoLes.* IdioTs."

Berle came away, back to the group, and said, very low and

calm, "They want some fuel and one of the cars. I said, 'Why not take it all?' —Meaning the fuel. The cars might do for us when Elios returns. We might still get back." *If Elios does return.*

Kelso stood where he was, watching the lawyer walk back. Freddie stayed with Kelso.

"We'll have to give them the remotes and encryption. I'll give them my car," Berle said. He held out his hand to Sheesh for the remote. To Mz. Bopoi, he said, "I'm sorry. You have to open your tank. You can do that from here. Don't move."

"Like hEll!" she snarled, starting toward them.

"They've got weapons." His hand was on her arm. She looked at it.

He said, "We're to keep the food. Blender's idea, I think. Not the lawyer's."

Her bosom heaved. "Big," she said. But she stood with the women and children as Berle went sloshing back to the outlaws.

Muttering together, Pegmo and Mz. Bopoi said, "How did they know?" "B'Stards followed the tech." They watched the small group working in the near distance to remove fuel and familiarize with Berle's flycar. It took off first. Then the architect and the others who were left climbed into their flyers and took off.

Quickly, Berle and Freddie climbed inside the remaining cars, and lifted them off, low, going slowly toward the hovel, the woodland edge. There they parked and climbed out, Sheesh and the children running toward them. The women followed slowly, Philipa's right arm akimbo, hand absently covering her concealed-carry. In the distance now they heard more coming. They moved downed limbs and, bumping over rocks, making ruts, drove the cars between woodland and hovel.

"Better go into the woods," said Berle grimly. "Before we're spotted. The next bunch might be more uphard."

"He's on his way to that disgusting compound of his," said Mz. Bopoi. "Wait till this settles!"

That's what will free us, thought Freddie.

—Or not, said HB in answer to Freddie's thought.

—BABY's getting born here quicker than BABY's getting born at home, said Fabian.

—Which BABY™ you talking about then, yo? said Jay.

—The second one, he said.

—How do we know it's not happening for real there? (HB was not thinking of the game.)

—It wasn't when we left 2017, said Fabian. It wasn't in 1900 either, of course. 1900 had no uncleri, I mean nukes, then.

Jay said, So you mean—?

Pomala finished. —That's how the world ends—the stars

226

fall? Like in the wallpaper? Fodder's deerskins?
    —It's in scripture, said Fabian, to which Jay said nothing.
    She seemed to consider, then added, *Your* scripture. —Eerie,
wee-eerd, but. Don't get me wrong. I'm a total materialist, meaning
I LIKE MATERIAL. (Followed by much personal-info-ranting dump.)
...But I seem to recall the aunts, grands, etc.; something about the
whole thing contracting to pre-BABY singularity—that's how I'm
putting it. Because, well—BABY! MACHOs, RAMBO's—all of it,
girls!! —That's the end!... And the beginning.... Tu. Now, Tu. Help
here, Tu.
    Pause.
    —C'mon, said Jay.
    —You are working here with two definitions of the world, the
terrestrial and the cosmic. And remember, they are embodied in
stories; these definitions of yours.
    —You mean turtles, said HB.
    —That's the metaphor.
    —Turtles, said HB. Turtles all the way down.
    —And, continued Tu, —Jay's cosmology—just her mythic
summary of it—is the real scientific formulation we've probably had
before and may get again. —Without all her distracting
personification, animism. Those stories are fine for little kids, but
you've got to get over it, both of you.
    —Let's smack him, Fabe.
    —When we get back, said HB. We've got a problem. It's
obvious The Dah is not going to help us with this. And. As far as
I'm concerned the problem is central to creation. No matter what
y'all say. All the materials can blow back—*if we survive*. And truth!
I don't call this survival.
    —You are contradicting yourself, Tu reminded him.
    —Yeah, I tend to do that. So, hoping we don't queue into a
loop, what's it to be? Wormholes (if we can find any)? Black holes
(same)? The sun? There it is!! (Indicating the circular disc sinking
into the mist.)
    —There would be a black hole, a great atom shredding abyss,
at the galaxy's center. But minute black holes dissipated after the
big event— (Tu begins dump).
    —OR—HOW 'BOUT HITOPOLIS!!!! (Jay)
    And they all looked eastward.
    And the HiTopOLites looked, from where they stood, small
and forlorn, outside the hovel, tools for its reconditioning still by the
door.
    The jetting whistle. The flash. The great glow in the east,
and then another flash. Shakings and rumblings and powerful
shiftings. Lightnings and thunderings. And more waves of shock

227

and shaking, as a liquefying of the earth. Suffusive glowing, and continual flashing, *basso profundo continuo*, howlings and coughings of earth in mighty upheaval.

Heavy dark turkeys flew off into the woods, scared, unawares. HiTopOLite MACHOs, wailing, reached for one another's hands. And it was all in the air, and dark, reaching past Elios westward, where more approaching flyers, like insects, had been hurled.

And, emotionally a'burst, eyes tight, SiXPointz 1900 EE friends embraced one another. Tightly. A group. Arms encircling. Heads bowed.

And the gang of WIMPs would see their MACHO friends and fight against RAMBOs no more. And would never play BABY with them again. And would not know what became of their friends where they huddled, trembling, far beyond the city. For the FivePoints WIMPs had immediately, and long before, concentrated themselves in the incineration/disintegration of HiTopOLis. And they followed together unawares into one of many minute traversable wormholes—opening-closing-opening-vacuuming of fission & fusion reactions— in the nuclear destruction of that city. And WIMPs, those *weakly interacting massive particles,* were no more.

TO 2017 CE?

Meantime

Scratching over parchment, the intricately star-made deerskin surface. *Scratching* in tallow-light, light made from the fat of the deer.... Such light would be soon gone. ...The ink in the quill was most gone, and too ink in the vial.

And what comes of the <u>What</u> <u>quest</u> *of the HiTopOLis claric, and meta-physician, he they call the scientist? And what became of the crystal giants, children of the other world?*

The questions remain (for some) but not for Father Domino, this brother. Friend of Leaping Fawn, friend of THE DEER. She showed me neither what they were nor what became of them. She chose not, mayhap knows not. *Scritch. Scratch.*

Father Domino heard a sound without, and came swiftly away from the dim cold cave into light. In one supple movement as though he had not been frail or stiff with cold, eyes and nose dripping, joints aching. He stood blinking, bewildered and very much formed—in the body. Filled with question and wonder. For there, many paces off in the light of damp spring-fallen snow, stood a dark A'ndyan woman, her cheek bones high and hair pulled back, wrapped in a blanket, one hand clutching it to her bosom. A real blanket, red, green and black with An'dyan design. Not deerskin, not catskin, but woven and woolen such as one saw in the Last World over the sea.

And this was Geagosasa! She who had before now worn only the hide of the deer, carried only the deerskin or rush pouch. She had a rush pouch with her now, he saw. And she had others of fabric, slung on the shoulder, and mayhap one of hide on her back. And with her stood an old brave in cloak. The old brave's head was most bald, but a flap of hair hung back, down its midst. And, in his hand a heavy muzzleloader, varnished wooden butt in the snow, its barrel long and cold. How Father Domino felt the cold in that barrel!

229

Dimly he thought it should have been sheathed with fringed hide.

"Father Domino," she was saying. *"Father Domino."*

He trembled, whether with cold or bewilderment she might not tell. Both, it must be both. He was in tatters, thin as the twigs, a wreath of tortured lines in his expressive face. Scars as a wreath of thorns buried in his flesh. "Father Domino," she said, going gently near. "We are come now to bring you back with us." She thought, *You have need we can cure.*

"Yes," she said, standing by him, close. She picked up his hand, as it were frail bird-bones. Something she had never done. Father Domino looked next to the old brave. Then the He-suit looked back at her. Breaking light from his gaze upon her, she now saw.

"Yes, Father Domino, it is I."

"Geagosasa?" It came half like the croaking, half like a flurry of bird wings. It had said nothing to anyone in so long. His voice had but spoken to himself alone—this voice, this one in his body, his throat, his mouth.

He continued looking bewilderment, but was glad. The glimmer-shimmer of early-morning half-light, on snow, lit the whole vale with its caked limbs and twigs of thorn-brush, swollen and red beneath their frost-white covering. The freshness was everywhere to his sensing, his breath, his sight. Then he half-turned toward his cave.

"We have come for you," he heard her say. "And for all your signals. See?" She held out a pouch. "You have many parchments, and we have many pouches for carrying. We will bring all with us. It is true, Father Domino, that the Longhouse does not care overmuch for them. But you do. And it is you I care for. You we come for. I have taught them to love you. We—I and my escort—and we are a few—." She gestured to a few others standing in snow-clad thickets. These he had not seen. "And you may write of Caht-Tail no more, but of Bird-Crest. We are come to bring you, and carry your knowledge in these pouches, to the long house in the mountains with us."

And you shall be fed and clothed on the way, she thought. *You shall be fed and clothed on the way.*

But he thought, *Will they know who they are, recognize themselves, remember? Will they Be?* Would they recollect this great disruption of their lives in the visitation of destruction on the city of HiTopOLis?

Meanwhile, huddled with the others inside a stone wall of the dark Akropolis Rural Cemetery, HBBBAH rubbed August sweat out of his big broom-cut, the shaved sides of his head glistening with remote light thrown down from the neighborhood. He muttered with extreme distaste, and looked about him with that special CossycSystems eye of his. "A line of 0's and 1's."

"Or, x's and o's." Pomala said this, the albino with blue tattooed face, smiling into the pod-lit dark.

Tu had worked the Hadesthon calculations. His black fringe of hair hanging, symmetrical Osiian features zoned in concentration, Tu had worked them again—just as the battery now gave out. The game display was suddenly and disconcertingly dark. And the cemetery around them, to which they had not been attending, was like a pit surrounded by hidden fire—from gas streetlamps and some thin old-fashioned household electric glow thrown down from beyond the wall. The alien neighborhood of Five Points 1900 A.D. was outside the Cemetery, still with rhythmic nightlife of horse-and-carriages, pool halls, bars, and neighborhood sociability—including kick-the-can. It was quieter now. Certain areas of the city had been in tumult. Remote fiddling and the tinkling of an upright piano drifted to them where they huddled beneath the wall. The FivePoints 2017 gang were wearing their jackets again, full of hope, ready for November and the fresh twinkle in time. The Hadesthon would get them back. Yes?

As the pod flicked off, Tu had felt a great elation and would have jumped in the air and floated, hovering, gently crowing the fact. But he was Tu, so instead he said only, "Got it. And just in time." He made an incoherent apology for taking so long, ending, "But you know what I mean."

"Sure we do," said HB.

They all looked at Tu, eyes goggling. *Just in time?* Jayrai had that deep rich complexion like Quad's but with rounder eyes. "Just in time? You mean as in the battery *is*—really gone?..." She waved her biomechanical fingers.

"You mean we're stuck here without games, apps, anime—anything?" Little Quadri's dark eyes were bewildered. He looked up at each in turn.

"This is it," said Fabian, affirming Tu. "No more anything if we don't get back to FivePoints." He shook back his long blond hair, dusted its center buzz-cut for sweat. He was lithe and slender, wore an earring, and star tattoos.

"FivePoints 2017," said HBBBAH. "How I miss the Prez." This was said with fervent affection for all things 2017 CE.

"The Prez!" exclaimed Jayrai. "What about chocolate cinnamon cappuccino? What about my upcoming baristaHood. My hoped-for job! What about Real-Life—*WorldCraft, Hadesthon*—Hadesthon—!! This. Better. Be. Right!"

Tu looked blank, but for him it was apologetic. "It's all we've got. Experimental, yes, be glad of that: At least it's not *gedankenexperiment*, it's probably not Schrödinger's cat I hope, but it may be an entanglement—the changing face of Pluto influencing throughout the entire solar system and on out toward the abyss at the center of the galaxy."

"Oh please," said Pomala. "Can we just get back on the wall?" She did not like the eerie feeling of the dark peopled with gravestones and the great shades of scattered mausoleums... though it was far emptier of monuments than she remembered from her escapades there in 2017. Maybe it was that, or the gaslight, or the shadows—so different from the artificial day-glow of the Akropolis light pollution that made FivePoints 2017 seem so much friendlier.

Through shadows they climbed up to settle on the stone wall next to gaslit Stock Exchange Street, where the occasional rider went by, horse and buggy. There to await the hoped-for return of 2017.

From beneath overhanging boughs, in tree-shadows, they watched the activity down at the corner. So different from what had been the boring traffic, with its homogenized lack of interest—only this morning!? *OMG!!* It felt like they'd been living in another universe! Oh, how *long is* life?! So *hoping* to see that great library again in a moment. After school in November ... would the sun be shining? They could not remember. Would *this* be remembered, Five Points 1900 CE? Right now no one cared.

"Let's hold hands," suggested Tu.

They looked at him. *Tu*?! He picked up Pomala's hand and held it. Tu. They groped shyly and held hands, Tu at the Five Points end, Pomala next to him. Then Jayrai, Fabian, HBBBAH, and Quadri.

"I felt something. Did you feel it?"

"Whatever it was it was massive. Somewhere off in the distance."

"Maybe another one of their riots?"

"Was it the rubber workers doing that?"

"Nevermind them!" said someone, meaning never mind everyone in old-time Akropolis. *"This Is It."*

"Can I be in the middle?" asked Quadri. He wanted, especially, next to Pomala.

Could the configuration make a difference? A scrambled consultation. They did not recall their exact positions from 2017 at the precise moment of the trans-chronic twinkle. Quad was the youngest. It was a BIG moment: Time to be merciful. Merciful, not teasing. He climbed over HBBBAH and Fabian, to sit between Pomala and Jayrai, holding hands. Together they waited. The churchtower clock, they had agreed, was all they had to go on. The UT clock was no longer streaming, automatically syncing in the pod from futureTime. As soon as Time twinkled the striking would stop, because clockworks were no more in FivePoints 2017—right? The UTC in the pods would start, and the game pick up where they left off. The batteries would still be good, said Tu, because these were still good in 2017 CE—. *If* all went well.

The hour was about to be sounded. This was *It*. Had. To. Be.

Oh. Please. (Pomala)

Jayrai was thinking, *It's only a game.*

Tu remembered, *It's a game based on science.*

Quadri was hopeful, looking round at them.

HBBBAH thought, *We're toast.*

"Look," said Pomala, pointing. "Here comes the autism girl and her keeper."

A small couple was coming from the intersection at Five Points, the boy Parry and the little girl who never spoke—on their way to the cemetery gate to find Willie, the young grounds-keeper, the grave-digger, Parry's big brother. It was late, time for Parry to collect him and go home.

As Parry and the little girl were passing, Fabian reached across Jayrai, squeezed Pomala's hand. And held it fast. Squeezed it so hard it hurt.

"Oww!!"

"Don't touch that girl, Pomala," he said. "Whatever you do. Don't. Grab. That. Hand. Just wave at'em as they go past. That's it. Wave."

SiXPointz HiTopOLis

s. dormAn

www.ingramcontent.com/pod-product-compliance
Lightning Source LLC
Chambersburg PA
CBHW050517260626
47157CB00004B/1357